WONDER RUSH
Copyright © 2021 by Dan McKeon

First edition May 2021

Cover design by Michael Corvin

ISBN: 978-1-7371325-1-6 (Trade Paperback)
ISBN: 978-1-7371325-0-9 (Paperback)
ISBN: 978-1-7371325-2-3 (eBook)

Library of Congress Control Number: 2021908914

Published by Hush Moss Press in Kinnelon, NJ

For more information contact:
dan-mckeon.com

DAN McKEON

HUSH MOSS
— PRESS —

Chapter 1

AMAYA

It had been two-and-a-half weeks since Wendy killed anyone, and she was getting antsy. The smell of popcorn wafting from the concession stand made her stomach churn; she didn't appreciate the reminder of her lost childhood. Amaya and Tommy argued about some stupid TikTok video while Meg attempted to intervene. Wendy's worn sneakers scraped the dry earth as she shuffled behind, allowing the meager crowd filling the football stadium to thin out. She spotted a handsome man in his early thirties fade into darkness under the athletic field. A warm rush of anticipation flooded Wendy's cheeks, and a sudden spike in adrenaline made her heart flutter.

"Go on ahead," Wendy said. "I'm just going to hit the girls' room. Meet you in the stands." Amaya waved her off, engrossed in her squabble.

She was lying, of course. She had no intention of using the restroom. Whether she would meet them in the stands later was still undecided. Wendy studied her friends as they blended into the crowd, memorizing each movement, in case this was the last time she saw them. She tucked her hair behind her ear, savoring the animated pitch of Amaya's fading quarrel as she and Tommy turned the corner and vanished from Wendy's sight. Her bones ached at the thought of leaving Amaya, but Wendy had one purpose for being on school grounds at such an ungodly hour on a Saturday morning, and she had just lost visual on him.

As she slinked beneath the stadium, the cement walls shaded the late-September sun and the temperature dropped ten degrees. Wendy wrapped her sweatshirt tighter around her torso, combating the goosebumps that crawled down her arms. She scurried toward the restrooms, her shoulders dropping in disappointment as the men's room door swung shut. She missed her chance. She furrowed her brow as she contemplated an alternative plan.

Reaching into her purse, she pushed aside her high school ID—the one that featured her overly energetic, toothy grin—the photo that captured everything she pretended to be, at least for now.

She dug through her bag. It was a cheap knock-off, but she didn't care. She pushed past a lipstick tube (Red Sunrise, Tommy's favorite), past a few broken pencils, their tips in a messy collection at the bottom of the bag, and past a barely wrapped tampon.

Wendy grabbed her wallet, unzipped the change pouch, and gripped a handful of pennies, nickels, dimes, and quarters. As the sound of running water echoed from the men's room, Wendy intentionally released the coins, watching them bounce on the solid concrete floor, their metallic *ting* reverberating off the walls.

"Oh, I'm such a klutz," Wendy said as Mr. Godwin exited the bathroom to find his third-period English student huddled over a mass of scattered money. "Who even carries change anymore, right? Ugh, I'm such a disaster."

"Let me give you a hand," Mr. Godwin said as he crouched down next to Wendy, prying up a dime with his perfectly manicured thumb nail. His eyes sparkled despite the sparsely lit basement. Wendy grinned, acutely aware of the intense jealousy her fellow students would feel being mere inches from Mr. Godwin's perfectly chiseled jawline. Wendy knew better, though. She was well-aware of the repulsive soul lurking beneath his flawless quaff of thick, wavy hair.

Wendy stood, reached back into her purse, and slipped something that resembled a joy buzzer onto her finger. From the outside, the contraption looked like a simple gold ring; however, inside her palm hid a small square sponge embossed in a plastic casing. Her thumb traced the groove that separated the lid as she flicked it off and reached for Mr. Godwin's hand.

"Thank you so much for your help," she said as she held Mr. Godwin's palm in hers, smearing a clear liquid that soaked the spongy patch of her "joy buzzer." She allowed his hand to linger in hers long enough for the poison to soak through his skin and long enough to bat her eyes as he smiled. Mr. Godwin almost expected flirtation from his students, and he wasn't one to discourage it. "Enjoy the game," she said, biting her lower lip, partially to play the role of doting teenage girl, but mostly to choke back the repugnance billowing in her gut.

Wendy slid the ring off her finger and back into the protective cover in her purse. She had administered a *transdermal-something-or-other* that contained *hydrochloro-blah-blah-blah*. She started ignoring the details of the briefings years ago. The bottom line was that the man would feel fine for the next day or two, slowly feel some stomach flu symptoms, and would be dead within a week.

* * *

The sun was almost blinding compared to the dingy undercarriage of the stadium. Wendy slid casually into the bleachers next to Meg, Amaya, and Tommy, the cold of the aluminum penetrating through her thin jeans. She considered bolting after her run-in with Mr. Godwin, but she didn't want to leave her friends behind. She couldn't leave Amaya. Not yet.

"Hey, Wendy, just in time." That was Meg. Sweet girl, but she tried a little too hard.

Amaya leaned back and flicked Wendy's right ear. That was the sort of attitude that drew her to Amaya almost instantly.

Wendy was a name she wasn't necessarily comfortable with, but it was fine for the time being. She wouldn't have it for long. To her it always felt a little too 1950s goody-goody, like she should be in a poodle skirt singing The Name Game.

Wendy, Wendy, bo-bendy. Banana-fana, fo-fendy.

Wendy Lockheart (for lack of better nomenclature) didn't normally gravitate toward the crowd that would spend a Saturday morning at a school football game, but this group was different. They weren't there because they were rah-rah cheerleader wannabes or because they were so cool that it was ironic to pretend to have school spirit. They just did whatever they wanted to do and yesterday Tommy said, "Hey, let's go to the football game tomorrow." Once she learned Mr. Godwin would be there, she was on board.

Tommy smiled at her, just barely catching her eye before looking down, as if something beyond fascinating was happening right at his feet. It was normal for a high school girl to crush on a high school boy, so Wendy played along. Tommy was cute enough, and she enjoyed watching him squirm as she gave him mixed signals. For her, it was a game. The agency taught her to remain unattached. Her time was always limited. But she kept up appearances, laughing at his lame attempts at jokes, going along with his banal, small-minded ideas (like this football game). In all honesty, it wasn't Tommy that brought her up from the stadium underground to watch her so-called peers smash each other's helmeted heads together. It was Amaya.

* * *

Wendy had found her way to countless different schools since her induction into the agency, and the first days were always similar. Some schools make you introduce yourself to the class. Other schools just tell you to take a seat and try to ignore you as best as they can until the blaring ring of the school bell.

The first afternoon in the cafeteria is generally the same, and it began as such at West Elmdale High School (Go Cardinals). Wendy collected her tray of somewhat discernible meat and potato product with a side of nearly gray string beans and found a corner of a scarcely populated table. This was her favorite part. She enjoyed seeing what types of people attempted to make contact. She was part space alien and part lab rat about to be dissected.

As she popped the lid off her Kiwi Strawberry Snapple, a girl named Lara at the far end of the table scoffed. "That is seriously revolting," she spat. Wendy scanned the area, searching for context. "Yes, you." She caught Wendy's eye.

"You don't like kiwi?"

"It's not your drink, you biohazard," Lara said, pointing at Wendy's forearm, which was bleeding onto the chipped particleboard table.

So much for blending in.

Wendy snagged a napkin and covered the cut she thought had healed. It was a souvenir from her previous target who got a little overzealous with a switchblade. She pulled a cardigan from her backpack and threw it over her Toucan Sam tee shirt, which she hoped would pass as vintage, but was really a Goodwill purchase.

"Ew, seriously? That's not much better," Lara said. "That sweater is literally falling apart."

Wendy tugged at a large hole worn through the left elbow.

Blood rushed to her face, partly because of embarrassment and partly out of rage.

"God, she's a mess," Lara said to a well-dressed girl to her right. "Stay away. She probably has lice."

"Lice? I got you, cuz." A strange little girl with dark-rimmed glasses and a streak of purple in her otherwise jet-black hair hopped up behind Wendy, a foot on either side of her on the cafeteria bench. The girl straddled Wendy from behind and feigned picking nits out of her hair like a wild monkey. She even threw in a few monkey noises as she did it. "Ooo ooo, eee-eee!" Her primal eyes scanned the room as she pretended to grab the lice and eat them. "There. Think I got them all. I'm Amaya Malone. At your service."

Amaya hopped from the bench, stood beside the table, and mimicked an overly exaggerated curtsy. And that was Wendy's first introduction to Amaya. It was instant chemistry. Lara rolled her eyes as she and her posse of prep school posers shuffled off in disgust.

"This here's my bitchy friend, Meg." Amaya gestured to a sweet-looking girl with braces and afro puffs with a zigzag part.

"She's kidding," Meg retorted. "She's always kidding. Hey, you're really pretty."

She wasn't.

"You have such pretty hair," Meg added.

She didn't.

"Pretty eyes, too." Meg shied away as she attempted that compliment.

Wendy's eyes were, in fact, unique. The agency had little control over that. The rest was all by design. It was part of her training. Don't be too attractive—attractive girls stand out. Don't be too homely either—ugliness garners as much attention as beauty. The idea was to blend in. To be as invisible as possible. Her eyes, however, were outside of the agency's oversight.

At seventeen years old, Wendy wore her brown, mousy hair in a shoulder-length bob with neatly trimmed bangs. She wore very little makeup—just enough to keep up with the status quo. She wasn't too tall, and she wasn't too short. Perfectly average. Her eyes were like a mosaic of different colored tiles. Similar to a chameleon, the primary hue shifted depending upon the surrounding colors.

When she was in Portland for six months, she had long blond hair and her eyes sparkled with a tinge of blue. She was a redhead in Decatur with grayish-green eyes to match. Today, in West Elmdale, New Jersey, her hazel eyes favored the light brown spectrum to complement her nondescript brunette bob.

"Thanks. I like your puffs," Wendy replied, nodding toward Meg's hair. "I'm Wendy."

She had been Wendy for less than twelve hours at that point, but the words rolled off her tongue as if she had been Wendy her entire life.

"I have an inverted nipple," Meg blurted out, immediately regretting it.

"I'm sorry. What's that, now?" Wendy asked.

"Nothing." She blushed.

"Why would you tell me that?"

"I don't know. We don't get many transfer students here. I got nervous. I overshare when I'm nervous." Meg pulled away and sat at the bench across from Wendy, her face turned down as she anxiously poked at her lunch.

"Doofus," Amaya chided, as she smacked Meg on the shoulder. "Don't scare the new girl away."

"Oh, I don't scare easily," Wendy explained.

"Good. For all intensive purposes, Meg is the saner one of us two."

"Um, did you say, 'intensive purposes'?" A tall, slightly muscular boy sitting at the table next to theirs had overheard the conversation.

"Stand up." Amaya gestured for the boy to rise. He did. Amaya had a commanding presence that didn't quite match her small stature.

"You know the expression is 'intents and purposes,' ri—?" Amaya slammed her knee into the boy's crotch before he could finish his question. Hunched over in pain, he stumbled back to his cafeteria bench.

"That's Tommy Vasquez, one of West Elmdale's finest," Amaya explained. "He's hot, but he's an asshat."

Wendy glanced over at Tommy and gave him a shy smile. "You know he was right, though. Don't you? About the expression?" Wendy asked.

"Doesn't matter. It's a little game I like to play," Amaya said. "I intentionally say an expression wrong and if anyone is douchey enough to correct me, I hit 'em in the balls."

"What if a girl corrects you?"

"Seriously? Nine times out of ten it's a boy trying to mansplain." Amaya made her way next to Meg and straddled the cafeteria bench.

"Well, what about that one time out of ten?"

"Then I punch a tit." Amaya shrugged as she tossed a tater tot into her mouth. "That's how Meg, here, got her inverted nipple."

Meg's eyes widened in horror. "That's not true. She's kidding again. She's always kidding."

* * *

The *buzz* of the scoreboard jolted Wendy back to the present. Her life left no room for sentimentality. She was going to miss her friends. Meg had a kind soul, and Tommy was nice to look at, but Amaya was something more. She connected with her in a way she hadn't with anyone else in any other town in this godforsaken country. She wasn't supposed to get attached, and it typically wasn't much of a struggle to abide by that rule, but it got lonely never having a genuine friend. For the first time, she dreaded what her next mission might be, or when it might begin.

She had no control over that aspect of the job. In fact, she had very little control over any facet of her purported existence. She even lacked the means to reach out with an inquiry, content to wait for instructions to reach her. Because the agency raised her, she never found the communication system aberrant, although she imagined outsiders may view it as somewhat peculiar.

Wendy received all intelligence via a stick of randomly flavored Wonder Rush Happy Funtime Bubblegum.

* * *

A middle-aged woman scratched an itch on her leg as she wrote her name on the whiteboard. Wendy's sensitive ears cringed at the sound of her wool skirt rubbing against her pantyhose.

The letters spelled out "Mrs. Ratchford."

The words almost teased the students as they read them. This woman needed no introduction. She was the go-to substitute teacher at West Elmdale High School and not well-liked.

Wendy could forgive the dated attire. She herself was no fashionista, but how Ratchford never seemed to notice the stale lipstick on her teeth, Wendy could not figure out. Once or twice, fine, but every day? At some point she must look in a mirror, right? A tight bun pulled her greasy hair to a slick shine, matting it to her skull.

"Class, I'm Mrs. Ratchford." She gestured to the whiteboard. "I'll be your substitute today for English Literature. Mr. Godwin has fallen ill."

So it begins.

It was Monday. Mr. Godwin was probably feeling a little

nauseous. Maybe some vomiting. If not, he would have that to look forward to soon. Maybe a slight fever—100, 101—nothing to cause too much alarm. Some Tylenol should keep it in check for now.

"I understand that you have been discussing Macbeth," Mrs. Ratchford continued. "We'll be watching clips from the 1971 Polanski film adaption today."

"Wasn't Polanski a rapist?" someone at the rear of the classroom asked.

There were scattered chuckles among the class, then another student piped up, "You showing us a rape film, Ratchford?"

"Who said that?" Mrs. Ratchford demanded. "Just settle down and watch the film."

Wendy wasn't sure what it was about substitute teachers that caused such disrespect, but it was the same in every school. Maybe it was the lack of recourse. Would a sub have the audacity to issue a detention? Does she even carry such authority? Would she send a student to the principal's office? Probably, if provoked enough, but she would surely let a minor infraction slide. She wanted to get through the day like anyone else.

It surprised her to see Amaya partaking in the antics, but she was pleased at how unique her approach was. Most modern TVs have "smart" capabilities, and Amaya downloaded the manufacturer's app months ago. Today was not her first tussle with a substitute. With a simple swipe of her phone, she could cast any video she wanted in front of the entire class.

Amaya gave Wendy a "check this out" nod and tapped a button on her phone. Instantly, the screen switched from Jon Finch rattling off some Shakespearean mumbo-jumbo to two frogs, mid-intercourse. Wendy laughed out loud, startling even herself. She rarely found standard teenage fare humorous, but Amaya seemed to know the right buttons to press.

"Oh, now what is this?" Mrs. Ratchford exclaimed, jumping

from her chair. "Must be a faulty connection or something." She jiggled the plugs on the back of the TV as if a loose wire could transform highbrow English drama into amphibious copulation.

After a hearty reaction from her peers, Amaya switched the video back to Macbeth. Mrs. Ratchford seemed pleased, as if her wire jiggling adequately addressed the problem.

"Here. Pick something," Amaya whispered to Wendy as she passed her phone.

Now Wendy faced a conundrum. The agency taught her to fit in with those around her, which would justify her casting a video and pranking her teacher. On the other hand, she was trained to stay out of trouble, which implied that she should quietly pass the device back to her friend. On the other, *other* hand, she was actually having fun. There wasn't a lot of that in her life, and she kind of liked it.

Wendy tapped a few buttons and an ISIS beheading video popped on the screen.

"Wendy! Oh, my God!" It was even a little too much for Amaya. She grabbed the phone from Wendy's hand and switched off the video just as a sword nearly sliced through the neck of a hooded man on his knees.

"Dude, you are seriously twisted," Amaya whispered. "I frigging like it!"

"Which one of you is Wendy?" demanded Mrs. Ratchford. One of the other students gestured, and Mrs. Ratchford grabbed Wendy by the arm and pulled her out of her seat. Sure, Wendy could have taken Mrs. Ratchford down easily, but she wanted to give Ratchford the win.

"And you." She pointed to Amaya. "Are you responsible for the fornicating frogs?"

"Guilty as charged, Ratchet."

"Excuse me, young lady, my name is Mrs. *Ratchford*."

Amaya clenched her fist and gave Wendy a look like she wanted to hit her for the correction. Wendy's eyes widened, and she shook off Amaya's gesture.

* * *

As it turns out, substitute teachers do have the authority to issue detentions. Wendy and Amaya sat in desks next to each other as the unlucky teacher whose turn it was to supervise detention unfurled a newspaper at his workstation. The room was silent as a few other students slumped in their chairs alongside the two girls.

Thugs. That's what Wendy thought they looked like. Then she chuckled out loud. Amaya gave her an odd look. Who was Wendy to think of these students as thugs? What could they have possibly done? Arrived late to class? Cursed out a teacher? Forgot their gym clothes at home? Wendy had literally just killed her English teacher. Okay, so he wasn't dead yet, but *alea iacta est.*

That phrase always stuck with her from a Latin class she had in… Des Moines? No, maybe it was Cleveland… No, it was Des Moines. She remembered the kid who sat next to her in Latin always wore an Iowa Hawkeyes tee shirt. It's funny the things that stick with you. The phrase meant, "The die is cast." Suetonius said it to Julius Caesar during one of the Roman wars. The Romans always seemed to be fighting someone. Once the die was cast, there was no turning back. For Wendy, her die was cast almost immediately after her birth, and she was never given an opportunity to stop it or even slow it down.

"*Alea iacta est,*" she mumbled.

"What is wrong with you?" Amaya whispered. "Don't tell me this is your first time in detention."

"No. Of course not," she whispered back.

It was.

She had stabbed people, poisoned others, strangled a few,

even shot one, but she always followed the rules at school. The agency insisted on it. There was no need to draw attention from teachers, the principal, or foster parents.

What would be the ramifications of this? Teachers always threatened to put things on your permanent record. She doubted there was such a thing. Even if there were, she figured she wouldn't be Wendy Lockheart much longer. Whatever identity she had next would have a clean slate. Maybe her foster parents would find out, but she doubted it. They didn't question her when she came home late from school. She could be at an after-school club meeting or hanging with friends. They gave her some leeway. Wendy never gave them any reason not to trust her—another edict from the agency. A suspension they would hear about, but probably not a detention. She thought she was most likely safe. She would be on Mrs. Ratchford's radar, but she was a sub—a temporary employee. Wendy leaned back in her chair, relaxing a bit. Things could be worse.

* * *

By the time Friday rolled around, Mr. Nelson, the school principal, joined Mrs. Ratchford in front of the English class.

"Class, this is difficult to say," he began. "As you are aware, Mr. Godwin has been under the weather lately. I'm very sorry to inform you he passed away last night."

Job complete.

"He went in his sleep and doctors say he didn't suffer."

That's disappointing.

"Mr. Godwin had some pre-existing medical conditions, and his immune system just wasn't strong enough to fight off the flu."

And there was the beauty of the entire plan. The agency knew exactly what pre-existing conditions Mr. Godwin had, and they knew his "flu" would be fatal. Such an elegant solution. There would be no investigation into foul play because he died of natural causes. They would never question Wendy or even suspect her.

"I know this can be very difficult for students to deal with," Mr. Nelson continued. "I imagine you may have a lot of questions or want to talk to someone. Counselors are available for all of you." Mr. Nelson hesitated. "You may also… hear some rumors… or read some things online."

"Guys! Godwin was a full-on pedophile!" exclaimed a student from the back of the class. He held up his phone, which displayed a news article.

There was some rumbling among the class.

"Now, let's allow the authorities to investigate," Principal Nelson interjected.

"Seriously," the student continued, "he had a hard drive full of kiddie porn and a studio in his house where he shot his own!"

This was not news to Wendy, naturally. It was all part of her briefing—the part to which she always paid attention. If she was going to eliminate the scum of the world, she wanted to know why. The rest of the details she generally ignored.

Removing dregs like Melvin from society was a tremendous source of accomplishment for Wendy. It's what kept her loyal to the agency. That, plus the fact that killing people made her feel really, *really* good.

Chapter 2

RYAN

The gentle click of the digital shutter seemed to attenuate the horrifying scene it captured. Detective Barnes missed the days when cameras held film and a temporarily blinding flash accompanied the rigid shutter snap. That seemed more apropos considering the grisly scene he was witnessing, like something out of an old black and white film noir.

He stepped over a placard, labeling an eyeball, staring him down from a dried crust of blood that had saturated the once-beige carpet. The optic nerve trailed from the back like an electrical wire, searching for its missing outlet. Barnes removed a handkerchief from his suit jacket pocket and grimaced as he covered his nose and mouth, attempting in vain to squelch the wretched stench.

"Two victims. One male, mid-sixties. The other female, late-fifties," Officer Hardison reported to Detective Barnes. "She's the one trying to peek at you from over there." Hardison gestured toward the eyeball on the carpet.

"Classy, Officer," Barnes retorted. "What are we looking at here?"

"Peter and Abigail McMahon, according to the neighbor who called it in and corroborated by the gas bill in the study," Hardison stated. "No sign of struggle from the husband. He has a fresh incision on his chest that's been sutured. Looks like a recent heart surgery. Poor bastard seems to have slept through most of the attack. Multiple stab wounds to the chest. The wife…" Hardison double-checked the name in his notebook, "… Abigail looks like the one who fought back, or at least attempted to." He gestured to her face and body. "Bruising on the neck, arms, and rib cage."

Blood stained the bed a dark maroon, almost black color, fading into a harsh crimson around the edges. Husband and wife lay side by side, Peter on his back. His gray beard blended into the matted, blood-soaked hairs on his chest.

Abigail rested on her side as if posed there intentionally. A dark caking followed from her left eye socket and onto the mattress, a remnant of what was once a violent flowing of sanguine fluid.

"Been sitting here probably three or four days," Hardison continued.

"No one noticed?"

"Neighbors called once the mail piled up. We'll check work records. If Peter recently had heart surgery, my guess is he had some time off from work."

"And her?" Barnes inquired.

"Not sure. Homemaker maybe?"

"How did she lose the eye?"

"The eye itself was punctured and ripped out of its socket."

"We talking about a knife? Screwdriver?" Barnes asked.

"The puncture wound is thin. Barely detectable. Maybe a surgical needle? The husband's chest has the same markings. Fifteen small puncture marks. Straight to the heart."

"So, we have a gentleman who we can assume was recently

released from the hospital, and the murder weapon is a syringe?"

"Seems to be."

"All right, let's get the hospital records. Crosscheck every doctor, nurse, technician, candy striper against the database."

"Givens is already on it."

"I want to know if either of these two made any enemies over there. What type of patient was Peter? Did he complain? Was he aggressive? Threatening? Did he eat all his Jell-O? I want to know everything. Let's find this miscreant."

* * *

A metallic *ting* emanated from a large kitchen knife as Grace Barnes slid it from the butcher block. She chopped a collection of peeled potatoes, sliding them from the cutting board to a large pot of boiling water.

"When's dinner, Mrs. B?" The small voice belonged to a crooked little boy with thick glasses.

"Not for an hour, sweetie. Do you want some carrot sticks to hold you over?" Grace asked.

"That's okay." He looked disappointed.

"What's wrong?"

"It's just that I need some help with homework, but you're busy."

"I can help him." Wendy bounced down the stairs, almost poetically.

"Oh, thanks, Wendy," Grace replied. "You're a doll."

"Aren't I, though? Come on, Corey. I'll give you a hand."

Corey had just turned six and was in Kindergarten. Born with cerebral palsy, he walked with the aid of a set of metal crutches. He hobbled over to a small table and took a seat. Wendy squatted into a chair that was clearly designed for someone at least half her size.

"What are we working on tonight? Algebra? Physics?

Voltaire?"

"Volt-what?" Corey giggled. "I have to color a picture of a tree at the park," Corey said, looking dejected.

"You don't like to color?"

"Well, my hands kind of shake and I can never stay in the lines." His head bowed in embarrassment.

"Hey, look at me." Wendy tilted up his chin gently with her index finger. "I have a secret and only you can know it."

He looked intrigued.

"The best things in life happen outside the lines. Why would you want to stay inside them? That's so boring. Let me show you."

Wendy picked a crayon out of a plastic tub in the middle of the table. The label called it "Electric Lime." She colored the top part of the tree, intentionally scribbling a good portion outside the black line, barely missing a bird flying overhead. "See what I mean?"

Corey smiled. "Yeah, it looks good." He reached for an asthma inhaler, took a puff, and grabbed another crayon— "Mountain Meadow"—and began scribbling wildly.

They both colored simultaneously, leaving the tree about twice its intended size.

"Now listen," Wendy said. "The entire world is going to give you lines to stay in. When that happens, just remember this tree. It's so much bolder and fuller and more exciting now that we made our own lines. Live outside the lines."

Corey gave her a big hug as the front door creaked open. Wendy quickly released Corey and quietly started coloring again.

"Hey, honey. Hi, kids." Detective Barnes kissed his wife on the cheek and removed his suit jacket, revealing a badge and handgun at his waist. He stepped over to a gun safe built into the wall, blocking it with his body as he entered a six-digit code. Removing his gun from his belt, he placed it carefully into the safe and closed the door, pushing a few more buttons to lock it into place.

Wendy paid no attention. Barnes was very secretive about the safe combination, and rightly so. Not even his darling wife knew the combination. Of course, Wendy already did.

About a week after she moved in with Grace and Ryan Barnes, the latest in a long string of foster families, Wendy deciphered the code. All she needed was a small slipup. Ryan must have had a particularly trying day, so he poured himself a whiskey before opening the gun safe. He placed the glass on a small shelf over a coat rack before retiring his firearm for the night. Again, he blocked the keypad with his body, but in Wendy's eyeshot was a distorted, mirrored image of the numbers reflected off the curve of the whiskey glass. She only needed to glance through her peripheral vision to pick up the sequence—1-0-1-7-0-6.

October 17, 2006? Maybe an anniversary. Maybe just random numbers. It didn't matter; she had the code. She tested it after school one day before Ryan was home and while Grace was busy upstairs with Corey. Ryan's service pistol was on him, but she was pleased to see a spare revolver in there. Loaded. Whether Ryan was home, she would always have access to a firearm.

The agency never distributed guns. They were too loud and drew too much attention. They were also too easy to trace. However, Wendy got extensive firearms training. Even if they would not give her a gun, she needed to know how to use one, and she needed to be clever enough to know how to get one from someone else if the situation warranted it. She didn't know if she would need Ryan's gun, but she rested assured knowing she could get her hands on it if things turned south.

Wendy's experiences with foster parents had been mixed. She lumped them into three different categories. The first she called "Sunnies." They were a constant ray of sunshine. Everything was wonderful and amazing and perfect. No matter what happened, Sunnies handled it with a smile and a hug. These were people who fostered because they truly wanted to help people while improving their chances to make it through the Pearly Gates. Sunnies usually wanted you to call them "Mom" and "Dad" and always talked about being one big, happy family. Sunnies made her want to vomit.

The second group she called "Breakers" because they would do everything in their power to break you. They weren't afraid to smack you around a little and they knew where to hit you, so the marks weren't visible. Breakers left scars—both physical and psychological. She was afraid of Breakers when she was little, but she almost looked forward to them as she got older. The look on a foster parent's face when you can take a punch and then return it with even more gusto was priceless. It also gave her an opportunity to vent some of her aggression. She had to be careful, though. Breakers often had difficulty knowing when to stop breaking.

Finally, there was a group she referred to as "Bambis," who were timid and unsure about how to handle foster kids. They were typically fairly new at fostering and acknowledged that they weren't your actual parents. They tiptoed around rules and problems to avoid conflict. The Barneses were Bambis. She liked Bambis. Bambis didn't hover or get in your business. It was a lot easier to get away with things with Bambis—detention, for example.

The twist with the Barneses, though, was Ryan's occupation. You would think having a detective in the house would complicate things for someone like Wendy, but she actually found it exhilarating. The imminent risk of capture would probably make most people apprehensive, but Wendy saw it as a challenge. She was also rather cocky, so thinking she was smarter than a trained detective, while imprudent, was also mentally stimulating. She needed a challenge sometimes, and Ryan was it.

"You know I hate bringing work home, but I just can't shake this case," Ryan said to his wife. Wendy continued coloring with Corey in the next room, indicating in no way that she could hear their conversation.

"We found a husband and wife brutally murdered on their bed," Ryan continued.

"How awful," Grace replied. "Were they shot?"

"No, actually. Stabbed."

Grace shuddered.

"With a syringe of all things."

Wendy's ears perked up.

"Yeah, I'll spare you the gruesome details, but I just can't get the image out of my head… or the smell. They sat there rotting for three or four days."

Wendy smirked and thought, *Five, actually.*

Chapter 3

POPPY

"I'm just saying, if you're gonna collect kiddie porn, why keep it on hard drives just lying around your house? Store it in the cloud, or something." Tommy seemed to have it all figured out.

"Is that where you keep yours, Tommy?" Amaya teased.

"Storing it in the cloud would make it too easy for authorities to hack," Wendy clarified.

"Oh…"

Silence.

Tommy contemplated this way too hard.

"You're not the brightest knife in the drawer, are you there, Tommy-boy?" Leave it to Amaya.

"Isn't the expression…?" Tommy stopped as Amaya got ready to kick.

"Don't you ever learn your lesson?" Amaya hit him twice in the shoulder instead. "Two for flinching."

"He probably just shouldn't have collected kiddie porn in the first place. Then he wouldn't have to hide it on a hard drive or a cloud or anything." Meg's simplicity brought a smile to Wendy's face.

It had been a week since Mr. Godwin died and was subsequently outed for his dirty hobby, but it was still anyone wanted to talk about. West Elmdale, New Jersey, was a relatively small town, and the biggest news before this was the Whole Foods that was going to open in the spring. All the lacrosse moms were excited to stock up on gluten-free bread or some trendy fodder like that.

The three girls strolled down the sidewalk in the town square while Tommy trailed behind.

"What if you just have, like, normal porn in the cloud?" Tommy asked. "Can the feds hack into that, too? I mean, like, hypothetically?"

"No one wants to see your collection of lesbo porn," Amaya consoled. "Relax and whack off with a clear conscience."

"Ah, cool!"

"Just make sure you cover your webcam."

"Wait, what? Why?"

Amaya ignored the follow-up question.

Tommy's step hustled as his concern intensified. "Amaya…?"

Amaya's face scrunched up as her walking slowed. "Hang on," she said. "I gotta sneeze." She cocked her head back, grabbed Wendy's arm and sneezed right into the crux of her elbow.

"Dude!" Wendy objected. "What's your deal?"

"They always say to sneeze into an elbow, so you don't spread germs."

"Yeah, your *own* elbow." Wendy shook her arm in exaggerated disgust, but she couldn't hold back her smile.

"Eh," Amaya replied. "Tomayto, tomahto."

Wendy wasn't accustomed to much human contact. She wasn't hugged often as a child. She never kissed a boy or even held one's hand. There was something almost intimate about Amaya's gesture. Disgusting, but intimate. It made her feel connected.

Up ahead, a familiar logo in a convenience store window caught Wendy's eye. The sticker bore the image of a yellow smiley face. Something like an emoji on steroids. The eyes were wide and blue, and it pursed its lips into a perfect O with a bright pink bubble protruding from them. It raised its eyebrows in a way that suggested that this little smiley face was exuberantly excited about the bubble it was blowing. A thumbs-up was superimposed on its side, showing approval of its gum choice.

"Hey, guys. I need to pop in here. I'll just be a sec," Wendy said.

"No biggie. We'll come with," Amaya replied.

The group entered the convenience store, and Wendy grabbed a pack of Skittles and a pack of M&Ms.

"Diet of champions," Amaya said.

Wendy smirked and tossed the bags of candy onto the counter. "I like to mix them," she explained to the cashier.

The cashier reached under the counter and grabbed a plastic bag and placed the Skittles and M&Ms inside.

"Three twenty-five," the cashier said.

Wendy gave her the money while peaking inside the bag. She saw her Skittles, her M&Ms, and a pack of gum bearing the same emoji image from the store window. The label on the gum read, "Wonder Rush Happy Funtime Bubblegum."

"That is so repulsive," Tommy said as they left the store.

"I rarely agree with Tweedle Dumbass over here, but that is a pretty nasty combo, Wen," Amaya concurred.

"I don't know," Meg said with an air of cheerful support. "It could be good."

"Here. Try it." Wendy called her bluff. She grabbed both the bag of Skittles and the bag of M&Ms in one hand and tore the top off both simultaneously. Wendy tipped the bags into Meg's hand, sprinkling a few of each together.

Meg tossed them into her mouth and reluctantly chewed. Her chewing slowed as she choked down the candy and feigned a smile. "It's not too bad." Her smile widened to reveal bits of candy stuck in her braces, but she looked like she wanted to regurgitate it all onto the sidewalk.

Wendy smirked. The saccharin sweet people of the world usually turned her off, but Meg was genuine. In all honesty, it was a disgusting combination. She never even tried it herself. It was a code the agency came up with, knowing no one would ever really combine the two, let alone feel the need to announce it to the salesclerk. It would be like ordering a pizza with extra anchovies. It was possible, but highly improbable. On the off chance that someone would not only buy Skittles and M&Ms intending to mix them and announce said plans to the convenience store clerk, well, all they would get would be a free pack of gum.

* * *

Her bedroom door creaked as Wendy gingerly slid it closed. She heard Grace and Corey talking about something downstairs, but she couldn't quite make it out. Wendy turned the lock clockwise until it clicked into place.

This was it. Wendy took a deep breath and sat on the side of her bed, tossed her phone next to her, and reluctantly opened the bag of candy. It was as if she were defusing a bomb, and if she cut the wrong wire, the whole thing would explode.

Wendy grabbed the pack of gum and tossed the rest of the candy aside. She stared at it for several seconds, rolling it around between her fingers, her knee nervously bouncing up and down. The rectangular package was banana blond with that godforsaken smiley face glaring at her in obnoxious neon yellow. She recalled fond memories of that smiley face as a child. It represented new and exciting experiences for her. She even named it "Poppy." Not the most original name, but she was probably five or six when she came up with it. She didn't know if the agency had a name for it and she never shared hers. She even wrote a jingle for Poppy when she was a child.

> *Poppy, the popping gum.*
> *Chew, chew, chew till you're all done.*
> *When the flavor starts to gush,*
> *That's the Happy Funtime Wonder Rush!*

Thinking of that jingle now just put a pit in her stomach. Today, she greeted Poppy with trepidation. Today, it represented the possibility of walking away from Amaya and her life as Wendy.

She picked at a small red tab sticking out from the side of the pack of gum, gripped it in between her unpolished fingernails, and slowly tore it off, leaving the top of the package resting like a hat on the sticks of gum underneath. Wendy took another deep breath, hoping for pink.

Wonder Rush Happy Funtime Bubblegum came in a pack of ten flat sticks of gum. Nine of those ten were wrapped in plain white paper. The tenth was color-coded, featuring a picture of Poppy in the center of the wrapper. If the paper was pink, it represented a new mission. However, a blue wrapper would inform her she was about to get a new identity. It was a signal for her to pack the few belongings she had and get ready to go somewhere else and be someone else. She hoped that paper was pink. She wasn't done in West Elmdale. She wasn't done with Amaya.

Wendy pulled the top off the pack of gum and breathed a sigh of relief.

Pink.

She inhaled deeply and then slid the pink stick out of the package and unwrapped it. It appeared to be a standard stick of gum. It was a deep rose color, somewhere between pink and red, rectangular and flat. It had no visible markings and wouldn't stand out in any way to the outside observer, but Wendy knew differently.

Opening her mouth, Wendy dragged the stick of gum slowly across her tongue and reached for her phone. The saliva uncovered a pattern across the gum, a collection of dots and dashes, squares and circles. It looked like hieroglyphics you might find inside a cave on a foreign planet, strange and alien.

Wendy tapped an icon on her phone in the shape of Poppy, which brought up the camera app with four right angle anchors, one on each corner of the screen. Holding the phone above the stick of gum, Wendy aligned it inside the four corner anchors. Immediately, a map popped up with a blinking yellow dot indicating a destination. A second blue dot appeared (Wendy's current location), and finally a red line connected the two. There was a date and time printed underneath. Tomorrow. 8:00 am.

Wendy slid the gum into her mouth and chewed away the evidence.

Strawberry. Her favorite.

* * *

Wendy hopped off the public bus with her backpack on her back and started walking. She was playing hooky, but she had to look like she was going to school when she left the house. A text alert vibrated her phone.

Amaya: *Dude, where are you?*

Wendy ignored the text. Then a few seconds later:

Amaya: *Pop quiz in pre-calc. Who am I going to cheat off of?*

Wendy smiled and shook her head.

Wendy: *Copy from Alex. He's smart.*

Amaya: *He also reeks!*

She included an emoji that looked like it smelled something rotten.

Amaya: *Seriously, where are you?*

Wendy: *Sick.*

She added an emoji with a thermometer sticking out of its mouth.

Amaya replied with an angry emoji. No "get better" or "I'm sorry you're sick," just an angry emoji. That made Wendy happy. She didn't need anyone checking up on her or offering to make her chicken soup. She never had a mother, and she didn't need one now.

Wendy turned a corner down a seedy-looking alley between two abandoned buildings. It was not the place you would want to be if you were an innocent high school girl. Luckily, Wendy was far from innocent.

She passed two men discreetly carrying out an illegal transaction of some sort, trying to be surreptitious. She caught their eye, and they quickly stuffed whatever it was they were dealing into their pockets. One man wore a black skullcap and a dirty tee shirt with the sleeves cut off. The other had a baseball cap on backwards and untied work boots.

"Hey, little lady," Skullcap shouted. "Ain't no place for no one like you 'round here."

Wendy put her head down and kept walking. She didn't want any trouble.

"Why don't you come here and give me a little sugar, baby?" Baseball Cap joined in.

Wendy kept walking, but they stepped in front of her, blocking her path.

"How's about you be a little more friendly?" Skullcap asked. "We're just lookin' to welcome you to our 'hood."

"I'm on my way to an appointment," Wendy explained. "I really must be going."

"An appointment? Oh… 'scuse me," Baseball Cap interjected. "We'll be nice and quick. Don't you worry that pretty little head of yours." He stroked Wendy's hair as Skullcap pulled a knife from his pocket.

Wendy laughed and shook her head.

"Something funny?" Skullcap asked.

"You guys have no idea what you walked into," she responded. "This is going to be fun."

Wendy kicked Baseball Cap in the crotch with a solid thud. As he bent over, clutching his jewels, she linked both of her hands together and sprung her arms up into his nose, bursting it instantly. Blood gushed from the center of his face. To put a cherry on top, she punched him directly in the windpipe, and he dropped to the ground like a marionette with its strings clipped.

Skullcap just stood there in shock with the knife in his hand. It had all happened in a matter of seconds, and he didn't have time to react. Wendy spun around and swept her leg at his feet. Skullcap fell hard, tossing the knife in the air as he lost its grip. Wendy caught the knife mid-air and slammed it into Skullcap's chest. She ripped off a section of his already torn tee shirt, wiped her fingerprints from the handle, and pelted it down onto Skullcap's stomach.

"Anything else you have to say?" she asked Baseball Cap, who was on the ground, grasping at his throat. He tried to speak but couldn't. He just pulled himself to his feet and hobbled away, gurgling as he tried to form words.

* * *

The large steel door looked old and worn through multiple layers of chipped paint, the outermost being a putrid green. In the lower corner was a Poppy sticker, its jovial countenance juxtaposed against the hideous filth of the decrepit building. She was in the right place.

Inside was dark and glum. An echo of dripping water pulsated through the room from some unseen, distant corner. Each of Wendy's steps reverberated loudly against the filthy linoleum floor. Suddenly, a flash of blinding light filled the room, accompanied by the electric hum of what sounded like a thousand bumble bees. Wendy shielded her eyes with her forearm, as if staring into the sun.

"Wendy Lockheart," a shapeless voice gestured to a chair in the middle of the room. "Have a seat."

"God, you always have to be so overdramatic," Wendy said. "How about a couch and a couple of normal lamps with those LED bulbs? Let's be a little environmentally conscious here."

"I'll be sure to install a suggestion box," the voice replied. Even before he stepped into the light, Wendy knew who it was. The strain on the vowels as he spoke failed to mask the Bulgarian accent.

"How have you been, Genko?" Wendy asked.

"We will skip the small talk. Yes, child?"

Wendy nodded. She knew by calling her "child," Genko was attempting to belittle her and assert his dominance. She was well-versed in the agency's mind games after all these years.

Genko handed her a tablet with a photo of a man in his mid-sixties with gray hair and baggy eyes. "The target is Peter McMahon."

Wendy flipped through a few pictures of him from different angles. She swiped through quickly until she reached a financial document. She glanced at it momentarily before swiping to the next one.

"I'm not an accountant, Genko. What am I looking at?"

"Peter McMahon is the President and CEO of McMahon Investments in the city," Genko explained. "He runs a Ponzi scheme where he swindles his clientele out of most of their money. Some are Wall Street pricks who deserve to be taken down a rung or two, but some are normal people just trying to save for retirement—teachers, nurses, middle management. A librarian gave him her entire life savings and *poof.* Gone. All of it. She hung herself and he bought a new shore house."

"Sounds like a case the feds can handle," Wendy said.

"They tried. Nothing seems to stick to this guy. He has offshore accounts funneling to other offshore accounts. Fall guys who get a slap on the wrist. McMahon always seems to walk away clean."

"Okay, so what's the play?"

Genko handed Wendy a wooden case about the size of a pencil box. She opened it up to find a syringe on one side and a dropper bottle filled with a blue liquid on the other.

"His lavish lifestyle finally caught up with him and he had a heart attack."

"I'm crushed," Wendy said sarcastically.

"Unfortunately, he pulled through. He's recuperating in the hospital now and being released this afternoon. He'll be back in his bed at home tonight."

"You want me to poison him?"

"No. The liquid is nothing more than a sedative. The same active ingredient as Ambien, which he already takes nightly. A little more in his system won't look suspicious. Give him a dropper full of that while he sleeps, wait thirty minutes, and he won't wake up for anything."

"What's the needle for?"

"He'll have a few sutures on his chest from where they made the incision for his surgery. Stick the needle right in there, straight into the heart, and just inject the air from the syringe."

"Air is going to kill him?" Wendy asked.

"His heart is weak. His chest was just opened. A little air in the heart will cause a gas embolism and lead to another heart attack. This time, fatal. In his condition, no one would be surprised or even suspect foul play. Easy-peasy."

"Any kids or a spouse I need to be aware of?"

"The kids are grown—out of the house. The bastard snores like a chainsaw, so the wife, Abigail, sleeps in a spare room. She shouldn't give you any trouble. Any other questions, child?"

"Just one," Wendy said. "On your way out of here, you may bump into a douchebag with a black skullcap and ripped tee shirt. Oh, and he also has a knife sticking out of his chest... Can you clean that up for me?"

Chapter 4

ABIGAIL

Wendy's gloved hand clenched the stiff doorknob. Locked. She assumed as much, but it was worth a shot. She pulled a kit from her backpack and slid out a pair of metal picks, placing one in the bottom of the lock and one slightly above it. With a twist and a click, the door latch relented.

A floorboard groaned as Wendy's body weight shifted to the rigid leg that had just crossed the threshold. She was careful to use the back door since a few thick trees and a privacy fence blocked it from the neighbors' view. Oh, how these arrogant pricks love their privacy. No alarm system. It surprised her, but she could disarm one if she needed. She was glad she didn't have to bother.

Her heart pounded through the labored silence, and she paused to allow her eyes a moment to adjust to the stark blackness of the unlit home. The clock above the stove read, "2:33 am." The tight ponytail Wendy had pulled her hair into tickled the back of her neck, and her black neoprene face mask itched her nose. She wore a skin-tight black Lycra bodysuit, finished with black sneakers on her feet. She carried a small, black backpack strapped across her shoulders, and black leather gloves shrouded her hands. She was the epitome of a walking shadow.

Wendy tiptoed to the staircase and slowly ascended. The third step creaked, freezing her in place. With her breath held, she shifted her weight to the other leg, straddled past the creaky stair and onto the next one.

A bead of sweat formed at her hairline as Wendy traversed the hall, peering into each room. She spotted an empty bedroom, a bathroom, and a home office. She pushed open a door that was slightly ajar and stopped the second the hinges broke the silence. Locked in suspended animation, Wendy prayed she hadn't woken the middle-aged woman lying on her side. Her sluggish, deliberate breath convinced Wendy the woman was fast asleep, and she continued toward the closed door of what she assumed was the master bedroom.

Soft moonlight trickled through the hallway window, illuminating her leather-clad hand as it reached for the knob and turned it. She pushed the door in slowly, pausing each time the slightest sound echoed off the hinges. Peter McMahon lay on his back, his grating snore reverberating through her like a jackhammer. The revolting man wore only boxer shorts, his legs splayed out in front of him. Wendy cringed. Then she spotted the stitches on his chest.

Setting her backpack onto the floor, Wendy gripped the wooden case that she received from Genko—sliding it out inch by inch as it rubbed up against the coarse stitching of her bag. She cracked it open and removed the dropper of blue fluid. Filling the dropper, Wendy hovered over Peter. His mouth was hanging open, and Wendy recoiled at the stench of his breath each time he snored in and out. She dangled the dropper over his gaping orifice and slowly gave it a squeeze. A few drops of blue fluid dripped into his mouth before his lips locked closed and he shifted in his bed. A single drop had fallen just as his mouth sealed and now trickled down his chin like the grease from his gluttonous supper.

Wendy pulled back immediately and disappeared into the shadows. Peter smacked his lips together, then kept snoring, his mouth agape once more. Wendy dribbled the rest of the fluid deliberately into the man's mouth, retrieved a tissue from her backpack, and dabbed his chin. She then stepped away. Glancing at her watch, Wendy grabbed her bag and slipped out of the room.

She bunkered down in the abandoned bedroom, removed her face mask, and inhaled a deep, satisfying breath. She had thirty minutes to kill. Wendy looked around and quickly deduced that she was in their son's old room. Genko acknowledged the kids were grown, but it was impossible to tell by looking at this room. They must have left it exactly as it was before he moved out. A shrine of sorts. There were posters of baseball players—Yankees mostly— along with a pennant, a signed baseball bat, and a few trophies, each with a brass batter resting on top.

She never met the boy, but she imagined he had a happy childhood, and his parents were probably proud of his accomplishments. She pictured them hugging him with a congratulatory slap across the back as he won each of those trophies. They probably beamed from ear to ear. Wendy had no one to make proud. No one to disappoint either, so that was the trade-off.

If she had parents or anyone who cared about her at all, would they be proud? How could they be? Look at her. It was nearly three o'clock in the morning, on a school night, and she was killing time in a house she broke into, about to end a man's life. It's the only world she had ever known, and it was exhilarating. But was it really what she wanted for herself? No one ever gave her a choice. What do you do when you have spent your entire life, since birth, being trained for a single purpose? What happens once you're old enough to question things? Is it too late? Has the die been cast?

Wendy shook these thoughts from her head. Now was not the time to lose focus. She had a purpose, and she was actually rather good at what she did. Even if no one else was proud of her, she could feel proud of herself. She excelled at… what? Killing people? She breathed a deep sigh, clenched her eyes, and then checked her watch. Close enough.

Affixing the mask back onto her face, Wendy rose, gripped the needle, shouldered her backpack, and snuck back into Peter's room. His sleep was so deep now that his snoring had stopped. He was so quiet that she took a moment to study his chest and make sure it was rising and falling. Yes, he was still breathing. She smacked him across the face to ensure he was sleeping. He barely budged. If his sleep wasn't deep enough, a needle straight to the heart would bolt him awake screaming. She had to be certain.

Her grip tightened around the syringe, and her pulse throbbed in her knuckles with each heartbeat. She drew in a slow breath and held it as she proceeded with the needle. Checking for any discernable response, she glided it in between Peter's sutures—one millimeter and then another. Nothing. She could feel the needle press past his rib cage and into softer tissue. She rested her thumb on the plunger, the barrel filled with air. Suddenly, a bludgeoning thud struck her mid-back, directly across the spine. Wendy dropped to the ground like a rag doll.

A nearly deafening ringing in her ears muffled a woman's frantic screams. Wendy turned toward the sound, but her entire field of vision blurred together, creating a dizzying mixture of light and color. She instinctively twisted as a baseball bat swung directly toward her skull, striking the floor less than an inch from her ear.

Is that the autographed bat from the boy's bedroom? He must have been thrilled to receive it. Probably signed by one of the greats. It's strange the things that come to mind at times like these.

"You get away from my husband!" The woman's scream narrowed into focus.

This must be Abigail. Not such a sound sleeper, after all.

"What are you doing to him?" Abigail's voice quivered. She didn't wait for Wendy to respond before swinging the bat again.

Now that more of her bearing had returned, Wendy rolled away from the impending strike and spun to her feet. Intuition kicked in, and she had no time to contemplate the fiasco this was about to become.

Priority number one was eliminating the bat. Abigail gripped it tightly with both hands, but she trembled in fear.

"Who are you? What do you want?" She swung the bat. Her teeth clenched, but her lips trembled.

Wendy intentionally did not respond. She still had the element of the unknown. Wendy was a mystery to her, and people fear what they don't understand. Once she spoke, Wendy would become an actual person. Now she was just a specter, a nightmare, a boogeyman creeping through their home in the middle of the night.

"Wake up, Peter," Abigail said as she nudged her sleeping husband with the tip of the bat. He didn't budge.

As her husband drew her attention, the needle still protruding from his chest, Wendy hit the woman hard in the solar plexus with her tightly clenched fist. Panic flooded Abigail's face as she gasped for breath. She hunched over, grabbing her chest, but she dropped the bat. Wendy picked it up and swung it at the woman. Abigail instinctively turned her shoulder toward the strike, and the blow landed on her arm.

Wendy adjusted her grip on the bat so one hand was on the narrow handle and the other on the wider barrel. She slammed the butt of the bat into Abigail's chest a few times until she fell to the bed next to her husband.

With Abigail subdued, Wendy dropped the bat to the floor.

Peter rested, sound asleep, next to his injured wife. Wendy knew there would be repercussions for her actions that night, but it could have been worse. She would finish up Peter and just let the wife sleep off her injuries. She never saw Wendy's face or heard her voice, and she left no fingerprints. That provided her with a modicum of solace.

Wendy bent down to pick up her backpack when something cold and hard pressed against her throat. She attempted to swallow but couldn't. Her eyes caught her reflection in a mirror across the room, and she saw Abigail behind her with her hands clasped on either side of the bat, Wendy's neck sandwiched in between the bat and Abigail's body.

Wendy slammed her elbow straight behind her with full force, knocking Abigail off her and relieving the pressure on her neck. Wendy coughed and grabbed the woman around the throat. Abigail responded in the same way. Now, both women's eyes locked, each grasping the other's neck.

A struggle ensued as they both fell to the bed next to Peter, who was now snoring again. Wendy was on top of Abigail, but Abigail was relentless. The woman's spryness shocked Wendy. She must do Pilates or something, Wendy thought. Zumba maybe.

Wendy eyed the syringe still sticking out of Peter's sutured chest wound, released her right hand from Abigail's throat, and grabbed the needle. She slammed the syringe directly into Abigail's eye, and she howled in pain as she loosened her grip on Wendy's neck. Wendy took a few deep breaths as Abigail lay lifeless next to her sleeping husband, the needle protruding from her left eye like a flagpole planted on newly discovered land.

Wendy reached for the syringe. She yanked it from Abigail's eye socket and the eyeball came with it, the severed optic nerve dangling from behind. Wendy stared at the eye, which glared at her from the end of the needle. She jerked the syringe toward the ground and the eyeball slipped off the end, landing on the carpet next to the bed.

Now out of patience, Wendy jabbed the needle into Peter's chest like a knife—once, twice, three times. Her blood boiled with rage and frustration as she continued stabbing Peter, overwrought with thoughts of how the agency would retaliate for this debacle. When she finally tired, she had left fifteen tiny stab wounds in a puddle of blood on his chest. Abigail lay on her side next to her husband, a river of thick blood and fluid running from her eye socket and onto the mattress.

Wendy panted like a dog in the blistering sun and pulled away from the bed. She completed the job, but it was an understatement to say that it did not go as planned. She glanced at herself in the mirror, her forehead and hair sprinkled with droplets of blood, the heavier flow hidden in the blackness of her bodysuit and face mask. She couldn't go home like this. Wendy grabbed the baseball bat from a puddle of blood on the floor and took it with her into the master bathroom.

She turned the squeaky knobs of the shower, waited a moment for it to heat up, and stepped in, fully dressed and holding the bat. She even left on her sneakers. The water ran bright red as it cascaded off her body and hair. She closed her eyes and let the soothing water run over her for a few minutes before rinsing the blood off the bat. Now she could see that Derek Jeter had signed it. Probably worth a few bucks.

Once the water ran clear, Wendy turned off the shower and grabbed a towel from the towel bar. She dried herself and the baseball bat. After slipping off her shoes, she also dried her feet. She didn't want to leave wet shoe tracks throughout the house. She would put them back on once she was clear of the McMahon home.

Wendy wrung out the towel, folded it tightly, and stuffed it into her backpack. Surely no one would notice a missing bath towel.

She grabbed the bat and stared at it, contemplating the best way to dispose of it. She could carry it home and deal with it later, but it was too cumbersome to hide. Plus, how would she get rid of it? Burn it? Toss it into a wood chipper? Unlikely. Ultimately, she walked the bat back into the McMahons' son's room and placed it on the shelf where she first saw it. Even if there were trace amounts of blood buried in the wood, it wasn't her blood. Abigail gave her a good struggle, but she never broke skin.

Before leaving the house, Wendy took one last look into the master bedroom. It was a ghastly mess. But hey, things happen, right? Truth be told, it was the most fun she had had in a while. Five days later, Detective Ryan Barnes, Wendy's foster father, would discover this gruesome scene, and the agency would undoubtedly pull Wendy away from West Elmdale forever.

Chapter 5

COREY

A hollow *ping* rang from the red rubber ball as Hannah bounced it three times in quick succession. She spit the hair from her mouth as the wind blew her blond pigtail into her face. At five years old, Hannah was already the star pitcher for the recess kickball team.

"Here you go, Corey," she shouted to the boy in the batter's box, which was nothing more than an area in the dirt where the leaves were kicked clean. "Let's see what you got."

Corey stood there, uncertain of himself, his body weight supported by a metal crutch in each arm. Hannah rolled the ball as slowly and carefully as she could, so Corey could have every chance to kick it. She did not grant such leniency to just anyone in the playground, but she liked Corey. All the girls did.

As the ball roll-bounced toward the indentation in the dirt they called home plate, Corey swung his right crutch and caught the corner of the ball. It bounced less than three feet in front of him, but that was enough to make him gleam with delight.

"I hit it!" he shouted without moving.

"You have to run," a girl on his team said. "Go! Run!"

Corey hobbled toward a rock they designated as first base, and the ball rolled slowly back to Hannah. She pretended to lose control of the ball as Corey inched his way forward.

"Oh, no. Corey, you really put some spin on the ball. I can't catch it," she said.

The rest of the team cheered as Hannah threw the ball to the girl covering first base, who intentionally dropped it. Corey was safe.

"Base hit!" Hannah exclaimed. "Great job!"

Corey jumped up and down in excitement as the first baseman high-fived him. In all the excitement, he almost forgot to breathe. He removed his inhaler from his pocket and took a deep puff. Off to the side, Corey overheard a group of boys talking.

"We're going to have cake *and* ice cream," Jordan exclaimed.

"Sweet… and a bouncy house too, right?" Marco asked.

"That's right!"

"Oh, man! It's going to be so fun!"

"Is the whole class coming?" Trevor asked.

"Well, all the boys are," Jordan clarified. "My mom made me invite them all."

"Even the cripple?" Marco pointed toward Corey, who pretended not to hear, but his smile slowly faded from his face.

"He's probably gonna pop the bouncy house with his crutches," Trevor added.

Marco laughed. "I heard he doesn't even have parents. He's so weird."

Corey had been looking forward to Jordan's birthday party for weeks, ever since the invitation was sent home in his backpack. He picked out a super cool Lego set that Mrs. Barnes purchased as a gift for the occasion. He even knew exactly what he was going to wear—his new red Converse sneakers and a Star Wars tee shirt.

Jordan talked about Star Wars all the time, so Corey was sure it would make Jordan like him.

"Corey, you have to run!" Hannah shouted. He wasn't paying attention and his teammate, Chloe, had just kicked the ball. He had to get off of first base.

Flustered, Corey gripped his crutches and headed toward second. His right foot wrapped around his metal crutch, sending Corey tumbling to the ground, his face scraping on the dusty gravel below. A group of girls all rushed over and surrounded him.

"Are you okay?" Hannah asked, looking down at him.

Corey looked back up into her bright blue eyes, her blond ponytails hanging down, tickling his face. His stomach turned, and he couldn't help but smile through the pain. He wasn't sure what a crush was exactly, but he guessed he probably had one. Hannah didn't laugh when Corey fell. She always sauntered next to him rather than passing around the side like most other kids. He was sure that Hannah would never invite him to her birthday party simply because her mother made her. She was kind, and she was gentle, and she helped him back to his feet.

By then, Mrs. Flowers, the recess monitor, had rushed over to the scene.

"Clear the way, girls," she said. "Corey, you know you're not supposed to overexert yourself."

Corey laughed, partly because he didn't know what "overexert" meant and partly because Mrs. Flowers had picked him up like a baby and the laughter hid the embarrassment. As she carried him off the playground, Corey wondered what Mrs. Flowers's first name was. He thought it would be funny if it was Rose or Daisy or Tulip. Then he laughed even harder.

* * *

Wendy's eyebrows puckered in concentration as she sat at the kitchen table typing a homework assignment into her laptop. Mrs. Barnes stumbled through the front door with an arm around Corey, who was balancing an ice pack on his forehead.

"Oh, my God. What happened?" Wendy asked as she jumped up from the table.

"Corey had a minor accident on the playground today. He'll be fine," Mrs. B assured her.

"Oh, Corey. Let me see." Wendy gently lifted the ice pack from his forehead to reveal a small red scrape. "Not too bad. It makes you look tough. Chicks dig scars."

Corey blushed.

"I have to help him change, and I need to start dinner," Mrs. B explained.

"I'll take care of Corey, Mrs. B. You just focus on dinner."

"Oh, thank you, Wendy. What would I do without you?"

Wendy had a feeling Grace would soon find out, but she remained silent.

* * *

Corey was already with the Barneses for about a year before Wendy joined them. Wendy had been there for less than six months, but she really cared for Corey as if he were her actual brother.

Corey's father, Dennis, left when Corey was very young. Supposedly that's common in families with a CP child. The disorder puts a lot of strain on families and marriages. All babies need constant attention, but you know they will eventually grow up and learn to take care of themselves. A disabled child will need continuous care. Forever. Not everyone is strong enough for that. Add in all the medical expenses, and Corey's dad just couldn't take it.

His mother, Karen, was a loving woman. She worked hard to make ends meet, bouncing around from job to job. Waiting tables at the local diner (there was no shortage of those in New Jersey), working retail, whatever she could pick up. She was so focused on Corey's treatments that she let her own care slip. By the time her doctors discovered the cancer, it was untreatable. It had started in her breasts and metastasized to her lungs, bones, and brain. Two months later, Corey was alone.

Karen reached out to Dennis before she passed, but he had moved on with his life long before. She couldn't bear to think of Corey ending up in "the system," but she had no close family and Dennis was really the only option. She begged and pleaded with him to take some responsibility for his son, but he refused.

Maybe it was for the best. The Barneses were good people, and they truly loved Corey. Dennis probably wouldn't have been as generous with his heart.

Corey sat on the edge of his bed in his SpongeBob pajamas as Wendy wiped his face with a soapy washcloth.

"There you go, Core," she said. "Good as new."

"Thanks, Wendy." He hugged her, and then his face grew long.

"What's wrong?"

"Do you think I would pop a bouncy house? With my crutches, I mean."

"A bouncy house? What are you talking about?"

"Well, I was supposed to go to Jordan's birthday party on Saturday, but some kids at school said I'll pop the bouncy house. I don't want to pop it."

"I bet you could leave your crutches outside and get a decent bounce going without them," Wendy said.

"Well… I'm not going anyway," Corey replied.

"You've been talking about this party for weeks. Why wouldn't you go?"

"The other kids don't really want me there. Jordan's mom

made him invite me."

"Hey, I'm sure that's not true."

"It is. I heard him say it. He didn't mean for me to hear, but I heard anyway. I thought he could be my friend."

"Let me tell you something, Core," Wendy said as she draped her arm around his shoulder. "Jordan doesn't deserve to be your friend. You're way too good for him."

"You think?"

"I know. Plus," she continued, "I heard he eats his own boogers."

"Aw, that's disgusting!" Corey laughed.

"Yeah, that's disgusting. Do you want to be friends with a booger-eater?"

Corey shook his head.

"Lie down and prepare yourself for Wendy's Wonderful Bouncy House!" She jumped on the bed and kicked her legs up and down as Corey bounced around, laughing hysterically. Wendy leapt in the air and landed next to Corey. "You think that's fun? Just wait until you're inside a real bouncy house."

"I can't wait!" Corey said.

"So, you going to go to that little booger-eater's birthday party?"

"I guess so…"

"You guess so?" Wendy leapt back on her feet and bounced Corey around on the bed again as he laughed uncontrollably. "You guess so?"

"Yes," he said through tears of laughter.

"Yes, what?"

"Yes, I'll go."

"Go where?" She kept bouncing him on the bed.

"I'll go to the booger-eater's party!"

"That's more like it. Now," she stopped bouncing and sat back on the edge of the bed, "let's go get some grub. I'm starving."

* * *

"He's going to have cake *and* ice cream," Corey said excitedly as he wolfed down his lasagna.

"Slow down there, sport," Ryan said. "You don't want to choke."

Wendy smiled at Grace as she nibbled at her dinner.

"Well, it sure sounds like it will be a lovely party," Grace assured him.

"Yeah, oh, and I got a base hit in kickball today," Corey added. "Well... then I kind of fell on my face a little." He pointed to the scrape on his forehead. "It's okay though. Hannah helped me up." Corey blushed.

"Ooh..." Wendy teased. "Who's Hannah?"

"She's just... well, she's my friend."

"Uh huh..." Wendy winked at her foster brother.

"Any news on that case you were telling me about, honey?" Mrs. B changed the subject but was careful not to use the words "double murder" in front of the impressionable children.

Ryan looked apprehensive, unsure of what would be appropriate to share. "Nothing much," he finally said. "A few leads."

"What sort of leads?" Wendy asked, a bit too enthusiastically. "We're doing a chapter on forensics in my biology class," she fabricated to reduce suspicion. "It would really help my grade to learn as much as I can."

"I can't say much about it. It's an ongoing investigation."

"Huh. Okay. No problem." Wendy feigned disinterest.

"The guy recently had some heart surgery. We're looking for a syringe that might have..." he stopped to censor himself in front of the kids. "We're looking at some leads from hospital staff."

"We're learning about how they take fingerprints and DNA samples," Wendy added. "Any of that?"

"No prints. The perp probably wore gloves."

Perfect.

"A few hair fibers. The lab is running those."

Shit.

"Cool," Wendy interjected nonchalantly. "Let me know if you learn more. Maybe I can get some extra credit."

Ryan just nodded, grunted, and kept eating.

Wendy was somewhat alarmed that they figured out that the murder weapon was a syringe. She was careful to take it home with her. She grinned, knowing that the key piece of evidence was in the same house as the lead detective on the case. The risk of being caught made it so much more exciting.

She took solace in the fact, however, that they were looking at hospital employees. The prospect of capture excited her. Actual apprehension did not. Ryan was bound to stumble over a hospital employee with a prior charge and no alibi for the night of the murders. That would slow him down until she got reassigned.

Wendy took a deep breath. She was aware her days there were minimal, but she was happy for the first time since she could remember. She thought of Amaya and how much she cared for her friend. She would miss Corey terribly, too. For the first time, she felt like she had a sibling, and she wanted to be there to protect and guide him. She shook it off. All she could do was make the best of her remaining days as Wendy.

* * *

Corey sat on the edge of his bed wearing his Star Wars tee shirt, his red Converse-clad feet dangling off the side. He leaned his crutches up against the bed on the right side, and a wrapped birthday gift rested next to him on his left.

He caught Wendy's eye as she walked past his open door. She doubled back and leaned against the doorway.

"Today's the big day, huh? The booger-eater's party?" Wendy asked.

Corey nodded. He tried to look excited, but his face was very pale. Gray circles had formed under his eyes, breaking up the otherwise white pallor. Wendy's eyes widened, and she rushed to his side.

"Hey, what's wrong?" she asked in a concerned tone as she squatted down in front of him.

"Nothing. I'm fine." He didn't believe that himself, but he figured if he said it out loud, maybe it would become true. "I just need to…"

At that, Corey projectile vomited directly onto Wendy's chest and stomach. She leapt back out of instinct but stopped herself from screeching out loud.

"I'm sorry… I…"

"It's okay. It's okay," Wendy tried to convince him. "Mrs. B!" she shouted. "Mrs. B, can you come upstairs…? Like, now?"

She heard Grace thumping up the stairs at a quickened pace. "What's wrong? What happened?" And then she saw Wendy covered in puke.

"Oh, boy. Okay," Grace said as she assessed the scene. "Wendy, go get yourself cleaned up. I got Corey."

Grace moved the gift and crutches out of the way and helped Corey to a recumbent position, with his head resting on his pillow.

"It's okay, Corey," Grace said. "Just rest."

She put her hand on his forehead and held it there for a few seconds. "Let me get the thermometer," she added.

Corey heard her fumbling around with various items inside the hall closet before returning with a digital thermometer. She placed it in his ear and it emitted a gentle beep.

"One hundred two point seven. Oh, Corey. I'm so sorry, buddy. It looks like you have a bit of a stomach bug."

"But what about the bouncy house?" he asked feebly.

"We'll just have to do that another day."

"But the party is today. Jordan won't turn six ever again."

"No, but other kids will. I promise we'll find you a bouncy house when you're feeling all better. Okay?"

He nodded, but his disappointment was clear.

"Mrs. B?"

"Yes, sweetie?"

"Can you get me…?" but it was too late. Corey turned his head and vomited on his bedspread.

* * *

Wendy pulled a clean shirt over her head and grabbed the soiled one, tossing it into a laundry basket after scoffing in disgust. She loved Corey. His partially digested breakfast? Not so much.

Wendy got a kick out of Ryan discussing the syringe she used to kill Peter and Abigail with, but she realized she had been sloppy with protocol. The agency was adamant about proper and timely disposal of all tools. That's what they called them—"tools." She pictured herself rummaging through a toolbox, pushing aside the hammer, a screwdriver, a wrench… ah, yes, there's the bloody syringe I was looking for. Exactly what I need to fix that leaky faucet. Do I still detect some ocular fluid on the needle? That made her laugh. She needed to get rid of that syringe, though.

Wendy opened her closet; nice wide double-doors welcomed her to a walk-in. It wasn't huge by any stretch of the imagination, but she never had a walk-in closet before. She crawled to the far corner, pushed aside some clothes that had piled up, moved her purse, and a few pairs of shoes. The Barneses had been very generous with her wardrobe when she first moved in. It was mostly hand-me-downs and thrift store purchases, but it was all new to her and she was grateful.

She pulled up the carpet in the corner of the closet and stuck her finger in a hole in the floorboard. With a slight jerking motion, she pried up the board and reached inside. When her hand reemerged, it was gripping the wooden box that Genko had given her. She cracked it open to find an empty dropper bottle and a clean syringe. She had at least remembered to disinfect everything. She snapped the box closed and tossed it into her backpack.

Wendy pushed the carpet back into place and replaced her shoes and clothes to cover it. As she grabbed the purse, she stopped. It was the same designer knock-off she carried the day she poisoned Mr. Godwin at the football game. She had forgotten all about it and failed to dispose of the "tool" inside there as well. She pulled the bag out of the closet, figuring she would eliminate all loose ends at once—the syringe, the dropper bottle, and the ring attachment she used on Mr. Godwin.

Peering into the purse, she saw her old lipstick and pencils. Even the school ID that she thought she lost. She grabbed that and slid it into her back pocket. She pushed some items aside to reach the bottom of the purse, but she couldn't find what she was looking for. Flipping the bag upside down, she emptied the entirety of its contents onto the floor next to her. No ring attachment.

Through her closed door, she heard Corey vomit again, and panic flooded her veins.

"No… no, no, no," she half-whispered.

"No, no, no!" she continued with increasing volume as she threw her door open and ran towards Corey's room. She could hear Mrs. B downstairs on the phone, filling Ryan in on Corey's illness.

"Corey… Corey!"

He removed his head from the trash can he just vomited into and looked at her with glassy eyes. "Yeah…?"

"Corey, did you go into my purse?" she asked, her voice quivering in fear.

"What? No," he replied.

"Ah, thank God." She breathed a sigh of relief.

"Not today, I mean."

"What?"

"A few days ago. I needed a pencil. Mine broke, and I had to finish my math. It was too hard to go all the way downstairs." he said. "But yours were broken too."

"Did you take anything out of there, Corey? Please try to remember. This is *very* important."

"You mean the joy buzzer?"

"The what?"

"The joy buzzer. You know, you put the ring on your finger and then when you shake someone's hand, it zaps them."

"Oh, God. Corey, did you take my joy buzzer?" Her eyes widened.

"It's in my junk drawer."

Wendy furiously opened drawer after drawer in his dresser. Just clothes.

"Top right," he specified.

There it was—the ring attachment designed to deliver a dose of poison to an unapologetic pedophile. A murder weapon sitting in the junk drawer of a six-year-old boy.

"It's broken though," Corey said.

"Did you use it on anyone?" Wendy asked feverishly.

"No. I tried it on myself first, but it didn't work. Just got me kinda wet."

"Shit! Shit-shit-shit!" Wendy exclaimed.

Corey laughed at her choice of words, the laughter morphing into a cough and finally into a dry heave into the trash can next to him. Wendy grabbed the "joy buzzer" and ran out of the room.

Grace was still on the phone as Wendy barreled down the stairs, tossing her backpack over her shoulders.

"Get him to a hospital!" Wendy exclaimed.

Grace moved the phone from her ear. "Wendy, what are you talking about?"

"Hospital! Now! I have to go, but promise me you'll take him."

"Hey, hey, hey, relax a minute. It's just a little stomach bug."

"Yeah, well… My English teacher had a stomach flu too. Remember him?"

Of course she did. The entire town talked about it for a week.

"He had a stomach flu," Wendy continued, "and he died. He died! Just like that. Maybe… maybe the flu is going around town."

"Wendy, honey, this is not the same—"

"Look. Listen to me. I need to go, but promise me you're going to take him to a hospital."

"Wendy…"

"Promise me! Humor me, whatever. Do you promise?"

"Um… okay, sure…"

"You promise? Say it!"

"Yes, I promise."

Wendy flew out of the house, slamming the front door behind her.

* * *

Sprinting down the street, Wendy charged toward the convenience store where she received her last pack of Wonder Rush gum. The sticker was no longer in the window, but she bolted through the door without noticing.

She knocked over a display of candy bars as she grabbed a package of Skittles and M&Ms. She fidgeted with them in line as she waited for the woman ahead of her to pick out a lottery scratcher.

"No... not that one..." the woman told the clerk as he attempted to retrieve her desired ticket.

"Come on, come on, come on..." Wendy mumbled to herself as she bounced on the balls of her feet, ready to pounce like a lioness on her prey.

"My son got me one last time... What was the name of that one...?" the woman contemplated.

Wendy was ready to jump out of her skin.

"I think it was a BINGO game... I remember scratching a bunch of little squares..."

The clerk behind the counter looked like he just wanted to get back to his Snapchat feed.

Wendy grunted. "Oh, my God. Come on!"

"Excuse me." The woman turned around to face Wendy. "You just wait your turn, young lady. You're being very rude."

"You're going to lose, anyway. Hang onto your dollar." Wendy pushed the woman aside, and she stumbled before catching her footing. Wendy slammed her candy on the counter and hurriedly shouted, "I like to mix them."

The clerk just stared at her. The woman scoffed and walked away, flipping Wendy the middle finger.

"I like to mix them," she repeated. "I like to mix them! Come on..."

"That's seriously disgusting." The clerk scanned the candy and said, "That'll be three twenty-five."

Wendy dropped her money as her unsteady hand reached into her pocket. She bent down, picked it up, and threw it on the counter. "Here. Money. Let's go!"

The clerk handed Wendy a bag with her candy. She looked inside. No gum.

"Shit! I like to mix them, I said," Wendy pleaded. "Where's

my gum?"

"You didn't buy any gum."

Wendy let out an indiscernible groan as she threw the candy on the ground and ran out of the store.

* * *

Wendy nervously tapped the seat in front of her as she mumbled to herself. "Come on, come on, come on. Can this bus go any frigging slower? Seriously?"

She leapt to her feet as the bus slowed, jumping out the moment the doors opened.

Wendy ran through the alley (quickly flashing back to the thug she stabbed in the chest) and threw open the cold metal door with the green, chipped paint. This was the building where she last met with Genko, although the Poppy sticker was now missing.

She shouldn't have been surprised. The agency never picked the same location twice, but she had to try something. She sprinted into the abandoned warehouse screaming, "Hello! Hello! Genko? Anybody here?"

Her own words echoed back to her, but the only reply she heard was the incessant dripping of that goddamn leaky pipe.

"Uhhh-ahhh!" she yelled as she ran outside and back to the street.

Wendy looked up into the cloudless sky, shouting, "Wonder Rush! Wonder Rush! Wonder Rush!"

Nothing.

Panicked tears welled in her eyes and her voice shook with fear as she started singing the jingle she made up as a child. She knew it only existed in her own mind, but she had no way to contact the agency, and she was desperate.

"Poppy, the popping gum," she sang at the top of her lungs. "Chew, chew, chew till you're all done."

Still nothing.

She wiped her leaky nose with the sleeve of her sweatshirt and continued. "When the flavor starts to gush, that's the Happy Funtime Wonder—"

A solid blow to the back of Wendy's head instantly silenced her. Her visual field went stark white before her body collapsed and she slumped onto the sidewalk.

Chapter 6

REBECCA

Isabella Martinez stood in the corner, fidgeting with a strand of curly raven hair that had slipped out from under the yellow ribbon that was struggling to hold it back. Her deep brown eyes angled toward the floor, unsure of what they expected of her. She wore a bright red tee shirt with a name tag pinned to the right side of her chest; however, the badge identified her simply as "6."

At eight years old, she was one of the younger girls, aged eight to ten, who filled the room, each wearing the same red tee shirt and similarly numbered name tag.

"In just a moment, the blue team will join you." The voice belonged to Gerald Holter, but that would be *Doctor* Holter to you—thank you very much.

Dr. Holter's credentials resulted from a Ph.D. rather than an M.D., but that never prevented him from correcting those who called him "Mister Holter," "Gerald," or, God forbid, "Gerry."

Dr. Holter forewent the formal white lab coat in favor of the more casual corduroy slacks and a loose-knit sweater. Why an experimental psychologist and university professor would even own a white lab coat is anyone's guess. Supposedly, he liked how official it made him look.

"There are six of you here on the red team," he continued, "and six more on the blue team." The door opened and six equally awkward looking eight to ten-year-old girls streamed in.

"You girls are in for a treat today." He mocked youthful excitement as only a childless adult can. "We have six big, delicious cupcakes for you."

A college-aged girl entered the room, placing a tray of cupcakes onto a table in the corner. Each sweet treat was piled high with a swirling mound of bright yellow icing covered with a generous helping of rainbow sprinkles.

"Now, there are twelve of you and only six cupcakes," Holter explained. "For each one you eat, your team will get one point. When the cupcakes are gone, the team with the most points will celebrate with a big pizza party!" There was that sickeningly phony excitement again.

"Otherwise," he concluded, "there are no rules. Now, go enjoy some cupcakes."

Rebecca Quinn sat behind a desk outside the room, looking in through a one-way mirror. She perched a clipboard on her lap, leaning on the desk in front of her. She scribbled a few notes as she observed. Rebecca was in her early twenties and a graduate student studying under Dr. Holter. She wore a loose-fitting flowered dress that would prove to be ankle length once she stood up, and she hid her looks behind her studious persona. It wasn't intentional. She was just always too focused on her studies and dissertation research to pay much attention to anything as trivial as makeup tutorials or hair trends.

Most of the young girls approached the table of cupcakes with some apprehension. Isabella stayed in the corner by herself. A gruff girl, who was a good three inches taller than any other girl there, plowed straight through to the table and grabbed two cupcakes. She wore a blue shirt with a number "4" name tag. A smaller girl (red, number "1") pushed her, although Blue-4 didn't budge.

"Hey," Red-1 exclaimed, "you can't have two. That's not fair."

"The old guy said no rules, so there." She pushed Red-1 to the ground and Blue-4 took a bite out of each cupcake—one in each hand.

Dr. Holter looked directly at the mirror, knowing Rebecca was on the other side. He gave a brief nod as if to ask, "Did you see that?" She had, and Rebecca scribbled another note.

"Messing with young minds today, I see." Ollie Hastings entered the room and quietly closed the door behind him. Ollie was about Rebecca's age, tall, too thin, and mildly handsome.

"The younger the better." Rebecca slid a chair next to her. "Here, pop a squat."

Ollie watched as Blue-4 devoured a cupcake, leaving her face coated in yellow icing and sprinkles. "What's the theory you're testing? Type 2 diabetes can start at any age?"

Rebecca laughed, and her eyes sparkled. She had the most intricate eyes, with a myriad of colors blending together. "No," Rebecca said. "Dr. Holter is studying aggression in pre-pubescent girls."

"That's my favorite age for aggression," he replied, "when they're still small enough for me to defend myself." Ollie put up his scrawny dukes like an old-time boxer.

By now, several girls were fighting over cupcakes. Others were looking over their shoulders as they nibbled, their senses heightened, ready to defend their treasure.

"We're conducting a version of a study done in the 1950s called 'The Robbers Cave Experiment.' It was a study in Realistic Conflict Theory. The experimenters took over a summer camp and two teams of boys competed for a trophy and prizes. The teams became verbally abusive, then physically abusive. One team even burned the other one's flag."

"And that's why I never went to summer camp. Plus, I burn like a tomato after being in the sun for more than, like, five minutes."

Rebecca smirked and continued. "It took less than three weeks for two groups of boys to despise each other to the point of physical violence, and there was no actual difference between them. The researchers randomly split them into groups. Dr. Holter wants to see if he can replicate the results in girls… in less than an hour."

"They say the female of the species is far more deadly," Ollie added.

"Here's the kicker," Rebecca added. "Dr. Holter randomly assigned these girls to each squad, but he told the red team that he grouped them together because they were a lot smarter and stronger than the girls on the blue team."

"What did he tell the blue team?"

"That they were much smarter and stronger than the red team."

Ollie snickered. "God bless psychologists."

Through the glass, Rebecca observed a young girl, Blue-3, holding a cupcake. She saw Isabella (Red-6 for this study) alone in the corner, so Blue-3 walked up to her.

"I don't care about the game," Blue-3 said. "Do you want to share my cupcake?"

For the first time, Isabella looked up from the floor with her big brown eyes, smiled, and nodded at Blue-3. Isabella reached for the cupcake with her left hand and sucker punched Blue-3 between the eyes with a right hook.

"Ooh!" Rebecca jolted up in her seat.

Blue-3 started crying, and Isabella quietly ate her cupcake.

"Wow! That girl packs a punch," Ollie said. "You're going to have some upset parents after this one."

"Actually, they're all orphans. We got a grant to work with the St. Agnes Orphanage for Girls over in Glascott."

"And what? Create psycho-children?"

"Of course not. Dr. Holter thinks if he can identify the source of aggression at an early age, he can reduce it and give these girls a better life. He'll pair positive behavior with a reward to extinguish the negative. He really cares about helping people. He truly is revolutionary."

Ollie nodded his head toward Dr. Holter, who bent down to talk to Isabella with a look of fascination on his face. He ignored the girl crying at the other end of the room. "If Holter is so interested in rewarding positive behavior, then why does he seem so much more interested in the mean girls?"

Rebecca wasn't sure how to respond. She hadn't noticed it before, but Ollie was right. He seemed to give more attention to the aggressive girls than the gentle ones. "That cupcake put the red team ahead," she said to change the subject. "I have to switch my observations to the pizza party."

Rebecca wobbled to her feet, revealing a rather well-developed baby bump. Ollie gestured toward it. "How have you been feeling?"

"Like a human being is about to burst out of me like that scene in Aliens."

"Alien."

"I'm sorry?"

"The movie you're referring to is 'Alien' from 1979. 'Aliens' is the 1986 sequel." Ollie drew out the "S" for emphasis. "No chest-bursting creature in that one."

"Wow, Ollie. What would I ever do without you?"

As they rounded the corner toward the pizza party observation room, Rebecca stuck out her arm, stopping Ollie in his tracks.

"Hang on," she whispered.

Dr. Holter had pulled Isabella aside in the hallway as the other girls filled the room.

"I am very impressed with how you got that cupcake today," he told her, squatting down so they could be at eye level. "That was very creative."

She remained quiet, staring at the floor again.

"I want you to have an extra special treat you can bring back to St. Agnes's with you. Would you like that?"

She nodded, and Dr. Holter reached into his pocket and pulled out a rectangular pack of gum in a pale yellow wrapper. Prominently displayed right in the middle of the package was a bright yellow smiley face, blowing a bubble.

* * *

"It was about blind obedience to authority." Dr. Holter stood in front of a lecture hall filled with college students. His excitement about the topic was evident in his vibrant inflection.

"Adolf Eichmann, the famous Nazi, was on trial for war crimes." He projected a photo of Eichmann on a whiteboard in front of the class.

"Stanley Milgram, a psychologist at Yale, sought to answer the question, 'Why do people follow orders from authoritative figures when they so clearly conflict with their own personal beliefs and morals?'" He replaced the photo of Eichmann with one of Milgram.

"So, this is how he answered the question. Milgram advertised a study on learning. The subject was told to push a button each time the 'learner' got a question wrong. The button did nothing, but the subject was told that it would send an electric shock to the learner, pairing punishment with failure."

The slide changed to a diagram of the experiment's setup. A

few students groaned.

"Each time the learner got a question wrong, Milgram increased the level of the shock. The learner was in a separate room, so the subject couldn't see him, but they could hear the screams as the subject administered the 'shocks.' Now, these were fake screams because the learners were in on the experiment. The subjects were reluctant to issue the shocks, but many of them did. Many of them administered shocks so strong that they would have been deadly. And why did they do this? Simply because they were told to."

Silence.

"Now, read the rest of the study in your textbook and send your analysis to my lovely Teaching Assistant, Ms. Quinn." He gestured to Rebecca, who was sitting in the front of the classroom. She gave a casual wave. "I will see you all on Thursday."

The students packed up their things, as did Dr. Holter. Rebecca grabbed his attention as the students filtered out of the room.

"Gerald?" she asked. Only Rebecca could get away with calling him that.

"Yes, Rebecca… due any day now, huh?" he responded, pointing to her ever-growing abdomen.

"Yes, any day now. Hey, listen," she said, changing the subject, "I wanted to talk to you about the St. Agnes study."

"It's going well, isn't it?"

"I thought the intention was to eliminate aggression in these girls, but it seems like you're encouraging it instead."

"My intention is to help more than just these girls by understanding aggression and how to trigger it." He swung his attaché case over his shoulder and gestured toward the door. "Walk with me. I have office hours." Holter charged ahead, and Rebecca trailed behind.

"You see," he continued, "there is so much more at stake than a few orphan children. What I'm working on is so much bigger."

"Why did you keep me in the dark? Am I part of the deceit built into your experiment?" Rebecca challenged.

"Look, Rebecca." He stopped in the hallway in front of his office. "You're a sweet girl." He stroked the sides of Rebecca's arms as he was saying it. "I just wanted to protect you from the ugliness of human nature."

She shook his hands off of her arms and said, "I am a grown woman, and I don't need you or anyone else to protect me. We're not done with this," she said as she walked away. "I will figure out what you're up to. These are young girls."

"They're orphans, Rebecca. Don't be so naïve."

As Rebecca walked away, pain radiated through her body. She clenched her stomach, let out an audible yelp, and collapsed to the floor.

* * *

Flashes of red permeated Rebecca's closed eyelids as she fought to remain conscious. She felt vibrations and a light breeze as she lay on her back. She was moving. Where was she? With great struggle, she opened her eyes wide enough to recognize that she was on a gurney, being rushed down a hospital corridor. A team of doctors and nurses surrounded her. She could only make out an occasional word, and those she heard were medical jargon that she didn't understand.

"What's going on? Where am I?" she managed.

"Hello, Ms. Quinn," a nurse responded. "It looks like you're ready to deliver your baby." She tried to sound as happy as possible, but Rebecca detected hesitation in her voice.

"What's wrong?"

"Well… you've had a placental abruption. Basically, it means the placenta has separated from your uterus prematurely and you've lost a lot of blood," the nurse explained.

"My baby… how's my baby?"

"We're detecting a very weak heartbeat. You're being prepped for an emergency C-section. Don't worry, Ms. Quinn, you're in good hands."

"Just save my baby. Make sure my baby lives."

Rebecca disappeared into an operating room.

Several minutes later, Ollie rushed into the hospital, running to the reception desk.

"Rebecca Quinn… she's giving birth," he nearly shouted at the receptionist.

"Prenatal is on the third floor. Sign in here, please." She failed to understand the urgency that Ollie felt. Ollie scribbled his name as fast as he could, grabbed a guest pass, and sprinted to the elevators.

The third floor looked different from the others, but Ollie barely noticed. He was laser-focused. There was soft, childlike music playing. The walls were decorated with Winnie the Pooh characters. He subconsciously noticed Eeyore from the corner of his eye. He was always Ollie's favorite. He wondered what that said about him, but he wasn't the psychologist.

"I'm here for Rebecca Quinn," Ollie repeated to the prenatal receptionist, who was also way too calm for his liking.

She tapped a few keys on her keyboard and raised her glasses to read the screen. "Uh huh," she said.

"What is it? Is she okay? I was told she collapsed in the hallway at the university."

"She's in surgery. Emergency C-section. Please have a seat in our waiting area and someone will come get you when she's out."

The waiting area shifted away from the Winnie the Pooh theme in favor of Disney characters. He sat on a chair in between a mural painting of Mickey on one side and a coy Minnie on the other. Several other nervous-looking men sat in the waiting room, along with a few excited future grandparents.

Ollie's heart pounded against his chest as he noticed a familiar-looking man stepping off the elevator and turning the corner with authority. The man was Dr. Gerald Holter.

"What is he doing here?" Ollie mumbled to himself while rising to his feet. Staying a safe distance away, Ollie followed Dr. Holter as he pushed through a set of swinging doors. Ollie remained on the other side, but he peered at Gerald through a small glass window in the door, his view obstructed by wire mesh embedded inside.

Gerald stopped in front of an operating room door and spoke to another man waiting outside. They both looked professional, like they had authority to be there. He didn't recognize the other man, and he could barely discern what they were saying. All he could distinguish was an Eastern European accent, and Gerald referred to the man as "Genko."

Gerald opened the operating room door but remained outside. He stuck his head in, made some gesture that Ollie couldn't decipher, and then closed the door and walked toward him.

Ollie quickly ducked so Gerald wouldn't see him through the window, and he shuffled back toward the waiting room.

Ollie sat, bouncing his leg with anxiety. Almost an hour passed before a doctor entered the waiting area. "For Rebecca Quinn?"

Ollie leapt to his feet.

"I'm very sorry to have to tell you this," the doctor said, "but there were complications with Rebecca's pregnancy and…"

Ollie's heart sank and his vision grayed.

"Neither the baby nor the mother survived. I am sincerely sorry."

Devastated, Ollie sank back into his chair and attempted to

pull himself together. The room spun, and a lump nearly burst out of his throat. Tears exploded from his eyes as he sobbed alone, his head at his knees.

A nurse handed him a tissue. After a long while, he rose and exited the waiting room. He failed to notice the nursery to his left as he passed by.

Bassinets filled the nursery, each holding a baby wrapped in either a blue or pink blanket. Each bassinet bore a tag with the baby's name.

All except one.

A little girl, wrapped in a pink blanket, slept soundly with no name. The doctor had been truthful about Rebecca's untimely death, but not about her baby's.

That baby would grow up to be known by many names, none of them her own.

She had had twenty-four identities to date, the most recent being "Wendy Lockheart."

Chapter 7

CANDACE

Wendy's head spun, and everything was black. She stretched her eyelids wide, and it felt like they were tearing. Was she blindfolded? Probably. She tried to move but couldn't, unsure if she was paralyzed or tied down. The latter seemed like the more realistic alternative.

Her memory jumped around like a frog searching out a lily pad. She couldn't remember who she was. Not because she had amnesia per se, but because she had been so many people in her short seventeen years, and she felt confused. She couldn't pinpoint who she was right now.

"Corey," she mumbled. She recalled that name with great urgency, but she couldn't quite figure out why. She needed to know about Corey. Who was he again? Was she drugged? Her parched lips rubbed together like sandpaper, and her tongue seemed glued to her mouth. So, being drugged was a strong possibility.

Maybe it would help if she ran through the list of people she had been.

What was first? Clare? She couldn't remember. In fact, she was never aware of her first identity. Who remembers anything from the early years of life? She was sure the agency changed her identity at least once a year since she was born, even before her training started, but her first actual memory was when she was Samantha. She remembered being Holly before that, but she had no memories as Holly.

They called her Sami. It was a cute name. She liked that one. She was five. She remembered that now, too. She had two foster mothers—what were their names? Something with an "M" and the other one was "L…" something. It was all foggy, like her brain was dragging itself out of a muddy swamp. It didn't cross her mind at the time, but they must have been lesbians. Hey, man, love is love.

There was a doll. Was it a Barbie? No, but something similar, just more… generic. Her name was Bibi. Yes, that was it. Somehow that was different enough to get past the trademark infringement. She loved that doll—took it everywhere with her.

Bibi had long, shiny blond hair that got tangled more and more each time she slept with it by her side or her foster moms tossed it into a travel bag. She had a tiny pink comb that Sami would use to straighten the doll's tangled locks, but it had gotten lost somewhere inside the house. Bibi wore a long, shimmering blue dress that made her look like a princess. Sami wished she had a magic potion to make Bibi her size, and then they could share clothes. Sami could picture herself in that dress, twirling around like royalty.

Sami had a few other toys, but not many. None that left a lasting impression on Wendy. Why did she remember Bibi so clearly above all else? Yes, she loved that doll to no end, but there was more. Candace. It had something to do with Candace. Who was she again?

Did Candace live next door? Maybe. No, they were in Kindergarten together. That was it. She could remember Candace's uneven haircut, like she had cut it herself. Thinking back on it, she probably had. A rush of nausea flooded her stomach when she thought about Candace. Why?

There was a playdate. She remembered that. M-Something and L-Something were in the kitchen with Candace's mom. Sami and Candace were playing with their dolls. Candace had an actual Barbie and a Barbie Dream House. Sami wasn't jealous, though. She was happy with Bibi. There was a fuzzy recollection of Bibi and Barbie playing in the Dream House.

"You can play with my Barbie if you want," Candace said.

"That's okay," Sami responded.

"Can I play with Bibi?"

Sami shrugged and reluctantly handed over her doll. Candace took one doll in each hand, facing each other.

"Hi, I'm Barbie," she said, bouncing her doll up and down.

"Hi, Barbie, I'm Bibi," she bounced Sami's doll. "You're so much prettier than I am, Barbie. It's too bad I have to live with Sami. She doesn't even have real parents."

Sami yanked her doll out of Candace's hand.

"I'm just kidding. Jeez," Candace protested.

Sami stroked Bibi's fibrous hair as if to soothe her.

"Come on, let me play with her," Candace demanded.

"No. She's mine. You can't have her."

"But you're s'pposed to share. My mommy said so."

"Not if you're a big, stupid jerk, you're not."

Candace's lower lip quivered and her eyes watered. "MOMMY!" she screamed at the top of her lungs. Her mother ran from the kitchen. M-Something and L-Something followed.

"Honey, what's wrong?" Candace's mom asked her crying child.

"Sami's being mean." Tears poured down her cheeks.

M-Something grabbed Sami and carried her into the kitchen, separating the girls. "Now, what is this about, Sami?"

"She's not being nice to Bibi, and I don't want to share her. She's my doll, and I don't want that stupid Candace playing with her," Sami told her foster moms.

This is normally when a parent would calmly explain the importance of sharing and using our "nice" words with our friends, but not these two.

"Bibi is your doll, and you don't have to share her if you don't want to," L-Something chimed in. "Plus, that Candace has an ugly haircut."

Sami looked shocked. "Really?"

"That's right."

"You know," M-Something added, "I have a way so Candace will never want to play with Bibi again."

Sami was listening.

"You walk up to her, show her Bibi, and break that doll in half. Right in front of her."

Sami looked confused and sad. "But I don't want to break Bibi. She's my friend."

"No," M-Something corrected. "It's a piece of plastic and you have gotten too attached to it. There's no room for sentimentality in this world. Now you do what we say. You march right over to that girl and snap that doll in half."

Sami was now crying, sniffling through her tears. "But... I love her."

"When an adult tells you to do something, Sami, you do it. No questions asked." That was L-Something. "Do you understand me?"

Sami nodded and wiped her nose on her sleeve, her hair drifting into her face. She warily grabbed her doll and headed over to Candace in the other room.

"You want to share Bibi?" Sami asked Candace.

Candace nodded through her tears, and her mother piped up.

"Now, isn't that nice? Thank you, Sami."

Sami held out her doll and looked back at her foster mothers. M-Something gave her a slight nod. Sami gripped Bibi with both hands—one near her head and one near her feet. She clenched her eyes, hesitated, and then snapped her doll in half. She was devastated, but she also liked the thrill of putting Candace in her place. Sami aggressively threw both halves of her doll at Candace, narrowly missing her face as she ducked.

"Here," she said angrily, "share that!"

Candace's mom scurried to her feet, flabbergasted as she grabbed Candace. "What sort of girl are you raising?" She didn't wait for a response before storming out of the house.

After Candace and her mom left, L-Something bent down, so she was eye-level with Sami. She pulled a pack of Wonder Rush Happy Funtime Bubblegum from her pocket and handed Sami a piece. "You were a very good girl," L-Something told her. "You get a reward."

Sami took the stick of gum, put it in her mouth, and chewed. Watermelon. Yum.

* * *

There was more to the story. Wendy could sense it, but she couldn't quite line up the details. Something about a dodgeball.

Red.

Round.

Bouncy.

A fat lip, maybe. Yes, that's what started it—the fat lip.

M-Something and L-Something… Seriously, what were their names? They were in the kitchen washing dishes when Sami's school bus pulled up in front of the house. Sami hopped off, looking down at the ground, trudging toward the house and appearing dejected. M-Something noticed immediately and turned off the sink water. By the time Sami walked through the side door, they both greeted her.

"Sami, honey, what's wrong?" L-Something asked.

Sami continued to stare downward and handed her a note. L-Something took it, unfolded it, and read it aloud. "Sami had a minor accident at school today. She tripped over the corner of her desk, fell, and bumped her lip. I applied ice and gave her hugs, and she's doing just fine. If you have any questions, please call. Signed, Nurse Nancy."

With her hand on Sami's chin, M-Something tilted her head up to get a good look at her lip. It was swollen and red, but not too bad. "Oh, Sami, are you okay?"

She nodded her head.

"I've never known you to be clumsy," M-Something said. "Did you really trip on your desk?"

Sami stood in silence.

"Sami?" L-Something asked. "Honey, it's okay. You can tell us the truth. Did you trip?"

Sami shook her head.

"I didn't think so," M-Something said. "What happened?"

"It was that stupid Candace," Sami finally said.

"Did she trip you?"

"No, Jimothy Patterson did."

"I don't understand. What did Candace have to do with it?"

"She went and told everyone at school about Bibi. She said I was crazy and then everyone started calling me 'psycho.' They said I'm psycho and I have no mommy or daddy because no one wants a psycho daughter." Sami didn't seem upset when she said this, she was more angry. Her fists whitened as she clenched the blood from them.

"Oh, sweetie, you know that's not true, right?" L-Something asked. "And what a terrible word to call you. You're not crazy.

You're strong and you're independent, and you're far better off in life on your own than tied down to anyone."

"So how did you do this to your lip?" M-Something asked as she examined the bruise.

"I went to sharpen my pencil," Sami continued, "and when I walked back to my desk, Jimothy stuck his foot out and tripped me. Everyone laughed."

"You know," M-Something added, "it's okay to hurt someone if they hurt you first."

"What? Really?" Sami questioned.

"Sure," L-Something confirmed. "I mean, it's only fair, right? If someone is mean to you, you should be mean right back. Give them a taste of their own medicine, as my mother used to say."

M-Something grabbed Sami's clenched fists and held them up in front of her. "You see this? You feel that anger inside of you?" Sami nodded. "Let it out. Show it to the world and don't hold back."

As Wendy struggled to put the pieces of reality back together, she had a clear vision of what came next. She remembered being back at school the next day, her lower lip still swollen. She was in gym class and they were playing dodgeball. She stood toward the back of the court as balls flew all around her.

"She can't catch the ball," Matthew teased. "No psycho like that could play dodgeball."

"Yeah," Taylor added, "what a total psycho."

"Hey, Jimothy," Candace called, "you should just trip her again. Bust her other lip." Jimothy laughed.

Rage grew inside her, and her knuckles turned cold as she tightened her hands into fists. She thought about what her foster moms told her about letting out her anger. The conversation happening around her was now a blur. She just remembered hearing "psycho" repeatedly. She wondered now what the gym teacher was doing during this harassment. She had no recollection, and it didn't even occur to her at the time. Shouldn't an adult have stopped this taunting?

A big, red, round dodgeball came hurling directly toward her face. Partly out of instinct and partly out of fury, she reached forward and caught the ball in a tight grip.

"You're out, Matthew," one of the other boys teased.

"Ha! I can't believe that psycho got you out," Jimothy said.

Matthew's shoulders sank as he walked off the court. Sami just stood there with the ball in her hand. "You're supposed to throw it," Jimothy badgered. "Oh my God, the psycho girl can't even throw." Then he got closer and started taunting her right to her face. "Throw it, psycho. Throw it."

Her ire was boiling as she squeezed the life out of the ball.

"Psycho," she heard one last time before she pumped the ball with both hands directly into Jimothy's face. That shut him up quickly. The ball bounced directly back into her hands as Jimothy stood there, stunned. Immediately, she pelted him in the face once more, and he fell to the ground. The entire class grew silent.

Sami went on a rampage, throwing balls as hard as she could in anyone's face that got in her way. Now the gym teacher was paying attention. "Hey, stop that," the teacher shouted, blowing her whistle. Sami never relented. She gunned down anyone she could find with that dodgeball, and then she located Candace, cowering alone in the corner. Sami approached her, a red ball in each hand. She chucked one ball at the back of Candace's head. When Candace turned, she hit her again with the other ball, directly in the nose.

Candace was on the ground, lying on her back, wailing and protesting. "Stop her, somebody stop this psycho girl!" she shouted as the gym teacher ran toward Sami. Sami repeatedly threw the ball straight down into Candace's face, over and over and over until her nose and mouth were bleeding.

The gym teacher grabbed Sami, who protested, swinging her arms and legs wildly. "You stop that right now!" the gym teacher shouted. Sami's foot caught her teacher directly in the shin, forcing her to drop Sami, who rushed back over to Candace. She threw one more ball directly at Candace's face, with all her power and anger behind it. She raised the middle fingers on both of her hands and pointed them down at Candace as she slowly backed away from her, never losing eye contact.

The school never allowed Sami to return. In fact, it was the last time she was known as "Sami."

Chapter 8

HEATHER

Her senses were returning, albeit slowly. The fabric tied across her face and covering her eyes was itchy. They had locked her wrists behind her back. She twisted her fists to no avail, burning her skin as the course rope dug in. They secured her to a folding chair—wooden. She could tell from the squeak against the concrete floor as she shifted her body weight forward. It would be simple to tip the chair over, but that would be pointless. She'd much rather be in a chair than squirming on the ground with her arms tied behind her back. They tied her feet, too. She knew that now. She was also certain now that they had drugged her. They needed her weak, and that's exactly what she was.

"Hello?" she called out. No response, but the hollow echo told her she was in a large space with a high ceiling and nothing soft to absorb the sound waves—no carpet, little to no furniture, nothing on the walls. They didn't bother to gag her, so she also concluded that she was in a remote location. Screaming would prove futile.

She thought about her memories as Sami. She was told that her training began at age ten, but she realized now that it started much younger. Before the physical training, they were preparing her psychologically for far longer. When did it start? Birth? Recalling L-Something giving her a piece of Wonder Rush gum clenched it for her.

Laurel! That was it. She finally remembered her name—Laurel. What was M-Something's name? It was still fuzzy.

Wonder Rush was an exclusive product of the agency, and it was unavailable to the public. Didn't she feel special? What an exclusive club to which she belonged! She felt like a Kardashian. Laurel giving her a stick of Wonder Rush proved she worked for the agency.

If Wendy was being molded at age five, it stood to reason that they started much younger. The simple act of changing her name at least once a year made that clear. The agency taught her not to get attached to anyone, not even herself. Did they strip her identity from her, or did she never have one to begin with? What exactly has her life been? When it's all you know, you don't stop to question it. Becoming a different person, adopting a new identity, a unique hairstyle, a fresh look, a new name, all just felt normal to her.

What exactly was the agency? She knew what little they told her. It had no official name. Naming it would make it real, and they worked in the shadows. The irony was not lost on her. The agency was nameless, as was she. She was an agent. She wasn't real. She was a pawn and nothing more. That's all they ever called it too— "the agency." Even referring to it as "The Agency" would be overkill. Common nouns only.

She was aware of other agents, but she wasn't sure how far the network stretched. Were they all like her? She didn't know, and they would never share that information. They were all teenage girls. She was certain of that much. Girls were less suspicious than boys. The younger the better. Who wouldn't trust a sweet, innocent young girl? Society saw girls as small and weak and defenseless and less significant than their male counterparts. It was the unfair, harsh truth, and it gave the agency an edge. Rather than trying to change society, they took advantage of its inherent bias.

Wendy deduced that psychological training began as young as possible, and physical training started at ten. Your first kill had to be by eleven or twelve, she was sure of that. It had to be before puberty, while you still had your youthful innocence. Before you knew any better. There was no room for moral judgement. They removed all morality during the psychological training phase.

She recalled being ten years old. She was known as Julia then. It was the first time she received a pack of gum containing a stick with a colored wrapper. Her foster father, Tate, opened the pack and pulled out a piece, wrapped in blue. It had a picture of the yellow smiley face on it. She liked the way it looked.

"This is a very special stick of gum," he said as he unwrapped it and handed it to her. "Here, take it, look at it."

She did.

"It looks like a regular piece of gum, right?"

"Yes."

"Now lick it. Right along the length."

She stuck out her tongue and gave it a lick.

"Now, look again."

"Wow," she gasped in amazement as the plain stick of gum became decorated with a myriad of symbols and shapes.

Tate took a cell phone from his pocket, scanned the gum, and a map popped onto the screen. "You see this yellow dot?" he asked. "That tells you where to go. This blue dot over here," he pointed to the screen, "is where we are now. And this red line," he traced it with his index finger, "is how you get there. The numbers on the bottom tell you when to arrive. Do you get it?"

"Yes, I understand," Julia confirmed.

"Good. Now, for the best part. No one can ever see this gum once you lick it, so you have to chew it. Get rid of all traces."

She put the gum in her mouth and chewed.

"What flavor did you get?" he asked.

"Cherry," Julia replied.

"Oh, that one's my favorite. Now, I won't be seeing you any longer. When you leave here, your life will change forever."

It sounded a little overdramatic, but he wasn't wrong.

* * *

She was rather perplexed when she arrived at what the yellow dot informed her was her destination. It was an abandoned warehouse store—maybe a Costco or a BJs or possibly a Sam's Club. The parking lot was empty, and not a soul appeared to be within a mile. Tate had given her a public bus schedule to get her as close as possible, and then she walked the rest of the way. She didn't have Tate's phone with her, nor did she have one of her own, so she was feeling her way around by memory. This couldn't be the right place. Could it?

The only glass on the building was the front entrance—the type with the automated sliding doors that part open like the Red Sea when you step near them. Only these doors remained stationary. She attempted to peer inside, but the glass was soaped up and opaque. Finally, she spotted something familiar. In the corner of the door was a sticker of an old friend she called "Poppy."

She found the correct location, but the doors were locked. She tapped on the glass, still unsure of herself. Glancing upward, Julia noticed a blinking red light on a security camera. She stared at it for a moment and the soapy double doors parted.

There was a wide-open space inside. A blue padded mat covered the floor where she imagined pallets of paper towels and toilet paper once sat. There were eleven other girls, all about her age, on the mat. It smelled musty inside and felt damp. A middle-aged man and a young woman stood in front of the group. A television stood between them, powered off. The man turned toward Julia as she approached.

"You must be Julia." He didn't wait for confirmation before adding, "Have a seat with the others. We're about to begin."

Julia detected some accent. What was it? Russian? Polish maybe?

The blue padding hissed and squealed as Julia stepped across it and sat cross-legged next to a dark-skinned girl with beautiful braids throughout her hair. Julia stared in amazement, wondering how she achieved such intricate designs. The girl caught her looking and just smiled in return. Julia smiled back, embarrassed.

"I'm Danika," the girl whispered.

"Julia."

The man in front spoke. "Eyes up here. Thank you." He waited for the girls to settle. "My name is Genko Krastev. Throughout this program, you will learn physical attack and defense techniques, weapons training, technology skills, and psychological manipulation. Those of you who pass the course will enter the program and become agents. Those who fail will return to the system and live the ordinary, boring lives of foster children. At least half of you will fail, so don't be surprised if you do. The other half will travel the country and live exciting lives. Your foster parents should have provided you with some basic information, but I imagine you have a lot of questions." Genko signaled to the woman next to him. "Izzy?"

"Good morning. My name is Isabella Martinez, but you can call me Izzy," the woman said. Izzy was now eighteen. She still had the long, dark, wavy hair that she had when she was eight and competing for cupcakes on the red team with Dr. Holter, only now she had tamed the unruly curls. Amazing what a good hair product can do for you.

"This program changed my life completely. I was a shy, weak, orphan girl just hoping and praying for a family to adopt me. I now lend my unique skills to the agency to train girls just like you. Every day is exciting and challenging. Most importantly, we're helping to make the world better."

"Thank you, Izzy," Genko continued. "Now we will watch a short video. Where is the popcorn?" No one laughed. "That was a joke," Genko clarified. "Okay. Here we go." Genko pushed a few buttons on a remote control and the TV screen powered on.

"WELCOME" danced across the screen in oversized letters. A man and woman appeared on the television, each holding the hand of a child who stood between them. They walked away from the camera in slow motion through a park, exaggerated smiles on all their faces. Soft, cheerful music played in the background. A tinny voice was heard but not seen. It reminded Julia of the poorly produced narration she once heard on an after-school special.

"Our world is beautiful and safe, filled with amazing people, just like you and me… But not all parts of the world are so lucky," the voice said.

The joyful music suddenly turned dark and a video of Middle Eastern soldiers wearing hijabs and shooting automatic weapons replaced the joyful family in the park. A terrorist fired a rocket launcher, blowing up a building in its crosshairs.

The girls squirmed.

"Some of these bad people are right here in the good ole U-S of A," the narrator continued. A video of an airplane flying into the World Trade Center filled the screen and then transitioned to a classroom of students on lockdown, practicing an active shooter drill.

"Sure, we have police…" The film showed police in hazard gear, attempting to calm an angry mob. "… and courts…" The image transitioned to old black and white footage of a comedy skit where a white-wigged judge slammed his gavel in over-exaggerated fast motion as his eyes spun comically.

Some girls snickered.

"But our police and our courts can only do so much," the voice concluded. The man behind the voice then appeared in frame, wearing a white lab coat.

"My name is Doctor Gerald Holter," the man said. "My friends and I have established this agency to stop evil dead in its tracks." Holter made a dramatic fist with his right hand and paused for effect. "With your help..." He pointed directly at the camera. "... we can make this world the amazing, safe place God intended."

A group of animated girls appeared on the video, each wearing a cape and superhero costume. In unison, they all put one fist in the air and flew up and out of frame.

"You," Holter continued in voiceover, "can be the heroes!"

Fade to black.

"Questions?" Genko asked, but he did not wait for a reply. "Good. I will leave you now with Izzy for self-defense training."

"Thank you, Genko," Izzy said. "When bad people try to hurt you, they may be much bigger than you. So, we're going to learn what we can do to stop them."

* * *

Wendy squirmed in her wooden chair, not attempting to break free but trying to get more comfortable. She had been sitting there for hours, and pins and needles were running down her legs. She never forgot that ridiculous propaganda video they showed her that day. She thought about Danika and her beautiful braids and how dejected she looked when she failed the program.

Wendy remembered feeling so sorry for her. She was a nice girl, and she wanted Danika to be a "hero" just like her. The agency made all the girls covet it—to crave something they didn't even understand. All they had to say was, "half of you will fail," and the girls all fought for it. The agency understood the psychology of competition. If you offer a prize and make that reward difficult to attain, people will desire it. They'll thirst for it. They'll go to war for it all without ever asking themselves, for more than a fleeting moment, if it would even satisfy them.

Wendy wondered what Danika was doing with her life. Maybe she was excited about her upcoming prom, or perhaps she was getting her college applications together. Maybe she even found a family that adopted her and loved her. She envisioned Danika with a happy life. One filled with so much promise. Danika, who she once felt sorry for, was free while Wendy, the star pupil in her training group, was blindfolded and tied to a chair somewhere in the middle of nowhere.

Why was she left alone for so long? It was a head game. Everything with the agency was. Yeah, she screwed up. Was this punishment? Partially, she figured. She also assumed they just wanted her to sit and stew in her own thoughts and memories. In fairness, they probably didn't expect the sedative to wear off as quickly as it did, but Wendy always had a fast metabolism. All her senses had returned, and she was thinking lucidly again. With her mental prowess intact, she wondered what would have become of her if she had just let Heather McCullough break free.

* * *

"Very good, AJ," Izzy encouraged as she walked among the girls on the mat. The girls were paired up, practicing self-defense movements. "Danika, make sure you turn your wrist toward Stacy's thumb, not away from it," she corrected. "Nice work, Julia." Izzy placed her hand on Julia's shoulder to show her approval.

The girls were practicing a strategy to break the hold of an attacker if he were to grab their wrists. The idea was to immobilize the attacker's hand, twist your arm to gain control, and then push the attacker's arm to the ground, leaving his face vulnerable to a blow with the other fist. It was a simple move, and Julia had it down. She partnered with a girl named Angelica, who was timid and unsure of herself. Julia knew Angelica wouldn't make it.

"Ow," Angelica yelled as Julia pushed her arm down a bit too hard. Julia did not apologize.

"Make sure we're not using full force, girls," Izzy announced. "We're just walking through the movements." Izzy returned to the front of the room. "I need a volunteer for the next move." She scanned the room. A few girls raised their hands. "Okay, you," she pointed. "Patrice, come on up."

Patrice walked to the front of the class, proud, as if she won something. Izzy lay on her back, her knees bent. "Now Patrice, I want you to straddle me on the ground here and put both your hands on my neck."

"I don't want to hurt you," Patrice said.

"Don't worry, you won't."

Patrice hesitantly knelt on top of Izzy and loosely grabbed her throat with both hands.

"Now," Izzy continued, "to get out of this position, I want you to cross your arms, grabbing your attacker's elbows with your opposite hand." Izzy demonstrated on Patrice. "Next shift your legs up, wrapping your ankles around the attacker's neck, push your hips up and your attacker's arms down." Again, she demonstrated on Patrice. "That one is more complicated, so I'll show you again." Izzy walked through the movements again from the beginning. "Cross, grip, wrap, hips up, elbow down. Got it?"

A few girls nodded. Others looked lost. "Okay," Izzy continued, "partner up and give it a try."

Julia turned to her right and found Heather McCullough. Julia rolled her eyes, but partnered with her anyway. Heather had been giving her trouble all day. It was clear that they were the top two students in the class, and Heather wanted to show her up. There was no first-place prize, but competition brings out the worst in people.

"Here, I'll get on the ground first," Heather snarled, as if she was doing Julia a favor. Heather lay on her back, Julia knelt beside her, swung one leg to the other side, and put her hands on Heather's neck. Oh, how she wanted to give it a nice tight squeeze, but she resisted. Heather performed the movements successfully.

Julia let out a slight groan as Heather pushed just a little too hard. "What's the matter, Julia? You can't handle the competition?" Heather taunted. "You know I'm the strongest girl here, right? I'm going to pass the program and I'm going to laugh so hard when you fail." Julia attempted to clench Heather's throat tighter, but she couldn't. Heather had applied too much pressure onto Julia's elbows.

"Okay, girls," Izzy announced, "switch positions."

Heather held Julia's arms down longer, staring her dead in the eye before she let up and pushed Julia off her. Both girls sprung to their feet, looking like they were about to fight. Instead, Heather knelt on the ground in position. Julia hesitated.

"Well, come on," Heather yelled. "We don't have all day."

Julia acquiesced and lay on the mat on her back, allowing Heather to straddle her. Rather than gripping Julia's neck, Heather made a fist and acted as if she was going to punch her in the face. She pulled her punch, but not before Julia reacted and hit Heather square in the mouth. Stunned, Heather let out a chuckle. She touched her lip and examined her hand, finding a single drop of blood.

"Okay," Heather said. "It's like that." Heather put both hands around Julia's throat and gave it a tight squeeze. "I'm going to enjoy watching you walk out of here and back to your foster home while I become an agent," Heather teased as she placed additional pressure on Julia's throat.

Julia refused to let the pain show. She struggled to breathe, but she didn't panic. She was confident she could hold her breath for a minute or more if she needed to. A strange thought flashed into Julia's mind. Looking up at Heather, she reminded her of someone. It was less of a physical resemblance and more of something in her disgusting personality. Lying there, her face turning red and then slightly purple, Heather reminded Julia of Candace. Suddenly, Julia thought about Bibi, her old doll, and the dodgeball game, and the kids mocking her and calling her "psycho."

Julia began the movements. She crossed her arms, grabbed each of Heather's elbows tightly, shifted her legs up in the air, wrapped her ankles around the back of Heather's neck, pushed her hips up and Heather's elbows down. She pushed them down hard, and Heather squealed. She squealed like a pathetic little pig. Immediately, Heather released her grasp on Julia's throat and the color on Julia's face faded back to normal. She gulped in a breath of air and kept pressing.

"Jesus," Heather shouted. "Okay, relax."

Julia loosened her grip a little but maintained her position.

"Let me go. My God, what is wrong with you?"

"Say I'm stronger than you," Julia demanded.

"No, I could have done the same thing to you when I was in that position, but I held back like we're supposed to. This is training, for Christ's sake. That doesn't make you stronger."

Julia applied more pressure, and she could see the pain in Heather's eyes.

"Say it," Julia demanded.

"I will not say it. You're not stronger than me. You're... you're... crazy is what you are!"

"What did you say to me?" Julia asked as she applied even more pressure.

"Ow!" Heather shouted. That got Izzy's attention.

"Girls!" Izzy yelled. "Stop! The exercise is over. That's enough. Heather, are you okay?"

"No," she managed through the pain. "This girl's a freaking psycho!"

At that, Julia slammed her arms down hard, applying all her pressure to Heather's elbows. She could hear bones snap as Heather wailed in pain, tears building in her eyes. Julia jumped to her feet and Heather stood there stunned, her arms dangling at her sides, bent in a way no elbow was designed to bend.

Heather was forced to drop out of the program. Julia was initially reprimanded, but that was mostly for show. This was exactly the behavior the agency sought. It's precisely what they rewarded. In fact, Julia finished her training at the top of her class.

Chapter 9

HARPER

Sporadic pinpoints of light broke through Wendy's blindfold, and footsteps echoed off the concrete. They were slow, deliberate, and heavy. It was a male gait. The *click* and *clack* suggested a hard heel but worn soles. Dress shoes, but old ones. Her ears picked up the scratching sound of suit sleeves rubbing against the man's sides as he sauntered toward her. Polyester. Cheap.

"Hello, Genko," Wendy said.

"What? You can see through the blindfold, child?" Genko asked.

"Let's just say you have a distinct sound."

There was a brief silence before she heard a second set of footsteps. This one was more hurried. Softer on the concrete. Sneakers. Casual, not running shoes. The trod was just as heavy, though. Male. She could smell a cheap cologne or aftershave.

While she was putting the pieces of the puzzle together (this was fun for her—like a riddle), a sudden blunt force exploded across the left side of her face. It stunned her as only an unforeseen blow could, but she shook it off.

"You had to bring in muscle, Genko?" Wendy asked. "Too much of a pussy to hit me yourself?"

A sharp jab drilled into her stomach and chest, knocking the wind out of her. She gasped for air, but none came. Rather than panic, she held her breath, counted to ten, and slowly inhaled.

"You've been a very naughty girl," Genko said.

He ripped the blindfold from Wendy's face, and she squinted as her eyes adjusted to the light. She now had a visual on the "muscle."

"Porter Moore," she said disappointedly, as if it were on the tip of her tongue. "The Axe body spray should have given that away. Ugh. A few more seconds and I would have had it."

Porter Moore was a weapon and tactical expert who was dishonorably discharged from the United States Marines, and he was an arms dealer before the agency handpicked him. He was the wrong person to provoke, but Wendy knew better than to show even an iota of fear. If they planned on killing her, they were going to do it, whether she exuded an air of confidence or fright. She opted for the former.

"How about you untie me and make this a fair fight?" Wendy taunted, but she knew it was a fight she would lose. Porter was a force to be reckoned with. "Why don't you tell me why I'm here?"

"You know exactly why you're here," Genko said. "Do you want to start with the Peter McMahon shitshow?"

Ah yes, sleepy Peter and his darling wife, Abigail. That felt like ages ago. How long had she been out? Hours? Days? She wasn't sure. Everything was still fuzzy. Maybe the sedative hadn't fully worn off yet.

"That was… unfortunate," Wendy replied. Kind of fun, too.

"Unfortunate? That's all you have to say? You took a quiet, inconspicuous heart attack and turned it into a gory double homicide. There weren't supposed to be cops. There wasn't supposed to be an investigation. You turned a page-five blurb into a front-page news story, and all you have to say is it was 'unfortunate'?"

"Okay, I messed up a little, but I improvised. Isn't that what we're trained to do? Not everything goes according to plan all the time. Plus, you're the one who told me not to worry about the wife. Why wasn't sedating her part of the script?"

"If she woke up groggy, she might have become suspicious. We didn't think it would be necessary," Genko said.

"Oh, you didn't want her to be groggy?" Wendy asked. "You'd rather her be dead?"

Genko signaled to Porter, who hit Wendy again, drawing blood from her lip.

Wendy cringed, fought back the pain, and spit a mouthful of blood onto the floor. "I'm just saying, we both have to take some responsibility for Peter McMahon."

"Let's agree to disagree on that. What I can't seem to understand for the life of me is what the hell you were thinking running around town screaming about Wonder Rush for the entire world to hear."

"Corey, oh my God…" Wendy's head ached and was foggy, but how could she have forgotten about Corey?

"*You* do not find *us*," Genko chastised. "*We* find *you*." Genko was now mere inches from Wendy's face, his index finger pressed firmly into Wendy's forehead. "If *you* have a problem, *you* deal with it. *You* do not pull us into it." Each time he said "*you*," he drove his finger harder into her cranium.

"You have to help Corey."

Genko ignored Wendy's plea. "You know better than this, child. Our entire operation exists because it's clandestine and you're running around town screaming about it at the top of your lungs."

This time Genko took the initiative, pulled his right hand back, and struck Wendy's right cheek with his open knuckles.

"There you go," Wendy encouraged. "Didn't that feel good?"

"You're reckless and we won't stand for it," Genko said as he backed away.

"If you can take a quick break from beating the living shit out of me, can you please tell me how Corey is?" Wendy pleaded.

"Who is Corey?"

"Corey's my foster brother."

"Why would I know anything about Corey?"

"Because," Wendy started, "that little contraption you clowns came up with to poison Mr. Godwin is now killing my foster brother."

"Wait, let me get this straight," Genko said. "You failed to dispose of a critical agency tool in a timely manner *like we trained you to do*, and this is somehow my fault?"

"Do you forget that I'm seventeen years old? I am a child. You gave a child a lethal weapon and you take no responsibility for it?"

At that, Porter hit her again. He didn't wait for a signal from Genko.

"I may call you 'child,' but you are not a child. You are an agent. That transcends age. You are a trained assassin, and nothing more. Do you understand?"

"Okay… yes, I understand. It's… completely my fault. I was careless." Wendy's head sunk. It was a harsh truth—one that she already knew too well. She had been beating herself up over it. It was not her intention to place blame on anyone. She was just looking for help—someone to fix the mess that she caused.

"Can you help him?" Wendy muttered, a sense of remorse in her voice. "He's a great kid, and he doesn't deserve to suffer because my life is a disaster."

"Help him how?"

"There must be an antidote or something, right? I mean, if we catch it on time."

"There is no antidote," Genko said. "What do you think this is? James Bond?"

"What can we do? We need to help him."

"There is no 'we,' child. *You* did this."

"Yes... yes, I know."

Genko saw the emotional pain on her face and softened a bit. "Look, we designed the formula specifically for Godwin. He appeared healthy, but he was not—high blood pressure, high cholesterol, he was pre-diabetic. As long as this Corey is healthy, he'll pull through."

"He has cerebral palsy," Wendy explained. "And asthma."

"Oh, well, in that case... he's dead."

"What?"

"Sorry, yes. Dead. It sounds like you became too attached to him, anyway. Now we move on."

"Move on?" Wendy objected. "I don't want to—" Another one of Porter's blows interrupted her.

"We have a new identity for you," Genko changed the subject.

"I don't want it," Wendy scoffed, spitting another mouthful of blood, narrowly missing Genko's feet.

"You don't have a choice."

"Well, then I'll walk away. Leave the agency."

"There is no 'walk away.' We know where you are and what you're doing at all times. You belong to us. You are our property. Do you not understand that?"

"Well, I don't want it anymore."

"What you want, child, is irrelevant. You work for us and you can't quit. You are in a unique position to help this world immensely. How could you give that up?"

Wendy's shoulder sank as she bit her lower lip.

"Think about all the scum you have wiped out," Genko continued. "Pedophiles, murderers, rapists, terrorists. *You* did that. *We* did that… together."

Wendy's eyes scanned the room mindlessly as she contemplated Genko's words.

"Look, I know this job isn't easy, but it is so rewarding. Think of everyone who would have suffered if you weren't there to save them. Think of the children, the women, the men. People spend their entire lives trying to make some difference in this world. You're seventeen years old, and you've already achieved more than most people will in their lifetimes."

Wendy took a heavy breath, held it, and slowly exhaled. She looked Genko in the eye and said, "What's my new identity?"

"Very good," Genko replied. "You will forget about this Corey?"

Wendy hesitated. It wasn't just about Corey. It was about Amaya, too—someone she finally connected with over her tumultuous seventeen years. Amaya, who would wonder where she was and why she ghosted her. Amaya, who would never and could never know the truth. Wendy would become just some girl she knew for a few months, while Wendy herself would cease to exist—discarded like a chewed-up piece of Wonder Rush. She thought about the pain she caused Corey. Did she even cost him his life? It seemed likely. She thought about her Bibi doll and knew it was time to break from Amaya and Corey the way she broke that doll.

"Yes," she finally said. "I'm ready to move on. No attachments, right?"

Genko's gaze rested on Wendy as he assessed her sincerity. "Cut her loose," he instructed Porter.

The stiffness in her newly freed hands was numbing, but she turned her wrists and splayed her fingers to get some feeling back. When Porter cut her ankles free, she stretched her legs but remained seated. She wasn't confident that her feet could hold her body weight yet.

Genko handed Wendy an envelope. She cringed as her hands, which had been stagnant for so long, worked through the pain. Inside was a driver's license, Social Security card, passport, and medical records—all forgeries. Tucked behind the documents was a new cell phone.

"You are now Harper Connelly," Genko said.

Harper—she liked the sound of it. Kind of trendy.

"The good news, 'Harper,' is that you no longer need to worry about foster families. You are now a grown-up, whatever that means."

"Harper" looked at the driver's license. She was now eighteen. Was she truly eighteen? An adult? She wasn't sure. She never knew her birthday. Each identity had a different one, but they were all "born" in the same year, so she had a general idea of how old she was. She never had a birthday party, either. Sure, some foster families would get her a cake and a few small gifts when it was whatever birthday the agency assigned that identity, but it wasn't a true celebration. She had no friends to invite, no family members either. She was alone in this world.

"Also, for some good news," Genko continued, "you will go to college. Maybe whatever angst you have been feeling lately will work itself out in a more sophisticated environment."

She had been so busy focused on missions that she never even gave college a thought. Where will she go? What will she study? Will she have a roommate? She thought for a moment before realizing the better question is, how many of her fellow students will she kill? She shouldn't fool herself. The agency wasn't putting her through college so she can graduate and become a hedge fund manager or something. They're intentionally positioning her at an institution where she can maximize her kills.

Was Amaya going to college? No, not yet. She was still finishing up her senior year at West Elmdale. Wendy— correction—Harper thought about the people she left behind. The agency always had a story they told the schools and the foster families when an agent moved on. It was often rather simple. Foster children were traditionally more unstable than your average child. They run away sometimes, get caught up in drugs or sent to juvie. Sometimes a biological parent comes back and reclaims them.

"What happened to Wendy?" she asked.

"I'm sorry?" Genko responded.

"I mean, how did things wrap up for her?" It seemed odd referring to Wendy in the third person, but she was now Harper and had to get used to it. "What story did you tell the Barneses?"

"Oh, don't you worry about that. It's all taken care of. Tied up with a little bow."

"I was just curious. I liked Wendy."

"No attachments, child. Now, Harper," he said, changing the subject, "your backstory is that you escaped a tough home life. Mom was a meth addict, and Dad was physically abusive. That will explain the bruises on your face. That will also explain why your family never visits you at college and why you don't go home for holidays. Make sense?"

Harper nodded.

"Some will ask why you're transferring in the middle of the school year. The story is, you were going to a local college, living at home. That became unbearable for obvious reasons, so you had to escape. You'll audit classes until the new semester starts. Sound good?"

She nodded again.

"As always, the agency will cover all expenses related to school, laptop, *et cetera*. Questions?"

Harper shook her head.

"Okay, good. Now, clean yourself up and Maureen will take care of your appearance."

Maureen was the same woman who did her last few makeovers when she adopted a new identity. She must have been in her sixties, but she always knew all the latest fashion trends and was a wiz with hair and makeup. Harper was excited to see what she came up with.

Chapter 10

RANI

The muffled sounds of the crowd melded into one cacophonous auditory blur. A loud *buzz* should have broken Rani's daydream, but it didn't.

"Rani, you're up," Nora said with an elbow nudge.

Rani sat on the floor, dressed in a tight, blue, sleeveless top and a blue and white cheerleading skirt. There was just enough belly showing to be considered tasteful. She sat among five other similarly dressed girls (Nora being one of them), with four guys standing behind them. The guys wore the same color scheme but were granted sleeves and long pants—bellies fully covered.

Rani snatched her pom-poms, plastered on a fake smile, and gave those pom-poms a shake. Jumping to her feet, she hollered, "Let's go, Rats!" It was an unfortunate nickname, but evidently "Rattle Snakes" was too many syllables for most sports fans to chant with any degree of repetition. The die-hards swapped back and forth between "Rats" and "Snakes" fairly indiscriminately, but at the moment, Rani was feeling "Rats."

The player at the free throw line wore a blue and white jersey with number 11 on the front. He wiped sweat from his brow, bounced the basketball three times, gave it a final spin-bounce, and then took his shot. Swish. The crowd cheered, and Rani did a backflip. The ref passed the ball back to Number 11, who followed the same ritual—wipe the sweat, dribble-dribble-dribble, spin-bounce, and then swish. Rani performed a second backflip, but this time followed it up with a high kick, a pom-pom shake, and another "Let's go, Rats!" For the cherry on top, she screamed, "Go Snakes!" Hey, why not mix things up?

The scoreboard now read:

HOME: 68
AWAY: 70

The timer showed 4.5 seconds on the clock and it was the Musketeer's possession. Things were looking bad for the Rats. Win or lose, Rani didn't care. She just enjoyed the crowd and the camaraderie. She even developed an unexplainable liking for the smell of the gym—a strange combination of sweat, floor polish, and desperation.

Musketeer number 8 was struggling to inbound the ball amid Rats number 21's tenacious defense. Knowing the time to inbound was critically diminishing, Musketeer-8 chest-passed the ball for his intended teammate, but Rat-21 got a finger on it. The ball deflected to no one in particular, and both sides hustled. Rat-17 grabbed the ball, tossed it to Rat-4, who was quickly double-teamed. With 1.3 seconds on the clock, he threw the ball to Rat-11, who was waiting on the left wing, just behind the three-point arc. He launched the ball, the buzzer sounded, the crowd jumped to their feet in utter silence. The ball bounced off the far side of the rim, hit the backboard, bounced to the other side of the rim, hung there for what felt like an eternity, and dropped into the basket. The Rats won, 71-70!

The crowd went wild while Rani and her squad kicked and cheered and tossed their pom-poms in the air. Friends hugged each other in the stands, beer was spilled, strangers high-fived. Is there anything better than a nail-biting, buzzer-beater win?

* * *

By the time Rani got back to her dorm, other students joined her fellow cheerleaders, who all chanted the school fight song with their arms draped around each other. Rani laughed as she stumbled over the lyrics. She should have them memorized by now, being a cheerleader, but she was still a freshman, so she wasn't too hard on herself. Rani broke from the mob as she reached her dorm room.

"Hey, Rani," Malcolm shouted, "afterparty at the Beta House. You coming?"

"Count me in," she replied. "I just need to get cleaned up."

Malcolm hooted and went back to chanting the fight song without missing a beat.

Rani tossed her pom-poms onto her bed, relieved to see her roommate out for the night. The rooms in Mulberry Hall were more spacious than some other doubles on campus, allowing students to perch one bed on either side of the room—no need to bunk them. It was still a little too close for Rani's taste. She rested her face in both of her hands, her jovial spirit wiped out in an instant. She sat there like that for several minutes, fighting back tears.

Finally, she got up, sat at her desk, flicked on the light above her mirror, and reached for a makeup remover wipe. She slowly and carefully abolished the caked-on makeup that made her seem larger than life in front of the crowd. Underneath, she was beautiful. Her deep amber eyes and jet-black hair, which shined like finely woven silk, complemented her caramel complexion. With the makeup cleanly removed, she opted instead for a subtle pink lip gloss and a basic black eyeliner.

Rani slipped out of her cheerleading uniform and traded it for a simple pair of form-fitting jeans and a black sweater. She clasped a thin gold chain around her neck—a simple gold cross resting over her sweater. She stood in front of the full-length mirror she had mounted to the back of her closet door. Taking a few deep breaths, she mentally prepared for the night ahead. She feigned a smile, as if practicing, wanting to know how the rest of the world would see her, but that smile quickly dropped to a stoic stare. Rani reached for her doorknob, ready as she ever would be, but an alert on her smartwatch interrupted her. The notification read, "Now."

She moved back to her desk, reached behind a stack of textbooks, and pulled out a medication bottle. Kicking open her small, dorm-sized fridge, Rani grabbed a water bottle, spilled one pill into her hand, popped it into her mouth, and washed it down. She placed the medication on her desktop as she put the water bottle back in the refrigerator. The prescription read, "Rani Bajwa—Zoloft—100 mg."

* * *

The Beta party was your typical college fare—obnoxious drunk guys hitting on equally drunk girls. Some played drinking games in the corner, others danced to the hideously loud music with way too much bass. Rani could feel her chest pound with each thud of the synthetic drum beat, but she danced anyway.

She wasn't necessarily comfortable in crowds like this, but she loved to dance. It's what made her join the cheerleading squad. As a child, Rani always loved dance class. Her mom took her to her first class at age four and it was instant love. Her high school didn't have a dance squad, so she joined the gymnastics team. She loved that even more. Once college rolled around, cheerleading seemed like the best of both worlds.

At parties like this, dancing gave her an excuse. She wasn't required to talk to too many people or drink. She thought about the surrounding people, all with a plastic cup, glass bottle, or beer can in their hands. She mused about people seeming to regress once they hit college—the baby bottle and pacifier replaced with Solo cups and vape pens. Finally, she concluded that most people her age were probably just as insecure as she was, and they needed some comfort object to hold on to.

As she danced with some of her cheerleading friends, she whipped her head around and noticed a guy standing by himself, leaning against a door frame. The obligatory security blanket that was a red Solo cup rested in his hand. Was he checking her out? She thought so, but tried to play coy.

As the music transitioned to a new song, Nora started jumping up and down. "I love this song," she attempted in vain to shout over the deafening music.

"What?" Rani screamed back, surprised to discover that she couldn't even hear herself.

"Never mind."

The girls danced more vigorously. Rani glimpsed back to where the guy once stood, but he was gone. She figured it was probably all in her imagination until she felt a hand on her shoulder.

"Can I get you a drink?" he asked.

"What?" No point in attempting dialogue in a place this loud.

He held up his cup to demonstrate. He gave it a little shake, offered it up in her direction with eyebrows raised as if asking a question.

"Oh, no thank you." She shook her head too, knowing he wouldn't be able to hear her reply.

He gave her a "come this way" wave and gestured toward the door. Nora grabbed her arm and shot her a concerned look. Rani shook it off. "I'll be right back," she yelled directly into Nora's ear. That she heard.

The guy wore a tee shirt with three Greek letters emblazoned on the front—Beta Omega Rho. He reached for Rani's hand. She took it and smiled. It was partially out of excitement that someone picked her out of a crowd and partly out of amusement that this frat guy, who was probably full of himself, wore a shirt that essentially said "BOP." Was she supposed to bop him on the nose?

He led her up a flight of stairs and she resisted. She feared where this was going. He turned and gave her a reassuring look. "It's okay," he mouthed as he pointed upward. She hesitantly followed.

They ascended another flight of stairs, and the music became more muffled. It was quiet enough to hear each other speak. "Where are we going?" she asked.

"I just wanted to talk to you. Come on."

"I can hear you just fine here."

He gave her a puppy dog look. "Trust me. You'll like it."

"Trust you?" she asked. "I don't know you. I don't even know your name."

"Kevin Mitchell. Now do you trust me?" His lower lip now stuck out to match the puppy dog eyes.

"No," she replied, but she followed him anyway. He was awfully cute, and when he smiled, she couldn't resist his dimples.

He climbed a set of narrow metal stairs and looked back at her waiting at the bottom. "Last set of stairs. I promise."

She followed him up and found herself on the roof of the frat house. It wasn't your standard slanted roof with asphalt shingles. It was a flat roof that the frat brothers used more like a balcony. The building itself stood three stories tall, and a railing surrounded the balcony, high enough to prevent any unforeseen drunken falls. There were a few lawn chairs and chaise lounges set up, and a small table with some playing cards and a few empty beer cans.

He sat in one of the chaise lounge chairs and gestured to the one next to it. She lay in the chair, staring at the night sky, which was clear and glistening with stars. "Wow," she couldn't help but say out loud.

"Isn't this much better than that horrible music downstairs?"

"You know," she said, "I was enjoying that horrible music."

"Oh, I'm sorry. You want to head back down?" he teased.

"No. This is amazing." Rani glanced up at the stars and took a deep breath. Kevin took a drag from a vape pen and offered it to Rani. "No, thank you," she said with a disapproving look. Kevin took the hint and put it back in his pocket.

"I'm Rani, by the way," she said.

"I know."

"I'm sorry. Were you stalking me?"

"Eh, a little."

"What?" Rani sat up in her chair and amusingly smacked his shoulder.

"I may have asked around a little after seeing you cheer."

"Huh," Rani said. "Okay. I see how it is."

"You sure I can't get you a drink?" Kevin asked. "Not to brag, but I know some people around here. I could make that happen."

"Wow," she said sarcastically, "you can track down a drink at a frat party? You must know people in high places."

"Something like that." He smiled and released the full power of those dimples. Rani melted.

"No. I'm fine," she said. "I don't drink."

Kevin noticed the gold cross hanging onto her chest. "Yeah, I don't drink much either."

She looked at him, surprised.

"Not on a Saturday night. I need to get up early for church tomorrow," Kevin explained.

She wasn't sure if he was sincere or if he was just playing her. Guys say anything they think a girl wants to hear. "You go to church?" she asked.

"Jesus and I are like this." He crossed his fingers, showing how close they were.

Rani nodded her head, not quite convinced. "Okay. Well," she said as she stood up, "maybe I'll see you there."

"Maybe you will," Kevin replied as he stood up, too. "Can I walk you home? Where do you live?"

"You don't know, Mister Stalker?"

He laughed and gestured toward the staircase. "Lead the way."

* * *

By the time they arrived back at Mulberry Hall, Rani was pretty smitten, although still leery. The beer-guzzling frat guy with all the right moves was not her typical type. Perhaps he was a smooth talker, but she was willing to see how things developed.

"Well, thanks for walking me home," she said. "It was nice meeting you." She hesitated. "I'm kind of glad you stalked me a little."

He laughed and said, "Me too." He leaned in and gave her a kiss. It was small and sweet and perfect. He didn't push things any further. He simply said, "Good night."

Rani entered her dorm room elated, but that feeling of euphoria quickly diminished when she spotted her roommate, Angela, asleep in bed with her filthy boyfriend, Todd. Todd was an upperclassman and had an apartment off campus. Why they needed to defile her personal space was beyond her.

Rani intentionally knocked into things and slammed drawers shut, hoping he would wake up and scurry away like a cockroach when the lights turned on. Instead, they both slept soundly. She tossed herself onto her bed. She would deal with her roommate in the morning.

Rani's sleep was choppy and disturbed. She couldn't shake the image of two people doing God knows what less than eight feet from her bed. The sun rose, and she heard rustling from Angela's side of the room. Rani feigned sleep as Todd clumsily gathered his clothes and shoes and slipped out through the door.

"Did you sin with him?" Rani asked.

"I'm sorry?" Angela asked.

"If people are fornicating in my bedroom, I deserve to know."

Angela had heard it all before and was at her wit's end. "First of all, Saint Rani, this is not *your* bedroom. It is *our* bedroom, and what I do on my side is entirely up to me. Second, I don't need your holier-than-thou attitude telling me what I can and can't do with my body. Do you understand?"

"Whatever, Angela. Just try to respect my values."

"Respect? Yeah, okay, Rani." Angela quickly threw on a tee shirt, grabbed her purse, and stormed out of the room.

"I'll pray for you…" Rani called out as the door slammed. "Ugh!"

Rani moved over to her desk and reached for a tissue, only to find the box was empty. Instead, she grabbed one from Angela's desk. Then something caught her eye—something in the trash can.

The next night, Rani lay in bed, waiting until Angela was sound asleep. At least Todd was in his own apartment that night. She could hear Angela's deep breathing, so she quietly got out of bed, slowly opened her desk drawer, and pulled out what she had found in Angela's trash that morning. Rani held it in disgust between the tips of her index finger and thumb, as if it were contagious. She placed the device next to Angela as she slept. It was a white plastic pregnancy test with two pink lines displayed in its little window.

Rani kneeled down next to Angela's bed, her hands clasped together and her head bowed down. She mumbled a prayer to herself. It's not that she hated Angela. She wanted to save her, and now she wanted to save Angela's unborn baby.

"Please, Lord, look after your daughter, Angela," Rani whispered. "Please protect her unborn child and give Angela the strength to raise her baby in the Christian faith."

Angela bolted up in bed, knocking Rani backwards. "What the hell are you doing?"

Rani got back on her knees and started praying louder. "Hail Mary, full of grace. The Lord is with thee…"

Angela spotted the pregnancy test on the side of her bed. She grabbed it angrily. "You went through my trash? What is wrong with you?"

"Look, Angela," Rani explained. "I can help you through this. There are resources at my church—"

"Church? Rani, do you think I'm really going to have this baby? I'm nineteen years old and still in school. I can't raise a baby."

"Wait, what are you saying?" Rani asked, not really wanting to hear the answer.

"Rani," she said, "I'm getting an abortion."

Rani stood in shock before dropping to her knees again. "Our father, who art in heaven, hallowed be thy name…"

Angela gathered a few of her things and stormed out of the room, saying, "Jesus, Rani. This is the last straw."

* * *

Later that afternoon, Rani returned to her dorm room to find Angela's side of the room bare. The bed was stripped down to the mattress. The closet doors were open, showing only a few stray hangers. Her desk was cleared off. Rani sighed as she sat on the side of her bed, looking at her half-empty room in disbelief.

"Rani Bajwa?" The voice came from a girl standing in her doorway, a backpack on her back and a duffle bag under each arm.

"Yeah?" Rani replied, confused.

"I'm your new roommate. I'm Harper Connelly."

Chapter 11

WENDY

She rarely had much trouble switching from one disposable identity to another, but there was something about Wendy she wanted to hold on to. Regardless, here she was, embarking on a new chapter in her life as Harper Connelly.

Harper remained in the doorway, biting the inside of her cheek and waiting for an acknowledgement from her new roommate. Her hair was now dirty-blond, hanging just above her shoulder. She had her bangs swept to the side, held back with a hair clip, exposing her forehead and no longer hiding her face. Her prismatic eyes sparkled aquamarine beneath a set of plastic tortoiseshell glasses—trendy, not dorky. She wore black leggings and a plain white tank top covered with a denim button-down that hung open. Casual black boots with a thick sole adorned her feet. Harper was more sophisticated than Wendy. She liked this look. Maureen, the agency's stylist, outdid herself this time.

"Oh… you didn't know I was coming, did you?" Harper asked a rather dumbfounded Rani.

"What…? No, I…" Rani tried to cover, but it was no use.

"Actually, I had no idea. I'm sorry. Didn't mean to make things awkward."

"The Housing Office told me a spot just opened up. Supposedly they emailed you about it," Harper said.

"I imagine they did. No worries. Come in."

Harper dropped her bags onto her cleanly stripped bed. "I assume this is my side."

"Nothing gets past you," Rani said, intending to be jovial, but realizing it sounded more confrontational. "So," Rani attempted to change the mood, "didn't work out with your old roommate?"

"Actually, I just transferred here."

"Mid-semester?" Again, she didn't mean to sound as harsh as she did.

"Yeah, well... long story." Harper had the backstory to cover her tracks but didn't feel the need to wheel it out yet. The few days she took to recuperate from Porter and Genko's little slap-fest healed most of her wounds. The swelling on her lip was down. She covered the crack with lipstick. Some bruising still colored her cheeks and eyes, but foundation hid most of that.

"I was actually on my way to church," Rani said. "Do you want to come with?" Rani asked this with some hesitation in her voice after her experience with Angela. It was also partially a test to see how her new roommate would react.

Harper had never stepped inside a church, but she was pretty sure she would spontaneously combust as soon as she crossed the threshold. "Um... raincheck maybe?"

"Sure thing. I can skip it if you want help unpacking."

"No. That's fine. I don't have much."

"Okay. Well... welcome." Rani paused by the door for a moment, wondering if she would scare Harper off like she did Angela. Angela was a sinner, though. She thought Harper looked nice. It was probably fine. Rani smiled and left.

Have you heard the one about the devout Christian and her professional assassin roommate? Harper couldn't help but laugh, although she had no punchline. She shook off the thought and unpacked her bags.

She laid out a set of sheets and a comforter on her bed and tossed a pillow on top. She haphazardly stuffed stacks of clothes into drawers and put some shoes at the foot of her closet. Her walls would remain bare. She had no photos of family or friends to hang up, and she was always too busy to keep up with the latest bands and movies.

Her side looked desolate compared to Rani's, which she decorated in an intricate and colorful tapestry that appeared to be floating magically on the wall above her bed. There must have been some university-approved adhesive keeping it in place. She also had a few pictures of friends, including some in her cheerleading uniform. There was a family photo on Rani's desk—her posing happily between an Indian father and a white mother. Leaning next to it was a small wooden cross.

Harper took her laptop out of her bag, put it on her own desk, and powered it on. She opened up a web browser and inhaled deeply. She should really let sleeping dogs lie, but she was curious. She keyed in "Corey Barnes" but stopped herself before she hit enter. Corey's last name wasn't Barnes. They didn't adopt him. What was his last name?

Harper deleted "Barnes" and tapped the laptop as she thought. It was something with a "V" or a "T." Now she felt like a carnival psychic staring into a crystal ball. *I see someone important in your life. Their very fate lies in your hands. Do you know anyone with a "V" or a "T" in their name?*

Lamont! That was it. Corey Lamont.

Or maybe the name starts with an "L," her imaginary psychic added with a very mysterious sounding inner voice.

Harper searched for "Corey Lamont" and scrolled through the results. Unless Corey was now a middle-aged balloon artist available for children's parties and corporate functions, she found nothing.

She thought about calling the house and asking for Corey. She would need to disguise her voice, but that wouldn't be a problem. If they put him on, then she would know he was okay. If they replied with something like, "I'm sorry to say this, but…" then she would know the news was bad. She just needed to know. Her new phone had none of Wendy's contacts in it, and there was no chance she could remember their phone numbers. I mean, she could barely recall Corey's last name.

Harper searched for "Ryan and Grace Barnes—White Pages." She found a link that looked good, clicked it and found one landline number available for Barnes in West Elmdale, NJ. For only $9.99, that information could be hers. All she needed was a credit card, which she did not have. She rummaged through Rani's desk drawers, hoping she was careless enough to leave a credit card in there. No dice.

Harper grabbed her cell phone, unlocked it, dialed 4-1-1, and waited for the automated voice.

"Thank you for calling Directory Assistance. For what city and state?"

"West Elmdale, New Jersey."

"Thank you. For what listing?"

"Ryan and Grace Barnes."

"One moment, please." Then: "I'm sorry. We could not locate the number you requested. Would you like to try another listing?"

She hung up the phone. Frustrated, she switched gears.

Harper typed "Amaya Malone" into the search box and hit "enter." She knew she had to tread lightly here. She couldn't leave any trace to Amaya from her new identity, but she was still safe.

She hadn't committed to anything yet. It was just a web search. It probably wouldn't even find the right Amaya.

Almost instantly, Harper was staring at a list of search results. There was an Amaya Malone who was a CPA in Cleveland—probably not her. Malone Funeral Home—nope. There was a link to an Amaya Malone on Instagram. Based on the URL that showed in the search result, the person's username was "LeaveMeMalone." That was Amaya. Her Amaya. Her instincts told her to click, but she hesitated. She needed to think this through.

She wasn't logged into her Instagram account. Actually, Harper didn't even have any social media yet, and there was no trace of Wendy on her laptop or phone. She could click the link without leaving evidence. Was Amaya's account private? She couldn't remember. If it was, she wouldn't be able to see anything anyway, so what's the harm? Maybe she was just rationalizing the decision. She was supposed to cut all ties with no qualms. That was the right thing to do. Close the browser, close the laptop, and walk away. Yes, that's what she should do. She decided.

Instead, she clicked the link.

Amaya's account was public. She could see everything. Harper bit down on the inside of her lip. Why was she so nervous? She never got nervous. She scrolled through her feed, stopped, and backed up. A photo got her attention. Harper clicked on it, enlarging a picture of a funeral card. Harper's jaw dropped, and she said out loud, to no one in particular, "Oh. My. God."

* * *

Amaya sat on her bed, her head propped up on two stacked pillows. Her laptop rested on her stomach and earbuds plugged each ear. The music streaming into them was too loud for her to hear the knocking on her bedroom door. Finally, her mom let herself in. This was ordinarily the time when Amaya would scold her mother for entering without knocking and her mom would chastise her for blasting her music too loud in her ears, but not today. Today was different.

"It's time," her mother whispered.

Amaya gave her a knowing nod, pulled the earbuds from her ears, took a deep breath, and got up.

Amaya had a strained relationship with her mother, Gina. Her father left when she was six, leaving her mother to raise Amaya by herself. Gina had little education and worked several poorly paying jobs. She wasn't home a lot and when she was, she was tired and stressed and worried that her daughter would follow in her regretful footsteps.

From Amaya's perspective, her mother just wasn't available. She wasn't there to help her with school projects or to listen to her teenage problems. Most nights, Amaya had to fend for herself for dinner. Laundry, dishes, vacuuming, all of those sorts of things, fell on Amaya. There was bitterness. Perhaps misplaced, but that's how she felt. There was resentment on Amaya's part, regret on Gina's, and constant consternation between the two of them. But today was different.

"Mom?" Amaya's voice trembled as her mother was walking away. Gina turned, and Amaya grabbed her, wrapping both arms around her tightly. Gina hesitated, taken aback, and then melted into the hug.

Tears were now streaming down Amaya's cheeks, and she was sobbing wildly. "I love you, Mom."

Gina was tearing up now, too. For her, it wasn't just about what today represented. For Gina, it was about every fight she wished she'd never had with her daughter. Every harsh word she wanted to retract. Each time she chose a double-shift over time with Amaya. Today put everything into perspective like nothing else could.

Gina placed her hand on her daughter's head, stroked her hair and whispered, "I love you too, sweetheart. Always."

* * *

The funeral parlor's utter silence exasperated the already somber atmosphere. Few people attended, and that made Amaya angry and sad. She glanced over at Mr. and Mrs. Barnes, who stood next to a closed casket propped up on a wooden stand. Corey was not with them. There were no photographs to display, just a framed printout on an easel.

Wendy Lockheart
Gone, but never forgotten

Meg and Tommy sat with Amaya in silence. A few students trickled in, but Wendy never made too many connections at West Elmdale High. Amaya scowled at her fellow students who couldn't bother with Wendy when she was alive and now showed up at her funeral. Hypocrites.

A few teachers joined. Mrs. Hampshire, Amaya's economics teacher, bent down and whispered to Amaya, "I'm so sorry for your loss. I know you two were close."

"Thank you," she mumbled, choking back tears.

Mrs. Hampshire then sat down next to Amaya, making her a little uncomfortable. She had never been that physically close to a teacher before. The chairs were rather narrow, and Mrs. Hampshire was rather wide, so her hips spilled over the sides and grazed Amaya. "How did it happen, if you don't mind me asking?"

"Wendy's foster mom said she became agitated about her foster brother's illness. She ran out of the house. Didn't say where she was going. Then she…" Tears welled in Amaya's eyes, and a solid lump in her throat prevented her from finishing.

"Oh, it's okay." Mrs. Hampshire grabbed Amaya's wrist and gave it a consoling rub. Amaya wondered what it was about funerals that made people feel like personal space vanished.

Meg, who was sitting on the other side of Amaya, heard the conversation and finished Amaya's thought for her. "She ran into the street, Mrs. Hampshire. She was upset, and she wasn't looking where she was going and…" Meg couldn't finish either, but Mrs. Hampshire got the general idea.

"Well, you let me know if I can help," Mrs. Hampshire said as she got up and walked toward the casket to pay her respects. That casket was empty, but Mrs. Hampshire didn't know that, nor did Amaya.

Toward the back of the room, Amaya spotted a middle-aged man who she did not recognize. Something about him seemed wrong to her. He was trying a bit too hard to go unnoticed.

* * *

Amaya tossed her purse onto her bed, slipped out of her black dress shoes, and fell face first onto her mattress and just lay there. Her hands grasped the bedspread, forming tight fists of fabric, and she sobbed.

After several minutes, she sat up, wiped her eyes, and unzipped her purse. Inside was a prayer card with Wendy's name, date of birth, and date of death on one side and a prayer to Saint Mary on the other. She scoffed. Wendy would have found the whole thing ridiculous, but this was Amaya's one last memory of Wendy. The one thing she could physically hold on to and think of her friend. A friend she didn't know for long, but one that would stay in her heart forever. Some people are like that. It's not the amount of time that they're in your lives that matters. They grab hold of some integral piece of you and never let go. That was Wendy.

Amaya placed the prayer card on her bed with Wendy's name and death date facing up, and she snapped a picture with her cell phone. She launched Instagram, uploaded the photo, and captioned it "RIP Wendy."

* * *

Harper stared at her computer screen, alone in her dorm room, glaring at the photo of her funeral card.

"The bastards killed me," she muttered.

It was a confusing feeling. She knew she wasn't dead, but she still felt a loss. She liked Wendy, and now she was gone.

Thinking about Amaya and how she must be suffering, upset her even more. She felt the loss of Wendy through Amaya, and tears formed in her eyes. She didn't want her friend to suffer, yet it seemed like she left a nasty wake of torment everywhere she went.

She wanted to leap through the computer screen and tell Amaya she was alive and well. She wanted to call her and hear her voice and give her some peace of mind and… what? Tell her she has a new identity? Tell her she's a professional assassin, traveling the country and killing people (but fear not, for they are bad people)? Tell her about the agency and her training and the brainwashing and the physical and psychological torture? No. There was no explanation she could give. Her only option was to move on. Leave Wendy behind. Leave Amaya behind. Wendy was gone.

Wendy was dead.

The only person who mattered now was Harper Connelly.

Chapter 12

KEVIN

Chester Pointe University wasn't the largest school in Southeastern Pennsylvania, but it still required more than a foldable campus map to find your way around. Harper figured that out pretty quickly as she attempted to navigate her way to Kensington Hall for the American Lit class she was auditing. She stood somewhere near the Student Center, or so she figured, trying to glance at the map without looking like a tourist. Students breezed past her, professors paid her no mind. She would be late on her first day, she was certain of that.

"Need a hand?" a guy called, rushing to class. He turned around and continued his trek backwards, waiting for a reply.

"Kensington Hall?"

"Yup. Follow me. That's where I'm headed."

"Ah, great," Harper said with relief. "This place is a maze."

"Don't you mean, this place is a-*maze*-ing? Go Rats!" He waved his spirit fingers.

"You could pass for the school mascot with those moves. Must have taken a lot of practice."

"More than you could imagine. I'm Kevin." He extended a hand. Harper shook it.

"Harper. Thanks for being my tour guide."

Kevin Mitchell (yes, Rani's Kevin), traded his Beta Omega Rho tee shirt for a tattered Beta Omega Rho hat. Harper pointed to it. "Is your frat seriously called 'BOP'?"

Kevin removed the hat and looked at the front curiously before putting it back on. "So it is. Whatta ya know. That's a 'Rho' at the end, though, not a 'P.'"

"Looks like a 'P' to me."

"We just call it 'Beta.'"

"I take it, three Greek letters is too much to say?" Harper teased.

"You know frat guys," Kevin said, "too dumb to remember four letters, so we only use three."

"I meant no offense."

"Some taken," he replied with a smile, but his dimples didn't have the same power over Harper. "You bruised my fragile male ego."

"Ooh, wouldn't want to bruise that. Sounds painful."

Kevin reached into his pocket, pulled out a vape pen, and took a drag. He blew the smoke out away from Harper and offered it to her.

"Didn't anyone ever tell you that shit will kill you?" Harper replied.

"Oh, but all the cool kids are doing it."

They had now arrived at a building with a placard on the side reading "Kensington Hall." "What floor are you on?" Kevin asked.

Harper checked her schedule. "Um... second... room 215."

"Cool. I'm on the first. I guess this is where we part ways, m'lady," Kevin said with an exaggerated bow.

"Does this cheese-ball charm ever work with the females

outside of a frat party?"

"Eh, a few drinks definitely help," he shrugged. "Welcome to CPU."

* * *

She knew she was late, so Harper snuck in and sat toward the back of the room. What she didn't account for was the fact that there were only twelve people in this class, and her late arrival was not as clandestine as she envisioned. As she entered, the professor stopped and the other students turned toward the door.

"Sorry," Harper whispered. "Carry on." She squatted down as she crept to a seat in the back, as if that was going to make her less visible somehow.

The professor was talking about someone named Faulkner. She had never heard of him. There was a lot of discussion about symbolism and metaphor, and Harper quickly realized that she was in over her head. Jumping around from one school to another her entire life wasn't exactly the ideal formula for a great education. Thankfully, she was only auditing this class. Still, maybe she would read some of this "Faulkner" character. The professor droned on about a book called *As I Lay Dying*. She figured it might be worth reading that one. She could consider it career research. That made her smile.

Harper had no idea how long the agency would keep her implanted at CPU, but she assumed it wouldn't be very long. A few months, maybe. Although they were smart to place her in a suburb of Philadelphia. There were a lot of colleges in the area—Villanova, Rosemont, Swarthmore, Haverford, Bryn Mawr, and Cabrini. Plus, there was another chunk of schools inside the city limits—Penn, Drexel, Temple, St. Joe's, La Salle, and Thomas Jefferson. She could really take her time working through the various student bodies, not to mention corrupt professors and staff. Then again, that might raise suspicion. She gave up trying to predict the agency's moves years ago. For now, she would learn as much as she could at CPU, starting with Faulkner.

What was the last book she read? A school in Maryland assigned *The Great Gatsby*. Did she finish that one? She couldn't remember, but she watched the movie. That took less time, and with all the agency's extra-curricular activities, school work was too much of a nuisance.

Harper reached into her bag and pulled out an open pack of Wonder Rush gum. It was from a previous mission, so the wrappers were all white. She removed a stick, folded it into her mouth, and chewed.

Peach. Not bad.

She liked that most about Wonder Rush—it was always a surprise. It kept you guessing. She thought it was a decent metaphor for work at the agency. There was always something new. Hey, maybe she should discuss that metaphor with her American Lit class. She laughed out loud, garnering a few looks from her classmates. Instead, she just blew a bubble until it popped, sticking to her lips.

* * *

There were two U-shaped upperclassman dormitories that faced each other like mirror images, leaving a large open area in between. The students commonly referred to this space as "The Circle" even though it was really more like an oval (Mathematics was not CPU's forte). There were a few benches and picnic tables on either side and a horseshoe pit off to one end. Otherwise, it was an open green space with a few scattered trees and scrubs. It was a popular hangout for all students as it sat in the center of campus. A pathway cut straight through the middle, connecting what students referred to as "North Campus" and "South Campus." The great seal of

Chester Pointe University adorned the center of The Circle where the path transected it.

The one and only piece of advice Harper received when she enrolled at CPU was never to step foot on the seal in the middle of The Circle. Supposedly, a cafeteria worker pushed a food cart through there a few years ago and it resulted in campus-wide run of food poisoning that shut down instruction for a week. There was another incident back in the '70s where the school mascot walked through the seal during a pep rally and the basketball team finished the season with its worst losing streak in school history.

It was all coincidence and superstition, as far as Harper was concerned. In fact, on her way back from her American Lit class, she intentionally walked straight across the CPU seal. A few students gasped, but she did not burst into flames. Instead, she made her way peacefully to a bench on the outskirts of The Circle.

Harper enjoyed sitting back and watching the world go by. She watched as some students meandered around, talking to friends. Others rushed from North Campus to South Campus, or vice versa. Some tossed around a Frisbee or kicked a hacky sack, while others caught some shade under a tree and studied. Other students, like her, just sat and watched. It reminded her of a time when she visited New York City. It was not nearly on the same scale, but it gave her the same feeling—a sense that anything was possible. She felt surrounded by so much potential. Whatever she wanted to do with her life, whoever she wanted to be, was all here for her to discover.

She felt free, and she felt something she hadn't in a long time—optimistic. For a moment, she wasn't thinking about the agency or her next mission or who she was going to be once they disposed of Harper. She looked around and wondered who was going to leave here one day and become a research scientist and change the world with some brilliant discovery. She thought about who in this cluster of students would become a surgeon and save some child's life. She wondered who would be the teachers, lawyers, nurses, writers, and artists. She briefly speculated whether she could be one of those extraordinary people, but she realized that such possibilities were not reserved for her. She was an agent and nothing more. She belonged to the agency. Yes, she benefitted the world in some way, but she questioned the agency's methods. Surely they could do better. They could be better. She could be more. But mostly, she wanted to choose. She desired some say in what her life represented.

"You look deep in thought." Harper didn't even notice Rani approaching.

"Hey, sorry," Harper responded, "just taking it all in."

"It can be overwhelming at first, but you'll get the hang of it. How was class?"

"Good… I guess," Harper said. "Confusing, maybe. I don't know. I'm definitely not smart enough to be here."

"Oh, whatever. I'm sure you'll do fine. You were smart enough to get accepted, after all."

Harper didn't know how to say that the agency of assassins that implanted her on this campus had a network of people in high places, and they got her into the school even though she never finished high school. She smiled instead. "So, you're a cheerleader?" Harper changed the subject.

"Yeah, how did you—?"

"I saw your pictures in our dorm room," Harper interrupted.

"Ah, right. I always loved to dance, and I got into gymnastics in high school, so…" It was almost as if Rani was making excuses, like cheerleading embarrassed her. "Honestly, I thought it would help me adjust to college. You know, meet some people."

"Did it?"

"Sure. I guess."

"I was never one to pal around with the beautiful, popular cheerleader, so I'm honored."

"Oh," Rani shook her head, "I'm not… wait. You think I'm beautiful?"

Most girls would mimic a false modesty, but Rani seemed genuinely demure. "Yeah. I mean, look at you," Harper said. "You're gorgeous."

Rani blushed.

"I can't be the first person to tell you that," Harper added.

"You'd be surprised." Rani looked at Harper, wanting to open up, but she hesitated. Finally she said, "If I'm being honest, I never really felt like I fit in anywhere."

"You're kidding."

"Where are you from, Harper?" Rani asked.

That wasn't a straightforward question she could give an honest answer to, but honesty wasn't Harper's forte, anyway. "I'm from Massachusetts." That was part of Harper's backstory, so it was a good enough response.

"I'm from Nebraska, and not one of the more tolerant areas like Lincoln or Omaha. I grew up in western Nebraska. My father's side of the family is Hindu from India and Pakistan. My mom is white, corn-fed, Catholic midwestern. There were minorities where I grew up, but very few. None in my class besides me. Don't get me wrong, everyone was nice. You'll never find better people than Cornhuskers. But I was just… different. I always felt different. The white kids didn't exactly exclude me, but they didn't welcome me much either. Same with the minorities. I just didn't fit in either way." Rani stopped herself and looked at Harper. "I am so sorry. I don't know why I'm dumping all of this on you. I've known you for, like, a day."

"No, it's fine," Harper said. "It's good roommate bonding." Plus, Harper could relate. She never fit in anywhere either. Mostly because she was never anywhere long enough to make connections. She didn't even have a family to return home to. It was a very lonely existence, and she could feel the same thing in Rani. "Have you found people here you connect with?"

"I have, yeah. Actually," Rani now whispered as if she was dishing some major gossip, "I met a guy."

"Oh, do tell." Harper wasn't one for relationship talk, but she knew it was the right facade for the occasion.

"He's sweet and popular and—"

"Talking about me?" Kevin interrupted as he walked up and sat next to Rani. His question was in jest, but it caught Rani off guard since she was, in fact, talking about him.

"What...? No, we were just..." Rani babbled.

"Hey, relax. I just saw you sitting here and wanted to say hello."

"Well, hello," Rani said. She turned to Harper. "This is Kevin. Kevin, this is—"

"Harper," he interrupted. "Did you find your class okay?"

"You two know each other?" Rani asked.

"Actually," Harper explained, "Kevin was kind enough to show me how to get to Kensington Hall."

"Practice, practice, practice!" Kevin said, cracking himself up.

"I think that's how to get to *Carnegie* Hall," Rani interjected.

"Eh, same thing," he said.

"I literally know two people at this entire school," Harper said. "What are the odds?"

"Huh, weird," Rani said, nudging her way closer to Kevin, feeling threatened and marking her territory. If Harper didn't know any better, she would have expected Rani to lift her leg like a dog and pee on him.

"Well, I should really get going," Harper said to ease the tension.

"Where you headed?" Kevin asked.

"I was just going to grab some lunch at the Student Center."

"Great, how about we all eat together?"

"Actually," Rani said, "I have cheerleading practice." She gestured behind her. "South Campus."

"Okay, no problem," Kevin said and turned toward Harper. "Me and you, then?"

"Oh, I don't know. Maybe I'll just—"

"No. Go ahead," Rani said, but her eyes said something else entirely.

"You know, Harper," Kevin said, "you haven't lived until you tried the triple chocolate chunk ice cream at the Student Center."

"And you want to live. Don't you, Harper?" Rani said with an edge to her voice.

"Sure. Okay," Harper conceded.

"Great," Kevin said.

"Yeah, great," Rani added.

"I'll... call you later," Kevin said to Rani as they all parted ways. Rani just smirked.

As Kevin and Harper crossed The Circle toward North Campus, Harper nearly stepped directly onto the CPU seal. "Whoops," Kevin said, wrapping his arm around Harper's waist and directing her away from the seal. "You must never step foot on the great seal of Chester Pointe University."

"I may have heard something about that," Harper said. Kevin's arm found Harper's waist, mostly out of sheer instinct, but it lingered longer than instinct would have dictated. Rani turned to look back at them just as the incident happened, and she shuttered seeing Kevin walking with his arm around Harper.

For Harper, the gesture made her feel ill. She couldn't quite describe the feeling, but she had a sudden urge to push him away and kick him in the crotch. She almost felt an electrical impulse rushing through her body. She didn't like it at all, but she just stepped to the side and put some distance between them.

* * *

Later that night, Harper sat alone in her dorm room, propped up in her bed, reading William Faulkner's *As I Lay Dying*. If she was going to try her hand at being a college student, she was going to give it her all.

In a jolt, the door swung open, and Rani stood inside the threshold. Brea, who lived across the hall, grabbed Rani's attention before she could enter the room.

"Hey, if you're looking to party later…" Brea lifted her sweatshirt to show Rani a vodka bottle, clinging to her stomach under the waistband of her jeans. "The offer stands for you too, new girl," Brea said to Harper. Harper just smiled and nodded politely.

"No thanks, Brea," Rani huffed.

"If you change your mind, it'll be in my fridge—room 6."

Rani ignored her and stepped into the room, slamming the door behind her.

"Kevin seems nice," Harper said.

"Uh huh," Rani replied.

"You two been together long?"

"Nope."

The tension was palpable. "Okay, well, I'll keep reading." She held up her book for Rani to see. "American Lit." Rani just nodded.

The two sat in silence, Harper in her bed, Rani at her desk. Rani highlighted something in a biology textbook, but she was distracted. Her smart watch buzzed and issued a reminder: "Now." Rani glanced at the bookshelf where she hid her Zoloft. *Later*, she thought.

Rani turned her head toward Harper and opened her mouth

127

as if to speak, but she held back. Harper kept reading, oblivious to her roommate squirming on the other side of the room. "Did you sleep with him?" Rani finally asked.

"What? God, no. Of course not."

"You kissed him, though?" Rani asked, fearing the answer.

"Rani, what type of person do you think I am?"

"I don't know, Harper. That's what I'm trying to figure out. I don't know you all that well."

"Look, Rani, we ate lunch, and we talked. He's a nice guy," Harper said.

"That's not a denial."

"It's not an admission either." Harper turned off the light she had clipped to the side of her bed. "I'm going to sleep. Goodnight." Rani said nothing.

Harper realized she was torturing her poor roommate, but it was fun to watch her writhe in agony. As Harper lay there, Rani stewed. She tried some breathing exercises that her therapist taught her, but they weren't working. Finally, she got into bed and started praying.

* * *

Harper learned to be a light sleeper over the years, like prey sleeping in the wild, never knowing what sort of predator was lurking and waiting to attack. True, Harper was typically the predator, but even a predator is vulnerable in deep slumber. So, when she awoke suddenly to find Rani crouched next to her bed, mere inches from her face, Harper leapt into defense mode. She struck Rani across the face, knocking her backward.

Harper rocketed out of her bed, grabbed Rani by the throat, and pulled her up to her feet. In absolute shock, Rani's eyes widened, as if they were going to explode out of her face. She tried to explain herself, but the words came out as mere gurgling. Harper released Rani's throat, gripped her wrist, and pulled her arm behind her back. She slammed Rani into the wall, her knee pressed firmly against Rani's back.

"What the hell are you doing in my bed?" Harper interrogated, but she had Rani's face pressed up against the wall with such force that Rani couldn't respond. Harper relented just enough for Rani to speak.

"Praying. I was just praying." Rani explained in sheer panic.

"I don't need your prayers," Harper said. She spun her roommate around to face her, slamming her forearm into Rani's chest and pinning her against the painted cinderblock like a specimen under glass. "You have no idea what I'm capable of." Harper stared directly into Rani's eyes, looking for some understanding, but all she saw was fear. Harper let go and Rani ran to her bed.

"I'm so sorry," Rani quivered as tears welled in her eyes. They were tears of absolute terror. "I was just praying for you. I didn't mean—"

"Praying for me?" Harper softened.

"Yes, I really like Kevin, but if he chose you over me, I just want you to be happy. I was praying for your happiness."

"Rani," Harper replied, "that may be the nicest thing anyone has ever said to me."

"You like him, don't you?"

"Not at all," Harper said.

"What?"

"Rani, Kevin and I ate lunch and talked about you the whole time."

"Really?"

"Yes, you nutcase. He's crazy about you. I won't even tell you what he said about your cheerleading uniform."

"Oh?" Rani could feel heat rushing to her face.

They sat in silence for a moment before Rani broke it. "Hey, Harper?"

"Yeah?"

"What did you mean when you said that I don't know what you're capable of?"

"Oh," Harper tried to cover for herself. "It was just talk. Trying to sound tough."

"I really thought you were going to kill me. Where did you learn those moves?"

Chapter 13

OREN

A dampness hung in the air along with a musty scent that lingered, weighing down upon her like a noxious cloud. She was alone in the paltry, cement-walled room, her arms and legs locked to a metal chair with steel brackets. How did she get there? Her memories abandoned her. Did they drug her? It was a possibility. She was ten years old again—the time when they called her "Julia."

The only thing in the room with her was a television set on a rolling cart, propped up at eye level. She wriggled in the chair, attempting to break free, but the brackets held her firmly in place. She heard a steady beeping noise that held for several seconds before the television powered up. It displayed a video of a couple arguing, although it was unclear what the quarrel was about. The video then changed to two men in a fist fight, blood exploding from one's nose as it contacted the other man's fist. She tried to turn away, but discovered her head strapped onto the headrest of the chair, preventing any movement.

The film transitioned to a couple holding hands, and a mild

shock crept up Julia's back. She wanted to jump out of the chair, but the restraints rendered her motionless. The image cut to a child stomping on another child's sandcastle at the beach, the second child in tears. At least the shocking had ceased. Again, the television switched to the couple. This time they were hugging. An even stronger shock pulsated through Julia's body and then stopped as the video changed to two dogs, growling and biting each other.

Anybody who took an intro psychology class would recognize this as classical conditioning, but Julia was only ten and saw it as torture. By the time the film transitioned to the couple in deep embrace, the electric shock was unbearable. Julia's body quivered in the chair, drool forming at her mouth and dribbling down her chin.

* * *

Harper jolted up in bed, gasping for air. It was unlike her to have nightmares, but at least now she understood why she had the reaction she did when Kevin put his arm around her. She had forgotten about that part of her training. The idea was to eliminate any desire for personal attachment. She was, after all, a trained killer. Nothing more. Her lifestyle prohibited romance and love. The agency stripped away her humanity at an early age.

She looked over to find Rani sound asleep in her bed, looking peaceful. Harper had difficulty thinking how two people could be any more different, but she liked Rani. She was her own person, and she didn't hide from it. Harper respected that.

She slid back down into her bed and contemplated the shock training the agency tormented her with. It explained her lack of romantic relationships. She thought about Tommy in West Elmdale, but that was innocent. He was kind of an idiot, but he was cute and harmless. Something stopped her from letting it get beyond flirtation, and now she understood why.

She came much closer to a genuine relationship when she was fifteen. She was living in the Florida panhandle with the Cabrera family. Mr. Cabrera was retired. He had worked in a box factory or something. Mrs. Cabrera volunteered at the local animal shelter. Harper wasn't sure what her profession was prior to that. They had three children who were older. Two had their own families. One, a son, was away at college. They must have been lonely in their empty nest, so they fostered a child.

She went by "Emma" at that point, and she was a sophomore in high school. The story the agency told the Cabreras was that Emma's parents both died in a car accident and she just needed someone to watch after her until she was old enough for emancipation. It was a straight-forward, simple story. Those were the easiest to keep straight.

She didn't miss the yellow flies, which could have been the official mascot of the Florida panhandle. The Cabreras also lived right near the border of the Eastern and Central time zones, and Emma got a kick out of watching her cell phone jump from one zone to the next indiscriminately. She felt like a time traveler.

She had been at Gulf Crest High School for about two months and kept to herself. She learned quickly that this was not the Disney type of Florida she had envisioned. This was Southern living, and she hadn't connected with anyone. To her, it seemed like a foreign land. She was walking down the hall after school, watching her phone change times between 2:40 and 3:40 and back to 2:40, when she literally walked directly into Eric Davies. He was getting books out of his locker and she smacked right into him, knocking the phone out of her hand and the books out of his. The crack remained on her cell phone screen until she left Florida, separating her display nearly in half with a jagged zigzag.

"Hey, watch it. What are you—" Eric said, but stopped when he caught sight of Emma. She was plain looking, but she had beautiful long wavy brown hair that she usually wore pulled back in a ponytail. Eric took notice, and that shut him up.

"I am so sorry," Emma said. "I really need to watch where I'm going. I just—"

"No, no, no, it's okay. I really need to adopt a more defensive locker strategy. Totally my fault."

Eric was tall and slender with some mild acne, and there was a kindness in his eyes. She was drawn to him immediately.

"You heading home?" he asked.

"Yeah, I most likely missed my bus at this point. I'll call for a ride."

"Don't you worry your pretty little head about it. I'll give you a ride," he said as he picked her cell phone up off the ground. "It's the least I can do after cracking your screen." Emma hesitated, but she smiled, took her phone back, and followed him outside.

He drove a pickup truck with a shotgun rack in the back. The rack was empty, but the hooks were worn. It had obviously seen some use. Eric noticed her eyeing it. "I ain't gonna shoot you. Guns are at home anyway. My daddy and I hunt wild hogs some weekends. Usually across the border in Georgia."

Emma's training kicked in. She had no one to kill at the moment, but she noted that she could obtain a gun if the need arose. She smiled and hopped in the car. They listened to country music on the way home and she laughed as Eric sang along, horribly off-key. There was something about country music that she just didn't understand, but Eric was adorable trying to sing it.

By the time she arrived back at the Cabreras' house, she was giddy, and Mr. and Mrs. Cabrera noticed. They were silent as they leered at the pickup truck through the window and glared back at her. The Cabreras were what Emma called "Breakers," so she treaded lightly. Breakers always looked for ways to break you down—either mentally, physically, or both.

She saw Eric after school and on weekends. He and his friends used to have bonfires on the beach, and Emma would join. Every time things got remotely physical between them, Emma pulled away and made an excuse. She enjoyed being in his company, though, and she appreciated having someone to talk to, even if she had to fabricate most of what she said.

Mr. and Mrs. Cabrera disapproved of Eric, and they made their opinion known. Emma faced many lectures regarding her "inappropriate" behavior that was "unbefitting" of a proper lady. She told them how innocent it all was, but that didn't seem to change their tune. They probably assumed she was lying.

When their son, Oren, came home from college for the summer, everything changed. He was handsome and sophisticated and spoke of important worldly things. It was safe to say she had a bit of a crush on him, but she kept it to herself. What would he want with an awkward teenage girl? Still, she enjoyed talking to him about politics and philosophy and culture. Everything that came out of his mouth fascinated her.

One night, Emma came home from bowling with Eric to find Oren alone in the house. Mr. and Mrs. Cabrera were out with some friends. Emma found it humorous that old people even had friends. What do they talk about? Being old? Oren had opened a bottle of scotch and was having a drink in the living room while reading a book. This was typically when the Cabreras lectured Emma. Since she wasn't aware that Oren was home alone, she attempted to sneak upstairs to her room with no one noticing.

"Come join me," Oren shouted from the living room. Emma froze with one foot on the first step, like he caught her in the act of some heinous crime. She followed Oren's voice to the living room and stood there like a dog with its tail between its legs. "Mom and Pop are out. You're safe." She loosened up enough to sink into the recliner across from him.

"Here, have a drink," he said, sliding a scotch glass across the coffee table. He had already poured it as if he had been waiting for her.

"Oh. No, thank you. I'm only fifteen," she replied.

"Well, silly me," Oren said. "I already poured you a glass and I can't rightly get it back into the bottle at this point. Shame to waste it. That's an eighteen-year-old scotch. Any idea how much that costs?"

Emma shook her head.

"That's about a hundred and fifty dollars a bottle." He slid the glass a little closer to her. "Now go ahead and drink up."

Emma gave him an uncomfortable smile and took a small sip. She coughed as it burned her throat. It was her first time drinking alcohol. She didn't really want it, but she didn't want to be rude to Oren, who she admired.

"It's a bit of an acquired taste. You'll get used to it," he said. "I betcha the second sip will go down much smoother. Give it a shot."

She managed another sip without coughing.

"Not bad, right?"

"I guess," Emma hesitated.

"I'm heading back to school in the morning," Oren explained. "I've enjoyed getting to know you, Emma."

"Same here. When will you be home again?" she asked.

"Probably not until Thanksgiving," he said, swirling the scotch mindlessly in his glass.

Emma had no idea if she would still be there by Thanksgiving, but she doubted it. She was disappointed. She enjoyed her time, as limited as it was, with Oren.

"Here's to Thanksgiving," Oren said, raising his glass. Emma mimicked him and raised hers as well before they both took another sip.

The scotch was strong, and Emma was already feeling kind of dizzy. She tried to hide it since she didn't want Oren to see her as an immature child, but the feeling was building rapidly. She didn't think she could be there much longer.

"You know what?" she said. "I'm going to go to bed. It's been a long night." Emma put her drink down onto the coffee table and stood up. She almost immediately collapsed, her legs sinking under her body weight.

"Whoa," Oren said as he leapt from his chair, catching her before she hit the floor. "You really aren't used to liquor, are you?"

Emma tried to respond, but nothing but gibberish came out of her mouth. Her lips were numb, and a tingling sensation ran down her arms and legs.

"Let me help you to bed," Oren said as he moved her arm across his shoulder. "There we go."

By the time they reached Emma's bedroom, she was barely conscious. Everything became hazy and dark and seemed to move in slow motion.

"You'll feel much better in the morning, Emma," Oren said as he laid her down on her bed. She just wanted the night to end, but Oren wasn't leaving. He sat down next to her and stroked her hair. "You're beautiful, Emma. Never forget that." He kissed her forehead.

Emma could barely hold on to a thought, but she was confused. She was fond of Oren and appreciated his kind words, but it felt wrong to her.

"I'll think about you when I'm back at school," he said as he gently kissed her lips.

Emma fought to keep her eyes open, but it was a battle she was losing. She could feel his fiery breath on her neck and his hand on her chest. She tried to tell him to stop, but her lips wouldn't move. She attempted to push him off her, but she barely grazed his shoulder. Emma focused and put all her blurred concentration into kicking her legs, but they failed her.

With each strained breath, she could smell him. A rancid mix of alcohol, sweat, and expensive cologne. She thought she might be sick, and a bubble was about to burst in her stomach.

She peeled her eyes open enough to see Oren's belt buckle drop to the floor, and she felt something tight pressing under her dress. It hurt. Her body was numb, but she could feel that pain and it wouldn't stop. Over and over. Then everything went black.

* * *

Harper wiped a tear from her eye as she lay awake in her bed, Rani now snoring across the room. She never saw Oren again, and the agency relocated her shortly thereafter. She recalled a feeling of confusion. She initially blamed herself for drinking too much that night. It was a full year later when it occurred to her that Oren slipped something into her drink. How stupid was that? She took three sips of scotch and blamed herself for drinking too much?

She hated herself for keeping quiet about it, but who would she tell? The Cabreras would believe whatever story Oren concocted. Plus, she wasn't innocent either. It's not like he poured the scotch down her throat, right? Anger rushed through Harper when she recalled that feeling of helplessness. She wished she could go back and help Emma, as if they weren't the same person.

Whatever shred of sexuality the agency didn't shock out of her in that metal chair, Oren stole from her that night. Still, she longed to love and be loved. Maybe someday, she thought as she finally drifted off to sleep.

Chapter 14

MARGOT

The Student Center at Chester Pointe University housed an à la carte dining facility (which was far superior to the all-you-can-eat cafeteria), a recreation room with a few pool tables and ping pong tables, several lounge areas, a convenience store in case you needed toilet paper in between classes, and a Starbucks. Not a generic coffee shop—an actual Starbucks. This morning, after her horrid night of sleep, Harper was beyond grateful for the CPU Starbucks, its green mermaid logo giving her a much-needed respite.

She placed her regular morning order—a smoked butterscotch latte (she didn't like her coffee to taste too much like coffee) and a blueberry scone. The barista handed Harper her cup and a bag, emblazoned with that savior of a green mermaid... or was it a siren? Either way, she was happy to see her.

She sat down on one of the lounge chairs that seemed to balance right on the cusp of retro and modern. She took a sip of her latte and reached into the bag for her scone; however, her hand detected something else inside. She pulled it out and sighed. She was ready for some excitement, but she just didn't have the energy today. Staring back at her was a pack of Wonder Rush Happy Funtime Bubble Gum.

* * *

The meet-up location was inside the Philadelphia city limits, and Harper was less than thrilled that the journey required both a bus and train ride. The faded sign outside of the building informed her it was once a rubber factory. Based on the smell outside, she concluded it had been a rubber factory fairly recently. The Poppy sticker on the corner of the door indicated she was in the right place.

When Harper entered the building, she was surprised to find a waiting area similar to the waiting areas in most companies across the country. It was well-lit with a row of chairs across each wall. End tables connected each section and contained a neatly organized spread of magazines. Soothing Muzak gently piped through speakers built into the ceiling. The walls were clean and white. This was a far cry from the abandoned warehouses to which Harper was accustomed. There was even a receptionist sitting behind a desk, typing into a computer and glaring at the screen through a pair of reading glasses resting at the tip of her nose.

"Can I help you?" the receptionist asked without looking up from her workstation.

Harper was nearly certain that she was in the wrong place, but she thought about the Poppy sticker outside. "Um… Harper Connelly?" she said and asked simultaneously.

"Take a seat, please. Someone will be with you shortly." She continued to type without looking up at Harper.

Harper hesitated, contemplated bolting, but stuck around. She sat in a chair and poked through the collection of magazines—*Field and Stream*, *Golf Digest*, *Popular Mechanics*, and *Sports Illustrated*. How's a girl to choose? A headline on *Field and Stream* caught her eye, so she grabbed that one. She figured if she had to wait, she might as well delve into "The Complete Guide to Spider-Rigging for Crappies." She did not understand what spider-rigging was or what crappies were, but she was a college girl now and had a newfound thirst for knowledge.

She was enthralled reading about the latest rod holders when the receptionist finally pulled herself away from her computer. "Harper Connelly?" she called out, as if there was anyone else in the waiting room.

"Yes?"

"Good morning," she said in an overly saccharine way. "What are your rubber needs?"

Harper now realized she was in the wrong place. "Uh… I'm sorry?"

"This is a rubber factory. What are your rubber needs?" The receptionist spoke with an edge to her voice.

"You know what? I think I'm in the wrong place. I'm just going to—"

The receptionist laughed. Cracked up, actually. She pulled herself together long enough to say, "I'm just messing with you. Follow me."

She led Harper to a conference room, which was equally bright and clean. A long table sat in the center, with eight chairs on either side. The receptionist sat down and gestured for Harper to sit across from her.

"My name is Margot LaRue," she said, and then stopped herself. "Actually, it's Enid Templeton, but doesn't 'Margot LaRue' have such a ring to it?" She gracefully posed her arms like an old Hollywood starlet.

Harper was unsure how to react to Margot/Enid. Eccentric didn't even begin to describe her. Her wingtip glasses hung from a pearl chain around her neck and draped over her loosely flowing dress, covered by not one but two different scarfs. "Should I call you Margot or Enid?"

That seemed to snap her out of her little daydream. "Ugh. Call me Enid." She looked dejected. Like someone killed all her dreams with a single blow. "*Enid*," she said again, almost mocking herself. "What a terrible name. At least you get assigned a new one periodically. I'm stuck with '*Enid*' until they toss me in the ground. And even then, it'll be etched into my tombstone for eternity."

"I'd be happy to call you 'Margot' if you'd like," Harper offered.

Enid perked up. "Really? Oh, I would like that."

"Well then, Margot, what's the assignment?"

Margot/Enid struck a Hollywood pose again, tossing her hair back and smiling to an imaginary set of paparazzi.

"Margot?"

"One moment, dear." She tried out a few more poses, mouthing something to her "adoring fans."

"Margot?"

"Uh, you're such a buzzkill." Margot grabbed a case from under the table, placed it in front of herself, and opened it. She removed a small wooden box and slid it in front of Harper. Harper flipped a latch on the side and opened the box to discover a vape pen inside.

"Oh, good idea," she said. "I'll get him addicted to nicotine and then just wait thirty years for him to drop dead from cancer. Nice play."

"You're a sassy one, aren't you?" Margot said. "I don't need your 'tude though, missy."

"Hey, just trying to have some fun."

Margot ignored that comment. "We filled that vape pen with a toxic mix of substances." She stopped herself for a moment and thought her statement through. "Well, it's filled with a mix of substances more toxic than normal. Your mark is addicted to these little contraptions. Swap out his vape with this one and his lungs will crystallize. It will work quickly."

"Won't that start an investigation into the manufacturer or something?" Harper asked.

"Yes, well, we thought of that. We used only chemicals he could get his hands on easily. To hedge our bets, we have one more goody. The *pièce de résistance.*" Margot pulled a piece of paper out of the case that she had folded over four times, resulting in a small square.

Harper unfolded it and read it out loud. "I can no longer live with the guilt. I feel horrible about what I did. Mom, Dad, please forgive me." She folded the paper back up and looked at Margot questioningly. "Suicide by vape? Is that really a thing?"

"A few isolated cases, yes. Our handwriting experts at the agency put that little note together. Not bad, huh?"

"Not bad."

Margot then pulled a small jar out of the case and placed it on the table in front of Harper. It looked like a travel-sized moisturizer or makeup bottle. "Since you will leave evidence behind, you'll need a dip." Harper was very familiar with dips, having used them many times in the past, so she just nodded her head.

If you have ever stuck your finger in candle wax right after you blew out the flame, then you're familiar with the basic concept of a dip. The dip itself is the agency's creation and is in liquid form at room temperature. You dip your fingers in and it quickly dries to something in between a paraffin wax and latex. It's meant to cover your fingertips and then easily peel off later. The layer is so thin that it's nearly undetectable, but it prevents any fingerprints from being left behind.

"What did this guy do to warrant death by vape?" Harper

asked.

Margot handed Harper a tablet which displayed a photograph of a mother and her two children—a boy around five years old and a girl around two or three. Harper swiped and a newspaper article displayed on the tablet. The headline read, "Hit and Run Kills Two."

"He was driving drunk and struck the woman's vehicle," Margot explained. "The two children, Garrett and Molly, were in the backseat. Molly had unbuckled her seatbelt and her mother, Katrina, was reaching back from the front seat trying to secure it, but she couldn't reach. Garrett, being the good big brother he was, removed his own seatbelt to help his sister. At that moment, the two cars collided. Both children died instantly. Katrina never recovered from the guilt of failing to pull over and fastening the seatbelts. A week after she buried her children, she shot herself. The other driver, our mark, just kept driving. The authorities never caught him."

"That's horrible," Harper mumbled to herself as she read the news article. "If they never caught him, how do you know we're targeting the correct man?"

Margot chuckled. "Oh, Harper, darling, the agency makes no mistakes. Our resources are far superior to any police department. Even the great city of Philadelphia."

Harper swiped the tablet again and her heart sank. The face staring back at her was one that she recognized. It was the face of a college-aged man, smiling with deep dimples. He was even wearing his ubiquitous Beta Omega Rho tee shirt.

"That's your target," Margot said. "His name is Kevin Mitchell."

* * *

A week and a half had passed since Harper's meeting with Margot.

She wanted to wait until the timing was perfect, but she knew the agency would soon grow impatient. Harper also delayed the inevitable because she really didn't want to kill Kevin. His actions were awful, but this was going to devastate Rani. Also, Kevin didn't seem like the type who would get behind a wheel drunk, kill two kids, and then drive away.

The agency left little opportunity for personal development. She didn't know Kevin before the accident, but she knew him now. Maybe the horrific event that unfolded that fateful night made him a better person. Maybe he learned from it and grew. However, nothing would change the fact that three people were dead and someone needed to pay for the crime. Kevin's stupidity and carelessness cut three people's potential short. Harper didn't want to kill Kevin, but she had to. It needed to be done.

The party at the Beta House was raging like any other Saturday. The basketball team was playing in Rhode Island, so Rani was away for the weekend, cheering. The timing was perfect.

Harper blended in with the crowd, going unnoticed. She had few acquaintances at CPU, and she didn't stand out in any noticeable way. In a packed house of a hundred drunk people, she was invisible. She carefully made her way upstairs, the loud thud of the deafening music finally abating.

The second floor was fairly deserted. A few couples were making out in various parts of the hallway, but they were too distracted to notice Harper. There were some socks on doorknobs. She knew enough about college culture at that point to understand what that meant. She snuck up to the third floor undetected.

The third floor was much quieter and empty. She spotted a metal staircase in the corner and checked her fingers. She touched each one to the thumb on each hand, making sure the dip held and her fingerprints wouldn't show. She climbed the ladder and pushed open the trapdoor leading up to the roof balcony.

The roof was deserted, so she waited. Rani loved to talk about Kevin in excruciating detail, so she knew he would come up there, eventually. She was also fairly confident that no one else would. Most students drank and danced into the wee hours of the night. Kevin needed a break periodically. He liked the fresh air and the quiet and some peace so he could hear himself think.

Harper tapped the back pocket of her jeans and felt for the note—still folded into fours. She rubbed the front pocket of her jeans and felt the vape pen.

The night sky was mostly clear. A thin wisp of clouds slowly pushed its way across the stretch of stars, hiding the bottom half of the crescent moon. It was late October, and the air was crisp. Not unbearably cold, but she was glad she wore her heavy cardigan. Perhaps it was too cold for Kevin to visit the balcony that night. Maybe she had delayed too long and lost her chance. Perhaps she would need to modify her strategy and catch Kevin after class sometime.

Harper chose this night intentionally. Not only was Rani in Rhode Island and out of her way, but the house was full. She considered seeing him during the day when only his frat brothers were around, but that seemed too risky. Her presence would appear unusual, and they would notice her. Ironically, the more people who were in the house, the less anyone would pay attention to her. The crowds increased her anonymity. Add the fact that most of the guests were three sheets to the wind, and she became even more invisible.

Just as Harper had almost given up hope Kevin would join her, the trapdoor squealed open.

"Oh, sorry. I didn't know anyone was up here," Kevin said, startled, before recognition took over. "Harper? Is that you?"

"Hey, yeah. Rani told me this was the best spot in the house when you needed a little peace. I hope you don't mind."

"Not at all," Kevin said as he made his way toward the railing overlooking the desolate backyard. As Kevin stared out into the night sky, he closed his eyes and took in a deep, cleansing breath. Harper snuck over to the trapdoor and surreptitiously locked it. "Beautiful night," he said. "Too bad Rani couldn't be here."

"Actually, I have something for you." Harper reached into her back pocket and pulled out Kevin's phony suicide note. "This is from Rani. Since she was out of town, she wanted me to give it to you."

"Thanks," Kevin said as he took the note and began to unfold it.

"But," Harper said with enough force in her voice to stop him, "she made me promise you wouldn't read it until you were alone in bed tonight."

"Okay. I'm intrigued." He folded the note back up and slid it into his pocket.

"You know," Harper began, "I wanted to apologize to you. Rani was pretty bent out of shape when you and I first met, and I never had an opportunity to clear the air."

"Oh? Why's that?"

"I guess she thought I was flirting with you a little."

"Oh, I don't—"

"Yeah, I… well, it wasn't my intention and I would never step on Rani's toes like that."

"You weren't even aware that Rani and I knew each other at that point. You have nothing to worry about."

"Thanks for saying that. Anyway," Harper reached into her pocket and pulled out the vape pen. "I got you a peace offering. I know you love these little cancer sticks." She handed him the vape and then rubbed her fingers together, making sure the dip was still in place.

Kevin took it and said, "That's sweet, Harper, but I quit."

Harper's heart sunk. "Really? Maybe one last drag for old time's sake?"

He looked at the vape, considering the offer. "I promised Rani, actually. She doesn't like it, and she's right. It's a terrible habit. Hey, you yourself said this shit will kill me."

Oh, you have no idea.

"Tell you what," he continued. "I'll give it to one of my frat brothers. They'll go crazy for it."

"No!" Harper interjected, grabbing the pen from Kevin's hand. He looked confused. "What I mean is, I'll smoke it myself… later. I keep meaning to see what all the excitement is about with these things." She slid the vape pen back into her pocket.

"All right," he said. "Just don't enjoy it too much. They're addictive."

Harper raised her hand with three fingers joined closely together. "Scout's honor. I'll take it slow." Harper had never been a Girl Scout and wasn't sure if she should use three fingers or two, but she remembered a three-finger salute from somewhere.

Harper contemplated her next move. She had the vape pen. She could just excuse herself, leave the party, and have the agency develop an alternative plan. Then it occurred to her; she already handed Kevin the note. Kevin lying in bed later that night, reading his own suicide note, would surely raise some questions. She needed to get the note back. She could see its outline in his front pocket. There was no way she could reach in and grab it, especially right after she apologized for "flirting." There was one other option.

Harper walked to the edge of the balcony and looked down. It was a three-story drop. She could push him off the side. The suicide note in his pocket would deter any proper investigation. She mentally played out that scenario. A fall from that height would probably just result in a few broken bones. If he went headfirst, that would do the trick, but it was too unpredictable. She didn't like unpredictability.

"Nice view out here," she said as she walked the perimeter of the balcony, looking for another option.

"I like it. Gets me away from the noise and the smoke."

As she surveyed the side of the house, she found her solution. The Beta House sat close to the house next door—some rival fraternity. A wrought-iron fence separated the property lines with a series of spikes running across the top. It was hard to tell from where she stood, but she estimated the spikes to be about eight to ten inches tall. Those could do some serious damage.

The railing around the balcony was an issue, however. It was about four feet high, wooden, with a flat top. It was probably too high to push him off without some struggle. She could easily assault him enough to weaken him and get him off the side, but that would leave marks. She needed to avoid any sign of foul play. Harper grabbed hold of the top of the railing and gave it a shake, testing its stability.

"It'll hold you, don't worry," Kevin said as he saw her testing the railing.

"Oh, I was just... it's funny the things that pop into your mind. This railing reminds me so much of the balance beam we used to use in gymnastics class when I was little."

She never took a gymnastics class.

"You said it'll hold me," she continued, "so here goes." Harper pulled herself up to the top of the railing and balanced on both feet, happy she didn't wear heels that night. She even put up her arms like she just stuck an amazing landing.

Kevin reached for her in panic. "That's not what I meant. Harper, get down from there. You'll fall."

"Not a chance," she said. She looked down to see exactly how far her fall would be, and her head spun. Three stories don't sound like much until there's only four inches of support under your feet and about thirty feet of free fall waiting for you on one side. Harper didn't have the luxury of fear, so she pushed those thoughts out of her head.

She promenaded around the balcony railing, one foot in front of the other as Kevin followed her closely from the solid roof. "Seriously, Harper. Get down from there. I'm not kidding."

"Oh, relax. I'm a trained professional."

Just not the way you think.

"Whoa," she said as her left foot slipped out from under her and she balanced herself only on her right.

"Harper!"

She laughed and returned her other foot. "I'm just messing with you. Tell you what," she said. "If you come up with me for a minute, I'll get down."

Kevin looked over the edge, contemplating the offer. "No way," he said.

"Fine, then," Harper replied as she continued her trek toward the side of the house. "Let's see if I can make it all the way around the house. Whatta ya think? Wanna place bets?"

"If you fall from there, the school will shut this frat down. Plus, Rani would never talk to me again."

Harper ignored him and kept walking, pretending again to slip. "Ah…" She appeared calm, but she was freaking out inside. She was almost near the wrought-iron fence, its spikes taunting her. One false move and the agency would be down one agent.

"Come on, Harper. This seriously isn't funny," Kevin protested.

"Then come on up and join me."

"Jesus Christ, you're insane!" he said. He gripped the top of the railing, clenched his eyes tight, and pulled himself up.

"Don't look down," she said.

The best way to get someone to look down is to tell them not to look down. "Oh, my God," he mumbled to himself as he peered over the edge. He assured his footing and said, "Okay. I'm up. Now please get down."

The only problem was, he had not yet positioned himself over the wrought iron spikes. "Just follow me for a few steps," Harper said.

"Hey, that wasn't the deal. You said—" His protesting caught him off balance, forcing his foot to swing around to catch himself. "Oh, God."

"Three steps. That's all. I promise."

"Fine... three steps," he reluctantly agreed.

He slowly and carefully took three small steps, but it was enough. He was in position. "Now can I get down?"

"Sure. I'll help you." Harper hopped off the railing and back onto the roof. She held out her hand to help Kevin, but pulled it away right before he took it. "One last thing," she said. "I want you to think about Garrett, Molly, and Katrina."

"Who?" he asked. That was the last word he spoke. Harper gave him a solid push off the railing. As he fell three stories down, there was finally an expression of recognition on his face, but it was fleeting. Within a second and a half, Kevin landed spine-first onto the wrought-iron fence. The pointy spikes skewering him through the middle of his torso. His legs hung on the Beta side, while his head draped over the other. His arms splayed out to either side, like he was being crucified.

You're hardly a martyr, Harper thought.

His open eyes stared back at her until all life faded from them.

Harper unlocked the trapdoor and made her descent back into the house. The third floor was still empty, the second floor still sparsely populated by sloppy couples. Finally, she made her way back to the first floor and disappeared into the crowd, the deafening music pounding in her chest.

As she walked outside, she heard a girl scream. A moment later, she heard another. The oblivious party goers kept drinking and dancing, and Harper simply walked back toward her dorm. She looked up to the stars with their gentle covering of thin clouds.

It really was a beautiful night.

Chapter 15

SOPHIA

Edgar Solomon flipped through the pages of the *Philadelphia Inquirer* business section. Resting one elbow on the steering wheel of his bus, he awaited its occupants. He scratched his white beard, slicked back the few gossamer strands of hair remaining on top of his head, and turned the page again.

His gruff appearance stood in stark contrast to the polished, high-tech interior of the bus. This was not an ordinary yellow school bus, but a deluxe luxury vehicle of mass transportation. The exterior was sleek black with deeply tinted windows. Inside looked more like a private jet—large bucket seats, television monitors in each headrest, soft cabin lighting, and a restroom in the back. Chester Pointe University was a Division III basketball school, but they spared no expense to get their team wherever it needed to go. In front of Edgar's bus, the engine idled on an identical polished-black luxury transport—one for the team and one for the cheerleaders and band. Tonight, Edgar drove the spirit squad.

In the distance, Edgar heard the approaching chants of "Let's go, Rats!" Without looking up from his periodical, he pushed the bus doors open. It was late, and he felt tired. The CPU Rattlesnakes had just finished game two of an evening tournament, yet their energy levels didn't wane. *Youth is wasted on the young*, he thought.

The basketball players loaded onto the front bus while the cheerleaders and pep band made their way onto Edgar's bus, singing the school fight song, pom-poms shaking. Rani's cell phone chirped, but she ignored it. Nora walked onto the bus behind Rani, and her cell phone vibrated. She ignored hers as well. Another chime echoed from the back of the bus, then another from the front. Soon, the whole bus sounded like a midnight swamp in late July, except text alerts and vibrations replaced the sounds of crickets and bullfrogs.

Rani continued the fight song as the rest of the bus's occupants quickly hushed, their disbelieving faces glued to their screens. "Fight, fight, fight!" Rani continued alone.

"Hey, Rani," Nora mumbled as she tugged at Rani's pleated skirt. "Rani, check your phone."

"What's going on?" Rani stood in the center aisle of the bus while everyone else sat in their seats, the glow of their smartphones illuminating their long faces. Rani reached into her purse, pulled out her phone, and read the tragic news about Kevin that had silenced everyone else. She raised her head in disbelief, dropped her phone to the ground, and collapsed.

* * *

Before Harper reached Mulberry Hall, she grabbed the vape pen from her pocket, tossed it onto the concrete sidewalk, and crushed it under her heel, the liquid oozing out of the center. She picked up the remains of the cracked plastic and tossed it into a dumpster. She would not make the same mistake she did with Corey and the "joy buzzer."

Oh, Corey.

Once inside, she slipped into the hallway bathroom and locked herself in a stall. Harper peeled the dip off each fingertip and dropped the thin pads (which looked like a layer of skin) into the toilet bowl. With a single flush, the evidence disappeared and her night finally ended.

* * *

After an overnight stay in Rhode Island, the basketball team, pep band, and cheerleaders headed back to CPU. Melancholy polluted the general atmosphere, and Rani had been utterly silent since her collapse on the bus. No tears, no sobbing, just shock and disbelief.

By the time Rani shuffled her way mindlessly down Mulberry Hall toward her dorm room, it was Sunday afternoon. A memory popped into her mind and she stopped, backtracked a few feet, and knocked on the door for room 6—Brea's room. Rani recalled Brea lifting her sweatshirt and offering her a swig of vodka. Rani hadn't had a drink in her life and less than politely refused Brea's initial offer. She figured now might be a good time to loosen her morals.

Brea answered the door hungover, her untamed locks falling over a stained tee shirt. "What do you want, Rani?"

Rani didn't answer, but she recollected Brea mentioning that the bottle would be in her fridge, so she headed straight there, almost as if hypnotized.

"Please, come on in," Brea said with groggy sarcasm.

Rani grabbed the bottle—still half-full—and walked out.

"Really, help yourself." Same sarcasm.

Rani swung open her dorm room door and tossed her bags onto her bed. Harper was out. Rani felt relieved. She craved some alone time. She placed Brea's vodka bottle on her desk, sat in her desk chair, and glared at it. Rani slowly turned the bottle around, studying its curves and textures, and contemplated her next move. After spinning off the cap, she tilted the bottle toward her and took a sniff. She didn't smell much.

She put the bottle to her lips and held it there. It wasn't too late to turn back.

Finally, she tossed back her head and took a swig. It was hot in the back of her throat, and she cringed as she swallowed. It burned in her esophagus as it made its corrupting journey down to her stomach.

Reaching behind her bookshelf, she grabbed her bottle of Zoloft, opened it, and popped one in her mouth. *This is what they're for, after all*, she thought. She washed the pill down with another painful mouthful of vodka.

Unlocking her cell phone, Rani scrolled through her camera roll. She found pictures of her with Nora and the other cheerleaders. She skipped past those. She swiped past photos of the basketball team, some of her friends. Then she found what she was looking for—a picture of her with Kevin. His arm was around her, and his smile showed off the deep crevices of his dimples. In the photo, Rani's face beamed with an emotion not short of elation.

She stared at the photo for several minutes and for the first time since she heard the news of Kevin's untimely passing, the waterworks opened. Tears poured from her eyes and she sobbed uncontrollably, gasping for breath in between wails and growling in mental anguish.

Rani slid another Zoloft out of the medicine bottle and washed it down with a gulp of vodka.

* * *

Harper sat in one of the Student Center chairs, her feet propped up on a small table in front of her. Her American Lit class had moved on to Emily Dickinson, so she read through a worn library book of her poems. Emily was comparing hope to a feather. Harper didn't get it, but at least it rhymed. She didn't understand poems that didn't rhyme. Harper looked up from her book, contemplating the words she was reading, when something caught her eye.

Across the Student Center, she spotted a display inside the convenience store near the cash register. Harper tossed her book in her bag and headed there. She picked up a prepaid credit card from the display and handed it to the cashier with a grin. At last, she could contact the Barneses and check on Corey, using the credit card online to get their phone number. It was perfect.

Harper handed the cashier twenty-five dollars in cash, and he handed Harper an activated credit card. As the card changed hands, Harper felt something else underneath it—a pack of Wonder Rush Happy Funtime Bubblegum.

So soon? What did it mean that they needed her so quickly? She acknowledged she veered from the agency's plan, but she had to improvise. She had no choice. It was that or get caught. Were they angry? Was there going to be some punishment? Perhaps she was reading too much into it. Maybe they had another mission for her, or another identity. She hadn't been Harper for long, but it wouldn't be the first time she got pulled from a post so soon.

No more Poppy stickers. No more mixing Skittles and M&Ms. The last two deliveries were handed to her, each by different people. First the Starbucks barista, now the Student Center convenience store clerk. What did that imply? It meant they were keeping a closer eye on her. It meant that the agency's network was even more widespread than she thought. They had people implanted everywhere. Who else was watching her? How many people on campus knew her identity and purpose for being there?

She thought about the various possibilities and implications as she trekked back from the Student Center to Mulberry Hall. She had time to figure it all out, but right now she wanted to log onto her laptop and get the Barneses' phone number.

When Harper swung open her dorm room door, it surprised

her to find Rani lying in bed. She had forgotten about Rani in all the excitement and how devastated she was going to be when she learned of Kevin's "suicide." Harper thought she should be the one to tell her, unless she already knew. News like that travels quickly.

Based on Rani's position in bed, Harper thought she might have already known. Rani was face down on top of her covers, her arms and legs sprawled out to the sides. Harper had never seen her roommate in that position. Rani was a consistent side-sleeper. Harper sat on the edge of Rani's bed and gave her shoulder a gentle shake.

"Hey, Rani?"

There was no response. She shook more aggressively.

"Rani, wake up."

Nothing.

Harper turned Rani over and gasped in horror. Her once caramel skin was now blanched gray. Rani's lips were blue and some unknown substance had dried white around her mouth. Harper slapped Rani's face gently. "Rani! Rani, wake up!" There was no response.

Harper lifted Rani's eyelids to find her once vivid amber eyes now lifeless. She put her fingers on Rani's neck and felt for a pulse. It was weak, but her heart was still beating. "Okay. Okay, that's good. Rani," she screamed louder, and she slapped her harder. "Rani, goddamnit, get up!"

Harper scanned the room for something, anything that could help her. She spotted an empty vodka bottle laying on its side on Rani's desk. Next to it was an empty medication bottle. Harper picked it up and read the label. "Shit."

Harper went back over to the bed and grabbed Rani. She propped her up and sat next to her, supporting all of Rani's body weight, and her unconscious arms slipped from Harper's shoulder where she placed them.

"Open your mouth, Rani," Harper said as she pulled down on Rani's jaw. Harper shoved two fingers past Rani's crusted lips and into her throat. "Throw up for me. Please, Rani, throw up for me." There was nothing.

Harper pressed harder and harder. Rani's tongue felt thick, dry, and lifeless to the touch, but then it moved—very slightly, but it moved. Rani's throat convulsed, and Harper felt something coming up. Something wet and slimy. She yanked her fingers out of Rani's mouth as she vomited.

"That's it! Good girl. Get it all out," Harper said as Rani regurgitated. Her entire body shook, but Rani was still weak and barely conscious. Soon, partially digested food and pills covered Rani's shirt and Harper's arm and leg. "Keep it coming," Harper added as she tilted Rani's head forward to prevent her from choking on her vomit.

Rani mumbled, but Harper couldn't understand what she was saying. "Shh, it's okay," Harper attempted to calm her down. "You're okay. Just relax."

"Ke…" Rani managed before collapsing back onto the bed.

"No, no, no. Stay up. Don't go to sleep." Harper pulled Rani back up next to her, grabbed her cell phone, and dialed 9-1-1.

"9-1-1. What's your emergency?"

"I'm at Chester Pointe University. Mulberry Hall, room twelve. My roommate took too many pills and vodka."

"What kind of pills, ma'am?"

"Um…" Harper reached for the empty bottle and read the label. "Zoloft."

"Is she conscious?"

"Barely, but yes."

"Okay. Help is on the way. Please stay on the line."

"Kev…" Rani got a little more out this time.

"Kevin, I know. I just heard about it. Rani, I'm so sorry."

Rani made a noise as if she was attempting to cry, but she could not produce tears because of dehydration.

"I'm so sorry, Rani." Most people say that when someone dies because they feel bad for what the person is experiencing. When Harper said it, it took on another meaning. She was sorry for what she did, but she knew deep down that it was the best option. Kevin needed to pay for his crime. But she still felt horrible for the impact it had on Rani.

Lights flashed through the window, and the squeal of the ambulance siren grew louder as it approached the building. Shortly thereafter, heavy footsteps approached the room, and muffled voices blasted through a handheld radio. A pounding knock shook the door.

"Come in. It's open," Harper announced, surprised to find her voice quivering. She wasn't one to get emotional. The agency trained that out of her, but a crack formed in her facade. As the EMTs carefully placed Rani on a stretcher, tears formed in Harper's eyes. That was also new.

"I see she vomited," one of the EMTs said to Harper. "Did she ever lose consciousness?"

"Yes," Harper replied, wiping a tear from her eye. "She was unconscious when I found her. I gagged her and made her throw up."

"Nicely done," he said as he strapped Rani to the stretcher. "You probably saved her life."

Harper remained on Rani's bed, covered in her vomit, as the EMTs rolled her semi-conscious roommate away. She contemplated the lives she had taken over the years. Bad lives, perhaps, but lives still the same. Even those who do bad things have people who care about them, and their loss affects them. How many others had she devastated like she did Rani?

She thought about the rush she got when she took someone's

life. The power she felt knowing she ended it. She thought about how delicate life is and what a fine line there is between a heart beating and knowing it can beat no longer. She thought about the empowering feeling when you push a life from one edge of the line to the other.

Then Harper thought about Rani. She thought about watching her nearly die and how she, Harper, pulled her back over that same fine line. The rush and excitement she felt saving Rani's life was far more powerful than any she ever felt taking a life.

Harper looked down at her vomit-soaked clothes and had one more thought. She needed a shower.

* * *

There was still a chill in the air, but the sun radiated in the cloudless sky. It was a powerful juxtaposition to what Harper had just endured. After she showered and calmed herself down, she slept. Not soundly, but she slept. It was Monday morning, but she couldn't bring herself to go to class. She needed to walk and think and clear her head.

Chester Pointe University had no dearth of large stone buildings, and McArthur Hall was no exception. The school used it mainly for office space—the Registrar's Office, Bursar's Office, things like that. There was a large stone arch that cut through the center of the building, an ornate corner stone supporting it at its peak. As Harper followed the bend in the path toward McArthur Hall, she spotted a woman walking through the archway. Her long, flowing dress and wingtip glasses gave her away instantly. It was Margot (or Enid, or whatever she preferred to be called).

In that moment, Harper realized she forgot all about her pack of Wonder Rush gum. Assuming Margot was here to track her down, Harper trudged toward her, prepared with an excuse. Instead, Margot approached two college girls who were talking on the far side of the building. Margot hadn't even seen Harper.

Harper halted, her shoes scuffing on the loose gravel under her feet. She ducked behind a large oak. Harper spotted them, but she was too far away to hear the conversation. One girl hugged Margot, while the other one waved awkwardly and walked away.

As she did, Harper quickened her pace to catch up to her. "Hey," Harper said, grabbing the girl's arm.

She looked annoyed. "Do I know you?"

"I'm sorry to bother you. Do you know that girl over there?" Harper pointed to the girl talking to Margot.

"Who? Sophia?"

"Sophia," Harper confirmed. "That woman she's talking to…"

"That's her mother."

"Her mother?" Margot not only had a daughter, but she was a student at the same university where the agency implanted Harper. What were the odds?

"Yeah," the girl continued. "Sophia's ex killed himself over the weekend. I guess her mom just wanted to check on her. It was a messy breakup."

"Kevin?"

"Yeah, you know him?"

Sophia's ex was Kevin?

Chapter 16

PORTER

The glare from the computer monitor illuminated Harper's face with an unnatural glow. She tapped the prepaid credit card mindlessly on her desk as she stared at Ryan and Grace Barnes's telephone number on the screen, contemplating the best play. An unopened pack of Wonder Rush gum sat next to her computer. She wasn't ready to deal with that yet.

She grabbed her cell phone, opened her settings, and turned off the "show my caller ID" feature. She knew the Barneses wouldn't recognize her number, but she didn't want to leave any trace. She entered the digits into her phone and hovered over the green call button, hesitating. She was always a "rip the Band Aid off fast" sort of person, so she tapped the call button and put the phone to her ear. How many people even answer calls from a blocked number, anyway? She would probably just get the voicemail. If so, she would just hang—.

"Hello?" It was Grace. Harper opened her mouth to speak, but words failed her. Even though she placed the phone call, she didn't expect anyone to answer. It was strange hearing Grace's voice. It transported her back to a previous life. Not to mention the fact that, as far as Grace knew, Harper (or Wendy) was dead.

"Hello?" she repeated, sounding annoyed this time.

Harper didn't want Grace to hang up, so she blurted out, "Hello."

She cleared her throat and put on a phony voice about an octave and a half higher than her own. "Hi, I was calling for Corey..." Harper's heart nearly burst from her chest. She needed to know what happened to him, but she dreaded the possibility that she killed him.

"Who is this?" Grace asked.

"Um... my name is Sheila." It was the first name that popped into her head. "I'm a distant cousin of Corey's. I've been looking for him for some time." Harper hoped that story was believable enough.

"I'm sorry..." Grace's voice trailed off. "Corey is no longer with us..."

Harper's jaw dropped. It was everything she feared. She knew it was a possibility, but she held onto the hope that he was okay.

Grace continued, "I—"

Harper hung up. She couldn't hear anymore.

So, it was true. Harper had no problem killing the scum of the world, but she had nearly killed Rani, and now she had confirmation that she was responsible for Corey's death. Who else did she leave in her wake of destruction? She never stuck around long enough to learn the ramifications of her actions. What was she doing with her life? The agency brainwashed her, starting at birth, but was she lacking free will? She wasn't a child any longer. At what point should she hold herself responsible for her own actions?

Harper picked up the pack of Wonder Rush and stared at it. What was her next move? She could meet up with Margot (or whoever the messenger would be this time) and kill her, but someone else would just take her place. She could toss the pack of gum and just run, but she knew the agency would hunt her down and kill her. She could go to the next meeting, act like nothing had changed, and just keep working for the agency. After all, she was ridding the world of horrible individuals. Then she thought of Kevin.

It was suspicious that Margot's daughter, Sophia, had dated Kevin. Add the fact that it was a "messy breakup," whatever that meant, and things got even stranger. Was Kevin even guilty of the things Margot claimed? Did Harper just carry out some personal vendetta and kill an innocent man?

Harper pondered that possibility and ran a web search for "Garrett Molly Katrina." She didn't recall their last name, but that should produce a hit. An entire family dying under those conditions would pop up on some news wire.

She scanned through Facebook listings, a few YouTube videos of people with those names. No news of a hit and run. Was Kevin innocent? She recalled Kevin's last word—"Who?" When Harper told Kevin to think about Garrett, Molly, and Katrina, his response was, "Who?" She remembered a look of recognition on his face right before those wrought iron spikes pierced his spine. Was that really a look of recognition? It happened so fast. Perhaps it was just a look of realization—knowing he was about to perish, and Harper was going to be his final vision.

She thought of the newspaper clipping Margot showed her. It looked legitimate, but the agency could have easily faked it. Harper never vetted her targets; she just trusted the word of the agency. They taught her to obey orders and never question them. Was that ingrained in her so they could more easily manipulate her?

Harper opened the pack of Wonder Rush and slid out the stick of gum wrapped in pink paper. She didn't unwrap it. She just looked at it and wondered. She wondered if Kevin was innocent. If so, were there others? Had she killed other innocent people on the whim of a corrupt messenger of the agency? Was the agency aware, or did Margot go rogue? There were too many questions, and she needed answers. There was one person who could provide them—Margot.

Harper unwrapped the stick of gum, licked it, and scanned the pattern with her smartphone. This was new. The screen flashed "expired" in bold red letters. She had waited too long. She never let an assignment expire before, and she was curious whether there would be ramifications.

With an expired assignment and an inability to contact the agency, all Harper could do was wait.

* * *

Stainless steel elevator doors slid open. Harper stood behind them, holding a small bouquet. She stepped into the sterile hallway of Grandview Medical Center, wondering what would be appropriate to bring someone who tried to kill herself with booze and pills. She picked up the flowers in the hospital gift shop, but she questioned her decision. She almost grabbed a stuffed "Get Well Soon" bear, but would Rani really want a permanent reminder of this ordeal? She figured the flowers would eventually die, and Rani could just toss them.

The receptionist in the lobby provided Rani's room number, and Harper headed to room 330. She tapped on the open door and peaked around the corner. Rani's name was on the tag outside the door, so she knew she had the correct room, but she still approached gingerly. Perhaps she was sleeping, or with a nurse or doctor. What if she was getting a sponge bath? Do they even do that? Probably not. Rani could surely walk to the bathroom on her own by now.

Harper reluctantly pulled back a hospital curtain and found

Rani alone in her bed. Harper immediately flashed back to the last time she saw Rani alone in bed and had to shake off a chill. Rani lay on her side, awake, with tears welling in her eyes.

"Hey, Rani," Harper nearly whispered. "Are you feeling better?"

Rani sniffled and sat up. She attempted a smile, more out of politeness than cheer. "Hey, Harper. Yeah, I'm doing okay. They pumped my stomach and gave me some fluids. They're just monitoring me now."

"Well, that's good, right?"

"I guess. You just missed my parents. They went downstairs to eat. I just feel…" Tears rolled down her cheeks and her lower lip quivered. Rani's eyes widened, pleading for comfort.

"Hey, it's okay," Harper consoled.

"I feel so embarrassed. My parents saw me like this. I had to admit to them what I did and… now they want to pull me out of school."

"You don't have to worry about that right now." Harper was still awkwardly holding the flowers, so she put them down on a table in front of the window. "You just have to concentrate on your recovery."

"I miss him," Rani mumbled.

"What?"

"Kevin… I miss him." Rani bit her lower lip to stop the tears that were threatening to unfurl yet again.

"I know, Rani. Part of you always will, but you have so much to live for. There are so many people that love you and care about you." Harper felt like a hypocrite considering she was the one who killed Kevin, but she meant what she said.

Rani looked off to the side and just nodded.

"Plus," Harper continued, "who else is going to pray in front of my bed as I sleep and totally freak me out? And trust me, I need a *lot* of prayers."

That got Rani to chuckle. "I would miss you threatening to kill me, too," Rani said with a smile.

Harper grinned.

"You know what?" Rani asked. "I'm so sad about Kevin, but I'm glad I'm still alive. I'm lucky to know you."

"Oh, don't say that," Harper said, knowing she was responsible for Rani's current situation.

"I'm serious. I know we're different people, but we don't have to be the same to be friends, and… well, I'm just glad you're my friend."

Harper grabbed Rani's hand and gave it a comforting squeeze. Honestly, she was happy Rani was her friend too, but she knew fairly soon she would abandon her. If Rani made it back to school, one day Harper wouldn't be there. No note, no explanation; she would just vanish.

* * *

Harper contemplated that notion as she left the hospital and walked toward the train station. A black sedan with darkly tinted windows rolled up next to her and slowed to a stop, its tires crunching the ground beneath. Porter Moore stepped out from the back seat, left the door open, and stood with his hands folded in front of him. The last time Harper saw Porter, he was using her face as a punching bag. He didn't speak a word, and neither did Harper. She just breathed a sigh of dejection and got in the car.

Porter and Harper sat alone in the back seat. She could only see the back of the driver's head and a glimpse of his eyebrows in the rearview mirror. No one she recognized.

"I didn't realize your work extended to the Philadelphia area," Harper said, breaking the silence. Most people who worked for the agency were fairly regional, but she encountered Porter Moore frequently in various locales. He had a unique skill set that she imagined was difficult to find.

Porter didn't answer her. He just sat in silence.

"So," Harper continued, "where we headed? Some shopping, maybe? Oh, I keep hearing about the King of Prussia Mall. Can we go there?"

Porter still said nothing, but he brushed his suit jacket to the side, revealing a pistol strapped to his belt.

"We can skip the mall. You know what? How about we just have some quiet time?" Harper relented. They remained in silence until the car pulled down a dirt road and stopped at an abandoned factory.

Porter gripped Harper's upper arm. His enormous hands nearly wrapped around her bicep as he escorted her into the building. Inside was dingy. No more clean, white office spaces. It was nice while it lasted. Porter led Harper to a dilapidated table and threw her into a rusty chair.

"I like what you've done with the place," Harper said. "Very shabby-chic." She didn't know why she resorted to sarcasm in times of stress, but it made her smile a little.

There was a *click-clack* of heels as Margot entered from another room and approached the table. She was no-nonsense today, a far cry from the glamorous starlet that gave Harper her last assignment.

"You missed your last meeting," Margot started.

"Look, Margot, I can explain. My—"

"Enid."

"I'm sorry?"

"Call me Enid."

Enid must be the Jekyll to Margot's Hyde.

"Okay, Enid," Harper corrected herself. "My roommate had an emergency and I—"

"You have no roommate," Enid interrupted. "You have no friends. You have no family or professors or hobbies or interests of your own. Do you understand me?" Enid was now in Harper's face, but she didn't flinch. "You only have the agency," Enid said, backing off slightly. "You do what we tell you. You go where we tell you, and you arrive when we tell you to arrive." Enid gave Porter a knowing nod.

Porter approached Harper, grabbed her arm, and slammed it onto the table, rendering it immobile.

"I may look like a harmless woman to you," Enid said as she put her foot up on a chair next to Harper. She pushed her dress aside, revealing a large knife strapped to her calf. She unsheathed the knife and eyed Harper's hand, which Porter held down onto the table. Enid slammed the blade directly toward Harper's hand.

Harper cringed, closed her eyes, and turned her head, bracing for the pain, but there was none. As she opened her eyes, she found the blade landed directly between her index and middle fingers, missing them both by less than half an inch.

"Next time you lose a finger," Enid said as she pulled the knife out of the table and put it back into the sheath strapped to her leg. "I don't want to hurt you, Harper. You're a valuable asset to the agency, but don't think for a minute you're not disposable."

"Got it," Harper said, her hand trembling in fear as Porter released his grip.

"Good." She glared at Harper for a moment before reaching into her bag and pulling out a tablet. "There's a domestic terror cell active in Center City. We had the leader isolated and vulnerable yesterday. That was the assignment you missed. Because of whatever drama you and your roommate concocted, we lost that opportunity."

Harper scrolled through the photos on the tablet. There were seven people—five men and two women—in the alleged "terror cell," and they all looked like normal people. She wondered if this was a legitimate operation or if Enid was going rogue again. Before Harper could scroll past the last member of the group, Enid stopped her. The photo showed a wiry, middle-aged man. His shaved head accompanied a scraggly salt-and-pepper beard.

"That's the leader of the group," Enid said. "Whatever happens, make sure *he* does not survive."

If Amaya had been there, she would have recognized him as the shady-looking guy hanging in the back of the room during Wendy's funeral, trying a little too hard to go unnoticed.

"They will meet tonight at an office building on Market Street," Enid continued as Harper flipped to a map of Center City, Philadelphia. A red star marked the location. Harper tapped the star and the building's blueprints displayed on the screen, the targeted meeting room highlighted in yellow. Enid removed a wooden box from her bag and placed it on the table in front of Harper, who opened it and looked inside. There was an army-green canister that had a pin at the top. It resembled an elongated grenade.

"There are two exits in the room. Your mission is to seal off one exit, pull the pin, deploy the gas, and leave through the other exit, sealing it shut on your way out."

"What about the canister?"

"Good question. Give it an hour. By then the gas will have dissipated and the air will be safe to breathe. Reenter and retrieve the canister."

Harper nodded.

"It's not the most elegant approach, and if we had more time, we would have come up with something a little more..." She searched for the right word. "... subtle, but your no-show yesterday put us in a bit of a bind." Enid looked to Harper for reaction or remorse, but she got none. "Questions?"

"Yeah," Harper said. "How do I know these guys are who you

say they are?"

Enid looked at her, dumbfounded. Finally, she gestured to Porter, who turned and hit Harper in the stomach. She doubled over and fell to the ground, coughing air back into her startled lungs.

"Are you questioning the authority of the agency?" Enid asked.

Harper regained her breath and pulled herself back up and into her chair. "Look, you're asking me to kill seven people. I just want to make sure they're guilty."

Again, Enid gestured to Porter, who jabbed Harper in the side, causing her to let out a yelp.

"Where is this coming from?" Enid asked. "I haven't been working with you for very long, but your reputation precedes you. The agency regards you as rather talented and loyal."

Harper didn't want to bring up Kevin, but she couldn't get him out of her mind. She thought about Rani unconscious on her dorm bed, her face pale and her lips blue. She envisioned Rani in her hospital bed, thanking Harper for being a good friend. She just couldn't let it slide. "It's Kevin," she finally said.

Enid looked confused. "Kevin Mitchell?" Porter wound up to hit Harper again, but Enid held up a hand, stopping him.

"I knew him," Harper said. "I also know that your daughter, Sophia, dated him."

"And how would you know—?"

"I tried to fact-check your story, and I came up with nothing. There is no news story about any car accident involving two children named Garrett and Molly. There's no subsequent suicide of a mother named Katrina. Did I kill an innocent man for... what? Revenge for a nasty breakup?"

Enid laughed and signaled to Porter, who hit her on the other side. Harper didn't even attempt to dodge him or fight back. She took her punches, not only because she was no match for Porter, but because she deserved it. She felt horrible about what she put Rani through and what she did to Corey. A solid beating wouldn't even come close to making up for that, but at least she was trying. She wanted Porter to hit her. She welcomed the beating, and she was happy Porter was there to give it to her.

"If it's going to make you sleep better," Enid said, "I'll give you the details on Kevin Mitchell."

Harper gestured for her to proceed.

"Garrett and Molly Westin indeed died in a car accident. Kevin Mitchell was behind the wheel, drunk, when his car struck Katrina's, killing both children. It is true Katrina later shot herself out of guilt. Every word I spoke to you was true. The newspaper clipping I showed you was legitimate."

"Then why couldn't I find it online?" Harper asked.

"Because, dear Harper, the Westin family wanted some privacy. They didn't want the names and pictures of two young children floating around the internet for the rest of eternity. Nor did they prefer to have Katrina's name and picture there, along with a flashy headline about her shooting herself in the skull. I'm sure you can understand the delicate nature of their situation."

"What about Sophia? It seems awfully coincidental that she dated Kevin. They had a messy breakup, and then you have me off him for you?"

"Do you want to know why the breakup was so messy?" Enid asked. "Would that make you feel better?"

"Actually, yeah. It would."

"Kevin felt so guilty about what he did that six months into dating my daughter, he confessed everything to her. That's how the agency learned of the situation. He felt horrible, and Sophia was trying to convince him to do the right thing and turn himself in. He refused, saying it would end his life as he knew it. It was a mistake.

It would never happen again. Blah, blah, blah."

"So why not go to the police? An assassination isn't the solution for everything."

"Because there simply was no evidence. He took the car to a chop shop. There was no CCTV footage. There was nothing. We checked."

Harper wasn't sure if she believed Enid. The story sounded a little too convenient. Every detail fit perfectly into place. On the other hand, if she were telling the truth, the details would also fit neatly into place. She was more confused than ever.

"Feel better?" Enid asked.

"I guess so," Harper said, mostly just to end the conversation. If Enid wasn't telling the truth, any further discussion would just be more lies. Why prolong it?

"Good." Then Enid turned to Porter. "Take her home."

* * *

The ride back to campus was equally quiet. Porter sat in silence, purposefully displaying his gun, as if Harper could ever forget it was there.

The black sedan pulled up to Mulberry Hall, and Harper opened her door.

"It's not your fault," Porter said as Harper exited the vehicle. Stunned, Harper froze, standing outside the car, its open door still propped in her hand. She had never heard Porter speak before. His voice was deep and gravely, exactly what she expected it to sound like. Why would he speak now?

"I'm sorry?" Harper asked.

"What happened to your roommate—it's not your fault," Porter repeated.

Was this a crack in Porter's tough facade? Did she have a new ally? Would he stop beating her every chance he got?

Harper opened her mouth to speak, her hand still on the open car door. Before she could get a word out, the sedan peeled out, and the door closed due to the force of acceleration.

Porter was gone.

Chapter 17

OLIVER

When most people picture the Philadelphia skyline, they envision the skyscrapers in Center City, several of which are on Market Street. The towering mammoths of modern architecture stretch hundreds of feet toward the heavens. At the corner of Market and 17th stands One Liberty Place, boasting over a million square feet of office space. In between 20th and 21st Streets, you would find the twin Commerce Square buildings combining for an additional two million square feet. There is no shortage of floor space on Market Street, so when Harper tracked down the location of her next target, it surprised her to find such a small building.

The structure was under construction and closed to the public. The weathered brick exterior combined with sleek steel support accents to blend with both the historic and modern flare of Center City. She was pleased to find construction halted. Based on the dates of the permits affixed outside, it appeared as if construction had been on hold for some time. Perhaps a budget issue or zoning problem. What it meant for Harper was that she had some privacy to get familiar with her surroundings. What it meant for a local terror cell was that they had an inconspicuous place to meet.

Harper was still unsure if she could trust Margot (she liked Margot much better than Enid and preferred to think of her as such). Her version of Kevin's story checked all the right boxes, but she had a feeling in her gut that she couldn't shake. The situation seemed off to her. Harper was determined not to make the same mistake with the alleged terror cell. She wanted to do some surveillance herself before she gassed seven people that night.

Margot failed to provide the names of the targets. After the doubt Harper cast upon the agency, she assumed Margot's omission was intentional. Lack of names prevented research. A web search of "domestic terror cell Philadelphia" surely would be fruitless. It's not like these organizations advertised. She could run an image search if she had the photos of the terrorists, but those stayed on the tablet and the tablet stayed with Margot.

The door to the building was locked, but locks were a mere speed bump for Harper. Construction inside was far more complete than Harper expected. There were some wires hanging from the ceiling and unpatched access panels in the walls, but there was already furniture occupying much of the space. "Furniture" may be too loose of a term—there were oversized beanbag chairs, a ping pong table, a few standing desks, and some large display monitors mounted on the walls. It appeared to be a tech startup that went under before it could start up.

Harper slipped on her thin black leather gloves—a second skin—and then she located the conference room where Margot's map showed the meeting would take place. It was what business types might call a "fishbowl," meaning it had a wall of almost all glass so anyone walking by could observe the "aquatic" life in a simulation of its natural habitat. Here, that habitat included an elongated conference table and some plastic chairs with metal legs.

Harper tested the light switch. The power was on and fully functional. She preferred rolling the canister into a dark room. It would add to the confusion and delay any response. By the time her targets realized what was happening, it would be too late. She made a mental note to look for a circuit breaker.

There was a door leading from the hallway to the fishbowl (Exit Number One). Inside the conference room was another door (Exit Number Two) leading to a Jack and Jill kitchenette area, meaning there was access from both the fishbowl and the hallway. There was a grated panel at the bottom of Exit Number Two, evidently to gain some ventilation if some overzealous worker put the popcorn in the microwave for too long. It was most likely required by building codes.

She would need to seal off the vent, but it provided her with the perfect hiding place. She could hide in the kitchenette and listen to what the terror cell was plotting. Assuming everything checked out the way Margot explained, she could roll the canister through the opening in the door and then seal it off again. She just needed to find something to cover the grate.

Further investigation of her surroundings led to the discovery of a circuit breaker behind a large metal panel in the wall. Unfortunately, the panel was in a utility closet, nowhere near the kitchenette. A small stumbling block, but she could work around it.

There was construction rubble lying around in trash barrels, where she procured a piece of cardboard and a half-used roll of duct tape. She also found some scraps of copper wire. Grabbing a handful, she stuffed them into her pocket. What she couldn't find was a screwdriver to loosen the screws in the grate, but she snagged a used plastic knife that she thought might do the job.

The knife broke almost immediately, but it gave her enough leverage to loosen the screws and finish unscrewing them with her fingers. Friction alone now secured the vent, making it easy to pull in towards her, release the gas canister, and then replace it. Finally, she tore off a side of the cardboard box, fitted it to the door opening, and taped it on all four sides. She taped only the top of the box to the door, creating a cardboard flap she could quickly secure on all sides when the time was right.

She knew she couldn't make it to the circuit breaker and back to the kitchenette to deploy the gas without too much time passing. Excessive time meant opportunity for her targets to out-think her. She didn't want that. Obviously, manually turning off the lights in the fishbowl wasn't feasible, so Harper would short out the circuit. She pulled a scrap of copper wire from her pocket and bent it into the right shape to fit neatly into one of the electrical outlets in the kitchen. She grabbed the remains of the plastic knife and taped the wire to one end. She wrapped a thick layer of duct tape around the shaft of the knife to insulate it thoroughly. The result looked like a sloppy, two-tined fork, but it would suffice.

Next, Harper mapped out her walking route. Once all seven people were inside the fishbowl, she would lock the main door. It worked with a simple push button. She tested it out, and it pleased her to learn that it was relatively quiet. She would then sneak around to the far side of the office to return to the kitchen without them seeing her through the large glass panel. She would lock Exit Number Two before anyone arrived. Easy-peasy.

As Harper turned a corner, she spotted a fire safety station built into the wall. There was a hinged door with a fire hose inside and a glass panel above it covering an axe, complete with red letters spelling, "Break glass in the event of an emergency." It even had a tiny hammer attached to a chain to break the glass with. Harper held the hammer in her fingers, scoffed, and jammed her elbow into the glass, shattering it onto the floor. She grabbed the axe and admired its clean, unused curves. "This could come in handy," she said to nobody in particular.

* * *

It was long past dusk by the time Harper took her position in the kitchenette. The room was pitch black except for the gentle green glow from the microwave clock. She had a flashlight built into her phone if the situation required it, but her eyes had adjusted to the darkness. Besides, any light seeping from under Exit Number Two would garner unwanted attention. She never understood why characters in movies snuck around in the dark with a flashlight. In her experience, it was the most obvious way to get caught. The only thing that draws attention in the dark more than a light is moving that light around wildly. *Think, people!*

Waiting was always the hardest part, staring at an unchanging watch, feeling your joints stiffen. The microwave clock showed "12:15" before she heard any rustling from the hallway. The muffled voices slowly became more distinct as they got closer to the fishbowl. In a sudden flash, light permeated through the grate in the door. She backed away out of instinct, but she knew there was no risk of detection.

Harper assumed a prone position on the floor, glaring out through the slats in the grate. She could make out three distinct pairs of shoes but couldn't see anything above shin height. One wore a pair of dirty brown work boots, another wore blue running shoes, and the third wore a pair of red pumps—two men and one woman.

Based on the conversation, Harper quickly learned that Red Pumps spent the weekend with family in South Jersey. Running Shoes was a little over exuberant in his replies to her lackluster story—he was a bad flirter. Work Boots seemed more the strong silent type and said little other than an occasional grunt or "uh, huh."

Black Dress Shoes, Sensible White Loafers, and Red High Tops joined that dynamic trio. The conversation was dull and mundane. They were clearly not well acquainted. It must be strictly business at these meetings and light on the small talk. After another agonizing ten minutes, Suede Moccasins completed the group. Seriously? Moccasins?

Harper had the army green canister by her side, the pin still firmly in place. She propped the fire axe against the far wall. She got into a push-up position, slowly and quietly pulled her legs toward her chest, squatted, and stood up. The door between the kitchen and hallway was heavy, but the hinges were silent. She snuck out into the hall, navigating toward the opposite side of the building in the dark. No need for a flashlight, thank you very much. Carefully approaching the fishbowl from the other side, she reached her hand over and pressed the lock button. She paused and waited for an acknowledgement from the "fish," but got none.

Back in the kitchen, Harper sat near Exit Number Two and listened. No need for a visual. She lost some valuable reconnaissance time on her trek to lock the door, so they were mid-discussion of their plans.

Harper detected a hum from a fan. Not the kind you would use to cool a room, but a miniature fan built into electronic equipment. The way the light through the slats dimmed and brightened again, she concluded it was a projector.

They were discussing "DC," presumably Washington DC. Was the target a government building or assembly? Perhaps they were just sharing pictures from a family trip to our nation's capital. Harper still was unsure if Margot was honest about this assignment, but the meeting was rather suspicious. If you're not planning anything shady, why meet in the middle of the night? Why meet in an unused office building? Why wear suede moccasins outside of the house? Okay, she could let the last one slide.

By the time she heard one of them mention "C4," she knew these weren't family photos they were looking at. Harper needed a visual.

She returned to the ground and peered through the slats. The bodies attached to the feet were now all seated, and she couldn't see much else. However, the conference table was glass, and she made out a distorted reflection from the projector onto the tabletop. What she saw looked like blueprints.

Harper couldn't hear everything they said, but the pieces she picked up involved "load-bearing pillars" and "weak points." She listened for names and heard "Carrie" or "Kerry" plus a "Donald," but the name she heard repeated most frequently was "Oliver." He must be the leader. Based on the fragments of conversation that she perceived, Oliver was the one delivering the presentation. Once she heard "detonate" and "explosives," she was ready to make her move.

Step one was to kill the lights. Harper grabbed her copper wire fork, adjusted the tines one last time, and held it up close to the electric outlet. She was pretty sure the handle was long enough to prevent the current from jumping from the outlet to her hand, but honestly, she wouldn't bet on it. She took a deep breath and slid the two ends of the copper wire into the outlet. Instantly, sparks flew, and she heard an almost deafening pop. It startled her, and she jumped back, leaving the contraption in the outlet. The smell of burnt copper and plastic permeated the air. The microwave clock was now dark. The light from the fishbowl no longer seeped through the vent in the door, and the hum of the projector fan slowly faded.

She heard rumbling from the conference room, but nobody seemed too concerned. They were, after all, in a partially constructed building. One would expect hiccups like this.

"Donald, check for a circuit breaker," someone said. It

sounded like the same voice as the presenter, so she assumed it was Oliver.

Harper heard Donald attempting to open the door. "The door's locked," he said in a confused tone.

She had to move quickly before anyone in the group became suspicious. Without the emerald glow from the microwave clock, the room was entirely black. So was the fishbowl. She carefully pulled the grate toward her, leaving an opening in Exit Number Two. There was enough commotion in the conference room that no one heard the slight scraping as she pulled the grate loose.

Harper yanked the pin on the gas canister, tossed it through the opening, put the vent back into place, and sealed it with the cardboard and duct tape. She heard the metal cylinder rolling across the room and then hit into something. A chair or a table leg, probably. She also heard some confused grumbles and a hissing sound—the gas was being released.

There was chaotic coughing, wheezing, and sneezing. They were running into each other, looking for an escape and some answers. What was happening to them?

Harper smelled the gas, a mix between sulfur and wet dog. There wasn't much noticeable clearance under the doorjamb, but she stretched out a piece of duct tape and covered it, anyway. She did the same around the door frame.

At that point, out-and-out screams of horror replaced the confused mumbling. Harper wanted to see what was happening, but she stayed put. If she could witness the destruction she was causing, she would see a group of people—five men and two women—clawing at the walls and doors, coughing uncontrollably, tears pouring out of their bloodshot eyes, mucus gushing from their nostrils, and itchy skin turning red and blotchy. She would observe Running Shoes literally throw Black Dress Shoes into the conference table, looking for an escape. This wasn't the type of gas where you drift off quietly in your sleep. This was the type that ate at your insides on a cellular level, causing a pain so excruciating that you prayed for death, agony so grueling that you would tear off your own skin if it meant a moment of relief.

She detected a random flashing of lights reflecting out of the fishbowl and into the hallway. A few of them must have activated the flashlights on their cell phones. She heard a thud on the kitchenette door and a desperate jab at the door handle. Harper stepped back, as if it would crash down upon her, but it didn't. She perceived a reverberating thud as someone attempted repeatedly to shatter the glass wall with one of the metal-legged chairs.

She didn't like that they now had a visual of the conference room, but she figured it was probably too late, anyway. There was kicking at the door and after several attempts, the cardboard flap that she constructed pushed in and the grate smashed into the kitchen, leaving a hole between Harper and the fishbowl.

Gas seeped in until a man's head pushed through the aperture. He got as far as his shoulders before getting stuck, blocking the flow of poisonous gas once more. The man's face was round and cherubic, bright red with splotches of white blistering sores. He moaned and screamed in between gasps of clean air. The top of his head was bald and shiny, and his face sported an unkempt moustache. She wasn't one to prejudge, but she guessed this was probably Work Boots. She couldn't see his shoes, but she thought it would be funny if he ended up being Red Pumps. That made her laugh out loud, drawing the ire of the man stuck in the door, appearing like some grotesque baby mid-birth.

"Why... doing... this?" the man grumbled through his deteriorating throat. "Please... help... us," he pleaded.

Harper moved to the far end of the room, picked up the fire axe, and charged toward him, holding the axe over her head. She let out a forceful grunt as she swung the axe directly into the top of his head, like a tennis player smashing the ball with a powerful overhead shot. That shut him up quickly. She left the axe lodged deep in the man's skull and made her way out to the hallway. She doomed these saps to a painful death, and Harper wanted a view of the extravaganza.

The few flashlights that illuminated the fishbowl swung around so frenetically that Harper couldn't decipher much of what was happening. She removed her own cell phone from her pocket and switched on the flashlight feature. The light reflected off the glass in the dark hallway, bounced back into her eyes, and temporarily blinded her. She turned her head, shielded her eyes, and pressed the phone directly up against the glass. What a view!

She counted five people dead. Two were on the ground, one was slung over the conference table, and one was draped over a chair. That left old baldy with the axe in his skull, his body lying limp on the conference room floor, his head jammed into the opening of the kitchen door, unseen from this angle. Harper turned the light toward that direction. What do you know? He had on work boots. "Well, hot damn!" Harper said. "Nailed it!"

That got the attention of Red High Tops and Sensible White Shoes. They both struggled to stand. Sensible held onto one of the conference room chairs, attempting to break the glass with it, but she was too weak. High Tops crawled toward Work Boots, Harper's light alerting him to the potential opening in the kitchen door.

High Tops pulled on Work Boots's legs, trying to drag him out, but the axe was preventing any further movement. "Maxine…" he managed. "Help…" Okay, so Sensible's name was Maxine. Mental note.

She dropped the chair and stumbled toward High Tops, both of them still coughing uncontrollably and leaking from every orifice they had, or at least the ones that were visible. "Coming…

Oliver…" she growled. Mental note number two—High Tops was Oliver. Harper recalled thinking he was the leader of the group. It was difficult to ascertain from his current condition, but Harper thought he bore a resemblance to the picture Margot showed her—skinny (bordering on emaciated), shaved head, scruffy salt-and-pepper beard.

They were both weak and probably unable to pull out Work Boots. They each grabbed a leg and gave it their all, though. In a sudden burst of adrenaline, the body came loose from the door vent and the axe dropped to the floor, halfway in between the kitchen and the fishbowl. Oliver stuck his head in the hole, took a deep, clean breath of air, backed out, and let Maxine do the same. Harper rushed back to the kitchenette to finish them both off.

By the time she got back, Oliver had gripped the axe and garnered enough strength from his recent gasps of clean air to hack away at the door. Maxine crouched toward the bottom of the door, trying to clear her lungs. As Harper rushed toward the door, Oliver finally made enough headway to kick it in the remainder of the way, sending Harper tumbling backward onto the kitchen floor.

Oliver and Maxine stumbled into the kitchen and toward the hallway. The gas reached Harper, and she coughed. She wheezed and dragged herself into the hallway, closing the kitchen door behind her to block much of the gas.

"Maxine, find the breaker panel. Let's get some light and then get the hell out of here," Oliver shouted.

Harper kicked out Oliver's legs, sending him to the ground, but he kept a firm grasp on the axe. He was still weak, but stronger than earlier. Oliver was not only wiry but also spry. He jumped to his feet, swinging the axe in the dark. Harper dodged, but he had her backed against the wall now. He swung again, slamming the wall directly behind her. Harper felt the breeze from the weapon as it narrowly missed her head. Oliver yanked the axe backwards, but it was stuck. This gave Harper an opportunity to slip out from under him.

Harper heard Maxine fumbling with something down the hall as Harper attempted to corner Oliver. He approached her, the axe at the ready, yet again. A small amount of moonlight coming in from the exterior window illuminated the hallway, but it was still too dark to make out any detail.

Harper couldn't get close enough to land a solid blow, so she waited for Oliver to make the next move. He charged toward her, holding the axe in both hands, and pressed the shaft of the handle into her chest. She dropped to the floor and Oliver mounted her.

"Tell me who you work for," he demanded. Harper was silent. He had her pinned down, but she didn't worry. She just smiled. She loved situations like this. It gave her a challenge.

Just as she was about to break free from his grasp, the lights flickered on. They could now see each other in perfect detail. Oliver looked at Harper and immediately relented.

"Oh, my God," he said. "Your eyes…" He marveled at them, now tossing the axe to the side but still straddling her. "I can't believe I found you. I can't tell you how long I've been looking for you."

Harper looked at him, her brows wrinkled in confusion. Oliver helped her up to her feet and examined her face, her features, and especially her eyes.

"My God. You look exactly like her."

"Who?" Harper asked.

"Your mother."

Chapter 18

MING

"She was the only one who got away with calling me 'Ollie.'" Oliver laughed, looking off to a distant corner of the restaurant. His memories painted a smile that slowly faded to a frown. He barely resembled the Ollie Hastings that rushed to the hospital to support Rebecca during childbirth. The harshness of life since then was clear in his graying beard, deep wrinkles, and sullen eyes.

The daily special at the Continental Diner was a stack of chocolate chip pancakes, a side of bacon, and an egg (any style—Harper chose sunny side up, although she wasn't feeling very sunny). Harper poked at the whipped cream dollop on the top of her pancakes with a fork. Ordinarily, she would wolf down a breakfast this decadent, but today her appetite escaped her. She was simultaneously nervous and excited. She never met anyone who knew her mother. She had so many questions, but they were all jumbled up in her head, rendering her speechless.

"Do you…?" Harper began but stopped herself. Could she handle the answer?

"It's okay," Oliver said. "Go ahead. Ask me anything."

Harper hesitated. "Do you... still keep in contact with her? My mother?" The agency told her nothing about her mother, and she didn't know she was dead. She figured her mom didn't want her, so she abandoned her. Now Harper hungered for all the details, but another part of her wanted none. If her mom tossed her aside, maybe any knowledge of her would just hurt too much. She used to dream about her mother coming back to her, but that ceased once it became too painful.

"You don't know?" Oliver asked. "They didn't tell you anything?"

Harper shook her head and looked down at her uneaten breakfast.

"My God. What animals," he said. "Harper, I'm so sorry to tell you this, but your mom died a long time ago."

She wasn't sure how to handle that news. She wanted to mourn for her mother, but she didn't even know her. Part of her felt somewhat relieved. Her mom didn't abandon her. It wasn't her choice to leave her behind.

"Actually," Oliver continued, "she died in childbirth."

"Giving birth to me." It wasn't a question. It was a revelation. Harper's first act as a living, breathing being was to kill her mother. She knew she was a killer, but she blamed the agency for that. Now she knew better. She was born a murderer.

"There were complications with the delivery..." Oliver trailed off, understanding how sensitive this would be for Harper. "It happens sometimes. It's nobody's fault."

He could tell she wasn't buying that.

"What..." she was still hesitant and conflicted. "What was her name?"

"Her name was Rebecca Quinn. She was the most beautiful, kindest person I ever knew. I never saw eyes like hers before. They were so complex and unique and multifaceted. Just like she was. In fact, the only other time I saw eyes like hers was last night when I looked into yours."

Harper shied away.

"You really look so much like her. It's uncanny."

"So," Harper continued, "you really loved her." Again, not a question.

"I loved your mother with every ounce of my being," he said with renewed life.

"I'm sorry. I don't really know how to ask this," Harper began.

"Just blurt it out. I can handle it." He smiled. Part of him felt like he was talking to Rebecca again. He knew that was silly, but seeing Harper brought back to life a part of him he thought he had lost forever.

"Are you…" Harper bit the inside of her cheek. "Are you my father?"

Oliver's face grew long, and he empathized with the pain Harper must have been feeling. "No, I'm sorry. I'm not your father." He looked down at the table before his gaze returned to Harper. "Your mother and I were close. Best friends for years. But romantically…?" He snorted a chuckle. "Let's just say we had a tendency to chase after a few of the same guys."

"Do you know who my father is?"

"Rebecca and I shared many things, but she kept some secrets close to her chest. She promised to tell me who your father was after you were born, but… she never got that chance. There was a grad student she dated off and on. I had my suspicions about him…"

"What was his name?"

"Everyone called him Mack." Oliver smirked. "It's funny. I don't think I ever knew his actual name."

"I've never had my own name," Harper said. "I mean, the

agency gives me a new one every few months, but I don't even know who I am. I mean, when I'm not working. I have no actual identity. Did she tell you what she wanted to call me?"

Oliver's heart shattered into a million pieces as Harper's pain wallowed in her eyes. He grabbed Harper's hands, which were resting on top of the table. "I truly am sorry, but she didn't. She said she wanted to wait until she saw you. To make sure your name fit you perfectly and represented you as an individual. Not just some name she pulled out of a baby book."

Harper's shoulder slouched in disappointment.

"Do you remember the day I was born?" she asked.

"Sure, I remember it well. What would you like to know?"

"I mean the actual date. Do you know the date when I was born?" Harper's nerves were getting the better of her, and her voice quivered. This would be the most information she ever knew about herself.

"They didn't tell you your birthdate?" It shocked him.

"No. Each identity has its own. The year is always the same, so I know my age—more or less."

Oliver scoffed in disbelief. How can you rob a child of her birthday? "It was April. I remember it perfectly. You were born exactly one week after your mother's birthday. April nineteenth."

"April nineteenth," she repeated in wonder. Wow, she had an actual, real, bona fide birthday. "So, I'm still seventeen."

"You're still seventeen," Oliver confirmed.

"What did she do? My mother, like, for a living?" Harper asked.

"Rebecca was finishing up her doctorate in Clinical Psychology. She did research under a professor named Dr. Holter at the university where she was studying."

Harper wondered why that name sounded familiar.

"She also worked in the Counseling Center on campus,

providing therapy for students. That's what she loved the most—helping people. I never met anyone who truly cared about helping people as much as your mother."

Harper thought about the five people she killed the night before, and a pit formed in her stomach when she heard Oliver's words. Her mother dedicated her life to helping people, and here she was hurting them. She would be ashamed of her.

"You said you've been looking for me," Harper said. It wasn't a question, but Oliver knew where she was heading.

"The doctors told me that both you and your mother died in childbirth. For a while I believed them. I mean, why wouldn't I? But there was something about Dr. Holter that I never trusted. He did these weird psychological experiments on kids, and… I don't know. I got suspicious. It wasn't until years later when I noticed some strange deaths in the area. Then these gum wrappers started popping up. Most people probably wouldn't think twice about them, but I had seen the design once before. Holter gave a pack of gum to a little girl after one of his experiments." Oliver reached into his pocket and pulled out an old, crumpled, faded Wonder Rush wrapper—a blue one with Poppy printed on the side. "Have you seen this before?"

Harper smiled, reached into her bag, and pulled out an open pack of Wonder Rush—nine pieces remaining, all in white wrappers. "The flavor is always a surprise. Want a piece?"

He chuckled. "I dug into some local deaths in the area, traced them back to a conglomerate of young girls, all led by—you guessed it—Dr. Holter."

In that instant, she remembered the training video she watched when she was ten. There was a Dr. Holter who explained how the agency worked. She never met him in person, but she could remember what he looked like in that grainy, poorly produced video. Then it hit her.

"So, Dr. Holter, who my mother worked for, and who also experimented with children, just so happened to start up the agency that employs me. That doesn't seem like a coincidence."

"That's what I thought," Oliver said. "I suspected he took you at birth and made you one of his experiments. By the time I tried to track you down, you had moved around the country so many times—each time with a unique identity. You were impossible to track. I came close in West Elmdale."

West Elmdale. She missed that sleepy little New Jersey town. She missed the people there. She missed Meg and Amaya. She thought about Corey and felt a bowling ball drop in her stomach.

"I was even at your funeral," Oliver said. "Well, Wendy's funeral. I got to West Elmdale too late. You had already left."

"How did you find me there?"

"I started checking local papers all over the country, looking for unusual deaths. I found one about an English teacher."

"Mr. Godwin."

"Right. I knew you would have been high school aged, so that was a red flag. Then when I read the news regarding that investment banker and his wife—in the same town—well, it was too much of a coincidence. I didn't know it was you, but I suspected the agency's involvement."

Harper glanced at a clock on the diner wall. She couldn't believe that just eight hours ago she was trying to kill the man sitting across the table from her—the only link to her mother and her past. She couldn't imagine Oliver was a terrorist, but she saw the blueprints reflected on the glass of the conference room table and she heard the discussion about explosives. She also thought about the axe that just narrowly missed her head.

"Can I ask you something else?" Harper asked.

"Of course."

"Are you a terrorist?"

"What?" Oliver looked shocked. "Is that what the agency told you? Was that your mission? To take out a terrorist cell?"

Harper nodded her head in embarrassment.

"Harper, I have not only been looking for you for years, but I have also been researching the agency and Dr. Holter. He is a dangerous man, and the agency is a terrifying organization."

Harper had her suspicions about the agency, but it felt strange to hear these words out loud.

"Most organizations are structured like a pyramid. There's someone in charge up top, managers under him, and employees under each of them. A president, some VPs, middle management, and then the worker bees. Make sense?"

Harper nodded.

"The agency works more like a spider web. They have branches and headquarters scattered across the country. Each one works independently, but they're all tied to each other by a thin thread. At the center of it all is a giant spider, just waiting for its prey. That spider is Dr. Holter."

"How did you discover so many details about the agency?"

"Well, I work in IT security. I uncover things that people want hidden. The only problem with the agency is a lot of their data access points block external networks, which makes it impossible to hack. I have learned a lot about them, but there's still so much I'm missing. Proof, for one thing."

"Okay, so what were you plotting last night?"

"The network is complex and difficult to track. They always meet in different locations." Harper was well aware of that. "But they have a few hidden facilities—research centers, manufacturing, training—I located one of them in Washington DC."

"You were planning to blow up a building?"

"Yes, but when it was empty. I promise. I have no intention to kill anyone. I just figured if I could stop some part of their network, even for a little while, I may save some lives."

"But they're terrible lives. The agency only targets bad people, right?" They instilled this in her since childhood, but she had doubts. She was looking to Oliver for validation. If the entire world told you the sky was green, and then you received evidence that it might be blue, you would question yourself too.

"Look, the agency has taken out some bad people—your English teacher, for example." It relieved Harper to hear that he was actually guilty. "But we have a judicial system for a reason. It may not be perfect. Sometimes they get things wrong, but people deserve a defense. They're entitled to a trial. We can't just go around killing people who we think warrant it."

"So, they are all bad people," Harper concluded.

"Not all of them. Running an operation like the agency takes a lot of money. There are many people to pay and bribe. The research is complicated and expensive. Early on, Holter had a financial backer, but they had a falling out of sorts. Since then, they have added in some contract killings. Those pay the bills. They tell the agents a made-up story and you girls go and unknowingly carry out the contract."

This news weighed heavily on Harper's mind. "Have you ever heard of Kevin Mitchell?" She was afraid to ask, but she wasn't sure she would get this opportunity again.

"Actually, that's how I found my way to the Philadelphia area. His suicide seemed a little odd to me, knowing what I know about the agency. I mean, if you're going to kill yourself, why do it in the middle of a frat party with so many people around? Suicide is usually a solitary activity." Oliver saw the hurt in Harper's eyes. "That was you, wasn't it?"

She nodded. "They told me he drove drunk and killed two kids. Their mother later killed herself. Do you know if that's true?"

"I researched that one," Oliver said. "I found nothing about a drunk driving accident."

"I was told that the family wanted it to stay private."

"There would still be a police report regarding the accident, but there wasn't. However, I wasn't looking for that specifically. I wasn't aware of the story the agency told you. What I found was dirt on a girl he dated—Sophia Templeton."

Margo's daughter.

"He supposedly cheated on her. She was... unstable. She threatened to kill him. He took out a restraining order. It was messy."

There was that word again.

"So, I killed an innocent man." Again, not a question, but a revelation.

"I couldn't say for sure, but it appears that way. I'm sorry."

Harper blinked away what was threatening to become tears.

"Oh, I almost forgot," Oliver said, reaching into his jacket pocket. He pulled out a burner phone and gave it to Harper. "In case you ever want pancakes again. The agency will track the cell they gave you, so..." He gestured toward the burner phone. "My number's programmed in there."

"Ollie... I mean, Oliver. I'm sorry I killed your friends," Harper said.

"They were decent people, Harper. Trying to make the world a little better. But I've been investigating the agency for a long time. I know them. I understand how they operate. They were using you to protect themselves. This is on them, not you."

Harper wanted to believe that, but she couldn't.

"One more thing," he said.

"Yeah?"

"I like when you call me Ollie."

* * *

Two weeks had passed since her breakfast with Ollie, and there was no word from the agency. No Wonder Rush, no Poppy stickers, no Porter dragging her to some abandoned factory to beat her senseless. She failed her last mission, and she had never done that before. Sure, she had to improvise a few times, but she always took out her intended target. Margot was clear that Ollie was her priority, and she let him walk. They must have known that by now.

She was aware of the agency's surveillance tactics, and it was reasonable to assume they were aware of her brief excursion to the diner with Ollie. So, what? Were they ghosting her? Maybe that wouldn't be so bad.

Harper sat up in her bed, reading Ralph Waldo Emerson, her latest American Lit assignment, but she couldn't concentrate. At some point the agency would contact her again, and she didn't know how to react. In the meantime, Ollie was trying to do some actual good and stop them. What was she doing to help? Nothing.

Suddenly, her doorknob rattled. Harper always kept it locked, so she leapt from bed, ready to defend herself. Keys jingled in the lock, and then the door swung open.

"Hey, roomie!" It was Rani.

Harper relaxed and smiled. "They finally let you out?"

"Yeah, well, once I stopped threatening to kill myself, they couldn't keep holding me."

Harper grimaced. She wasn't sure if Rani intended that as a joke or not, and she was uncomfortable laughing.

Rani tossed her bags onto her bed and gave Harper a big hug. Harper froze. She was still apprehensive about people touching her, but eventually she warmed up and hugged her back.

"The doctors had me cooped up for weeks," Rani said. "You up for a walk around campus? Get me some fresh air?"

* * *

It was late November, and even a non-denominational institution like Chester Pointe University was decorated for Christmas. The air was frosty and there was a light flurry of snow, but neither girl minded.

"Rani," Harper started, "there's something I need to tell you about Kevin." She knew it would upset Rani, and she wasn't sure if she was strong enough to hear the truth, but Harper felt like she deserved it. She couldn't go on lying to Rani. She spent her life lying to people, and she wanted to be a better person.

"Actually," Rani said, "my therapist told me not to talk about Kevin. At least for now. I'm sorry."

"No, it's okay. It can wait." Harper wasn't looking forward to that conversation, anyway. "Nora stopped by looking for you a few times."

"Oh, yeah?" Rani's voice raised an octave. She didn't want the entire cheerleading squad gossiping about the crazy freshman who tried to off herself.

"Yeah, she just said she missed you, and she said something about a tumbling pass and a... basket toss, or something like that."

"Did you tell her anything?"

"I told her your grandmother was sick, and you had to go home for a few weeks, and you left your cell phone here."

Rani's voice returned to a normal octave. "Wow. That was smart. Thanks."

Lying came so naturally to Harper that she didn't think twice about it.

Rani grew silent, and there was a tension in the air that was palpable. "Everything okay?" Harper asked.

"Well, I'm not coming back to school after winter break. I'm going to finish up the semester—my professors allowed me to make up a lot of work on my own—then I'm going to go back to Nebraska. My parents just want to have me close by. You know?"

"I totally get that. Nebraska's lucky to have you."

Rani smiled. "I really can't thank you enough for what you did for me."

"Really," Harper said, "don't thank me. I don't deserve it."

"I wonder what might have happened if you didn't... well, do what you did." Rani teared up. "I just... I'm happy I have a second chance, that's all."

Harper couldn't let Rani go on thinking she was a saint. She wouldn't have had to save Rani if she hadn't killed her boyfriend. "Rani, there's something you should know—"

Just then, Harper's hair wafted in the breeze as a knife whirled past her head and landed in the stone wall behind them. Her first thought was, *What was that?* Once she saw the knife protruding from the mortar in between two stones, her second thought was, *What kind of force is required for a knife to penetrate cement?*

Harper pulled Rani to the ground. "Rani, get down."

"What's happening?" Rani asked, confused and disoriented.

Another knife flew by her head and landed behind her.

"I finally want to live, and someone is trying to kill me?" Rani said.

They were backed up to a building surrounded by woods. Harper could tell the general direction from where the knives were coming, but she couldn't see anyone in particular.

"They're not trying to kill you," Harper said. "They're trying to kill me."

"Why would anyone—" Another knife interrupted her question. "How many knives does this person have?"

Harper pulled two knives out of the wall and looked toward the woods. "Rani, get out of here. Go back to the dorm."

"I'll get help."

"No! Do not call for help. Do not involve anyone else. Do you understand me?"

"But Harper—"

Another knife shot from somewhere in the woods, and Harper swatted it away with the blade she held in her right hand.

"Promise me," Harper said. "Promise you won't tell anyone about this. I can explain later, but let me handle this."

"I can help you," Rani offered, with little intent behind it.

Harper snickered. "Trust me, Rani, I got this. Now, go! I'll cover you."

Rani ran off, mumbling to herself. "Cover me. She has to cover me? What is this, a shootout? Dear God, please let me get back to Nebraska in one piece!"

Harper charged into the woods, a knife in each hand, ready to attack. She didn't understand what she was running into, and her assailant had the upper hand, but Harper was a proactive girl. If someone was trying to kill her, she was going to kill them first.

Leaves rustled to the left, then a twig snapped. Harper changed direction and ran toward the sound, but she lost it. She turned in a circle, on high alert, looking and listening for any signs of movement. Just then, she heard a scream from above her as a young girl dropped from a tree branch onto Harper's back. The girl held a knife to Harper's throat, forcing Harper to drop her blades and grab the girl's wrists to prevent her from slicing her open.

Harper kept one hand firmly on the wrist of the girl's hand that bore the knife and moved her other hand to the girl's elbow. Harper jerked the girl's elbow forward, ducked down, and rolled her forward, off her back.

They now stood face to face, about ten feet apart. Harper glared into the eyes of an Asian girl who appeared to be around fourteen. She panted like an animal eager to attack, a knife still in her right hand. Harper eyed the two knives she dropped, which sat partially buried under leaves a few feet away from her. She made a move toward the blades, but stopped when the girl stepped closer, like a cat about to pounce. There was no doubt the agency sent her. Two weeks of silence and now they were disposing of her.

"Let's calm down a minute," Harper said, holding both hands up. "I don't know what the agency told you—"

"What do you know of the agency?" The girl asked as she stepped even closer, her knives at the ready.

"Look, I'm an agent too," Harper explained.

"Liar!" the girl screamed as she charged toward Harper. Harper ducked as the girl lunged toward her. Harper jerked her body upward, and the Asian girl flipped and landed hard on her back.

Harper straddled her, grabbed the girl's right hand, which still held the knife, and pressed it to her throat.

"Now, stay there. Don't move," Harper said as she kept one hand pressed against the knife. With the other hand, she reached into her pocket. The girl jerked forward, but Harper pushed her back down. "Hey, stay put. I want to show you something."

Harper pulled her pack of Wonder Rush from her pocket and held it up for the girl to see. Harper could feel the pressure on her hand subside as the girl tried to make sense of what she saw. She lay there, confused.

Harper rose and reached out her hand. After a moment, the girl took it, dropped her knife, and Harper helped her to her feet.

"I told you," Harper said. "I'm an agent. My name is Harper."

The girl looked at her distrustfully. "I'm Ming."

Chapter 19

SARAH

Ming's fingers cascaded poetically across the ivory keys of the baby grand that sat in the oversized marble solarium. The early morning sun trickled in through the floor-to-ceiling windows, interrupted only by the flickering shadow of the autumn leaves as they danced in the gentle wind. Beethoven's Ninth Symphony echoed harmoniously through the two-story conservatory. As Ming's dexterous fingers transitioned to the fourth movement, a cacophonous thud sharply interrupted her dulcet tones. She struck the key repeatedly, but the lumbering *clank* remained unchanged.

"That's the one right there. Hear it?" She wasn't deaf. The man standing beside the gloss-black baby grand piano adjusted the silk pocket square in his overpriced suit jacket pocket. It was a perfect match to his imported Italian tie.

"I hear it," Ming said as she got up from the padded bench. "Might need a new string, Mr. Coulson."

"Bernard, please," he corrected. "I appreciate you coming so early. I'll be in meetings all day and I need this fixed before the gala tonight."

Ming smiled, a bit disgusted at the extravagance surrounding her.

"You look so young," Bernard continued. "I expected them to send someone more…"

If he says "experienced," I'm going to kill him, Ming thought.

"… experienced," he concluded as he glanced at his Rolex.

That's it, you're a dead man, she thought through gritted teeth, but then she shrugged it off. She was going to kill him, anyway.

"I can see you're in a rush," Ming said. "Give me a hand. I can finish in no time."

"Uh… sure, I guess," he said. "What do you need me to do?"

Ming opened a metal toolbox, grabbed a pair of pliers and a stretch of piano wire. Standing on the side of the piano, she reached across and hit the dead key one more time. She located the bad string with her eyes and put an index finger on it.

"Right here," she said. "Can you just hold this string for me?"

"Okay," he replied as he put his finger on the string. Ming moved toward the back of the piano and got to work. The string was not only loose but also frayed. She just needed to line things up perfectly and physics would take care of the rest.

"There's a string on the far side that appears loose, too." She plucked another string further down. "Can you grab that one for me?"

He leaned in and reached for the other string, his head now buried in the back of the piano. "This one?"

The pulse in his jugular vein throbbed in his neck with each pounding beat of his heart. It was almost lined up, but not quite. "Actually, I think it's the next wire."

He adjusted his hand, and now everything was in perfect line. "This one?" he asked.

"Yup, that's it."

"Hey, is this even safe? These wires are—"

"I'm a trained professional," Ming interrupted. She didn't specify what she was trained in, however. She grabbed the pliers, pinched where the piano wire had frayed, and turned her head just as it snapped, whipping toward Bernard, striking him directly in the jugular vein. Before he even realized he was injured, he stood up, confused. He reached for his neck, dabbing the spot where he felt a sudden sharp sensation, like he was just stung by a bee. He pulled his hand away when he felt moisture and looked back at Ming, eyes wide, as he studied his blood-stained hand.

"Get... help," he muttered.

"Oh, my... how did that...?" Ming feigned surprise. "I'll call for help immediately."

She pulled a cell phone out of her bag and tapped the dark screen. "Beep, boop, beep," she said as she pretended to dial. Bernard furrowed his brow in confusion as he collapsed to the ground. She tossed the phone aside.

Her instructions were to let him bleed out, but she was getting fidgety. He didn't have long to live, but she did not excel at restraint. The agency tried to tamper her thirst for destruction, but they were unsuccessful.

Ming slipped on a pair of thick leather gloves, wrapped a piano wire between her hands, and bound it around his neck. Bernard's eyes protested as he gurgled an objection, but he was too weak to stop her. With a quick jerk of her hands, the wire cut directly into Bernard's neck, leaving him nearly decapitated.

Ming stepped back and smiled as she looked at her handiwork. Running the piano wire through her gloved thumb and forefinger, she wiped off the blood. Ming rolled up the wire, put her tools and her gloves in the toolbox, and glanced at her watch. She was running late.

* * *

The school bell rang out through the nearly empty halls as Ming rushed toward room 205, swung the door open, and slipped into the back. Her algebra teacher gave her the evil eye but let her tardiness slide. She slid into a desk toward the back of the room and removed a notebook and pencil from her bag.

"Psst..." Arnold, an awkward boy with greased back hair, hissed in Ming's direction. She ignored him.

"Psst..." When she ignored him again, he added, "Hey, Ming."

"What?" She finally snapped to shut him up.

"Can I copy your homework?"

"What? I'm Asian, so I'm automatically good at math?" she snorted. "Racist prick," she added under her breath as she turned her attention to Mr. Hawthorne's lecture.

"Ming..." He seemed panicked now.

Ming reached into her folder, pulled out last night's homework, and slapped it on the greaseball's desk. "Fine. Here, it just so happens I *am* good at math, but you're still a racist prick."

"Thanks, I owe you." Like he could ever repay her.

Mr. Hawthorne droned on about polynomials, but Ming covered all this material in her last school, so she zoned out.

"Ming..." It was Arnold again. Seriously, high school boys made her want to puke. She ignored him. Why not? It worked so well last time.

"Ming..." This kid was relentless.

"What, Arnold? What else could I possibly do for you this fine morning?" she whisper-yelled.

He just pointed at her leg. She was wearing a short blue dress with a pair of yellow leggings underneath. She immediately found the spot he was pointing to—a quarter-sized red bloodstain. She quickly crossed her legs the other way to cover the blood.

Arnold snickered. "Oh, my God. You're having your period

right in the middle of algebra class." A few heads turned, and Ming bolted from her desk toward the door. She assumed telling Arnold it wasn't her blood would raise more questions than it would answer.

"Miss Quan," Mr. Hawthorne shouted, stopping her. "Where do you think you're going?"

"Bathroom."

"You need a pass, you can't just—" But she was already gone.

* * *

Ming stood in front of the bathroom sink, rubbing the bloodstain with a wet paper towel—not the absorbent quilted type, but the industrial flat brown type. She might as well have used a sheet of paper from her notebook. It was useless. She slipped into a stall and removed her leggings. As she did, two giggling girls entered the bathroom.

"I know, right?" said one of them.

"Arnold said she was having her period right in class," the other one added.

Ming peered through the narrow opening between the door and the frame. She didn't know either girl. They weren't in her algebra class. Did Arnold text the entire student body already?

Ming watched as the girls primped their already perfect hair. One was a brunette and the other one blond.

"What a freaking loser. Buy a tampon. Oh, my God!" the blond said.

"She probably can't afford one," the brunette added. "I heard she lives in a group home or something."

Ming had heard enough at that point. She kicked the stall door open, her yellow leggings in a ball on the bathroom floor. She grabbed a handful of curly brown hair and slammed the girl's head into the mirror. Not enough to crack it, just enough to show she meant business. Blondie froze.

"Wow, your hair's so soft." It caught Ming off guard, and she relented. "What do you use?"

With Brunette's face pressed against the mirror, her answer came out a bit distorted. "It's... Argan... oil."

"Hm, nice." Ming pushed Brunette's head a little harder. She was still raging. "You got something to say about me? Say it to my face!"

"Um, she can't," Blondie said. "You have her face pushed into the mirror."

Ming let go and grabbed Blondie by the throat, pushing her back against the wall. "How about now? Can you see my face now?"

Brunette started slapping Ming, so she grabbed her hair again, threw her down to the ground, and stepped on the side of her head. Her other hand never left Blondie's throat.

"You got something you want to say to me?" Ming demanded. Blondie couldn't speak, so she just shook her head. Tears swelled in her eyes. Ming wanted to keep squeezing harder. She had just killed Bernard Coulson an hour ago, but it didn't quell her hunger.

"Let her go!" Brunette screamed from the floor.

She preferred not to have a mess to clean up, so Ming let go and both girls darted out of the bathroom. She had a switchblade in her backpack, but she left that in the classroom. If she had it with her, maybe she wouldn't have exercised such restraint. It was probably for the best. She really liked knives.

* * *

Ming's scheduled bus stop was three blocks from her group home. Considering the school itself was merely a quarter of a mile away, she typically walked. It gave her some alone time before entering the chaos of sharing a room with three other girls.

Today, as she walked past a bodega a block and a half from her home, she spotted a sticker in the window. It bore an image of a yellow smiley face, blowing a big pink bubble, and giving his gum-chewing experience a solid thumbs-up.

Ming entered the store, grabbed a pack of Skittles and a pack of M&Ms and placed them on the counter. She looked the clerk dead in the eye and said, "I like to mix them."

* * *

Ming sat behind a chipped wooden table, blowing a bubble. Enid (she was always "Enid" to Ming) slid a tablet onto the table facing Ming. It displayed a photo of Harper.

"Her name is Harper Connelly," Enid explained. "She's a freshman at Chester Pointe University, and she's the number one supplier of fentanyl at three different local colleges."

Ming scanned through the photos showing Harper in the middle of a drug deal, purchasing from a supplier, even taking the drugs herself. They were Photoshopped, but Ming didn't know that.

"Can I stab her?" Ming asked eagerly.

"Now hold on," Enid said. "There's more. Her supply is responsible for the deaths of four different college coeds."

"Okay, can I stab her?"

"Ming, darling, you're incorrigible." She said *darling* like an old time Hollywood starlet—*dah-ling*. She tossed her hair to the side dramatically and walked toward the other end of the table.

Enid grabbed a small wooden case and handed it to Ming. "She drinks a butterscotch something-or-other at the Student Center every morning," Enid said as Ming opened the wooden box, revealing a single sugar packet. "That's not sugar in there. Go to the Student Center, make some casual conversation with her, then make sure she adds the contents of this sugar packet to her drink.

Got it?"

"Got it," Ming repeated.

"Exquisite. Now, if you'll excuse me, I have tickets to the theater." *Theater* came out as three dramatic syllables—*thee-ah-tear*.

Ming grabbed the box and headed outside. As she turned the corner out of Enid's eyeline, she tossed the wooden case into a dumpster.

"I'll stab her," Ming said to herself.

* * *

Ming followed about a hundred feet behind Harper. She recognized her from the pictures Enid showed her, but she wasn't alone. She was walking with an Indian girl. *No problem*, Ming thought, *I'll just kill them both.*

As Harper and the Indian girl crossed behind a large stone building, Ming slipped into the woods. Her targets seemed lost in their conversation and stopped walking. Ming opened her backpack, pulled out a large felt package, and unrolled it in front of her, revealing a lineup of ten shiny steel knives. Holding up one of the blades, she watched in awe as the light bounced off it. A few snow flurries gently dropped onto the steel, melting instantly.

She assumed her position, cocked back the knife, and let it fly. "Oh, so close," she mumbled, as the knife narrowly missed Harper's head and stuck in the stone wall behind her. Ming grabbed another blade, gave it another admiring look, and sent that one flying. "Missed again. That's okay," she said, encouraging herself.

Ming grabbed a third knife, tossed it through the air, and narrowly missed her target again. The Indian girl ran away and Harper charged toward her, a knife in each hand.

Ming ducked behind a tree, watched as Harper turned in her direction, and scurried up a tree branch. She perched atop the branch, looking down at Harper. She bellowed a scream as she dropped from the branch, landing directly onto Harper's back.

* * *

Ming lay on the ground with Harper straddling her, holding up a pack of Wonder Rush gum. Ming eased back and Harper helped her to her feet.

"I told you. I'm an agent. My name is Harper."

Ming wasn't sure if she could trust her yet. "I'm Ming." Ming brushed the leaves off her jeans and her coat. "If you're an agent, I assume 'Harper' is just your current identity. What's your actual name?"

"I... I don't know," Harper said.

"What do you mean, you don't know?"

"I mean, I never had one. They took me right from birth," Harper explained.

"They took you... Wait... Oh, my... Wow, you're her," Ming said with great excitement. "You're the Purebreed!"

"What are you talking about?" Harper asked.

"The Purebreed. I heard stories about you during training. You're special. The only agent to begin her training at birth. They say you're the best!" Ming was losing her mind at this point. "Oh, my God. You're... I can't believe I almost killed the Purebreed. How could I almost kill the Purebreed? Harper... can I call you Harper?" She didn't wait for an answer. "Pure... wow, they wanted me to kill the Purebreed. Why would they...? Gee, you must have really pissed them off. What did you do to piss them off so badly?"

"Ming, listen to me," Harper said. "It is 'Ming,' right?"

"Ming, yeah. Well, my actual name is Sarah, but I'm Ming now."

"Okay, Ming—"

"Sarah," she interrupted. "Call me 'Sarah.'"

"Okay, Sarah—"

"I can't believe you're calling me 'Sarah.' Ha! The Purebreed is calling me 'Sarah.' Ha! I love it!"

"Sarah," Harper continued. "The agency is not what you think. You cannot trust anything they say."

"Of course not. They almost had me kill the Purebreed."

"Enough with this Purebreed stuff. This is serious. What did they tell you about me?"

"Um…" she tried to remember, but she wasn't really paying attention. "They said you were a drug dealer, I think."

"Drug deal… Wow, unbelievable. I'm going to stop them, Sarah. Are you with me?"

"Sure!"

"Really, just like that? You don't feel any allegiance to them?"

"Nah, I just like to stab things. I don't really care who. Can I stab someone?"

"Sure, I guess."

"Great. I hate those assholes anyway. Listen to this. I've been Ming, Song, Chen, Fung, and Jing. And those were just my *last* five identities. Can you believe that? All Chinese names."

"So?"

"So, I'm Korean!" Sarah said, flabbergasted. "Racist pricks. I'll take them all out just for that!"

"Perfect. We need a plan, but first we need to make sure my roommate doesn't completely lose her shit. Follow my lead."

* * *

Rani sat on the edge of her bed, rocking. She held her cell phone in between both of her hands, debating whether to call 9-1-1. Suddenly, the phone buzzed, startling her, and she threw it on the ground.

"Uh, what's wrong with me?"

She picked the phone up and viewed the alert on the screen.

"Now," it read.

Rani's shaking hands struggled to open her medication bottle. "I could definitely use one of these," she snickered. She popped the pill in her mouth, opened the fridge, and pulled out a water bottle. She took a sip just as her dorm room door swung open, causing her to spill water down her chin and all over her shirt. "Ah!"

Harper entered the room, laughing.

"Harper, you're alive! Oh, thank you, God," Rani said as she made the sign of the cross. "Wait, why are you laughing?"

"Well, it's a funny story, really," Harper said as Sarah joined her. "This is my friend, Sarah."

"Hi," Rani said nervously.

"Go ahead," Harper said to Sarah. "Show her."

Sarah put her backpack on Harper's bed, unzipped it, pulled out the felt roll of knives, and laid them all out in front of her.

"You're the one who was trying to kill us?" Rani asked.

"No, see, that's just it," Harper said with a chuckle. "Sarah and I have this little game we play where we throw knives at each other."

"What sort of sick game…?"

"They're not real. We were never in danger."

"They sure looked real when they—"

"I haven't seen Sarah in months. She came out to visit before break and she was playing a joke on me."

"They're not real?" Rani asked.

"I come from a family of carnival performers," Sarah said. "You know the act where the guy is blindfolded, and he throws knives at the girl and they always narrowly miss?"

"Yeah…"

"These are those knives. They always miss. They're trick knives. You don't think anyone would really risk being stabbed to death on stage, do you?" Sarah added.

"Um… I guess not." Rani reached for a knife. "Can I—?"

"Nope!" Sarah quickly rolled up her collection of knives. "They're very expensive."

"Look, Rani," Harper said. "Sarah invited me to spend Thanksgiving with her family. Since I'm only auditing my classes this semester, I'm just going to take off early."

"Oh," Rani looked sad. "You know I'm not coming back after break."

"Yeah, I know." Harper was upset too, but she couldn't stay there. The agency would just keep sending more agents to kill her. She couldn't be a sitting duck. She needed to move, and she needed to do it post-haste.

"When are you leaving?" Rani asked.

"Now, actually," Harper said as Rani looked dejected. "I'm sorry. Sarah has a train ticket, and it's nonrefundable. I didn't know you were coming back today and—"

"Right," Rani said. "It's fine. I'll be fine."

"Look, Rani," Harper said. "I'm glad I got to know you." Harper tucked her hair behind her ear, stifling genuine emotion. "You make me want to be a better person."

She had told Rani so many lies in the short time she knew her. She was relieved that the last thing she ever said to her was the truth.

Chapter 20

CHARLES

The cinder block walls were cold and damp, etched in white efflorescence from too many harsh rains. Harper saw the morning frost on the newly fallen leaves through the small, warped egress window carved high into the wall. The aged, cheap glass distorted her view. Harper tilted her head to the left and then the right, watching the leaves shift and morph through the crooked glass. This was her biggest source of entertainment over the past three days.

It was barely seven in the morning, but the thud of footsteps above her and the squeals of children heard through the splintered floorboards suggested a much later hour. As the hinges of the basement door screamed out, Harper tucked herself tight into the corner behind an old, musty armoire. The footsteps on the stairs were light and cautious. Harper remained silent and still until she heard a dish scrape against the concrete floor.

"Breakfast," Sarah whispered. A whisper was all she needed in the confined basement of the group home, as it reverberated to all corners.

"Anything yet?" Harper asked, whispering back.

"Nope." The footsteps trailed off, back up the stairs.

Harper crawled out from behind the armoire and staggered to the bottom of the stairs. Sarah left her two slices of white bread (not even toasted) and a bottle of water. *I feel like I'm in prison,* Harper thought. *I might as well eat like I am.*

Harper needed to disappear. There was no chance she could stay in her dorm without the agency discovering her. Hiding out in the basement of Sarah's group home seemed like a good idea. She just wasn't sure how much more solitude, darkness, and cramped space she could take, but she sat tight. She had been through worse, and she could withstand whatever was required of her. After all, she and Sarah had a plan.

And it was a good one.

* * *

On the evening of the fourth day, Sarah made her way down the basement stairs, placed a dish of dinner on the ground, and whispered, "Tomorrow morning. Eight AM. Clean yourself up."

This was it. Harper wasn't hungry, but she picked up the plate, which consisted of a roll with butter (more prison food), a scrap of meatloaf, and an open pack of Wonder Rush Happy Funtime Bubblegum—nine pieces remaining. All in white wrappers.

* * *

A folding table and chair were set up in the middle of a large, wooden, oblong floor. The curved, padded wall surrounding it, along with the dust-covered pinball machines and arcade games off to an adjacent room, suggested that Sarah was in the middle of an abandoned roller rink. There was even a large silver disco ball hanging overhead, although it was powered off.

Margot slid across the floor, shoes in hand, spinning and

gliding to some imaginary music that only she could hear. "This place brings back some fabulous memories," she said as she leapt and twirled. "I was the queen of the 'Ring-a-Ding Roller Rink' back in my day." Margot bowed and curtsied as she made her way to Sarah's table.

"Anyway," Margot said before stopping herself. "Wait, one more." She kicked and spun and bowed one last time. "Okay," she said as she dramatically primped her hair. "Back to business. I've got a good one for you this time, Ming."

Just hearing the name "Ming" made her blood boil. "Actually, I have a good one for *you*," Ming said.

The disco ball immediately powered up, and tiny white lights reflected and spun around the roller rink. ABBA's "Dancing Queen" piped in through the speaker system.

That wasn't part of the plan, Sarah thought. *But it's a nice touch.*

"What is this? What's happening?" Margot looked around anxiously. *She* was supposed to be the one in control.

"Hello, Margot," a voice boomed from the loudspeaker.

"Margot? No one calls me..." Then it hit her, just as Harper emerged from the darkness.

The light from the disco ball speckled her body as ABBA informed them all of their options to both dance and jive.

"What's wrong, Margot? You look like you've seen a ghost," Harper said.

"Ming!" Margot demanded. "Your mission was to terminate this target."

"Well, it turns out, I don't die very easily," Harper explained.

"Then we will eliminate both of you," Margot said as she pointed back and forth frantically between Harper and Sarah.

"Or," Sarah interjected, "you can hear us out. We have a proposition."

"You're in no position to..." Then both girls surrounded her, and Margot was well aware of their capabilities. "I suppose it doesn't hurt to hear you out."

"We want positions of greater authority," Harper said as Margot scoffed. "I'm almost eighteen. Soon enough, I won't be able to... blend in... as well anymore. I have dedicated my life to the agency and I just want to provide my service at a higher level."

"What makes you think you're in any way qualified for a position like that?"

"Well, most agents begin their training at age ten, right?"

"That's right."

"My training began at birth."

"What do you mean?"

"I have been an agent literally my entire life. If I understand correctly, I may be the only one."

"Since birth? Wait... you're not... oh, my... you're the Purebreed." Startling realization hit her like a Mack truck.

"I have dedicated every moment of my life to the agency. I am strong, I'm smart, capable, and I have killed a *lot* of people. I'm good at it and I don't want to stop."

Margot mulled over her options. "Okay. I can make a phone call. You just have to do something for me first." Margot pointed to Sarah, but kept her eyes locked on Harper. "Kill her."

"Excuse me," Harper objected.

"Excuse *me*," Sarah objected as well.

"Ming, you failed your mission," Margot explained. "When you fail a mission, there are consequences. If you're worthy, maybe you just get a beating. Get put back in your place. But you, Ming, are not worthy. You're impulsive and careless and a risk that this agency is no longer willing to shoulder."

"She's also a child, Margot," Harper said. "She's fourteen years old, and all she did to deserve this life was to have the misfortune of losing her parents at a young age. So no, I won't kill her."

217

"Then there's no deal," Margot said. "You can both turn around, go on your merry way, and wait to be plucked from existence."

"I have one more proposal," Sarah said.

Margot was skeptical but ready to listen. "What's that?"

Sarah placed her foot on the folding chair, yanked a knife out of her boot, and planted it deep into Margot's chest. "You can die."

ABBA was still having the time of their lives as the disco lights continued to shimmer. Margot fell to the ground and gurgled out her last breath, the look of shock now glued to her face forever.

"Well, that definitely wasn't part of the plan," Harper said.

Sarah just shrugged. "I never liked her much, anyway."

Harper patted down Margot's jacket and dress, although there were no pockets. "Check her purse," Harper instructed.

Sarah dug around and pulled out a cell phone. "This should help."

Harper grabbed the phone, but it was locked. She held it up to Margot's lifeless face, and the facial recognition instantly kicked in, unlocking the device. Harper adjusted the phone's settings to no longer require a password. "Might come in handy later."

Harper scrolled through her text messages as Sarah looked over her shoulder. "That one," Sarah said as she pointed to an entry labeled "Dad."

"You want me to text her father?" Harper asked.

"She told me that her dad died a few years ago. Cancer or a heart attack or something. Maybe old age. I don't know. That woman drones on. I usually tune her out."

Harper checked the date of the message. "If her father died years ago, why was she texting him last night?"

"Exactly."

Harper scrolled through the messages.

Dad: *Looking forward to your birthday tomorrow. Let's meet for breakfast. 8:00 am?*

    Enid: *Just name the place.*

    Dad: *Where we celebrated your thirteenth. The Ring-a-Ding.*

    "It's code," Harper said, as if it wasn't obvious to Sarah.

    "Scroll up more." Harper did.

    Dad: *Shame about the ex.*

    "Must be referring to Kevin," Harper said.

    "Who?"

    Harper shook her off and kept reading.

    Enid: *One last chance?*

    The timestamps showed a gap of two hours before "Dad" replied. He was probably checking with the higher-ups to see if Harper deserved to live long enough for another mission.

    Dad: *Last chance.*

    Harper scrolled down some more. There was some coded discussion that appeared to be about Ollie's band of "terrorists," then finally…

    Dad: *No more chances.*

    The order to kill Harper came from upper management. How high up it went, she wasn't sure. She recognized another opportunity. Harper keyed in a message to "Dad."

    Enid: *We need to meet. Now.*

    "Let's just wait and see—" Harper said as a buzz from Margot's cell phone interrupted her. The reply contained nothing but a string of numbers.

    "Did he turn into a robot or something?" Sarah asked.

    "No. They're coordinates."

* * *

    "What can I get yous?" The voice came from a vendor inside a food cart.

    "You sure this is the right place?" Sarah asked Harper.

"Just a sec," Harper told the vendor as she pulled Sarah aside. "This is where the coordinates placed us." She looked around. They were back in Center City, Philadelphia, and the morning commuter crowd wasn't making it easy to determine who might be "Dad."

"There." Sarah pointed to a man wearing a derby hat and a wool overcoat. His perfectly pressed slacks and expensive loafers suggested to Harper that this guy was more likely a business executive waiting for a client. "I've seen him before."

Sarah flashed back to a particularly brutal beating she encountered after she failed to "show restraint." The man she spotted on the steps of a Philadelphia high-rise wasn't the man who beat her (he would never get his hands dirty), but he was there, whispering something to someone as she suffered each blow.

Sarah charged toward him; Harper followed. "Sarah, are you sure this—"

"Enid sends her regards," Sarah said to the man, who looked down at her in disgust. It took Harper a minute to realize she was talking about Margot.

"Ming. Not who I expected," the man spoke.

"Please, call me Sarah," she corrected him. Then, under her breath, she mumbled, "Racist prick."

His eyes widened as he looked Harper up and down. He grabbed her arms and shook his head in amazement. Harper pulled away instinctively. "Alas, our paths cross. You are a bit of a legend in our circle. Sad that our experiment with you didn't turn out so well. Shame. What's your current name?"

"Harper."

"Yes, Harper. I'm surprised to see you amongst the living, Harper." He then turned toward Sarah. "Ming, I see you failed your mission."

"Sarah," she corrected.

"Let me tell you why we called this meeting," Harper said.

"Why *you* called…?"

"Sarah and I are seeking a more active role in the organization. We brought our proposal to Mar—" She corrected herself. "Enid, and we had a… difference of opinion."

"I see," he answered. "And where is Enid now?"

"I stabbed her!" Sarah jumped in. Harper raised her hand to suggest a little more subtlety.

"You what?" the man asked.

Harper spoke up. "Unfortunately, the agency has an opening for a new messenger."

"And you think one of you should fill that position? What qualifications do you—?"

"No, no, no," Harper interrupted. "We're far too skilled to waste our talent being messengers. No. We're looking for positions a little… higher up."

The man laughed. A little too hard. "You're serious? You're what? Seventeen?" he asked Harper.

"Yes, but I'll be eighteen soon. Too old to be an agent much longer."

"And you," he turned to Sarah, "you're what? Fourteen?"

Sarah nodded.

"I'm sorry, but the agency doesn't allow children to run the operation."

"No," Harper corrected, "but you allow children to carry out your dirty work."

"And if I don't agree to this little proposal, I'll end up like Enid? Are you planning on stabbing me right in the middle of the street?"

"Here's the bottom line," Harper said. "We're strong, ruthless, we know a *lot* about the agency. Wouldn't you rather work *with* us than *against* us?"

He thought about that for a moment. "All right. Sarah, there's really no way I can sell a fourteen-year-old agent rising up the ranks, but I'll let you live. How's that? You can continue working as an agent. Fair?"

Sarah just gave him the evil eye.

"And you, Harper. You are coming of age, it's true. The agency is prepping Project Arabella and could use some fresh blood. Killing you didn't work out the first time, so let's see what you can do."

"What's Project Arabella?" Harper asked.

"I've probably said too much as it is," he said. "I'll take a chance on you, Harper. Just don't let me regret it."

"Fair enough," Harper said, extending her hand.

The man shook it and said, "Now that we're colleagues, you can call me Charles."

* * *

As they walked away, Harper reached into her pocket and pulled out the burner phone Ollie gave her. She turned to Sarah and said, "I have someone I really need to talk to."

Chapter 21

BARB

"One for you," Ollie said as he handed Sarah a burner phone. "And one for you." He gave Harper an ordinary-looking Timex watch.

Harper studied the watch, confused. "What is it?"

"You've never seen a watch before?"

"Well, sure, but…" Harper flipped it over, searching for a clue. "What am I supposed to do with it?"

"Tell time, I guess," Ollie said with a smile. "Just kidding. The agency may check you for smartphones or smart watches, anything with digital capabilities. They won't confiscate an ordinary Timex. But," Ollie emphasized, "I implanted a Bluetooth chip and a 5G radio inside of it. Remember when I told you how the agency keeps much of their data on private networks?"

Harper nodded her head.

"Well, if you can get within thirty feet of any Bluetooth device—a computer, a mouse, a keyboard—I can connect through the watch and transmit the data through a cellular network."

"How will I know if I'm connected?"

"Here, I'll show you. Put on the watch." She did as Ollie took out his cell phone and switched on Bluetooth, which he had turned off for the demonstration. Harper felt a distinct vibration on her wrist—*buzz-ba-ba-buzz.*

"That pattern tells you you're connected," Ollie explained. He then flipped open a laptop and Harper felt a *buzz-buzz.* "Two elongated vibrations like that mean my software has completed a scan of the network."

He turned the laptop so Harper and Sarah could see the screen. It displayed a list of files from the phone. When he lifted the phone and scanned it around the room, the laptop displayed the video. A perfect hack.

"Keep in mind, this is one device on a simple network, so don't expect it to work so quickly on the inside."

"What cool stuff does this do?" Sarah asked, holding up the burner phone Ollie gave her.

"It makes phone calls," he explained.

"And what else?"

"That's basically all it does," he said. "Sorry, Sarah. Since you'll still be acting as an agent, you can keep an eye out for anything unusual and you can use this phone to get in touch with either of us. We're both programmed in there."

"Uh, that's so boring." Sarah wanted more action.

"Listen," Ollie said. "It's important that you do nothing to get on the agency's bad side. Just do exactly as you're told and don't improvise. Got it?"

"I guess. So, I keep on killing people?"

"Unfortunately, yes. For now. What we're working on is much larger. We need to sacrifice for the greater good."

"One question," Harper said. "Ever heard of Project Arabella?"

Ollie thought about it. "No, I haven't."

"Charles mentioned it, and then it seemed like he immediately regretted it. I'll see what I can figure out."

* * *

The rattle and mechanical hum of the large steel barrels was nearly deafening. Five different oblong drums spun slowly on a narrow tilt, like a cement mixer keeping its supply viable and homogenous. Each barrel was open on the front end. Four out of five displayed a mass of a clay-like substance, each a different color. The fifth remained empty, the motor off.

Harper looked down at a scrap of paper, unsure whether she had the correct address. She stood on a metal platform overlooking the operation. A set of narrow steel stairs flanked either side. One worker, a woman who looked much older than her fifty years, spotted Harper up above. She made no gesture but removed her gloves and hard plastic earmuffs and trudged up the stairs.

"You Harper?" the woman asked.

"That's right."

The woman wore a blue-gray, full-body jumpsuit. The name "Barb" was stitched onto the chest pocket. Barb pointed to the name. That was the extent of her introduction.

"Nice to meet you," Harper said. Barb shrugged.

"You drop outta school or something?" Barb asked as she eyed Harper up and down.

"Gap year." It was a reasonable lie and a decent enough answer for Barb, who was apathetic at best.

Harper got the impression that going by "Barb" instead of "Barbara" was probably about as carefree as she got. "Barbie" was surely out of the question. Barb had a face that looked like it would shatter into a thousand pieces if she forced it to smile. A full head of frizzy red hair, tucked into a hairnet, framed her face. Her gray roots peeked out around her scalp.

"Welp," Barb said, "this is the operation. I'm about to start a new batch. I'll walk you through it. Ain't nothin' to it, really." Barb walked down the stairs without looking back to see if Harper was following her.

"We'll have to shout to hear each other above the machines," Barb yelled, handing Harper a hairnet and a pair of gloves.

They approached the fifth barrel, and now Harper could see the entire assembly line. Attached to the barrel was a large rectangular machine, followed by a conveyor belt, another round machine, a second conveyor belt, yet another machine, another belt, and finally another contraption on the end. The room was enormous, like a... well... factory.

"Here, we'll git'er started, then I'll show you the other machines. They're farther along," Barb said.

She flipped a switch, and the machine hummed. There were large plastic tubs, ten gallons each. Barb grabbed one by the handle and signaled for Harper to do the same. One by one, they dumped the contents into the steel mixing barrel.

"This is the gum base," Barb explained as she deposited another bucket of what looked like large, colorless pellets. They seemed far from edible. "Grab one of those." Barb tipped her head toward a gallon-sized bottle of red liquid.

Harper lifted the bottle, opened it, and hesitated.

"Yup, just poor 'er on in," Barb instructed as she grabbed a similar-looking bottle. "This here's the color and flavor."

Barb pulled a lever and a thick, transparent liquid slowly trickled into the mixture. "Corn syrup and softener," Barb explained.

Barb pushed a button and large metal arms started spinning, slowly mixing the ingredients together. She made a gesture toward the machine next to them, and Harper followed.

"This one's a bit farther along." Barb pointed to a large,

doughy red mass that was being pushed through the rectangular contraption. "That there's the extruder. It smooths it all out."

Long red ropes of chewy mush oozed from the extruder and onto the first conveyor belt, which attached to another machine. "That one there flattens it out," Barb explained.

Flat, soft, red sheets made their way onto another conveyor belt and into yet another machine. "That's the cutter," she said as she pointed. What came out onto the last belt finally resembled sticks of gum. The sticks continued their journey to the last machine and came out wrapped.

Harper picked up a pack. *Still warm*, she thought. She looked at the label, expecting it to bear an image of her lovable friend, Poppy, but it didn't. "Bubba Bomb?" Harper asked as she read the package.

Barb smacked it out of her hand. "Ain't supposed to touch it."

"What's Bubba Bomb?" Harper asked.

"That's what we're making. Ain't no one told you that?"

"Do you make Wonder Rush here?" Harper asked.

"We make all sorts of gum here. Bubba Bomb's our biggest client. Do we make Wonder Rush?" she thought out loud, looking up to the corner of the ceiling for the answer. "Can't say for sure. We make a lot of things."

"Do you... work for the agency?" Harper hesitated to ask.

"Agency? Well, I'm in the union, if that's what you mean. Suppose you are too. You better be. I ain't workin' with no scabs."

"Union, yeah, of course," Harper said to calm her down. "That's all there is to it?"

"That's everything. Keep your fingers out of the machines. Shadow me for a few days. Then you'll be golden."

Why would Charles send her here? This wasn't even an agency building. It's like they subcontracted part of their manufacturing. Harper figured there wasn't much Wonder Rush produced daily.

Its customer base was rather small. No need to spin up a factory to run a machine a few times per month.

When Harper asked for more responsibility within the agency, gum manufacturing wasn't exactly what she had in mind. This was hardly the place where she could infiltrate a national organization of assassins.

With the constant rumbling of the equipment, Harper didn't know if her Timex watch buzzed or not. She assumed there weren't any wireless devices on the factory floor. Even if there were, they surely didn't hold any agency secrets.

She needed a promotion.

* * *

On the third day, Barb spotted Harper as she walked into work. She took a final drag from her cigarette, flicked the butt onto the ground, letting it burn, and followed Harper inside.

"Got something for you today," Barb said.

"Oh, yeah? What's that?"

"It was Wonder Rush you were asking about, right?"

Harper nodded.

"We got an order for that today. I seen it before. Just forgot the name. We need an add-on."

"What's an add-on?" Harper asked.

Barb gestured; Harper followed. There was a different machine that clicked into the last part of the assembly line. "They have a different wrapper for some of their gum. Not sure why. Kinda weird. This doohickey will sort 'em out. They got a more complicated flavor pattern too."

You never know what flavor you'll get, Harper thought.

As they processed the batch, Harper could see some sticks of gum running through the add-on machine. She knew an invisible pattern of dots and dashes and shapes were being sprayed on as the final product came out in pink and blue wrappers, Poppy staring right at her.

One piece of specially wrapped gum got mixed in with nine other plain-wrapped sticks and came out in one complete package. As the packs of Wonder Rush stacked up, Harper noticed something she never had before. The UPC code was different on each pack. Typically, identically packed items bear identical UPC codes, but not Wonder Rush. Harper smirked and mumbled under her breath, "Brilliant."

She realized they couldn't print the encoded symbols on the pink- or blue-wrapped gum each time they summoned an agent to a particular location at a particular time. It wasn't workable. They needed to manufacture the gum long before they established the mission. The unique UPC code on the wrapper allowed a messenger to scan the pack and link the encoded stick of gum to the mission at hand. "Brilliant," she repeated.

"Hey, Barb," Harper shouted. "Where do these orders get processed?"

"It's all computerized. Above my pay grade, but I can show you when we finish this batch."

* * *

Floyd Gleason sat behind his desk, typing something into the computer in front of him. His short-sleeved dress shirt was probably once white, but he had washed it too many times. A necktie hung loosely around his collar, falling too short onto his stomach. His office had a full glass wall that overlooked the factory floor. Floyd jumped as Barb busted through the door, Harper in tow.

"Jeez, Barb. What gives?"

"Oh, relax, Floyd," Barb said. "Why you always so on-edge?"

"What do you want, Barb?"

"The new girl wants to check out the computers behind the operation."

"Hi, I'm Harper," she said.

"I've seen you on the floor," Floyd said. "You're a good worker."

"Thanks." Harper took a step closer and extended her hand to Floyd. As she did, she felt the *buzz-ba-ba-buzz* of her Timex. She figured there wasn't much going on in this network, but she had access nonetheless.

"All the orders process through here." Floyd tapped the side of his computer, almost with pride. "It's a simple database, mostly. Web front end. Keep studying and maybe you can be management like me someday."

A girl could dream.

Harper noticed a family photo on Floyd's desk—him alongside an equally homely wife and two awkward looking children. "Beautiful family," Harper lied.

"My pride and joy!" Floyd beamed as Harper felt the elongated *buzz-buzz* of her Timex. The network scan was complete. As Floyd was gushing over his family, Harper noticed Barb's face grow even longer than usual.

"I appreciate you letting us barge in like this," Harper said.

"I encourage your curiosity," he said. "Now, go make some gum!" He let out a jovial laugh.

"I'm on break," Barb said.

* * *

Harper pushed open the large metal door to find Barb outside, sitting on a decaying wooden bench with a cigarette in her hand.

"Mind if I join you?" Harper asked.

"Didn't know you smoked."

"I don't. I'd just rather hang out here with you than in the break room with all the sweaty guys."

Barb shrugged and made room for Harper on the bench. Harper thought about Barb's reaction to Floyd's family picture.

"Are you married, Barb?"

"Yup," she responded. Short and sweet.

"What does your husband do?"

"Not a whole hell of a lot," she responded as she angrily flicked ashes from her cigarette.

"Any kids?"

"What is this, Twenty Questions?"

"Sorry, just thought I'd get to know you. I'll leave," Harper said as she motioned toward the door.

"No kids," Barb said, stopping Harper in her tracks. "Not anymore, anyway."

"I'm sorry to hear that."

"I had a boy. Philip." Barb took a long drag from her cigarette, contemplating whether she wanted to open up to a girl she had only known for three days. "We lost him a few years back. Leukemia."

"Oh, Barb. I didn't know."

"Why would you?" she snapped. Then she softened a bit. "Probably be around your age by now." Barb crushed out her cigarette butt on the corner of the bench and tossed it into a garbage can. "Life goes on," she said as she stood and shuffled toward the door and back inside.

It's funny. Harper had seen so many kids orphaned at a young age, but she never saw it from a parent's perspective. She knew how hard it was to grow up without a mother or father. She never even considered what it was like for a parent to lose a child.

She thought about Katrina, the woman who allegedly committed suicide after Kevin hit her car during a night of drinking. But that was a made-up story. A manipulation to get her to carry out a phony mission. Barb was living it. Barb was real, and

Barb's response was simply, "Life goes on."

She saw the pain and indifference on Barb's face every day. Now she knew its source. Barb was in constant mental anguish, but her life carried on.

Harper thought about that for a minute, and she contemplated everything she had been through herself. Her struggle began at birth, with her mother dying, and it snowballed exponentially from there, but all she could do was move forward. Everybody struggles with something in their lives. Sure, some people have it easier than others, but nobody's life is a fairytale. No matter what, life has to continue.

She figured there were three types of people. There are the Katrinas (real or imagined) who can't deal with their pain and give up. Then there are the Barbs, who keep moving forward but aren't living their best lives. They're stuck in a routine but unable to move past the pain. Harper wanted to be part of the third group—the group that acknowledges their pain and struggle. The group that mourns and never forgets but uses their past to make their futures better.

Harper dreamt of a future where she was free of the agency, and she could provide these young girls with a better life. She thought of her mother, a woman who dedicated her life to helping people but was cut short of achieving all she wanted. She would fight for her mother. She would fight for the orphans caught in the agency's grasp, and she would fight for herself.

Life goes on, Harper thought. *So it does.*

Thanks, Barb.

* * *

The apartment that the agency secured for Harper sat above a bakery three blocks from the factory. The room itself was tiny—a single bedroom large enough for a twin bed and dresser, a small bathroom, and a kitchen. It looked like it was last renovated in the '80s, but Harper didn't mind. She lived in greater squalor in the past, plus she had the smells of the bakery wafting in from early in the morning until late afternoon. When the wind was just right, the scent of the confections below her mixed with the sweet breeze from the gum factory.

Harper pulled a lockbox out from under the bed, unlocked it, removed Margot/Enid's old phone, and sent a text to Charles.

Enid: *You have to get me out of the gum factory.*

She stared at the screen for a moment; then finally he replied.

Charles: *Stop using this phone.*

Harper rolled her eyes, put Margot's phone back in the lockbox and picked up Ollie's burner phone. She wanted to call him but didn't feel safe. This was an agency apartment, and she suspected they might be listening. Instead, she opened a secure messaging app called SpecterText, where she could send anonymous messages under the username "NoName3399."

NoName3399: *I got you into the network. Anything?*

She tossed the phone on her bed, not expecting a reply for a while, but it buzzed almost immediately. She picked it up and saw a reply from "Twist00"—that was Ollie.

Twist00: *Not much. Just candy orders.*

NoName3399: *I have an idea...*

Harper tapped the screen mindlessly with her uneven fingernails, pondering her plan. Finally, she sent one last message.

NoName3399: *But it's too soon. I need to get in deeper.*

Chapter 22

WALLY

The sun shone through the large glass panels that enclosed the reception area. The *click-clack* of Harper's boots echoed off the solid marble floors, reverberating around the sparsely decorated walls. She had to pass a security checkpoint, complete with a walk-thru metal detector. They confiscated her cell phone, just as Ollie predicted, but she kept her trusty Timex. The tip of the Washington Monument loomed in the distance, and Harper wondered if this was the building that Ollie and his friends were planning to demolish.

Harper wasn't sure if Charles took her request for a promotion seriously, but she cast that doubt aside for now. This was a big upgrade from the gum factory. Harper approached a receptionist seated behind a large oval desk filled with four computer monitors and a phone system with a myriad of blinking lights.

"Good morning. I'm Harper Connelly. Reporting for my first day of work."

"Please have a seat," the woman said. "Someone will be with you shortly."

Harper sat in a plush waiting area, and it reminded her of her first encounter with Margot. Were they planning on tricking her like Margot did? This seemed like a sophisticated operation, so she doubted it.

"Harper Connelly?" a man asked as he entered the waiting area.

"Yes," she said as she adjusted her glasses, hoping they made her look more professional.

They walked in silence to the elevators, and Harper noted the keypad went to the tenth floor, but the man pressed number three.

This was a large building. Was the entire thing run by the agency, or was it just the third floor? Or was this similar to the gum factory, where the agency subcontracted tasks? It wasn't clear, and there were no company names posted anywhere.

"Right this way," he said as the elevator doors opened. He led her down a long hallway and into an area of cubicles. She thought it probably looked like a million other office spaces across the country.

"This is Wally." He gestured to a man in his mid-twenties who sat inside the cubicle. "He'll get you up to speed."

Wally rose awkwardly and attempted to brush the wrinkles out of his dress shirt and khaki pants. "Hi, I'm Wally," he said as he extended his hand.

Harper shook it. "Nice to meet you. I'm Harper."

Wally was tall and fit. A bit disheveled, but not unattractive. Harper noticed immediately that his left shoe was untied. "You don't want to trip," she said as she pointed out the loose shoelace.

"Ugh, these are always coming untied," Wally said as he reached down to tie his shoe.

"I highly recommend the double-knot," she said. "It's a pretty effective strategy."

"Noted," he said with a chuckle. "Nice to have some fresh

blood in our department. We've been pretty swamped with Project Arabella coming."

There was that name again.

"What is Project Arabella?"

"Honestly, I'm not sure. The higher-ups keep talking about it, but they didn't give us peons any details. Have a seat." Wally gestured to an open desk with a computer.

As Harper sat down, her Timex vibrated almost immediately. *buzz-ba-ba-buzz*

A series of rather sophisticated printers and computer equipment populated the area next to her workstation. "So, what is it we do here, Wally?"

"They didn't tell you? Of course they didn't tell you," he said, answering his own question. "Why would they tell you? Everything's a big old secret around here. Why tell your workers what they're doing for a living?"

"Hey, Wally," Harper stopped him. "Take a deep breath, buddy."

"Yeah, sorry. So, we're in charge of identities."

This was more like it.

"We research people who might have died recently that match the age and demographics we're looking for. We look for people who maybe changed their names at some point. It happens more than you think. Then we print out identification materials—driver's licenses if they're old enough, passports, birth certificates, things like that."

"Great. Sounds easy enough," she said.

"I hope you're okay with bending the rules a bit. The agency does a lot of that. I'm not sure what they're up to, but my paycheck keeps coming, so I don't ask too many questions. Not that they would answer them, anyway. It's always girls too," he said.

"What's always girls?"

"We always get new identities for girls. Usually teenagers. Not sure why."

"Huh," Harper said. "As long as they keep sending the paychecks, right?"

"Ha!" Wally laughed. "That's what *I* always say."

buzz-buzz

The vibration on her wrist informed her that the network scan was complete. That one took a while. Ollie must have gotten a lot of useful information.

"I'll walk you through the first one," Wally said as he pulled a file folder from a drawer and tossed it onto the desk. Harper flipped it open to find a photo of a blond girl alongside a very basic description—"Caucasian, brown eyes, twelve years old."

That was the only important information to the agency. They could adjust everything else.

"Now we scour the web for an identity we could use," Wally said. "I bookmarked some funeral homes I get a lot of excellent information from. Also, various local newspapers that print obituaries. This part can be time consuming, so don't expect—"

"Got it," Harper said as she hovered her mouse over an obituary for a twelve-year-old brown-haired, brown-eyed girl named Maribell.

"You got...? Well, beginner's luck. How 'bout that?" Wally said, slapping his knee. "You're a natural."

He pointed to the photo in the file folder and said, "Looks like you're going to be a brunette from now on, 'Maribell.'"

So that's how they decided. Harper assumed the agency selected each new look so nobody would discover the previous identity. Instead, she had been playing dress-up her entire life. Somewhere out there was the family of the real Harper Connelly— a girl with dirty-blond hair and tortoise-shell glasses—who lost her life too soon. And here she was walking around with her name, her passport, and her birth certificate. She was suddenly nauseous.

"Do you think we're helping these girls?" Wally asked.

"Helping them?"

"Yeah. I mean, if things got so bad for them they needed new identities, don't you think maybe we're doing something good for them?"

Oh, Wally, if you only knew.

"I think you're right, Wally," she said instead. "I think we're really helping them out." It was a pleasant thought, even if it was fleeting.

"Yeah. It feels good to do something positive with my life," Wally said.

Harper wanted to grab him and tell him to run. She came across many terrible people in her seventeen years. Wally wasn't one of them. He had a good heart. That was clear to her. Here he was helping the agency assign identities to brainwashed orphans-turned-assassins, and he thought he was doing something beneficial for the world. The more she learned of the agency, the more revolted she felt.

"Hey, I'm going to go get some hot water," Wally said, rolling his chair over to his desk. He pulled a box out of his desk drawer, holding it up for Harper to see. "I have a nice selection of herbal teas. You want some hot water too?"

That solidified it for Harper. Have you ever known an evil person to drink herbal tea?

"We can celebrate your first new identity," Wally said with a big, goofy smile.

I truly wish it was my first, Harper thought, but instead she said, "Sure. Some herbal tea sounds good."

* * *

Shortly after Wally left the cubicle, a man walked in and placed a security badge on Harper's desk. "Harper Connelly. Welcome aboard."

The voice was familiar, although she had only heard it once prior.

"Porter Moore," she said. "You sure get around."

"I'm Head of Security, so I go where I'm needed," he said in a gruff tone. "This is a secure building, so this ID badge will grant you access to the floors and rooms to which you're authorized. There's a scanner at each door. Scan the card. A green light will appear, and the door will open. If you don't have access—"

"Let me guess," she interrupted. "A red light?"

"I encourage you to scan a secure location. Just so you can familiarize yourself with the procedure."

"I'm sure I can fairly accurately imagine what a red light looks like."

"I still recommend you try it. The basement, for example. That level has the highest security. That's a decent place to test it."

"Um… okay," she said. "You're mysterious as always, Porter."

He left without another word.

Why would he encourage her to use her ID badge in a secure location? Then she remembered the only other thing he ever said to her—"It's not your fault." Rani was in mental anguish, and Harper was beating herself up over it. Porter simply said, "It's not your fault." She recalled thinking that maybe Porter wasn't as bad as she thought. She also remembered every time he punched her and kicked her. So the jury was still out. Regardless, he had piqued her curiosity.

* * *

She waited until the area in front of the third floor elevator was vacant before she entered, pressed the "B" button, and quickly hit the "door close" button repeatedly, as if that would make it close faster.

When the elevator opened again, Harper stepped out onto a cement floor. It was a far cry from the marble that covered the lobby. She walked around, looking for a secure area, but it was empty. There were four large support pillars at each corner, which appeared to be hundreds of yards away from each other. Harper recalled the blueprints she saw reflected on the conference room table the night she gassed Ollie and his friends. This could be the same place, but most office basements probably look similar.

She snuck her way around the dimly lit basement, careful to keep her weight on the balls of her feet to eliminate the echo from her heels, which the hard concrete walls of the silent basement would surely magnify. She spotted a doorway to the side, a security scanner on the right.

Harper scanned her ID. The light blinked green, and the bolt unlocked. Perhaps Porter wasn't such a company man.

The door opened to a small landing and a set of stairs going down. She followed them down one flight, to another landing, and then down another. She repeated this so many times she lost track of how many stories she descended. There were no other doors at each landing, just more stairs.

By the time she reached the bottom, her thighs and calves burned and she dreaded walking back up all those stairs, but adrenaline kept her going. There was another security scanner on the side of the door. Part of Harper wondered if this was just a cruel joke. Porter sent her all the way down here just to force her to trudge all the way back up. Such sadism wouldn't surprise her from Porter, having witnessed his cruelty first hand countless times. She estimated she was probably about a hundred feet below ground.

Harper grabbed her ID badge, held her breath, and scanned it. Nothing. No green light, no red light, nothing at all. "Thanks a lot, Porter," she said as she looked upward to all the stairs she would need to climb. She waved the badge over the scanner again. Over and over and over. Finally, the light blinked green, and the bolt unlocked.

* * *

Harper's eyes had grown accustomed to the low light of the basement and stairwell, so when she pulled open the heavy metal door, the flood of bright fluorescent lighting nearly blinded her.

The entire ceiling was a panel of tube light bulbs illuminating every corner of the office space. A few people hustled by and paid her no mind. She clipped her ID badge to her blouse and did her best to blend in. A man nearly collided with her as he bolted out of an enclosed room. He wore scrubs and latex gloves. "Excuse me," he said through a surgical mask.

Harper peered into the room as the door closed, but she saw little. There was a table with something on top. Was it a body? Human? She couldn't tell. She held her ID up to the security scanner, but it blinked red. *Touché, Porter*, she thought.

As she made her way around the basement, she came across a large, glass-enclosed room containing twenty or thirty workstations. There were about a dozen men and women working, each wearing a white lab coat, gloves, goggles, and masks. Some looked into microscopes, others examined complicated looking scans on computer monitors.

Harper didn't understand what was going on in there, but she knew she needed to get near a computer. She continued to walk past the glass-enclosed laboratory and found a row of abandoned desks. She snuck behind a cubicle wall, reached around to the computer, and powered it up. The machine let out a loud chime— *da-dong!* "Shh…" Harper whispered, as if that would quiet it down.

As the computer booted up, she felt the *buzz-ba-ba-buzz* of her watch. She was connected. Now, she just needed to wait for the *buzz-buzz* to know Ollie was in, and then she would hightail it out of there.

"What are you doing here?" The voice almost made her jump out of her skin.

"I was just—"

"We decommissioned these workstations months ago," the man continued. "You must log onto one on the east side of the building."

"Right," Harper said. "I was just looking for a quiet place to work, but I'll head back to the east side."

"Very well," the man said as he left.

East side? Should I walk around with a compass down here? Harper wondered.

Regardless, she didn't want to draw too much attention, so she headed to the other side of the building. As she walked past the laboratory again, she couldn't help but look in. She needed to know what was going on in there. The entire room was open and bright. There was no way she could sneak inside.

It distracted Harper as the laboratory door swung open. "Pardon me," a man said as he walked past her. Harper froze, and a lump dropped in her throat. She knew that voice. She watched as the man in the lab coat disappeared around a corner.

Regaining her composure, Harper followed him, her heart pounding in her chest so strongly that she could hear the blood pulse through her veins with each heartbeat. She thought about this moment for years—what she would say, what she would do.

The man disappeared into a bathroom. Harper stopped, looked around, and followed him in, locking the door behind her. She was now alone in the bathroom with him. She could play this so many ways and her mind was racing with the possibilities.

He stood in front of a urinal, his back to Harper. He was

vulnerable. She could take him out right there and end it, but she needed to talk to him first. Harper heard his urine stream stop, his fly zip up, and then he turned around and halted—startled to see Harper there.

After a moment, he continued to the sink and washed his hands. "You know this is the men's room," he said. "The women's is next door."

He didn't even remember her.

"I'm exactly where I intended to be, Oren."

He immediately stopped washing his hands, shook the water from them, and turned around. "Do we know each other?"

As Harper looked into his eyes, she immediately became that scared fifteen-year-old girl again. Everything she always wanted to say to him just evaporated instantly. She felt small and weak, unable to move, like he had her pinned down on that bed all over again.

"It's been a while, but yes." She could still feel him on top of her. His smell was etched into her brain.

"I'm sorry," he said. "I meet many people. What's your name?"

Harper's jaw trembled, and she wasn't sure if the words would leave her mouth. "You knew me as Emma," she finally managed. "I was fifteen, staying with your parents in the Florida panhandle." Sweat formed in her clenched fists.

"Oh, Emma, sure. I remember you. How have you been?" Oren was not only friendly but downright jovial. Did he really forget what he did to her, or did he just assume she was unconscious the whole time and had no memory of the event?

"I've been better, Oren. I have to say, I'm surprised to see you here."

"Same here," he said. "Are you new to this department?" He was still far too amiable.

"What I mean is, I'm surprised to see that you work for the

243

agency." Her confidence was slowly returning as she transitioned from Emma back to Harper.

"Oh, right. Well, they paid my way through college. I work in the Research and Development wing now. It's a good job."

Harper scoffed. "So, were you working for them when you drugged me and raped me?"

"Now, Emma—"

"It's Harper now," she corrected.

"Harper, look. It was nothing personal. You understand that. I'm not a bad—"

"Not personal? I'm sorry, Oren, but I don't think rape could get any *more* personal. Is there something I'm missing?"

"Harper, I'm sorry. I truly am. The agency gave me direct orders. If I didn't obey, I would have lost my scholarship. I didn't have a choice."

"You *always* have a choice," she snapped back.

"So you willingly did everything the agency told *you* to do?" he asked.

"It's not the same thing. They started brainwashing me at birth. You..." Her blood boiled. "You just wanted to... what? Finish college? You were an adult, Oren. I trusted you. You were old enough to know right from wrong. You're trying to compare that to a child who they conditioned to obey every order they gave her literally since the day she was born?"

"Since birth? Wait a minute... are you...?"

"Yeah, I'm the Purebreed, okay? Big freaking deal."

"Wow," Oren said in amazement as he approached her more closely, examining her face and eyes. "I had no idea. Holter talks a lot about you."

"You know Holter?"

"Sure. Look, Harper, you were getting too close to that Arnold kid."

"Eric," she corrected.

"What's that?"

"Eric. My boyfriend's name was Eric, not Arnold."

"Sorry. You were getting too close to *Eric*. Agents can't have attachments like that, and they definitely can't date."

"So you just raped away my relationship with Eric and the potential of any future relationships?"

"That's a crude way of putting it."

"Oh, really? Is that description inaccurate?"

"Harper, I'm sorry to have to put it this way, but you're an agent. Nothing more. You belong to the agency. You do what you're told and you accept any recourse for your actions. Don't think of it as rape. Think of it as... part of your training."

"You know what else was part of my training?"

"What?"

"This." Harper slammed her elbow into the bathroom mirror, shattering it into hundreds of pieces. She tore off her blouse, which was covering a plain black tank top, wrapped it around a large glass shard, and buried it deep in Oren's throat. The tip of the shard poked straight out of the back of his neck.

Shock flooded Oren's face as he gurgled blood from the gash in his throat and fell to the ground. Harper hovered over him, watching as he took his last breaths.

Her ID badge was still clipped to the blouse that protruded from Oren's neck. She unclipped the badge, washed it and her hands in the sink, and slipped out of the bathroom.

* * *

By the time she returned to her desk, Harper was sweaty and out of breath.

"Hey, where you been? Your tea got cold," Wally said.

"Forget the tea, Wally. You deserve to know what the agency

is up to."

"What are you talking about?"

"We need to leave," she said as she nervously scanned the room.

"Okay, well—"

"Now!"

"All right." He bolted up in his seat.

"Look, you're not helping these girls. What you're doing for the agency is bad. I promise you."

"But—"

"Come with me and I'll explain, but you can't keep working here."

Wally hesitated.

"Now, Wally. Let's go."

He jumped to his feet and followed her. Then he asked, "Hey, did you change your shirt?"

In all the commotion, Harper failed to realize that she never felt the final *buzz-buzz* from her Timex.

Chapter 23

VIRGINIA

The occasional horn honk was all that interrupted the rumble of traffic above them. The smell of gas exhaust mingled with the scent of the frigid Potomac River, an odd mixture of dead fish and storm runoff. Harper studied a graffiti tag spray-painted onto the stone wall speckled with moss and lichen. Was it a name or a symbol? Maybe just a design. It didn't matter. She watched Wally huddled in the corner as they hid under the bridge on a patch of dead earth bordering the river.

"Assassins?" Wally asked rhetorically. He just kept repeating that question since Harper told him the truth about the agency.

"I called for help. We need to hide a little longer," Harper said. She wanted to get up and charge ahead, but she promised Ollie she would wait.

"Assassins," Wally repeated. This time it was a statement rather than a question. Perhaps that was progress.

"I'm sorry I dragged you into this, but you deserve to know the truth, and you can't keep helping those people." Harper attempted to console him.

"I didn't even know we had a basement," he responded.

"What do you mean?"

"The basement. I didn't even know the office had a basement. You were working there for what? An hour or two? In that time, you not only discovered the basement, but you killed a researcher working there?"

"He was an evil man, Wally. Trust me, the world is better off without him."

"How many?" Wally asked.

"How many what?"

"How many people have you killed?" Wally trembled, partly because of the cold late-autumn breeze drifting off the Potomac and partly out of fear of Harper's response.

"Honestly, I have no idea."

"Oh, God. That's a lot. I know exactly how many people I've killed—zero! When the number is low, it's easy to remember. Even if I killed one person, I would remember that. Two or three, no problem. You don't know how many people you've killed? At what point do you stop counting? Ten? Twenty?"

Harper interrupted him. "This isn't helping, Wally."

"Oh, my God." Something had just occurred to Wally, and he sat up, suddenly alert. "I *have* killed people. Oh, my God. I don't know how many either!"

"What are you talking about?" Harper was losing patience.

"I mean, how many girls did I assign new identities? They were all assassins? Doesn't that make me, like, an accomplice, or something?"

"Wally, you didn't know what you were doing," Harper consoled. "We just need to stop them and get out of DC."

Wally curled up with his knees to his chest, trying to generate warmth. Harper was on high alert for any member of the agency who might hunt her down. So, when Ollie charged down the slope and around the corner of the bridge, Harper knocked out his legs, straddled him, and cocked her arm back, ready to attack.

"Oh, Ollie," Harper said, relaxing her fist. "Sorry about that." She got off him.

Ollie brushed himself off. "Not exactly the greeting I was expecting. Come with me."

* * *

The hotel room Ollie booked on short notice in DC was surprisingly spacious. Harper sat on a couch in an office area while Wally rested on a recliner, heavy blankets covering them to break the chill. Ollie sat across from them, leaning forward in a desk chair, his elbows on his knees.

"Did you get any information from my network scan of the basement?" Harper asked.

"It was too far underground. There's no cell signal down that far. I got nothing."

"How about the third floor?"

"I got a little, but nothing that can take them down. Partial information, circumstantial evidence. Like I said before, everything the agency does is so… compartmentalized. Like a web. It really is the best description. Oh, that reminds me," he said. "Project Arabella…"

"Did you find out what it is?"

"Not exactly, but I found a few articles about a spider named 'Arabella.'"

"A spider?"

"Yes, NASA sent a spider named 'Arabella' to space in the '70s to study the effects of web spinning in zero gravity. After some initial disorientation, the spider could do it."

"So, what does that mean?"

"Well, I'm not entirely sure."

"The agency is going into space?" Wally offered.

"I doubt that," Ollie said. "It may mean they're experimenting with new technology, or they had a breakthrough with some research, or maybe they're planning an expansion—not literally to space—but wider than their current reach. I'm not sure."

"That makes sense." Wally suddenly perked up. "There's a big summit the agency has been preparing for."

"Summit? When is it?" Ollie asked.

"It's actually next week," Wally said, "in Toronto."

"Oh, my God," Harper said as she covered her mouth in shock. "They're going international."

"There are thirty-seven million people in Canada!" Ollie said. "We have to stop this."

"Remember when I told you I had an idea regarding the gum factory, but it was too soon?" Harper asked.

Ollie nodded.

"Well, I think it's time."

* * *

The elevator emitted a gentle chime before the mahogany-paneled doors slid open. A woman named Virginia stepped into the lobby, her briefcase in one hand, a coffee cup in the other.

"Good morning, Virginia," a receptionist spoke as Virginia passed her.

"Morning, Kim," she responded. "How was Morgan's recital?"

"Oh, it was adorable. She got so nervous that she stayed backstage for the first half of the dance."

"They're so precious at that age," Virginia replied. "Any calls this morning?"

"Henry called from Internal Audit and Mark from Legal," Kim said.

"Get Mark back on the line and patch him through, please," Virginia said as she entered her office. She put her briefcase on her desk, hung up her jacket, and powered up her computer.

Suddenly, the entire building shook, and Virginia heard a massive explosion. She held onto her desk to steady herself before calling out to Kim. "Was that an earthquake?"

"I'm not sure. Look out your window."

As Virginia peered down at the crowd below her, she found it curious that a mob had formed, all looking up in confusion.

"What's going on out there?" Virginia charged into the hallway, enveloped in a light cloud of smoke. She hit the elevator button, but nothing happened. "Elevators are out."

People pushed passed her in a panic. Virginia followed them to the stairwell. Her office was on the eighth floor, so she didn't have too far to go. Clusters of people rushed from higher levels, coughing on dust and tripping over each other.

By the time she found her way outside, the curious mob she saw from her window was running and dodging falling debris. Virginia craned her neck to see the top of the New York City skyscraper that housed her office and froze, shocked to see an airplane protruding from the side.

"What's happen—?" Virginia couldn't finish her sentence before a frantic onlooker pushed her out of the way, forcing her to the ground. As she attempted to rise to her feet, a large iron beam came towering down, crushing both of her legs. Virginia let out a scream so intense that she surprised herself.

* * *

Genko fiddled with the keys in his wool overcoat pocket, unlocked the front door of his home, and grabbed the mail from the bin attached to the brick siding. There were three letters—probably bills—and a small cardboard box. He knew what that was.

Once inside, he tossed his keys into a ceramic bowl that rested on an antique console table, hung his coat in the closet, and placed the mail on the desk in his study.

"Hi, honey. I'm in the kitchen," a woman's voice called out.

Genko entered the kitchen, bent down, and greeted his wife, Virginia, with a kiss. She looked noticeably older since she lost her legs that fateful day in September, but her smile shaved off at least a few of those years.

"How was your day?" she asked as she rolled her wheelchair over to the stove to stir a pot of boiling pasta.

"Fine," he said in his Bulgarian accent. "Do you need help with that?"

"I'm perfectly capable of cooking dinner on my own, thank you very much. You relax a bit. Dinner will be ready in half an hour."

"Sounds wonderful," he said as he kissed her again.

Back in his study, he pulled a metal letter opener from the top drawer of his desk and opened the mail. He was pleased to find only two items were bills. One was junk mail. Genko used the tip of the letter opener to pierce the tape that enclosed the small cardboard box. He pulled the flaps open and stopped.

"What is this?"

Inside the box was a case of gum, which he expected. What surprised him was the brand.

"What the hell is 'Bubba Bomb'?"

* * *

There was a steady *beep-beep-beep* from the semi-truck as it backed into the docking bay. One of the warehouse workers slid the truck door open once it came to a stop. Two others wheeled out dollies and unloaded large cardboard boxes. Still another worker cut the tape seal and removed the packages from the boxes.

Inside the store, an employee wearing a Walmart vest stocked the shelves with various products. He loaded several boxes of Wonder Rush Happy Funtime Bubblegum onto the shelves of the candy aisle.

The same thing occurred all over the country at every Walmart, Target, Stop & Shop, Kroger, Wegmans, 7-Eleven, Quick Chek, Wawa, and local grocery and convenience stores.

A four-year-old girl picked up a pack, drawn to the bright yellow smiley face blowing a bubble. "Mommy, can I have this?" the girl asked.

Her mother glanced at the pack of gum and tossed it into her shopping cart.

* * *

Sarah grabbed a bottle of Dr. Pepper from the refrigerator display at her local deli and brought it to the counter. As she was reaching for her money, she spotted a full box of Wonder Rush mixed in with the rest of the gum and candy.

She just chuckled to herself and said, "Nicely played, Harper. Nicely played."

And just like that, the agency's communication system was temporarily offline.

* * *

Sarah walked down the sidewalk, took a sip from her soda, but failed to notice the white van slowing beside her. The sliding door flew open and two large men emerged. She screamed and squirmed as one put a black hood over her head while the other grabbed her legs and threw her into the back of the van.

The Dr. Pepper bottle crashed to the ground, dark liquid fizzing over the sidewalk.

* * *

She smelled an odd mixture of peppermint and body odor, but the hood remained on her head, so she saw nothing. Sarah's arms and legs were tied behind the chair on which she sat.

"I understand you two have a bit of a partnership," Genko said. "Before I kill you, I need to find her."

"I don't know who you're talking about," Sarah protested.

"You know exactly who I'm talking about—the girl that just won't seem to die—Harper Connelly."

Genko ripped the hood from Sarah's head. The two large men that grabbed her were still there, standing behind Genko and trying (successfully) to look intimidating.

"I was planning on torturing you until you revealed Harper's location, but that won't be necessary," Genko said as he held up Sarah's burner phone. "Shall we call her together?"

Sarah shook her arms and convulsed her body to free herself from bondage, but her attempts were in vain.

Genko hit the number on Sarah's contact list. "It's ringing," he teased as he put the call on speakerphone.

"Sarah," Harper said through the phone. "I'm glad you called."

"You might not be too glad, child."

"Genko," Harper said. "Where's Sarah?"

"Harper, I'm right here," Sarah yelled. "Don't do anything he says."

Genko signaled to one of his bodyguards, who walked over to Sarah and secured a stretch of duct tape over her mouth.

"Sarah, are you okay?" Harper asked.

"Sarah's not having a good day, I'm afraid," Genko said. "I will kill her shortly. *But* I am willing to trade."

"What do you want?"

"Isn't it obvious?" Genko asked, "You, child. I want *you*."

Silence.

Genko was about to speak up, questioning whether Harper was still there. Then Harper broke the silence. "Okay. I'll make a deal. My life for hers."

Sarah squirmed in her chair, squealing an objection through the duct tape that covered her mouth.

"Very good."

"Where are you?" she asked.

"I'm sure you can easily track this phone, burner or not, but I'll save you some time. We're in New Jersey."

"Where?"

"West Elmdale."

Chapter 24

ANT

The evening sun set earlier this late in the year, so Harper had the mask of darkness on her side. She perched on a thick tree branch fifteen feet off the ground, directly across from Ryan and Grace Barnes's suburban colonial. Ollie and Wally were doing reconnaissance, locating where Genko was holding Sarah, but Harper wanted to be more prepared for the eventual encounter.

She knew Genko wouldn't be alone. He was also expecting her, so she lost the element of surprise. Her usual physical prowess wouldn't be enough tonight. She remembered the gun that Ryan kept in his safe (combination 1-0-1-7-0-6). She just needed to get inside unnoticed.

It felt strange scoping out the place she once called home, albeit briefly. She always liked the Barneses, but seeing the house now made her miss Corey. She felt horrible about what happened to him and her role in it. She wondered if they had any other foster children at the moment or if their experience with her and Corey soured them on the venture forever.

She didn't have the best view inside the house, but she saw shadows. Based on the movements and the gait, she could tell which shadow belonged to Ryan and which to Grace. She counted two shadows, so she assumed no new foster children were nearby. Given their history with her and Corey, she doubted they were allowed to continue fostering. A wave of guilt flooded over her.

She lingered as the dark gray of the night faded into solid black and a deep silence fell over the neighborhood. In an instant, the Barneses' porch light flicked off, followed by the interior lights of the first floor. They always left an upstairs hallway light on, so she wouldn't wait for that to extinguish.

Harper gave it another hour to ensure Ryan and Grace had settled into bed and were asleep for the night. Not only did she want to avoid detection, but she also didn't want to give either of them a coronary. The last time they saw her, her name was Wendy, and they were lowering her body six feet into the ground.

Sliding from the tree branch, Harper descended to a thinner limb and grabbed it with both hands. The uneven bark of the oak branch dug into the bare skin of her palms as her body swung down. Loosening her grip, she dropped silently to the ground. It was her intention to pick the back-door lock, but the Barneses left a window cracked open. She snuck toward the window as she slipped on her leather gloves. She slowly and quietly slid the window up and climbed in.

The lower level of the house was dark, but she remembered the layout well enough to find her way around. It smelled of a warm mix of lilac and fresh-baked sugar cookies. Harper inhaled slowly and smiled as a tender nostalgia rushed over her.

As she crept from the living room to the hallway where Ryan kept the gun safe, Harper bumped into a side table, which let out a jerking *thud* as it stammered across the hardwood floor. *That's a new table*, she thought with a grunt. She froze for a moment, rubbing the pain from her shin and making sure she didn't wake anyone.

Harper slunk to the gun safe, entered the combination, and smiled as the lock clicked and the door latch released. Before she fully opened the safe, footsteps pulsated above her, growing louder as they approached the stairs. The first-floor hallway light flicked on as a heavy stride moved closer. She could tell it was Ryan based on the weight and step pattern. Harper ducked behind a sofa, but she looked back and noticed the gun safe was still open.

"Who's there?" Ryan asked while opening the safe door fully. She listened as he picked up the guns (both the house gun and his service pistol), examined them, and put them back in the safe.

"Whoever you are, I'm a West Elmdale police officer and I am armed," he said. "Please show yourself." Ryan cocked his service gun.

She searched left and right, but there was no escape. Nervous sweat dripped from her forehead toward her eye, but she didn't dare move to wipe it. All she could do was hope that Ryan wouldn't check behind the sofa. She didn't like leaving things up to chance. She was typically the one in control. At that moment, she had none.

"You are in a private residence and I am within my rights to shoot you," he said as his voice grew closer.

She put her head down and cowered into as small a position as she could, hoping that would somehow make her invisible. Harper heard his footsteps approaching. Then he was so close she could hear him breathing.

"Why don't you come out from behind there?" Ryan asked. Harper looked up to find him staring directly at her, his pistol held steady.

"I'm unarmed," she said as she crawled out from behind the couch with her hands up.

When he saw who it was, he decocked his firearm and put it at his side. "Harper Connelly," he said. "What a surprise."

In her fear, she nearly missed the fact that he called her "Harper" instead of "Wendy."

"You don't look too startled to see me," she said. "How do you know my name? I mean, my new name?"

"Have a seat, Harper," Ryan said as he gestured to the couch. "I tried hard to conceal the safe combination from you, but I can't say I'm surprised you figured it out. I know your training was rather extensive."

She wasn't sure how to respond, so she sat quietly.

"That combination. 10-17-06. Do you know its significance?" he asked.

She recalled thinking it might have represented a date— October 17, 2006—at least that's the mnemonic device she used to remember it. "No, I don't," she said.

"It's a date."

I knew it.

"Two very important things happened to Grace and me on October 17, 2006. First, our beautiful baby girl was born— Adelaide Jane Barnes."

"I didn't know you had any children," Harper said.

"That's the second major life event that happened on October 17, 2006. We lost our only child—Adelaide Jane Barnes. She lived for exactly thirty-three minutes."

"Oh, I'm... I'm so sorry to hear that. Truly," Harper said.

Ryan just nodded and remained silent for a moment.

"We tried again to have more children, but we couldn't. The doctors said it was a miracle we conceived initially." Ryan placed the gun on a coffee table and sat in a chair across from Harper.

"Dr. Holter," he continued, "showed us great kindness. Grace was... well, she wasn't handling the loss very well, but he helped her tremendously. He gave Grace her life back. He also gave us an opportunity to foster children in need. It wasn't the same as raising our own child, but it filled a hole for us both, especially Grace."

"So, you work for the agency now," Harper said, drawing her own conclusions.

"I have a position of authority with my job, and I use it when the agency needs me. How do you think you skated so easily after that fiasco with the McMahons? I mean, you dug the woman's eye out with a syringe."

"You knew about that?"

"I did, and I protected you. That was part of my job. I directed the investigation to the hospital staff. It's still an open case. Probably will be forever."

"I didn't know," Harper said.

"That's the point. The agency is looking out for its best interests, even if you don't realize it."

"*Its* best interests," Harper emphasized.

"That's right," Ryan responded. "It was in *their* best interest that the authorities didn't catch you. They don't consider *your* best interest. I want you to understand that point, Harper. They don't care about you. You're inconsequential to the grand scheme. It's the agency first and the agency only."

Harper nodded her head. "I'm realizing that, yes."

"I know you want to kill Holter. I know you're back in West Elmdale to save your friend. But Harper, you need to exercise extreme caution. I don't need to tell you how dangerous these people are."

Harper and Ryan both turned as they heard rustling near the top of the stairs. "Ryan, honey. Everything okay down there?"

"All is fine, dear. Why don't you come downstairs for a minute?" he called up.

Harper looked confused and ready to hide again.

"She'll kill me if she knew you were here, and she didn't get to see you," Ryan said to Harper. "You made an impression on us both. You're a good kid, Harper. Don't lose that. And don't let this agency cut your life short. Sometimes you have to let things go. Certain battles are too big for you to take on."

Grace came into the living room, tightening the belt on her terrycloth bathrobe. She stopped immediately the second she saw Harper. "Oh, my…" she managed. "Oh, dear. I never thought I would see you again." Grace grabbed Harper's face with both of her hands and studied every inch of her. A tear welled in Grace's eye. "What is your name now?"

"Harper."

"Beautiful name. I love the blond hair too, and those glasses are adorable," Grace added.

"Oh, thanks," Harper said, removing the glasses and looking at them. "They're just clear glass, but it completes the look, I guess."

Harper grew glum as her gaze fell to the ground.

"What is it, sweetie?" Grace asked.

"I'm so sorry," Harper said, fighting back tears. "I'm so sorry about Corey. It was all my fault. I was careless, and it killed him."

"Oh, Harper," Grace said, "Corey isn't dead."

"Wait, what? But I called here…"

"I thought that might have been you," Grace said.

"You said that Corey was gone. That he died."

"No," Grace clarified. "What I said was that Corey was no longer with us. You hung up before I could explain any further and you blocked your phone number, so I couldn't call back."

"He's no longer with you?" Harper asked.

"That's right. He had an aunt who wasn't very close to the family. When she learned Corey was in the foster care system, she came and picked him up. We still see him occasionally."

"Corey's alive?" Harper asked.

"Corey's alive," Grace confirmed.

Harper was so overcome with joy and relief that she jumped from the sofa and threw her arms around Grace. Her emotional catharsis instantly overwhelmed her body's ingrained repulsion for human contact, and she squeezed harder. "He's alive! I can't believe... oh, thank you!"

"You saved his life," Grace added.

"What?" Harper asked as she pushed away, wiping her nose on her sleeve.

"I wouldn't have taken him to the hospital. I thought it was just the flu. You were so insistent that we take him in, so we did. The doctor said it saved his life. You did that," Grace emphasized. "You saved him."

"I don't think that really counts," Harper protested. "I put him in that position in the first place."

"Look, Harper," Ryan interrupted. "It really is great to see you and we would love to catch up more, but we never know who might be watching. You should move on."

"Right," Harper agreed. "I'm sorry I broke into your house."

"You break in anytime you want, dear," Grace said.

Harper smiled, thinking Grace would have been a wonderful mother.

As Harper approached the front door, Ryan stopped her. "Aren't you forgetting something?" Ryan reached into the safe and pulled out his revolver.

"I thought you told me to drop the whole thing with Holter."

"I did," Ryan confirmed, "but I know you won't."

Harper smiled and took the gun. Ryan handed her a box of ammunition. "Be careful," he warned.

"No promises."

As she left, Harper received a text message on her burner phone. It was from Sarah, but she knew it was really from Genko.

Elmdale Diner. Table in back.

A moment later, there was a final text.

Now!

* * *

Harper fidgeted with a loose seam in the car's backseat while Ollie drove with Wally beside him.

"Sarah's in a white van with two large armed bodyguards," Ollie said. "From what we can tell, Genko is alone in the diner."

"Got it."

"Harper," Ollie said, "are you sure you want to do this? I mean, I understand wanting to save Sarah, but is it worth putting yourself at risk?"

"I can handle myself. Sarah's just a kid. She doesn't deserve this."

"Neither of you do, and let me remind you, Harper, you're a kid too."

"I don't know if I ever really got to be a child," Harper explained. "Sarah still has a chance. Plus," she added with a smile, "I have you two to protect me."

Twigs snapped under the weight of the car as they pulled up to the diner and parked in the rear lot. The white van idled on the far end.

"Wish me luck," Harper said as she reached for the door handle.

"Hang on," Wally said, stopping her. "The first thing they'll do is search you for weapons. You'll lose Ryan's gun and they'll just be more heavily armed."

"He's right," Ollie agreed.

"I'll take it," Wally offered. Ollie and Harper both hesitated. I mean, the guy had trouble keeping his shoes tied.

"Do you know how to handle a gun?" Ollie asked.

"Well, I'm an Eagle Scout," he said.

"Of course you are," Harper mumbled.

"If I need to pitch a tent, I'll call you," Ollie said. "In the meantime, I'll take the gun."

"I have two shooting merit badges," Wally said. "Three, if you count archery. Plus, I won first prize in the Boy Scout Rifle and Pistol Shooting Competition my senior year of high school."

Ollie and Harper exchanged surprised glances.

"Good enough for me," Harper said, handing him the gun and the box of ammunition.

* * *

Genko sat in front of a half-eaten slice of blueberry pie and a newly refilled cup of black coffee, his back to the wall.

"Smart," Harper said as she approached the table and dropped into the booth across from him.

"Pardon me, child?"

"Smart meeting in a public place like this," she said. "You know I won't kill you in the middle of a diner, even if it is sparsely populated." She looked around at the few late-night patrons—a handful of drunk high school and college kids, and some older regulars who were most likely avoiding going home.

"Works the other way around too," Genko interjected. "You know I won't kill you in an open space."

Harper laughed. "*You* kill *me*?"

"You know," he said, "your overconfidence—no, cockiness—is going to be your downfall."

"We'll see about that," she said as a waitress approached the table.

"What can I get ya, hon?" the waitress asked as she scratched her head with the tip of her pencil.

"Nothing for me," Harper said.

"Please, eat something," Genko said. "You never know when

264

you might eat again." There was a threatening tone in his voice that Harper didn't appreciate.

"I'm not hungry," she said firmly, staring down Genko.

"All right, fine," the waitress said, holding up her hands, separating herself from whatever drama they were stirring up.

"Walk me through this," Harper said.

"All business, huh?" Genko smiled. Harper didn't. "Very well. Sarah is outside with my colleagues. I assume you have some... company... with you as well."

Harper nodded.

"My associates will release Sarah to your friends and take you in her place. Simple and clean," Genko explained.

"And what will you do with me?" Harper asked.

"Oh," Genko said, surprised. "I thought that was obvious, child. I'm going to kill you." A laugh escaped from his clenched mouth. "Once and for all, I'm going to kill you!"

Harper finally smiled. "This sounds like fun," she said. "Life is boring without an occasional challenge."

"You really think you can handle me and two armed men?"

"Don't you know who I am?" Harper asked before leaning in and getting mere inches from Genko's face. "I'm the goddamn Purebreed!"

* * *

Outside the diner, Genko led Harper to the rear parking lot. He held her arm with a firm grip which she easily could have broken, but she needed to make sure Sarah was safe. She knew Genko wouldn't kill her in the parking lot, nor would he risk it in a moving van—too unpredictable. She would wait to see where they brought her and assess the situation then, knowing that Ollie, Wally, and now Sarah would follow them.

The two bodyguards escorted Sarah from the van toward

Ollie's car. She looked worn and disheveled. Her usually silky black hair was tattered and matted. Sweat and tears stained her cheeks and eyes. They had bound her arms and legs and taped her mouth shut. Ollie took hold of Sarah as Genko handed Harper off to a bodyguard.

"You okay, Harper?" Ollie asked.

"Just peachy," she replied.

The bodyguard pulled Harper's arms behind her back with a great deal of power, forcing her to wince. "This isn't necessary, boys. I go willingly."

Both guards grabbed her and threw her into the back of the van.

Genko reached into his pocket and pulled out a switchblade. He flicked the knife open and cut Ollie's tires. "Just in case you plan on following us," he said as he jumped into the driver's seat of the van and peeled out of the parking lot.

* * *

Harper scanned the back of the van. It was bare. Nothing she could use as a makeshift weapon. She figured Genko had everything cleared out. He wasn't taking any chances. There was a duffle bag. Maybe there was something in there she could use, but she probably wouldn't have the opportunity to check it out with these two goons watching her every breath.

Goon number one held Harper's wrists together as goon number two wrapped them in duct tape. They then grabbed her ankles and did the same.

"I told you, I'm coming willingly," Harper repeated. "This isn't necessary."

"We just do as we're told," Goon One said as he secured the tape to her ankles.

"Good point," Harper said. "It's important to do as you're

told. You know who else did as they were told?" Neither goon replied. "The Nazis!"

Supposedly Goon Two didn't appreciate being compared to a Nazi, so he hit her hard—right across the jaw with a solid fist. It hurt, but she would never let them know that. Harper shook off the pain.

"What's your name?" She asked Goon Two, but he remained silent.

Goon One chimed in instead. "He's Clark. I'm Ant," he said as Clark smacked him on the arm. "What?" he asked.

"Why do you want to know our names?" Clark asked.

"Well, I just like to know the names of people who would beat a bound, defenseless teenage girl. It takes a unique person, don't you think?" Harper asked.

Clark had little to say in terms of a retort, so he hit her again. This time, harder.

Harper gestured toward Ant with a nod of her head. "Why do they call you 'Ant'? Is that short for 'Anthony'?"

"Nah, it's on account of the fact that I can lift more than my body weight. You know, like an ant."

"Ants also blindly follow orders from their leader," Harper said. "Not much room for independent thought."

"Hey," Ant objected. "I can think for myself."

"Yeah?" Harper asked. "So you think this is all okay? You agree with beating and killing teenage girls?"

Clark hit her again. This time in the stomach, and it knocked the wind out of her. Harper knew physical weapons were not the only ones in her arsenal. The agency also trained her in psychological warfare. If she couldn't injure these goons physically, she could at least get inside their heads.

"Hey, Clark," Ant said. "That's enough."

She was getting to them. Well, at least to Ant.

"You have kids, Ant?" Harper managed through shortened breath.

"Nah. Got a girlfriend, though. Like to have kids one day," he said.

"Would you want a couple of well-built, handsome young men such as yourselves laying a hand on that child?" Harper asked.

Clark pulled his fist back, ready to strike, but Ant grabbed his arm before he could attack. "I said it was enough."

She had Ant in the palm of her hand. Now she just needed to work on Clark, but it looked like she wouldn't get that chance. Clark grabbed the roll of duct tape and ripped off a piece. "Enough talking from you," he said.

Before he could get the tape across her mouth, there was a deafening crash, and Harper's body slammed into the side of the van. She tumbled as her head hit the van wall, then her back hit, and she landed on her stomach. The van had flipped. Because she was now lying on the headliner of the van's roof, she deduced it landed upside down.

Clark lay toward the back of the van, unconscious. Ant was next to him, bleeding badly but awake. "What... happened?" He asked.

"I don't know," Harper said, blood trickling down her forehead. "An accident, I think."

"Can you walk?" he asked.

Harper slowly moved her taped up legs. "Yeah. I think so. You?"

"A little. Yeah," Ant said. "Come on. I'll get you out of here."

"What about your orders?"

"Sometimes we have to think for ourselves, right?"

Chapter 25

CHIP

Chip Rafferty stood in the middle of a boxing ring, his punch mitts raised, ready for the next hit. Across from him, Trey Greene (late-teens, spry, and ready to train) bounced on the balls of his feet. With his sparring gloves laced up, he jabbed and hooked as Chip caught the punches in his mitt.

"Watch your back leg," Chip instructed. "Keep it angled a bit." Trey adjusted his stance.

"Nice. Much better. Can you feel the difference?" Chip asked.

"Yeah," Trey managed in between punches.

"Now, try a jab, hook, uppercut combo with your left. We gotta strengthen your weak side."

"Like this?" Trey asked as he attempted the combination.

"That's it," Chip said as he caught Trey's punches.

"One more time. Same combo. First with the left, then the right," Chip instructed.

Trey completed the punch combination.

"Okay," Chip said as he removed his mitts. "Not bad. I want you to work a little more on your footing for next week and don't forget the cardio."

Trey groaned.

"I know it's no fun, but you don't want to lose because you got winded, right?"

Trey nodded.

"Good. Go on, get out of here."

Chip switched to a pair of bag gloves and moved over to the heavy bag. He hit it repeatedly—left, right, uppercut, hook. Sweat beaded on the muscles of his arms, exposed through his sleeveless shirt.

"Don't drop your shoulder," a man called out from behind him. Chip turned to find Charles, the man who granted Harper her recent promotion.

He still wore an expensive tailored suit and looked out of place in a boxing gym.

"Hey, Dad," Chip said. "What are you doing here?"

"I've got a job for you," Charles responded.

"*That* kind of job?" Chip asked.

Charles gave him a knowing look.

"I'll clean up and meet you out front."

* * *

Charles waited outside of his black Mercedes as Chip emerged, a gym bag over his shoulder.

"What's the job? Security? Training?" Chip inquired.

"Something a little different this time," Charles responded. "I have an agent. She's gotten a bit too big for her britches."

"You want me to take her out?"

"No, we tried that. She's," he searched for the right word, "resourceful. Says she wants to move up in the organization. Maybe she does, but I don't trust her."

"Send her to the gum factory. Let her think she's doing

something important without giving her any real responsibility."

"Great minds, son," Charles said. "That's exactly where I started her, but she grew restless. Here's what I'm thinking. I'll bring her to the DC office. Give her a job assigning identities."

"Sounds harmless."

"I want you beside her. Monitoring her. Figure out what she might be planning. Who else might be working with her. Get her to trust you. Come across as a little weak, maybe. Vulnerable. She likes to save people, so give her someone to save."

"I can do that."

"I just want you to observe and report back to me. I don't want her blood on your hands. Got it?"

"No problem. I'll keep her in the dark with the agency's plans, obviously."

"Yes, but give her something. She needs to think you can be a resource for her. Give her just enough to keep her interested," Charles said.

"What about Project Arabella?" Chip asked.

"Don't give her details. I already let the name slip out, so you can reference it."

"How about the summit?"

"She won't live long enough to make it to the summit, so feel free."

"Very well," Chip said. "She might put together the fact that you're my father, considering our names."

"Well," Charles said, "you're in charge of identities now. Come up with one of your own."

"Okay." He thought for a moment. "From now on, you can call me 'Wally.'"

* * *

Wally turned the corner around a section of cubicles, a Styrofoam cup in each hand. He had replaced his sweaty tank top with a wrinkled dress shirt and khaki pants. His hair was intentionally disheveled. Not messy, just enough to make him appear a little awkward.

"Okay, I got our hot water," he said as he turned into his cubicle, expecting to find Harper there. "Where did she go?" he asked himself.

He put a cup down on her desk and one on his own. He grabbed a tea bag from his box of assorted herbal teas—he chose lemon hibiscus—and dipped it in the cup of boiling water. He took a sip and scowled. "Ugh, how does anyone drink this stuff?"

After twenty minutes passed, Wally became worried. He grabbed his cell phone from the top drawer of his desk and considered calling his father. His only job was to monitor Harper, and he already failed. He decided to let it go for another ten minutes.

When those ten minutes passed, he felt like he had no other choice. He tapped the contact number for his father and took a deep breath as it rang.

"Yeah," Charles said through the phone.

"Um, hey, Dad," Wally said. "So, I think I lost Harper."

Silence.

"Dad?"

"I heard you. What do you mean, you lost her?"

"I went to get tea and when I got back, she was gone."

"Well, find her. What do you want me to do from here?"

"I don't—" he said, but the line was dead.

Wally put the phone back in his desk drawer. He didn't want to risk Harper finding it and discovering the connection between him and his father.

Wally roamed the halls. He even peeked into the women's bathroom, but there was no sign of Harper. His concern sprouted beads of perspiration on his forehead. He returned to his desk and waited, going over all the various possibilities in his head.

Just then, Harper appeared in the cubicle, sweaty and out of breath.

"Hey, where you been? Your tea got cold," Wally said, trying to feign calm.

"Forget the tea, Wally," Harper said. "You deserve to know what the agency is up to."

* * *

Wally shivered as he sat under the stone bridge on the banks of the Potomac River. This wasn't part of the assignment, and he wasn't sure what to do. He left his cell phone in his desk drawer, but even if he had it with him, he didn't know how he would explain this to his father.

Harper had just told Wally everything she knew about the agency. It was old news to him, but he couldn't let on.

"Assassins?" he asked, trying to sound nervous and frightened. The only thing that scared him was his father's inevitable reaction. At least he was still with Harper. He would continue to monitor her. That was his mission.

"Assassins," he repeated, staying in character.

By the time Ollie showed up and dragged them to a hotel room, he knew there was no turning back.

* * *

Wally sat in the passenger seat of Ollie's sedan, parked in the rear parking lot of the Elmdale Diner. Harper was about to go inside to meet with Genko. He knew she had Ryan's gun on her and he couldn't let her go into the meeting armed. Charles gave Wally instructions to observe and report back to him. He specifically told Wally not to get directly involved. These seemed to be extenuating circumstances, however.

Harper reached for the car door handle, and Wally knew he had to stop her. "Hang on," he said. "The first thing they'll do is search you for weapons. You'll lose Ryan's gun and they'll just be more heavily armed." He thought that sounded fairly reasonable. It was a decent bluff.

"He's right," Ollie agreed.

Then Wally said, "I'll take it."

* * *

As the white van peeled out of the Elmdale Diner parking lot, Ollie examined his flat tires, throwing up his hands in disgust. "We have to follow her," he said.

"Yeah, well, looks like we're stuck," Wally said.

Ollie signaled to Sarah in the backseat. "Help me untie her," he said, carefully pulling the tape from her mouth.

"Ah!" Sarah screamed.

"Are you okay?" Ollie asked her.

"Yeah, I'm fine," Sarah said, wiping sweat and tears from her face. "We can't leave her with them. They're animals."

Sarah wiggled her feet and wrists as Wally cut them loose.

"Come on," Ollie said. "Help me find an unlocked car." Ollie pulled on the door handle of the car next to his. Locked. He tried a few others. No luck.

Wally just stood and watched, hoping Ollie's efforts would prove fruitless.

Alas, a door opened. Ollie checked the glove box—no keys. He flipped the visor down, and out fell a set of car keys. "Bingo!" he said. "Let's go!"

Sarah hopped in the backseat. Wally stood motionless.

"Wally, let's go," Ollie repeated.

"I'm afraid I can't let you do that," Wally said as he drew

Ryan's revolver.

"Wally, what are you doing?" Ollie asked.

"Get out of the car," Wally said. "Both of you."

Sarah stayed put, and Ollie remained in the driver's seat. "Look, Wally," Ollie said, "whatever it is—" Just then, Ollie slammed on the gas pedal and the car took off.

Wally attempted to shoot out the back tire as the car tore away, but he missed. "Shit!" he screamed. "Dad's gonna kill me."

Wally bolted to an older-model sedan. He was fairly confident he could hot-wire a car that old. He slammed his elbow into the driver's side door, shattering the glass. He reached inside, pulled up the handle, and got in. Ripping the panel out from underneath the steering wheel, Wally grabbed some wires, stripped them, and struck them together. The car engine revved and then purred. "Yes! Thank you," he said to himself.

Slamming the gas, Wally ripped out of the parking lot, and turned in the same direction he saw Ollie and Sarah go. "Come on, come on," Wally said. "Where are you?"

He sped past each car in his way, rolled through stop signs, and ignored traffic lights. Finally, he spotted the taillights of Ollie's stolen car. "There you are," he said, accelerating even faster.

As he got closer, he discovered that Genko's white van was directly in front of Ollie. Wally couldn't let them catch Genko. He sped up faster until he drove directly next to Ollie, oncoming traffic narrowly missing him. Wally drifted his car into the side of Ollie's. Sarah screamed from the backseat.

Ollie drifted back, bumping Wally's vehicle. Genko must have seen the commotion in his rearview mirror, and his brake lights illuminated, but neither Wally nor Ollie noticed. Ollie's car slammed directly into the back of Genko's van. Wally continued driving forward, drifting into the side of the van.

There was an intense scraping as steel dug into steel. Wally slammed on the brakes, narrowly missing the top-heavy van as it flipped over, rolling off the side of the road, and landing face down, its wheels spinning in the air.

Chapter 26

AMAYA

Ant crawled over to Harper in the back of the van, flipped open a switchblade, and cut the duct tape that was holding her arms and legs.

"You need to run," Ant said.

"Come with me," Harper offered.

"I can't. They'll kill me for being a traitor."

"I could—"

"Just go," he said. "Seriously, if Genko is alive up there, you need to disappear."

"Hey," Harper called out as she reached for the door handle, "I hope you and your girlfriend have those kids someday."

* * *

The exhaust from the upturned van clouded the frosty night air. Harper wiped the blood from her forehead with the sleeve of her jacket. Her right leg screamed in pain, but she fought through it. There were two cars, badly wrecked, that she didn't recognize. A man stepped out of a late-model sedan, a gun at his side.

Is that Wally?

Through the other car's windshield, Harper saw Ollie behind the wheel and Sarah in the backseat.

Why were they in separate cars?

Wally raised the gun to Harper as Ollie shouted out, "Harper, get down!"

"What?" Confused, she ducked behind Ollie's car as Wally fired the pistol, missing.

"Why is Wally shooting at me?"

"He's not who he appears to be," Ollie said. "Run and stay away from him."

Harper noticed Sarah bleeding and disoriented in the back seat. "We need to help Sarah."

"I'll take care of her," Ollie said as Wally fired again. "Just get out of here."

Harper ducked behind the van, blocking Wally's view of her. Sirens wailed in the distance, growing louder, and Wally shouted from the other side of the van. "Harper, time's up. There's no escaping this time. Show yourself."

Harper hid on the van's far side, off the road. A steep ravine hung five feet to her right. In the darkness of night, she couldn't see how far the drop was, but her options were certain death at Wally's hands, or potential death at the bottom of the ravine. Although risky, the latter seemed the better option.

Harper tucked her body in and rolled. The ravine's precipice dug into her back as momentum carried her off the side. Her knees pressed into her chest, and she buried her face in her arms. Her tightened torso bounced off boulders and tree branches as she groaned and grunted through the sharp pain. Her body reeled as it launched off of a ledge jutting out of the earth. She was airborne momentarily when she thought about Rani and actually prayed. The half-second freefall felt like an eternity as she flailed her arms, searching for stability. Her back protested with a loud crack as she hit the ground with a solid thud and continued to roll into an icy stream.

The frigid temperature gave her aches and pains a much-needed reprieve. She soaked in the cold of the trickling stream, panting as she regained her strength. The gentle light from the night sky permitted her to see Wally looking down from above. Having witnessed Wally's view firsthand mere moments ago, she knew all he could see was darkness.

As satisfying as the icy water felt, Harper was cognizant of the fact that she needed to disappear. Not only to get away from Wally, but to dry off before hypothermia set it. She was angry with herself. She shouldn't have trusted Wally to begin with. He worked for the agency. Why did she ever think she could trust him? "Stupid," she scolded herself.

Shifting her body weight to her feet, a screaming pain shot through Harper's right leg. She limped along the side of the stream until she spotted a light through the trees.

Harper dragged herself through the woods and stopped as she reached the property line of a suburban backyard. The exterior house lights were what she had spotted through the trees. A swirl of gray smoke from the chimney made her envious of the warm people inside. What she wouldn't give for a dry blanket and ten minutes in front of that fire. Instead, she lumbered along.

Doing her best to stay out of the pathway of the light, she limped in between houses and out to the road. It was a cul-de-sac that looked vaguely familiar. Harper dragged her leg to one of the connecting streets, unsure what she was hoping to find.

"Harper," Wally hollered.

How did he find me so fast?

She could tell by the intonation of his voice that he hadn't spotted her yet. He was calling out. Fishing.

"Har-per," he repeated, almost in sing-song.

She thought a neighbor might hear him and come out to investigate; however, he probably sounded more like someone looking for a lost dog.

"Harper, where are you?" he continued as she tucked her body flat against the siding of a home, lost in a deep shadow.

Wally was across the street now. There were no streetlights in this neighborhood, and that worked to her advantage. However, there were enough houses with their exterior lights on to provide more luminance than what made her comfortable.

Harper spotted Wally two houses down from where she was hiding. They were on the same side of the street. He stopped calling out for her, supposedly realizing how counterproductive that was. He gripped the gun at his side. He didn't know her location, and he wasn't as alert as he should have been. She could capitalize on that weakness.

She scanned the area for anything she could use as a weapon. All she found was a trash can off to the side of the house, near the street. At least it was metal. She grabbed the lid and held it by the center handle, feeling like a cheap knock-off of Captain America. She was confident that aluminum wouldn't be too effective at blocking bullets. Instead, she gripped the lid with both hands on one side and waited in silence as Wally approached.

His steps were slow and methodical, scanning each dark crevice of the neighborhood as he moved forward. As he got closer to Harper, she cocked back her arms, holding the trash lid over her head like a large Frisbee. At the exact moment Wally peered down the side of the house where Harper was hiding, she slammed the side of the trash can lid directly into Wally's neck.

Completely startled, Wally dropped the gun and slammed into the metal garbage can. The *clanging* sound echoed through the quiet neighborhood, garnering the attention of the home's owner. The outside lights flicked on as Harper searched for the gun. It must have slipped into the bushes because she couldn't find it.

Wally lay beside the trash can, garbage spewed all around him. As Harper attempted to run, Wally grabbed her foot, tripping her. She fell to the ground and Wally pounced. He straddled her as he locked his hands around her throat. She could ordinarily get out of that position fairly easily, but her leg was badly bruised.

She panicked as she fought to breathe. He was a lot stronger than she thought. Harper looked around for anything she could use to fight him, but all she found were food wrappers, some pizza crust, a few empty Chinese food cartons, and… that could work.

Harper picked up a pair of chopsticks, stained brown with soy sauce, and held one firmly in each hand. Mustering all her strength, Harper slammed the chopsticks directly into Wally's ears, one on each side. A look of shock froze on his face as blood rolled down his cheeks and onto her chest.

Wally collapsed on top of her, dead, a wooden chopstick protruding from each ear, buried deep in his brain. A woman screamed, but the weight of Wally's body on top of Harper muffled the sound.

Harper rolled Wally's dead body off of her and looked up at the source of the scream. She was a teenage girl, around Harper's age. She wore an oversized West Elmdale High School sweatshirt and fuzzy plaid pajama pants. Her raven hair had a purple streak down the side, and now Harper realized why the neighborhood looked so familiar.

The girl looked at Harper in shock, then horror, then confusion, then recognition, then confusion again. Her mouth hung open, and all she could muster was, "Wendy?"

* * *

Harper perched on the corner of Amaya's bed, her wet clothes in a pile on the floor. She imagined her subconscious brought her to Amaya's house when she needed help. She would have to remember to run that one by Holter, right before she kills him.

Harper cringed as she examined the discoloration on her leg.

"That looks bad," Amaya said.

"I bruised the bone, but it's not broken," Harper said.

"We should get you to a doctor, anyway."

"They'll just tell me the same thing and then charge a few hundred dollars for it," Harper said. "It will heal. Really, I've had worse."

Harper slipped on a pair of Amaya's sweatpants. "Thanks for helping me…" Harper wasn't sure how to finish that sentence tactfully.

"Drag a dead body into the woods? Hose his blood off the sidewalk?"

She missed Amaya's bluntness.

"Yeah. Thanks for that."

"Eh, it's just a typical Saturday night for me," Amaya said with a smile. "So am I, like, an accessory to murder, or something?"

"Technically, I guess so," Harper replied. "Does that bother you?"

Amaya thought about it and then said, "Not as much as it probably should. Is that wrong?"

They both laughed. Harper looked in the mirror. She didn't even notice the large crack running down the middle of the left lens of her glasses. She took them off and tossed them into the trash can. She wasn't even sure why she kept them as long as she did. They served no purpose other than to make her look more like the real Harper Connelly, the one whose identity she stole. She wiped the dried blood from her forehead with a wet washcloth, pleased to see that the cut itself was mending.

"Seriously, though, isn't someone going to find his body?"

Amaya asked.

"Eventually, yes, but the agency will cover it up. No one will even hear about it."

"The agency," Amaya said. Harper caught her up as best as she could as they were disposing of Wally's body, pulling some spare bullets from his pocket, and digging Ryan's gun out of the bushes.

Harper looked around Amaya's room. Her eye caught Wendy's funeral card, the one she posted on Instagram.

"It was a nice funeral," Amaya said. "You should have been there." She winced as she heard the words come out of her mouth. "Sorry, I didn't mean it like that."

"It's okay," Harper said. "It's not like there's any etiquette for how to talk to your high school best friend after she returns from the dead."

"Best friend, huh?" Amaya teased.

"Yeah, well, 'friend,' I guess. I don't know." Harper attempted to make things less awkward but failed miserably. "When will your mom be home?" she asked, attempting to change the subject.

"Not until morning," Amaya said. "She's working the late shift."

Harper picked up a photo pinned to Amaya's wall. In the picture, Amaya had her arms around Tommy and a big smile on her face. "Is this a thing?" Harper asked.

"Yeah, sorry," Amaya said. "I know he's a pain in the ass, and you were maybe a little into him, but he was really supportive after... well, after you died."

"It's totally fine," Harper said. "I'm happy for you both. Really."

"You know, Wendy, you can stay the night," Amaya offered.

"Harper."

"I'm sorry?"

"It's Harper now."

"Right. Old habits."

"*Harper*, you can spend the night."

"I've already been too much trouble. I couldn't impose any more than I already have."

"Look," Amaya said. "Let's cut the bullshit. This is weird and a little tense, and I don't want to dance around it anymore. I'm just really frigging glad you're alive and in my house right now, okay? I don't care about whatever agency you work for. I don't care that you're a trained assassin. I don't care how many people you've killed." She stopped herself. "Wait, how many people have you killed?"

"I have no idea," Harper replied.

"Well, shit. That's a lot then."

"Yeah, it's a lot," she agreed.

"As long as you promise not to kill me in my sleep, spend the night."

"I really have to find Ollie and Sarah," she said. "I have a burner phone." She dug through her pile of wet clothes and found the pocket of her jeans. She pulled out the crumbled remains of a cell phone. "Huh. I guess I will spend the night."

Harper grabbed her wrist in a panic and checked her Timex. It was still working. *Takes a licking and keeps on ticking*, she thought. She remembered that old ad from somewhere.

Amaya lay in bed and turned off the bedroom light. Harper lay beside her. There was a long silence before Harper spoke. "Hey, Amaya?"

"Yeah?"

"I, um… I really missed you."

"All right, whatever-your-name-is, don't get all sappy on me." They both laughed.

"Yeah, sorry," Harper said. "Good night."

"Night."

There was another long silence before Amaya piped up. "Hey, Wendy? Shit! I mean, hey, Harper?"

Harper chuckled. "Yeah?"

"I really, *really* missed you, too." Her words broke up as she choked back tears. Then Amaya threw her arms around Harper and gave her a big squeeze.

They stayed like that for a few minutes—Harper on her back, Amaya with her arms around her. Amaya sniffled, rolled back to her side of the bed, and then said, "All right, go to sleep, you big freak."

* * *

The early morning sun shone through Amaya's bedroom window. Harper was already awake, putting on last night's clothes, which were still wet. Her leg was stiff, but she slept like a brick, and that made it feel a little better.

"Take some of my clothes," Amaya said.

"Sorry, I didn't mean to wake you."

"Nah, I always wake up at the butt crack of dawn on a Sunday morning," Amaya said.

"Here," Amaya said while rising from bed. "I'll find you something that will fit."

Amaya pulled some clothes out of her closet and tossed them onto the bed. "So, where to next?"

"I have to go to Toronto," Harper replied.

"What's in Toronto?"

"Oh, the less you know, the better, probably. For your own safety."

"Maybe I can come with you," Amaya offered. "I mean, I've always wanted to visit our neighbors to the North."

"It's not exactly a sightseeing tour," Harper said.

"The truth is," Amaya said, "I just don't want to lose you a second time. If you walk out of my house this morning, will I ever see you again?"

Harper thought about what waited for her outside of the safety of Amaya's home. "I really can't promise anything."

"Then take me with you," Amaya said. "Please."

"It's extremely dangerous, Amaya. I couldn't live with myself if anything happened to you."

"So train me."

"Train you?"

"Yeah, we can do one of those movie montages where we condense two weeks of training into two minutes and at the end, I'm just as good a fighter as you are." Amaya said. Then she raised her eyebrows up and down, playfully. "Maybe even better."

"If it were only that easy," Harper said. "Plus, you have school."

"It's almost Christmas break. No one cares anymore. The teachers barely teach. It's all holiday parties and movies."

"What about your mom?"

"I'll come up with something. She's been pretty cool since… you died."

"You love saying that, don't you?"

"It is fun, yeah. Honestly, I don't think I've had this much fun since… you died."

"Okay, okay," Harper said.

"I can come?"

"You got a passport?"

"Yup. Do you?" Amaya asked.

"That's one of the agency rules—always carry your ID and passport. You never know when you'll need them," Harper said. "The passport will be wet, but it's in that pile somewhere." She gestured toward the mound of wet clothes on Amaya's floor. "Do you have access to a car?" Harper asked.

"I have one of those annoying late birthdays, so I don't have my license yet. Meg could drive," Amaya offered.

"No." Harper was firm. "I'm not dragging Meg into this."

"You don't drive?"

"The agency gave me a license for identification, but I've been too busy to learn how to drive." she added.

"You have the license. You can fake it, right?" Amaya asked.

"If I'm going to die on this mission, it better not be because of my driving."

"We could take a train, or a few trains," Amaya offered.

Harper considered the risk she would take if Amaya came along. She also agreed with Amaya, though. She really didn't want to leave her again. "You know this is a monumentally bad idea, right?"

"Harper, my friend," Amaya said as she put her arm around Harper's shoulder, "sometimes the best ideas in the world at first seem monumentally bad."

"Tough to argue with such sound logic. I guess we're going to Toronto."

Chapter 27

JEROME

The trees and buildings zipped by in a blur as Harper leaned her head against the train window. It felt nice to rest, but her jaw clenched with concern. It was a mistake allowing Amaya to join her, but she just couldn't let her go again. What was she thinking? Yes, Harper was a rather worldly and experienced teenage girl, but she was still a teenage girl. Teenagers don't always make the best decisions. Could she live with that rationale if something horrible happened to Amaya?

"What did your mom say?" Harper asked.

"She said, 'Viva la Canada,'" Amaya said.

"You didn't tell her, did you?"

"She was asleep when we left. I'll call her later."

"Do you know what you'll say?"

"I have a decent story cooked up, yeah."

"Then call her," Harper insisted.

"Maybe later."

"Now, Amaya, or I will have them turn this train around," Harper joked.

"I like feisty-Harper," Amaya said. "I didn't know you wielded such godly powers."

"Oh, you have no idea what I'm capable of," Harper snickered, recalling the same words she once spoke to Rani.

"All right, fine," Amaya agreed with a smile. She grabbed her cell phone and dialed her mother.

After a few rings, her mom picked up. "Hi, Amaya," her mom said. "What's up?"

"Hey, Mom," Amaya began. "Remember my friend Wendy, who died a tragic death? Well, she's alive now, so we're going to Toronto to take down an evil agency of assassins. Call you later. Bye."

Amaya ended the call as her mom's voice echoed through the receiver, saying, "What? Amaya? No—"

"That was your big, elaborate plan?" Harper asked.

"I never said it was elaborate," Amaya confessed.

Amaya's phone immediately lit up—an incoming call from "Mom." Amaya hit "decline" and tucked her phone away. After further thought, she pulled it back out and sent her mother a text message: *I'll explain later. No need to worry.*

"So, you going to show me some moves?" Amaya asked.

"Here on the train?"

"Sure, why not?" They were riding in the coach car, which was all they could afford based on the cash Harper and Amaya could scrounge together. The seats were positioned similar to those on an airplane—a center aisle with two chairs on either side. They even featured the same fold-down tray tables as the airlines. The only thing they were missing was the instruction sheet on how to handle a water landing.

"There's not much room here," Harper said, trying to think of some basic tips she could posit to her friend. "When in doubt, hit the soft spots and hit them hard. Those would be the groin—"

"I'm good at that one," Amaya interrupted.

"Yes, I remember that. Target the groin, eyes, throat, and ears. Most of all, stay out of the way. Let me handle anything that comes up."

"Kay," she said. Then: "You realize we're going to Toronto based solely on an offhand comment from the guy who's rotting in the woods with my used chopsticks sticking out of his head, right?"

"Yeah," Harper said, her eyes drifting off as she gazed out the window.

"So, the whole thing could be bullshit or worse," Amaya said. "It could be a trap."

"Yup, that occurred to me too."

"So, why are we doing this again?"

"It's the only information I have, and I need to try something. I can't just sit idle while the agency kills more innocent people and poisons more young girls' minds."

"So, you don't know what we're walking into?" Amaya asked. "Or exactly where we're going. I mean, Toronto isn't tiny."

"Right again," Harper said. "I really wish I had a way to reach out to Ollie and Sarah. We may need them." She thought about that and then turned to Amaya. "Take our picture."

"Huh?"

"Take a selfie of us."

"Okay," Amaya said, confused. She removed her phone, launched the camera app, and held it out in front of them. "Smile," she said. They both made a goofy face, and she snapped the picture.

"Now, post it," Harper said. "Say we're traveling to Toronto. I don't have a way to track down Ollie, but he may see that and at least he'll know where we're headed."

"You really think this Ollie guy is going to check my Insta?"

"Not specifically, no, but he's a tech guy. If he runs any facial recognition on the web, he might find it," Harper said.

"Sounds like a longshot."

"A longshot is better than no shot," Harper said.

"What if the agency uses the same facial... whatever that Ollie uses?" Amaya asked.

"I'm sure they will," Harper admitted. "I'm ready for them."

"You realize posting this picture is basically announcing to all of West Elmdale High that you're alive."

"Keeping it a secret at this point only protects the agency," Harper explained. "I'm done doing that."

"Fair enough," Amaya said as she tapped the upload button. "Done."

Before she could pocket her phone, it rang again. It was her mother. "Hey, Mom," she said into the receiver. "Of course I was kidding," she answered her mother, "unless you know some magical way to bring a teenage girl back from the dead."

There was a long pause on Amaya's end as she flapped her fingers and thumb together, mocking her mother's rambling. "I'm with this girl, Harper," she said. "We met in Yearbook Committee." She then mouthed to Harper, *I'm not even on Yearbook Committee.*

"We're touring some local colleges," she added. "Still finishing up those applications." *No, I'm not,* she mouthed to Harper.

"You know me," she said into the phone, "always planning for the future." Amaya turned to Harper, wrapped an invisible noose around her neck, and pretended to hang herself with it.

"Kay. Love you, too," she said as she ended the call. She turned to Harper and said, "She's been up my butt since... you died."

"There you go again," Harper mumbled with a half-cocked grin.

"I kind of miss the days when she would just ignore me."

"You know, you're lucky to have her."

"Sometimes I feel like I won the parent lottery," Amaya

replied sarcastically.

"I mean, it must be nice to have someone who cares about what happens to you."

"Ouch." Amaya just realized how insensitive she was being. "Sorry. I didn't mean to be a dick about it." Harper stayed quiet. "You really never knew your mom?"

"Nah, but it's okay." Harper shrugged. "It's not too bad only having yourself to look after. Just lonely, I guess."

Amaya grabbed Harper's hand, a gesture that was getting more comfortable for her. "You got me, okay?" Amaya said. "I care about what happens to you. I may not be blood, but I can be your family." Harper smiled. "You're in a unique position, my homicidal friend," Amaya continued. "Most people are stuck with their douchebag families. You get to pick yours."

"So eloquently put," Harper said.

"If I'm known for anything, Harper," Amaya said, "it's my frigging eloquence."

"That's the other thing," Harper said, "I don't even know who I am. I'm 'Harper' now, but that's just a stolen identity. My whole life I've been using other people's names and appearances. I mean, who am I really?"

"Dude," Amaya said, "you're seventeen. None of us know who we are. We're all still figuring it out." She grabbed her purple streak of hair and held it out in front of her. "Do you think someone who knows herself does this?"

That made Harper laugh.

"We're not defined by whatever name our parents gave us," Amaya continued. "My mom was so looped out of her mind on pain meds after I was born that when she told the nurse she was naming me 'Amanda,' it came out 'Amaya,' and it stuck. Do you think my life would be any different if my name was 'Amanda'?"

"I guess not... *Amanda*," Harper teased and then scrunched

her face. "Yeah, that doesn't sound right."

"I think we figure out who we are based on our life experiences and the different people that impact us. People who come in and out of our lives shape who we are, even if we don't realize it."

Harper thought about the various people she encountered—foster parents, agency operatives, targets, people who supported her, and even those who stabbed her in her back. Amaya was right. Each one of those encounters shaped her personality and made her the person she was today. She may not have a name of her own, but she was figuring out who she wanted to be. An agent was not one of those things.

Amaya continued, "You, 'insert name here,' can be anyone and anything you want to be." Amaya thought for a minute. "Except a cow. I used to want to be a cow when I was a kid, believe it or not. You can't be a cow. That was a tough lesson to learn. Lots of tears."

Amaya's cell phone chimed again—not the standard text alert or ringtone, but that obnoxious siren that you can never seem to turn off quickly enough. In the aisle next to them, another cell phone echoed the same alarm, like a foghorn that just ingested helium. Behind them, the same. Soon, the entire rail car was echoing a steady digital scream.

"Um, Harper," Amaya said, staring at her phone. "I think the agency found our Instagram picture." She turned her screen for Harper to read.

EMERGENCY ALERT:
Two female teenage fugitives on the loose. Last spotted on Amtrak Maple Leaf train from New York, Port Authority to Toronto, Union Station. Considered armed and dangerous. Reward for capture DEAD OR ALIVE.

"Any possibility they're talking about two other teenage girls?" Amaya asked.

"Not likely," Harper said. "This train is probably fifty or sixty cars long. There must be many pairs of teenage girls traveling together. We just need to lie low and not raise suspicion."

There was grumbling among the passengers. There's nothing like armed fugitives on a moving train you're stuck on to raise concern. It surprised Harper that the agency went to this extreme, but she was also impressed. She lifted her head over her high-back seat to look for anything or anyone suspicious.

"Harper," Amaya said, "what's that red dot on the back of your head?" Then it suddenly occurred to her what it was. "Get down!" she screamed as she grabbed Harper's waist and pulled her downward. A bullet flew overhead and landed in the train's side, creating a hole that tore straight through to the outside, a thin beam of light streaming into the rail car. The assailant's weapon must have had a silencer, because all Harper heard was a piercing as the bullet ripped through the air.

"So much for lying low," Harper said as they crouched to the ground. "We need to get out of this car."

"No argument there, but how? We're sitting ducks."

"I'll create a diversion and you head for the next car" Harper reached into her bag and pulling out Ryan's pistol. "I'll be right behind you." Still crouching, Harper pointed the gun straight above her, into the ceiling. "Cover your ears," she warned.

Harper blasted a round straight into the ceiling. She didn't have a silencer, so the explosive sound caused panic among the passengers who began scurrying around, screaming. There was enough chaos to camouflage their disappearance. "Now," Harper said to Amaya, nudging her.

Amaya ran for the door that separated the rail cars, smacked the big black button that read "Press," and waited as the door slid open. That second and a half felt like an eternity. "Harper, come on," she screamed as she slipped in between rail cars. Harper followed closely behind, her gun at alert in case anyone attempted to follow.

Amaya hit the button on the next door, and they entered another passenger cabin. People ran as they saw Amaya and Harper trudging toward them, Harper with her gun at the ready. She tucked it into her pants, realizing she was scaring people.

They ran to the next car, looking back to find the assailant following a car behind. They were now in the dining cart, which was mostly empty. They greeted the few patrons as casually as possible before darting into the next car. This one was a sleeper car. A narrow center aisle separated a row of private rooms on either side. The doors were mostly closed, and they breezed past the ones that were open.

Harper spotted a staircase on one side. "Down here," she said. They fumbled down the stairs to a lower level, complete with a luggage compartment, a pair of bathrooms—men's and women's—and a shower. Harper slipped into the women's room, Amaya followed, and they locked the door behind them.

Amaya crouched into the corner, panting. "Oh, my God. So, is this, like, a normal Sunday for you?"

"Not exactly," Harper said, checking her gun. She was glad they were on a train rather than an airplane where the security checks were much more stringent. The train stations only performed random bag checks, and who would stop such sweet looking teens on their way to scenic Canada?

"We can't stay in the bathroom until we get to Toronto," Amaya said. "That's, like, eleven more hours."

"We won't," Harper said. "We just need to get our bearings."

"I guess we shouldn't have posted that Instagram pic," Amaya said.

"I don't think that's what triggered this. That guy shot at us with a semi-automatic handgun with a laser scope and a silencer. He's with the agency and was already looking for us."

"What about the Emergency Alert blast?"

"Instead of a handful of people hunting us, it turned the entire train into scouts. Also, it allowed this guy to shoot at us on an open train with no one stopping him. They all think he's the good guy. It's a brilliant move, really, and it's no coincidence that he waited until the alert came and everyone read it."

Suddenly, there was a pounding on the bathroom door that could only be from a large male fist. Harper and Amaya froze. Harper put her finger over her lips, instructing Amaya to keep quiet. The pounding repeated, followed by a jiggling of the door handle.

"I'm in here," Amaya yelled out to him in a fairly decent impression of an older woman. "I may be awhile. Word of advice, avoid the breakfast burrito."

The man grunted and his footsteps faded as he walked away.

"Not bad," Harper said.

"Eh, I'm good for something every once in a while," Amaya said. "So, what's the plan?"

"The train stops in Schenectady. We get off there as long as they don't discover us first."

"How long until we're in Schenectady?"

Harper looked at her watch. "About an hour. We need a new hideout, though. At some point, that goon is going to come back. That story won't work twice."

"So, where to?" Amaya asked.

"Not sure. We have to find somewhere we can blend in." Harper hesitated. "Amaya?"

"Yeah?"

"I'm sorry I got you into this."

"As long as you get me out of it, no hard feelings."

"All right. Let's move." Harper carefully opened the bathroom door, her gun at her side. She looked in both directions and stepped out. Amaya followed.

They slowly climbed the stairs back into the sleeper car area. Harper led the way down the narrow corridor when a set of large black hands reached out of one of the sleeper rooms and pulled Harper inside. They reached out a second time, grabbing Amaya. He yanked Harper with such force that she dropped the gun.

Harper kicked and punched the man, but it was like hitting a pile of stone. He was about six foot five, and solid muscle. His shirt seemed to be losing the battle of keeping his arms covered. Each time he moved, his bulging biceps pushed his sleeves further toward his shoulder. He picked up Harper's gun and closed the door behind him.

Harper and Amaya both showed him their open hands. "That was our only weapon," Harper said. "Please don't shoot us. We're not who you think we are. We're not fugitives."

"I know that," the man growled. "I also know exactly who you are, Harper. You," he signaled to Amaya, "I'm less familiar."

"Um, I'm Amaya," she said, unsure if she should extend her hand to be polite or keep it raised.

"I'm Jerome," he said. "Relax. You two are safe here."

"You're not with the agency?" Harper asked.

"I am, actually," Jerome said. "They sent me here to kill you, but I won't. Much like you, I have been working inside the agency to take them down. Nasty people. Here, take this." He handed Harper a flash drive. "I have a copy, too. You may get this information out easier than I can."

"What's on it?" Harper asked.

"It's a financial analysis of the agency and all of their

beneficiaries. Very incriminating, but not enough by itself. The agency keeps everything so separated, like a…" He struggled to find the right analogy.

"Like a spider web?" Harper offered.

"Yes, exactly."

"Why trust me?"

"I've been studying you for a while," he said. "You got guts. More than I do."

Harper pocketed the flash drive. If she ever found Ollie again, he would know what to do with it.

"I assume you're headed to the summit," Jerome said.

"We're trying to get there, yes. Do you know where it's being held?" Harper asked.

"Holter built a new facility—enormous building—right near High Park, overlooking Humber Bay. He created a tech company as a front. Called it 'Arabella Industries.'"

"Project Arabella," Harper said to herself.

"You know it?"

"Only by name."

Suddenly, there was a pounding at the door, much like the one earlier at the bathroom—heavy and fierce. Jerome grabbed the gun from his belt (Harper's was on a table next to them). "Get in the bed," he instructed the girls. "Quick."

Jerome pulled a blanket over them and threw some clothes and his suitcase on top. It was a slipshod means of concealment, but it would have to do in such tight quarters.

Jerome opened the door to find the assailant who was hunting Harper and Amaya. "Hey, Dale," Jerome said. "Any luck?"

"I lost the scent," he said. Jerome's hulking torso blocked the entrance almost entirely. He probably had to walk through the narrow door sideways to get into the room, but Dale could see around him a little. The pile of blankets and clothes on the bed caught his eye. Dale gripped his pistol tighter. "Everything okay here?" he asked suspiciously.

"Yup, all is well." As Jerome turned his head to look back into the room, Dale saw a gun sitting on a small table next to the bed. It was a firearm he didn't recognize. The agency didn't issue it, and he never saw Jerome with it before. He glanced back at the mound on the bed with renewed curiosity.

"Who's in there with you?" Dale asked.

"What? No one. I'm alone."

"Jerome," Dale said. "Didn't the agency teach you anything? You're a terrible liar." Dale raised his gun and shot Jerome twice in the chest.

He staggered backward, his tight shirt slowly turning red with blood. In his dying breath, Jerome lifted his own gun and fired three shots. One hit Dale in the leg, one in the arm, and one directly between the eyes.

Jerome collapsed to the ground inside the bedroom. Dale sank to the floor of the narrow hallway. Kicking the blanket off of them, Harper and Amaya emerged in shock.

"Oh, my God," Amaya said. "Are they both dead?"

There was no question about Dale. It's difficult to survive a gunshot wound to the head. Jerome had a chance, albeit slim. Harper put her index and middle fingers on the side of Jerome's neck, checking for a pulse. Nothing. Harper shook her head.

"Help me drag Dale in here," she said, thanking her lucky stars that Jerome wasn't the one in the hallway. She didn't think they could drag him.

They each grabbed a leg and started tugging. "When I helped you drag old 'Chopsticks' into the woods last night, I assumed that was a onetime deal," Amaya said. "If this is going to become a habit, I'm going to have to charge you."

"Put it on my tab."

"At some point, won't someone run across these two dead bodies?" Amaya asked.

"Sooner rather than later, as long as there's a trail of blood leading to the room," Harper said, pointing at the streak of red running from the corridor to the cabin. "This whole train already thinks we're wanted killers. Let's not give them more reason to believe that. Come on, we need to disappear."

They moved forward a few more rail cars, finding another sleeper car that was fairly deserted. Shortly thereafter, there was an announcement over the loudspeaker: "Next stop, Schenectady, New York."

"That's us," Harper said. "We need to get off without drawing attention. My guess is there are agents at the train station too, so be on the lookout."

"After today," Amaya said, "I'm sure I'll be on the lookout for the rest of my life. How do you live like this?"

As the train slowed, Harper and Amaya meandered to the nearest exit door, doing their best to blend in.

* * *

The train station looked newly renovated, but they breezed past the "History of Schenectady" display. Maybe another time. There were large monitors overhead displaying the train schedules. Every few seconds, a photo of Harper and Amaya, alongside the same Emergency Alert message, replaced the schedules. It was the photo Amaya posted on her Instagram page.

"Well, that's not good," Harper said.

As a family walked by, a young boy looked up at the monitor and then at Harper and Amaya. "Hey, Mommy," he said, tugging his mother's coat. "Those are the girls on the TV."

His mother validated her son's observation and shouted, "Those are the fugitives! Someone stop them!"

The crowd of people looked around as Harper and Amaya bolted, not knowing where they were running.

A man chased after them, grabbing Harper and slamming her against the wall. He slapped a pair of handcuffs on her wrists before grabbing Amaya and doing the same. Harper caught sight of the man and squinted her eyes. "Ollie?"

"Play along," he whispered.

He grabbed each girl by the arm and led them away. "I have apprehended the fugitives," he announced. "Everything is under control."

* * *

Outside, Ollie escorted the girls to the backseat of his car, got behind the wheel, and took off as fast as he could.

"I sure am glad to see you," Harper said.

"I've heard a lot about you," Amaya said, struggling with the handcuffs behind her back. "I'm Amaya."

"Hey, Amaya," he said. "Let's get you two far from here."

"Where did you get the cuffs?" Harper asked, struggling as much as Amaya was.

"At a sex store, believe it or not," he said. "There's a button in the middle of each cuff. It even has a little pink heart on it. Just push it and it will unlock."

"Huh," Harper said, holding up the now open handcuffs. "That's... disturbing, actually."

"Did you find us with my Instagram post?" Amaya asked.

"What Instagram post?" Ollie asked. "Harper, you still have your watch on. I tracked you with that."

"Ah," she said, looking at the Timex. "Then why didn't you come find me last night?"

"I got... tied up," Ollie said. "I escaped, but they took Sarah."

Chapter 28

HOLTER

The morning sun reflected off the still autumn waters of Humber Bay, creating a dazzling light show on the crisp, blanched side of the Arabella Industries building. The parking lot was nearly full, although a few stragglers trickled in. The summit was about to begin.

Harper and Amaya waited in the car with Ollie for the last of the late arrivals to clear out.

"Harper, you know the plan?" Ollie asked.

She nodded. "Oh, before I forget," Harper said, pulling Jerome's flash drive from her pocket. "You'll want to see this."

"Should I ask?"

"What? And spoil the surprise?"

Ollie smiled and pocketed the flash drive. "All right," he said. "Amaya, stay in the car. This is far too dangerous. Got it?"

"I wouldn't dream of leaving this car," Amaya said.

"Good. Harper, let's do this."

* * *

The lobby of Arabella Industries was a mostly open space. There was a seating area on either side with a reception desk in the center. To the outside world, it had to appear like an ordinary tech company, so security was clandestine. No metal detectors. No armed guards—at least not at this section of the building. Everything looked new and clean and shiny. It even smelled new—a combination of freshly laid carpet, floor and wood polish, and furniture straight from the factory.

Ollie walked through the front door looking well-dressed and professional, an attaché case slung over his shoulder.

"Can I help you?" the receptionist asked.

"Yes," Ollie began. "Dr. Holter sent me to triple-check the security feed. You know him, overly cautious."

"I see," the woman said. "I'll need some identification, please."

"Of course," Ollie replied, reaching into his jacket pocket for his wallet. He handed the woman a card as Harper and Amaya walked in behind him.

"Sir," the receptionist said, "this is a library card."

"Oh," Ollie said, "how silly of me."

"I'm going to have to call security," the woman said as she picked up the telephone receiver.

"That won't be necessary," Harper said as she darted behind the desk, flung her forearm around the woman's neck, and immobilized her in a choke hold. "Now," Harper yelled to Amaya.

"Oh, jeez." Amaya squirmed as she jabbed a needle into the receptionist's arm and injected a clear fluid. Harper held on tightly as the woman grew weaker and eventually fell unconscious.

"I can't believe I just did that," Amaya said. "I guess I'm pretty much a doctor now."

"Let's not get ahead of ourselves," Harper said, patting her friend on the shoulder.

"Amaya," Ollie scolded, "I told you to stay in the car."

"Yeah, well, that didn't happen," she said as Ollie pushed the receptionist to the floor and took over her seat.

"You said you wouldn't dream of leaving the car," Ollie added.

"I *wouldn't* dream of it," Amaya responded. "That would be a weird dream."

"You're untrained, Amaya."

"I've got her back," Harper said.

"Plus," Amaya added, "I probably already committed a felony." She kicked the unconscious receptionist to prove her point.

Ollie groaned, realizing any further argument would prove futile. "I can monitor the security cameras from here and see what I can find on their network. Harper, you have your new burner phone?"

She held it up to show him.

"Good. Don't break that one," he said with a wink. The girls turned to leave before Ollie stopped them. "One more thing," he said. "Don't die."

* * *

Harper and Amaya shuffled through a reception hall. There were remnants of breakfast leftovers, but the guests had abandoned the premises. The waitstaff cleaned up as Amaya grabbed a Danish from a plate just before a busboy lifted it from the table.

"Amaya!" Harper scolded.

"What? It's peach," Amaya said. "I love peach." She took a bite, gagged, and tossed it onto the table. "Never mind. It's apricot."

"Excuse me," Harper said to a server clearing a nearby table. "We're late for the summit. Can you tell us where it's being held?"

"Third floor," she replied. "Take a right off the elevator, then straight ahead."

"Thanks." The server ignored her and continued cleaning.

* * *

As the elevator doors slid open, Harper stuck out her arm, holding Amaya back. She peered into the hall, and retracted as two gentlemen walked by, deep in conversation. After they passed, Harper dropped her arm. "Let's go. *Quietly*," she emphasized.

They turned right, as instructed, and headed for a set of large double-doors. Harper stopped as the doors opened. A woman exited, and Harper grabbed the door before it closed.

* * *

Inside was a three-story auditorium, the type that could house a decent-sized concert. There were several rows of theater-style seating, positioned in a U shape all around the back and sides of the auditorium. The same setup was below on the second and first floors. Harper and Amaya sat in the back row, avoiding detection in the dark assembly hall. They glanced down at a stage on the lower level, jutting out into the middle of the curved seating area.

Charles stood on stage with a set of graphs on a large monitor behind him. He still wore the expensive suit and designer shoes. He seemed way too enthusiastic for a man who lost his son mere days earlier. Was he really that cold-hearted, or was he unaware his son was dead? Maybe Wally was still lying in the woods behind Amaya's house, undiscovered, with a pair of dirty chopsticks buried in his brain.

"As you can see," Charles said into the microphone, "the numbers speak for themselves. What we have developed here at the agency is truly groundbreaking. We've been keeping America safe, and now we're extending our reach to you."

There was polite applause as Harper tried not to puke. "And now," Charles continued, "I would like to introduce you to our lead combat trainer, Isabella Martinez. Izzy?"

The audience applauded as Isabella took the stage. She appeared noticeably older now, but she was the same woman who trained Harper many years ago, when she was called 'Julia.' Unbeknownst to Harper, Isabella was the same little girl that her mother met in a psychology laboratory, fighting over cupcakes at age eight.

"Thank you, Charles," Isabella began. "We train our girls in several disciplines of martial arts and self-defense. The agency's proprietary technique is a marriage between Jiu Jitsu, Judo, Karate, Taekwondo, Kung Fu, Aikido, and Krav Maga. We ensure that once our girls have completed their training, they are not only apt fighters, they are warriors. Lethal weapons."

"I didn't know you were a lethal weapon," Amaya whispered to Harper. "Which one are you, Mel Gibson or Danny Glover?"

"Shh," Harper hushed her friend.

"What better way to show you how effective our training is than with a simple demonstration?" Isabella asked the crowd. "Penelope, Trina, please come join me." Two ten-year-old girls walked on stage, one on either side of Isabella. They both wore a uniform of sorts—black leggings, a flaming red pleated skirt, a bright yellow blouse, and a pair of black Doc Marten boots. They looked like private school girls whose school was an insane asylum.

"Did you get one of those... interesting outfits too?" Amaya asked.

"No," Harper replied. "Those are definitely new."

Penelope and Trina performed their well-choreographed routine. There was no genuine risk of injury, but Harper thought their form was good.

"Thank you, girls," Isabella said as the crowd applauded.

"Now, we have something very special." Thirty girls emerged from backstage, all between the ages of fifteen and seventeen, and all dressed in the same obnoxious, misogynistic uniforms. They took their position, fifteen girls on either side of the stage.

"Let me introduce you to our distinguished guest," Isabella continued. "Ming Quan." Genko walked on stage, dragging Sarah (bound and gagged) behind him.

"Shit, that's Sarah," Harper said, fighting not to jump out of her seat.

"Why'd they call her 'Ming'?" Amaya asked.

"Because they're racist pricks." Harper smirked, knowing Sarah would appreciate that comment.

Isabella continued to speak as Sarah fought to break free from Genko's grasp. "Ming is a defector of the agency, and what you will witness today, live on stage, is what we do to our enemies. You will have a first-hand account of the raw power and skills of our finest agents." She then turned to Genko. "Cut her free. Let's give Ming a fighting chance."

"They're going to kill her," Harper said. "We have to get down there. Come on." They leapt to their feet and bolted for the stairs.

On stage, Sarah fought off the first girl. She threw punches and kicks, and she took even more. Isabella gestured to the girls, and another one joined in. Sarah was doing her best to fight off both girls at once, but there were dozens more waiting in the wings.

Harper and Amaya burst through the first-floor doors and rushed the stage. "Sarah," Harper shouted, "we got your back."

"Harper," Sarah panted in between blows, "I'm sure happy to see you."

All thirty girls now pounced on the three of them. "What do I do?" Amaya asked, a bit panicked.

"Just remember what I told you," Harper said.

"Right," Amaya recalled. "The soft spots. Irregardless, this won't end well for me."

A girl stared down Amaya, hate brewing in her eyes. "Dumb-ass, 'irregardless' isn't a word."

Amaya smiled. It was exactly the opening she was looking for. She cocked back her knee and slammed it directly into the girl's crotch will all her strength. The girl's mouth dropped as she fell to the ground. "Ha!" Amaya exclaimed. "I did it!"

Before she could congratulate herself any further, another girl grabbed her from behind and threw her to the ground. With the girl on top of her, Amaya considered the various soft spots that Harper mentioned, and she poked the girl directly in the eye. The girl recoiled, grabbing her eye in pain.

"Dude," Amaya said to Harper, "my finger was actually on her eyeball. Like, I touched the actual ball of her eye. That was so nasty, but so cool!"

Harper was in her own battle, fighting off three different girls at once. It was total mayhem, but the audience was eating it up like it was a WWE Divas match.

"ENOUGH!" a voice bellowed from the loudspeaker. Isabella grabbed Sarah and Charles held Amaya back while Genko zapped Harper with a Taser and pulled her off two different girls. "Bring her to me," the unseen voice demanded, like the Wizard of Oz behind his curtain. Harper's body stiffened as fifty thousand volts of electricity pulsated through her.

* * *

Genko tossed Harper into a chair inside a large control room overlooking the auditorium. There were computer monitors and switchboards lining the walls, and surveillance cameras in each corner. Harper's heart raced and her fingers tingled, but she felt the *buzz-ba-ba-buzz* of her Timex almost immediately.

"Leave us," a man demanded. Genko submitted. The man

sauntered toward Harper, squatting down so they were at eye level. "Do you know who I am?"

Harper looked at him through blurry eyes. He looked familiar, but she couldn't place it. Then it occurred to her. She saw him once in a training video when she was ten years old. "Holter," she managed.

"That's right," he said. "And you, Harper Connelly, have been a pain in my side for far too long."

"You think you can kill me?" Harper taunted. "You're a tired old man. What makes you think you can accomplish what so many have failed to do? Only one of us is walking out of this room," Harper threatened, "and it sure as hell won't be you."

Harper then felt the long *buzz-buzz* on her wrist.

* * *

Back at the front desk, Ollie hunched over his laptop, Jerome's flash drive sticking out of its side. He scanned through spreadsheets, bank statements, and account summaries. "Oh, this is gold," he said to himself as an alert popped up on his screen. Ollie clicked the notification, and a window opened, showing him Dr. Holter's private network. "Nice work, Harper."

Ollie discovered the surveillance video feed from Dr. Holter's control room, and he watched as Holter interrogated Harper. He hit a few buttons and patched the live feed to the large overhead screen in the auditorium. Now the entire audience could see and hear each exchange between Harper and Dr. Holter.

As Ollie delved into Holter's files, he spotted something strange on the security monitor next to him. A van pulled into the underground parking garage and a woman exited the vehicle. She opened the back and removed blocks of explosives. He squinted as he studied the screen closer, tapped a few buttons, and enlarged the feed.

The night Harper gassed Ollie and his friends, only two people escaped—Ollie and the group's explosives expert.

"Maxine?"

* * *

Dr. Holter backed away from Harper, who remained seated, attempting to regain her strength after her run-in with Genko's Taser. He was so focused on Harper that he failed to notice that their encounter was being broadcast to the audience below.

"I have significant plans, Harper, and I won't let you interfere," Holter said.

"I know all about your plans," Harper said. "Project Arabella."

"Is that right? Why don't you tell me what you *think* you know about Project Arabella?"

"I know that the United States wasn't enough for you. After the mess you made there, you decided to spread your venom into Canada."

Dr. Holter laughed. "Let me show you something." He pulled up a map of North America on a computer monitor overhead. "This is the agency's current foothold." He hit a button and red interconnected dots spread across the United States. It looked like one of those cell phone commercials that bragged about their coverage. It also looked, as Ollie predicted, like a spider web. A big, messy web covering all of America. Harper cringed.

"Now," Holter continued, "let me show you what will happen once Project Arabella is complete." He hit some more buttons and the map of the United States expanded to a map of the world. Red interconnected dots appeared throughout Canada and Mexico and then into Europe, Asia, Africa, and Oceania. "One hundred and fifty countries. A worldwide spread. Agents everywhere, keeping order and making this planet a safer place."

"A more corrupt place," Harper corrected. "You have no right to be judge, jury, and executioner. You're not the world's police. The agency may eliminate some bad people, but aren't they still owed their day in court? Besides, sometimes the agency is wrong."

"Nonsense," Holter scoffed.

"The agency kills innocent people either because they made a mistake or because you took a payoff. The agency is riddled with corrupt operatives. Do you know I had an assignment to kill a man simply because he broke up with my messenger's daughter?"

"I'm sure we can explain that."

"Yes, you can," Harper said. "The explanation is this entire agency is rotten at every level. Why are you telling me all this anyway if you're just going to kill me?"

"You're strong, Harper. You're a fighter, but I don't want to fight you anymore. I want to work with you. I want you to work for me. You have proven yourself."

"How many people have you sent to kill me? Huh? Do you even know? Now I'm supposed to turn around and work for you?"

"You have always been special. You're not like these other girls. I designed you as my greatest experiment. I thought I failed once you turned on us, and I was prepared to cut my losses, but you have shown me just how resilient you are. My experiment wasn't a failure after all. You truly are—"

"The Purebreed?" Harper interrupted.

"Yes, my pure breed," Holter said, making it two words. "Do you know why I call you the Purebreed?"

"Because unlike these other girls that you abduct at age ten, you kidnapped me at birth and forced me to grow up under psychological torture."

Holter laughed. "Your upbringing was only part of it, dear child. You began your training at birth, that's true, and no other girl has undergone such extensive instruction. There's more to it, though."

He bent back down in front of Harper. He wanted to see her eyes as he spoke these words. "You are the only agent in the history of this organization to have my blood coursing through her veins."

"Impossible."

"It's true," Holter said, caressing Harper's hand. She jerked it away in revolt. "Your mother had a bit of a school-girl crush on me. Taken by my intellect and power. She desired to help people, as did I. We just didn't always see eye to eye on technique. She didn't think big enough."

"I don't believe you."

"Take any paternity test you like. You are my daughter."

"My mother could never love an animal like you."

"Oh, I doubt very much that it was love," he said. "When she became pregnant, I saw an opportunity like no other. A chance to raise my daughter from birth with no attachments whatsoever, shaping her pliable mind through every developmental milestone."

"You had this idea when she got pregnant?" Harper asked. "She died because of complications in childbirth. You couldn't have predicted that."

"Complications can also be planned and helped along."

Harper turned stark white, the blood rushing from her face. She took a few deep breaths to prevent herself from fainting. "So you... you killed my mother."

"It was for the greater good," he explained. "Think about the thousands of people saved because of your work. Isn't it worth the sacrifice of one life for thousands?"

"It's never worth the sacrifice of one *innocent* life."

"I vehemently disagree."

"You're a monster," Harper growled. "How can you live with yourself? And how could you abandon me knowing I was your daughter? I'm seventeen years old and the only time I ever laid eyes on you was in a training video."

"An agent can have no attachments," he said. "Not even parental ones. Look, Harper, if you could have killed Osama bin Laden prior to the 9/11 attacks, wouldn't you have? How about Hitler before he occupied Germany? Or what about these school shooters? Or the guy who brought a diseased bat to a Wuhan wet market? Don't you see? What we're doing here is good. We do good for the world."

Dr. Holter was still unaware that the entire audience was watching his every move from the overhead display, but they were all frozen, watching in wonder.

"What about these girls?" Harper asked.

"What about them?"

"They carry out your dirty work and then what? You toss them aside when they get too old?"

"Some may rise in the ranks, like the opportunity I'm offering you, but most will be disposed of, sure."

"How can you say that so casually? These are human lives. They're children. They did nothing to deserve what you're putting them through."

"Harper, don't be so naïve," Holter said. "These are orphans. No one wants them anyway. Society has already disposed of them. I'm at least giving them something constructive to do for a few years."

* * *

Down below, the group of uniformly dressed teenage girls snapped out of whatever daze the agency had them in. They finally saw Holter and the agency for what it truly was. Now, they were not only pissed off teenage girls, but highly trained, pissed off teenage girls. They turned their sights on Isabella, Charles, Genko, and the agency's security guards and esteemed guests. It was total pandemonium as no one was safe from their wrath.

313

* * *

Ollie found Maxine in the underground parking garage, strapping C4 to the support beams.

"Maxine, what are you doing?" Ollie asked.

"Oliver," she said, "I'm happy to see you. Help me finish what we started. I'm going to blow up this facility."

"There are people in that building," he objected. "There's a better way. I'm working on a plan."

"A plan?" Maxine appeared disheveled and distraught. She barely resembled the woman Ollie knew in Philadelphia. She was jumpy and malnourished. The bags under her eyes were heavy. Her hair even seemed thinner. "*I* have a plan. There's a summit going on in there right now. We have to strike immediately. We can take them all down in one shot."

"Maxine, slow down. You look like you haven't slept in days."

"Days? Ha!" She laughed. "I wish. I haven't slept for over twenty minutes at a time in weeks. How could *you*? Don't you remember what that girl did to us? To our friends? I can't close my eyes without seeing her face. Without smelling that putrid gas and feeling it eat away at my lungs. This is a major agency facility. A brand spanking new one, and I'm taking it down. Down to the ground," she shouted.

"Maxine, there are innocent people inside."

"No one associated with the agency is innocent."

"This was never our mission. We had no intention of hurting anyone. We only planned to destroy the agency's resources and networks."

"Things have changed," Maxine said. "Everything changed that night."

"Listen," Ollie said, "there are people I love in that building and I won't let you do this."

"Well, you don't have a choice, Oliver." Maxine pulled a gun from her waistband and pointed it at Ollie with a shaky hand. The fire in her eyes convinced him she would not back down.

* * *

Holter stood in front of the large glass window overlooking the auditorium. His mouth agape as he witnessed the chaos below him. He studied the live feed of his control room on the screen above the assembly hall.

"You did this," he said to Harper. "I don't know how, but you're responsible for this. My own daughter." He snickered as he shook his head in disbelief.

"I'm not your daughter, and you're not my father. There are things much greater than blood. You're nothing to me."

"I'm ruined is what I am. Look at that." He gestured to the crowd below him. "I'll be a laughingstock in the international community."

"I'm afraid you have a lot more to worry about than that."

"What do you mean?" he asked as Harper's burner phone rang.

"Yeah?" she said into the phone. "What? Slow down, what are you saying?" She listened in disbelief. "Okay. I'm on it." Harper hung up the phone and headed for the door.

"Where are you going? I'm not done with you," Holter said.

"I don't answer to you anymore." She exited through the door before turning back. "You need to leave. The building's going down and everyone has to evacuate. Even a piece of shit like you."

* * *

Sarah continued swinging her fists as Harper pulled her off Isabella. "Sarah, help me get everyone out of here. We need to clear the building."

"I'm not done with these assholes," she objected.

315

"The building is about to explode. Everyone needs to get out. Now!"

Sarah joined Harper in breaking up the melee. Spotting Amaya in the fetal position under a pile of girls, Harper pulled her up. "Don't hurt me," Amaya pleaded.

"Amaya, it's me," Harper said. "We have to clear the building. Help me get everyone out."

Harper stood on top of a large speaker, grabbed the microphone, and shouted to the unruly assembly. "There is a bomb in the garage of this building. Everyone must evacuate immediately!"

The fighting ceased and panicked people ran for the exits, trampling each other. Harper remained behind to make sure everyone escaped. As the room cleared, the floor shook, and the building rumbled. Pieces of plaster fell from the ceiling. Harper darted for the door.

* * *

Ollie gathered people outside in the parking lot as ambulances, fire trucks, and police sirens wailed in the distance. The facade of the building peeled and drop to the ground, exposing the steel beams inside.

"Come on, Harper," Ollie said to himself. "Where are you?"

As the roof of the building toppled in, Harper pushed through the front door, Amaya and Sarah in tow. Ollie ran toward them, hugging Harper. "Thank God you're all right," he said.

"Where's Holter?" she asked.

"He hasn't come out."

"I'm going back in," Harper said as she bolted back toward the building.

"What are you doing?" Ollie asked, running after Harper. "Let him die in there. It's what he deserves."

"No," Harper said. "What he deserves is to be held accountable for everything he's done. I won't let him take the coward's way out."

"It's too dangerous," Ollie objected. "Look, fire trucks are on their way." He pointed to the lights in the distance. "Let them dig him out."

"There's not enough time," Harper said. "This building will crush him in minutes." She ran into the crumbling building.

"Harper!" Ollie screamed to no avail.

* * *

Harper found Dr. Holter still in his observation room, watching everything collapse around him, both literally and figuratively.

"Let's go," Harper said as she grabbed his arm.

"A good captain goes down with his ship," he said.

"Not this time," she said as a chunk of the ceiling fell, narrowly missing both of them. That seemed to snap him out of whatever delusion of martyrdom he was suffering.

"Aren't you the same girl who was just threatening to kill me? Make up your mind, Harper."

"I would love to see you crushed in here," she said, "but I realized something after our conversation earlier."

"What's that?" he asked.

"I realized that I'm better than you," Harper said. "The person your twisted agency molded and shaped would have killed you on the spot, but I'm not that girl anymore. I've been a killer my entire life. *You* turned me into that, but that's not who I really am. It's not who I choose to be. I'll get much greater pleasure from watching you rot in prison than watching you take your last breath in this building."

There was a deafening crackle above them as a wood beam crashed down, narrowly missing Dr. Holter's head.

"Okay, I don't want to die in here," he said.

"Then let's go."

They ran for the door as another lump of cement crashed down onto his leg. He yelped as Harper pulled his leg out from underneath. The bone protruded through the skin of his calf.

"I can't make it," he said. "Go on without me."

"I got you," she said as she put his arm around her shoulder and dragged him out of the room.

Holter screamed in pain as his lame leg sputtered down each step. On the ground floor, a pile of rubble blocked the doorway. "Hold on to this," Harper said, placing his hands on a metal railing.

She dug out the blocks of concrete and rebar. The building shook as she jerked the door open. The whole thing was about the collapse, and she knew it. Harper grabbed Holter's arm, put it around her shoulder once more, and pulled him through the threshold of the door and over a toppled pillar. Just then, the building emitted a final groan and crumbled into a mountain of dust and debris.

* * *

Ollie watched from the parking lot as Arabella Industries suffered its final blow and fell into a pile of concrete, glass, and metal. Harper was nowhere in sight.

"Harper!" Ollie screamed as he ran toward what used to be the front door. Frantically, he threw aside hunks of concrete and steel. "Harper, are you in there?" He grabbed a metal beam, but it wouldn't budge.

Sarah ran and joined Ollie. Amaya followed. The three of them dug through stone, metal, and rubble, trying to find any sign of life. "Harper!" Amaya shouted.

"We're coming for you," Sarah yelled. "Don't give up. We're going to find you."

They dug, and they dug, but it was like trying to move a mountain with a teaspoon. It felt useless, but they refused to admit defeat. "Damn it, Harper," Ollie shouted. "I told you to stay out of there." Ollie cried and screamed as he threw chunks of mortar, glass, and brick haphazardly.

Suddenly, a mound of crushed cement stirred. "Harper!" Ollie yelled. Ollie, Amaya, and Sarah dug out the pieces of debris until they could see flesh. Harper's bloody hand emerged from the wreckage, and Ollie grabbed hold with all his might. He pulled, and he felt the strength in Harper's arm.

Harper emerged from the building coughing, plastered white with cement dust.

"Harper!" Amaya and Sarah screamed simultaneously as they both embraced her.

There was a cavernous opening within the wreckage from where Harper surfaced, and Ollie saw Dr. Holter struggling inside. He reached in and called out to Holter. "Grab my hand," Ollie shouted. "I'll pull you out."

As Holter gripped him by the wrist, Ollie felt his skin crawl. His touch revolted him, but he did it for Harper. Ollie extended his other arm toward Holter, grabbed him tightly, and pulled him from the wreckage. Holter had sustained serious injuries and was semi-conscious, but he was breathing.

The ambulances, fire trucks, and police cars sped into the parking lot. EMTs leapt from their vehicles, grabbed Harper, and sat her on the curb. They shined a light in her eyes and checked her vital signs.

A second ambulance stopped and loaded Holter onto a stretcher. A Mounty emerged from his police cruiser and stood beside Ollie. "What the hell happened here?" he asked in shocked disbelief.

"There was a summit," Ollie said. "It didn't end well."

Chapter 29

QUINN

The April sun glistened through the tall oaks and maples and meandered its way down to the newly blossomed azaleas, giving their natural pink color a bright glow. The daffodils and tulips that Ollie planted in the backyard opened wide, basking in every drop of spring daylight. He had hope for the dogwood blossoms too, but it was still early for them.

In her bedroom, Harper smacked her lips together, spreading her blush lipstick evenly as she glanced in the mirror. She had dyed her hair back to its natural brown, or at least as close as she could remember it. As she checked her watch, she felt nerves spin around in her stomach. It was a feeling she was unaccustomed to, but this was an unfamiliar experience for her.

Harper skipped down the stairs and into the kitchen. "Wow, Sarah, that looks amazing," she said as Sarah piped a ribbon of pink icing around a white-frosted birthday cake.

"Hey, don't look," Sarah objected, trying to block Harper's gaze with her body.

Harper swiped at the frosting with her index finger and gave it a taste. "Mmm... that's good."

"Go outside," Sarah commanded.

"All right, fine," Harper agreed, raising her hands in mock surrender.

Outside, Ollie grilled hotdogs and hamburgers, and Harper took in a big, satisfying whiff as she stepped through the sliding glass doors to the backyard. The grill rested next to a long folding table, covered with a checkered tablecloth and helium balloons on either end. "It smells great out here," she said.

"Nothing like a spring barbeque," Ollie said. "I just heard a car pull up." There was that nervous stomach again.

A wooden fence with an ivy-covered gate enclosed the backyard. As the gate swung open, Harper heard Amaya and Tommy bickering. Meg trailed behind, shaking her head. "It never stops with those two," Meg said to Harper as she handed her a wrapped gift with a balloon tied to it. "Happy birthday," she said as she hugged Harper.

"Yeah, happy birthday," Amaya said as she breezed past her and kept arguing with Tommy.

"Thanks, Meg," Harper said. "I told you not to get me anything," she added as she held Meg's gift up to her ear and gave it a little shake.

"It's a purse," Meg said.

"Doofus," Amaya chided, smacking Meg's arm. "You're not supposed to tell her."

"Thank you, Meg," Harper said. "I'm sure I'll love it."

Tommy grabbed Harper from behind and gave her a big bear-hug. "Happy birthday, girl," he said. She was actually starting to appreciate an occasional hug here and there. Her therapist would call that progress.

"Thanks, Tommy," Harper said. "Burgers and dogs are on the grill."

"I'm not one to pass up charred animal flesh," he said, heading for the table.

Amaya punched him in the arm. "See, that's what I'm talking about," she said. "That's disgusting. Why would you say that?"

"Give them five minutes," Meg said. "They'll be making out again."

Harper laughed and put Meg's gift on the table. From the corner of her eye, Harper spotted another car pull up. It was one she recognized from what felt like another life. She walked to the gate to greet them.

"It's great to see you under happier circumstances," Harper said as she extended her hand. Ryan Barnes shook it and then pulled her in for a hug.

"You did it," he said. "You took down the agency. I'm proud of you."

"Thanks." She felt herself blush. Truthfully, she was proud of herself.

"Wendy!" a voice yelled from the car. Grace Barnes helped Corey out of the backseat and onto his crutches. An instant warmth filled Harper's body. She hadn't seen Corey since the night he got sick—the night when she thought she killed him.

"Corey!" she shouted, running toward him. She wrapped her arms around him and lifted him off the ground. "It is so amazing to see you. I missed you so much."

"I missed you too," he said. "Happy birthday, Wendy." She didn't have the nerve to correct him. Plus, she really liked the way he said "Wendy."

"Happy birthday, honey," Grace said as she gave Harper a hug.

"It's great to see you all," Harper said. "I'm so glad Corey's aunt let you borrow him for the day." Then she squatted down and looked Corey in the eye. "I have a huge surprise for you."

"Really?" he asked. "But it's *your* birthday."

"I know. It's actually for both of us," she said. "Close your eyes."

He closed them, and Grace led Corey to the backyard.

"Okay, open them," Harper said.

"Whoa…" Corey's mouth dropped open in amazement as his eyes couldn't believe the big, brightly colored, inflatable bouncy house that stood in the backyard. "I won't pop it?"

"You won't pop it," Harper said. "Come on. Let's bounce."

Corey radiated happiness as he laughed and bounced with Harper. Meg and Sarah joined them, and they bounced and sent Corey high into the air.

Harper then noticed another car pull up. She thought all the guests were already present, so she was confused. An elderly couple exited. The man walked with the aid of a cane as the woman linked her arm in his.

"I'll be right back," Harper said as she slipped out of the bouncy house and put her shoes back on. She approached Ollie, who was still working the grill.

"Hey, Ollie," she said. "Do you know those people?"

"Oh, they made it," he exclaimed. "Tommy, can you take over the grill?"

"What?" Amaya said. "He's a man, so only he can work the grill?"

"You're right," Ollie corrected. "Amaya, would you please take over the grill?"

"I would love to," she said. She took the spatula from Ollie and poked around in disgust at the hotdogs and hamburgers. "Hey, Tommy, can you do this?"

"Ha!" he said. "I thought you wanted the job."

"I wanted to be *considered* for the job," she clarified. "The job itself? That's all yours," she said, patting his shoulder.

Ollie held the gate open for the elderly couple as Harper waited for an introduction. "Thank you, dear," the woman said to Ollie.

"Please, have a seat." Ollie led them to a picnic table with folding chairs on either side. "You too," he said to Harper. "Have a seat." Confused, Harper sat down across from them.

"I would like to introduce you to Miriam and Thomas Quinn. These are Rebecca's parents," Ollie said to Harper. "They're your grandparents."

Harper's mouth hung open. She was rarely at a loss for words, but she didn't know if she could speak. Her heart swelled with emotion. These people were the only blood relatives that she ever met, besides Dr. Holter, but he didn't count. They were a genuine tie to her mother—the woman she spent her life wondering about and hoping to meet one day.

Miriam placed her hand on Harper's cheek and stared into her eyes. "My Lord," Miriam said as a tear formed in her eye. "I feel like I'm looking at my Rebecca again after all these years. Your eyes… you have your mother's gorgeous eyes." She turned to her husband. "Doesn't she look so much like our Rebecca?"

Thomas was speechless. He opened his mouth to talk, but his lower lip just trembled as he fought back tears. "Beautiful," he managed. "You're beaut…" That's all he could say before the waterworks started. Miriam handed him a tissue.

Harper turned to Ollie and gripped his hand tightly. "Thank you," she said as tears welled in her eyes, too. "Thank you for finding them for me." Ollie smiled and squeezed her hand back.

"I read all about you in the paper," Miriam said. "You are a brave young woman. Your mother would be so proud of you."

"I never liked that Holter," Thomas said, regaining some composure.

"No, we didn't," Miriam confirmed. "We met him a few times

when we visited Rebecca at school. I never understood what she saw in him. I can't believe what he did to you, and to my sweet daughter."

"Well, he'll be in prison for a long time," Harper said. "Ollie turned over a massive amount of evidence against him and several key players in the agency. The warrants and subpoenas dug up a lot more. He'll have his trial," Harper added, "but he won't be able to hurt anyone anymore. That's for sure."

"I'm glad to hear it," Miriam said.

"We read about your case, too. What did the lawyers call it?" Thomas asked.

"Duress," Miriam added.

"That's right," Harper said. "They held none of the girls accountable for the crimes committed under the instruction of the agency. They said we were acting under 'extreme duress.'"

"Wonderful," Miriam said. "I'm so happy you're safe now."

"What are you going to do next?" Thomas asked.

"Well," Harper said, "I'm finishing up my last semester at West Elmdale High School. Then I'll be heading to college." Harper turned, looking for her friend. "Amaya," she called out, "come here." Amaya joined them at the table.

"At your service," Amaya said as she took a bow.

"This is my friend Amaya," Harper said. "She's going to be my roommate."

"I'll make sure she's not partying too hard and occasionally gets some work done," Amaya said.

"Well, it's very nice to meet you, doll," Miriam said.

"Do you know what you're going to study?" Thomas asked.

"Actually, yes," Harper said. "I'm going to be a social worker in the foster care system. There are a lot of kids out there who need someone to give them a chance. I think I can help them."

"God bless you," Miriam said, taking Harper's hand in hers.

"Time for cake," Sarah cried out as she carefully balanced her beautifully decorated cake and placed it on the table.

Harper joined her behind the table, put her arm around her and whispered, "It's perfect. Thank you." As people gathered around, Harper spoke out. "Before we cut into this incredible cake, I just wanted to say a few words." The nervous feeling in her stomach returned.

"Today is my eighteenth birthday, and this is actually the first real birthday party I've ever had. I couldn't be happier spending it with all of you. I'm so excited to meet my grandparents today," Harper said, gesturing to Thomas and Miriam. "I grew up without a family, but a wise woman once told me that blood doesn't necessarily define family, and I am in a unique position to choose my family."

"That was me," Amaya said. "I'm the wise woman."

"Yes, that was Amaya," Harper said. "I truly love you as if you were my sister."

"All right," Amaya said. "Don't make me cry. I bought the cheap eyeliner."

Harper continued, "I also grew up with no identity. I have had something like twenty or thirty different names. I don't even remember them all, but I never had a name of my own. It was always assigned to me. Stolen from someone else," she said. "Well, today I have decided who I am and who I want to be for the rest of my life. On Tuesday it became legal and official. The name I have chosen is 'Quinn Hastings.' 'Quinn' after my mother, Rebecca Quinn.'' She noticed tears welling up in Thomas and Miriam's eyes again.

"Hastings," she continued, "after my new *adoptive* father, Oliver Hastings." Ollie gave her an emotional hug and everyone cheered. "One more thing," she said as she pulled Sarah close to her. "Ollie adopted Sarah too. I'm so happy to have a sister." Sarah and Quinn embraced, and the applause continued. Amaya even threw in a "Woot! Woot!"

Quinn's eyes scanned the backyard, taking in the faces of everyone there. The faces of people she genuinely loved and cared for. The realization that these people cared about her too was almost overwhelming. She suddenly felt struck by a magnificent rush of… well, wonder. She simultaneously smirked and cringed at her mind's choice of expression.

"So," Quinn continued, shaking off the thought, "without further ado, let us eat cake!"

Quinn looked down at the cake. Written across it in perfect cursive pink lettering was "Happy Birthday, Quinn."

"I'll cut it," Sarah said as she grabbed a large kitchen knife.

"No, no, no," Quinn and Ollie both objected as Ollie took the knife from her.

"What?" Sarah asked. "I wasn't going to stab anyone."

* * *

Quinn sat behind a table at the college library, mindlessly twirling a strand of hair between her fingers, a textbook propped open in front of her. Amaya stormed in and tossed her backpack on the table with a solid *thud*.

"No one ever told me college would be so much work," Amaya nearly shouted.

"Shh…" a student at the next table whispered.

"All right, relax," Amaya said. "It's not like you're over there curing cancer or anything."

"Tough class?" Quinn asked.

"Yeah. Can you believe we have to write a paper *and* take a test on Plato's *Republic*?" Amaya asked. "Like, seriously, make up your mind—one or the other—we don't need both."

Quinn closed her book and slipped it into her bag. "I have

class in five," she said. "Walk with me?"

"As you wish, master," Amaya teased.

Quinn stepped outside, took a deep breath, and smiled.

"You're not getting weird on me again, are you?" Amaya asked.

"Just enjoying the day," Quinn said.

As they walked past the library, toward the center of campus, Quinn put her arm around Amaya and kissed the top of her head.

"What was that for?" Amaya asked.

"I'm really happy to be here with you," Quinn said.

"Disgusting," Amaya joked, playfully wiping Quinn's kiss from the top of her head. Then she smiled. "I'm happy to be here with you too."

As they walked past the student store, there was something unusual in the window, but Quinn didn't notice. That's fine. It wasn't intended for her. In the corner of the window was a sticker. It bore the image of a bright yellow smiley face with bright blue eyes, blowing a big pink bubble. It raised its eyebrows in exuberance, and a thumbs-up was superimposed on its side, indicating approval of its gum choice—*Wonder Rush Happy Funtime Bubblegum.*

About the Author

Dan McKeon is the author of four feature-length screenplays as well as several short stories. *Wonder Rush* is his first novel, and he is excited to share it with the world.

Dan's interest in writing blossomed during a film analysis class he took while studying psychology at Villanova University. In addition to his Bachelor of Arts from Villanova, Dan also holds a Master of Science in Computer Information Systems from Boston University and a Professional Certification in Screenwriting from the University of California, Los Angeles (UCLA).

When he is not writing, Dan works as a software developer and enjoys spending time with his wife, Rosa, and his two sons, Justin and Brandon.

dan-mckeon.com

Made in the USA
Middletown, DE
19 May 2021